CW00456205

The Spindrifter

– MICHAEL GOODALL –

FASTPRINT PUBLISHING
PETERBOROUGH, ENGLAND

Michael Goodall

THE SPINDRIFTER
Copyright © Michael Goodall 2009

ISBN 978-184426-470-4

First Published 2009 by
FASTPRINT PUBLISHING
Peterborough, England.

Printed by Lighting Source

Michael Goodall

The opening and closing quotations are from Henry Vaughan, '*The Retreate*'.

Extracts from *Peter Pan* by J.M.Barrie are by kind permission of the Great Ormond Street Hospital for Children.

For Elizabeth, with love, yet hardly a dent in the debt I owe.

Michael Goodall

CHAPTER ONE

'Happy those early dayes! When I
Shin'd in my Angell-infancy.
Before I understood this place'

When the first crash came she was on her knees, sliding a finger round the inside of a jam jar for the last smears. By the second, an instant later, she was already up and running, bare feet thumping across the grass, still fiercely clutching the jar despite the screaming whistle and roar of explosions around her.

She scrambled down into the cool darkness of the Anderson shelter and scurried to the farthest end, away from the door and the noise like thunder, wrapping herself into a small, tight ball.

Within moments her mother broke into the damp murkiness and flung herself to the ground with a yelp. Together they lay motionless as the bombs tore into the landscape around them. It was as though the fragile tin bolt-hole had been snatched up and shaken by an enraged hand. In the brief lulls between the deafening bursts the girl thought she could hear her mother's heartbeat drumming against the floor. The woman stretched out and anxiously encircled the child's thin ankle with a moist hand. There had been no warning this time, no siren wail floating eerily across the valley, nothing at all.

At the touch of her mother's hand the girl stared out wide-eyed. The woman's face was hidden but through the gloom she could see that the golden hair was flecked with dirt and that she was clutching something, wrapped hastily in a tea towel, close to her. The girl knew it was the big photograph of Daddy, the one that hung in the hall, all smart in his blue uniform and shiny peaked cap. It was the first thing you saw as you came into the house. She always brought it. Every time there was an air raid the three of them were there together.

The woman stared at her wedding ring, concentrating on it to shut out the air-splitting din but it would not be held back. Then she thought she could hear the aeroplane moving away to the east, floating higher with a new lightness, turning back to sea. What she did not know was that it was a holed stray, cut off from the main thrust of the raid; a string of jagged punctures along its fuselage, chunks of aluminium pulled off by its own hurtling speed as the wounded pilot arbitrarily released the few remaining bombs. Already far behind and below it were the billowing parachutes of the escaped crew. Then it would wheel away, trailing burning oil, and out at sea, five minutes into the future, plunge down and hit the water with a booming slap, settling briefly on the surface before starting a slow, spiralling descent with its lone dead pilot to nestle forever in the weed, sand and gloom of the English Channel. Above, a pall of smoke drifted across the silvered sea, a momentary hissing on the water, an angered sea god's disapproval.

Those last bombs shook the earth below and the air around them. A scorching blast filled their mouths and eyes with gritty smoke. They both stayed completely still, caught in their awkward positions, and stifled their choking as if the slightest cough might somehow give them away, might challenge the beast.

The woman imagined she could hear Hadley, their home, ripped suddenly apart by the bombs so casually jettisoned. She could hear the roof slates rippling and crashing to the ground, walls crumbling in a rumble of showering bricks and plaster. She saw the precious tea service sliding and smashing into a thousand fragments against the kitchen flagstones, furniture smashed and burning, charred wooden rafters poking through the remains of the roof. She had seen in town the great mounds of rubble and wreckage after raids like this. Houses, streets, mangled beyond recognition so that even the familiar was utterly transformed, beyond redemption, incapable of ever having been the scene of normal life. It was not England. It was some hellish place beyond imagining. She began to weep silently and, as she did, the sudden, sure and entirely practical knowledge that she had left the wireless blaring compounded the nightmare. She wept, accompanied by a thin rain of falling earth beating a brief, irregular jazzbeat on the roof of the shelter.

The little girl, who could not really remember a time before the bombs, was thinking of her father and how it must be worse for him. She was remembering when he had last been home from the sea. They had taken a picnic to the nearby green slopes overlooking a sea blue with the promise of summer but grimly barricaded, fortified by much more than castles of sand. She couldn't remember paddling in the sea but could recall, just, Daddy swimming far out one day and her being frightened. Nor could she remember making sandcastles although she had seen children in picture books making them and they looked happy. Daddy had taken a photograph of her at the picnic and, when it came back from the chemist's shop, she looked squinty-faced and serious in it. She asked if there were pirates at sea and he had laughed.

'Pirates? Hundreds of 'em. And smugglers and cut-throats.'

She wanted to know what the big things sticking out of the water were for. He said to keep Adolf out. Then he said that one day soon he would teach her to swim. She asked if the water was cold and again he laughed, leant forward and wiped the remains of the picnic from her face with a big, white handkerchief.

'Not really. When you get used to it.'

'And are there monsters?' But already he had turned to her mother and did not hear her.

High above, a fragment ripped from the stricken aircraft completed a graceful curve and, gathering speed, plummeted down and sliced through the thin roof of the shelter with a sudden, metal-rending wrench. Hardly bigger than a man's hand, it thudded into the floor, the rushing noise of it filling the cramped space. They both cried out but, as they looked up and saw the unexpectedly small hole, their cries became sobs of relief and they fell into each other's arms, the photograph pressed between them.

A triangular, five-inch patch of daylight had joined them underground, stabbing a beam of light to the floor. Unconsciously the mother rubbed her child's back comfortingly. It was not until they were once again outside, blinking against the sun and registering with incredulity that Hadley was completely untouched, that the woman saw the weeping blood on the girl's arm. The plunging fragment had scored an arc, several inches long, on the inside of her right forearm, as if the white skin had been gently touched by a gull's feather dipped in red. Though bloody, it was not a deep wound and the woman hugged the child, uncaring of the blood staining her dress. The child's fingers finally released the jam jar and it fell to the ground with a dull thump, unnaturally loud in the newly reclaimed silence. Then the woman unwrapped the photograph and put it carefully down before loosely bandaging the wound with the tea towel.

And out at sea as the plane crashes, a sound like the crack of a great sail turning into the wind rushes back over the waves towards the primed, deserted shore.

CHAPTER TWO

'Jump!'

It was a stern, impatient voice spilling over with frustration.

She stood at the very end of the pier, speckled with goose-bumps despite the sun. A wet, woollen costume hung on her skinny frame and dripped a slow, cold puddle onto the planks beneath her feet. A borrowed rubber bathing cap clung to her head. It was too big and felt clammy and uncomfortable.

'Will you jump!' It was not a question but an irritable command. Without moving her head she looked out to where the man was treading water. His face was indistinct in the dazzle from the sea. She did not want him to know she was looking. It would somehow bring the moment of jumping even closer.

She stood with her hands clasped together, knees slightly, reluctantly bent, eyes shut tight now. She was counting to three but not out loud. At three she felt something inside rise up as though she were on tiptoe, tipping forward, already travelling through the air although in fact she had not moved at all. She opened her eyes. The warm flood of relief at finding she had not actually jumped was balanced exactly by the fear she had felt in that rising up and the imagined leap into the terrible unknown. She looked down. It was different here. In the shallows the sea was warm and sparkling and there were all the sounds of fun; children shrieking, running and splashing, dogs barking, the chunk of a bright new tin spade cutting into firm, yellow sand. But here the sea was green and dark with secrets. There might be monsters, sea snakes.

'Come on!' The strident voice stretched out the last word into a hoarse bark. They had been at the beach for an hour when he got up from his deck-chair, struggled through a prolonged changing ceremony beneath a large, striped towel and marched down to join her.

His stocky body, dominated by a ballooning white stomach spread across with coarse hair, loomed over her as she played happily at the water's edge. He seemed implacably oblivious to his comic, bloated shape as he stood, beaming with dark purpose.

'Now,' he said importantly, 'watch closely so you can copy what I do. I promised your mother I would teach you to swim and it's high time at your age young lady.'

His tone lit a fuse of quiet panic inside her. He hadn't looked at her when he spoke. He rarely looked directly at her. Within his voice she sensed that she was just an obstacle to be overcome, something temporarily separating him from the fulfilment of that promise. She shrank inside. It would be another slow torture to be endured. Grown-ups seemed to want her to do things their way all the time.

He strode purposefully into the sea until it surrounded the bulging stomach. Turning briefly to check she was still paying attention he plunged headlong, swimming out with slow, exaggerated strokes. She did not want him to stop.

She wanted him to keep swimming far out to sea and forget his promise. She watched, with growing dread, as he forced his way through the water, knowing that when he stopped it would be her turn. The childhood sounds of the beach were stilled. All she could hear was the rhythmic splashing as he rolled inelegantly on.

He stopped, turned and pushed back his wet hair. Then he plunged back to shore with those same ponderous strokes, puffing loudly, until he stood squarely before her. The sun had caught him during his deck-chair hour and he shone pink at the edges. Heavy salt droplets hung from the clipped bristles of his moustache and in the greased, crinkled hair.

The next hour was misery, dispelling all the happiness that lay, along with her abandoned spade, on the beach. She did not like him holding her in the water with his fleshy hands while she had kicked like a frog and pumped fruitlessly with her arms. She felt frightened. He might let go at any moment and she would sink. He made her duck her face in and blow bubbles. The salt water hurt her throat and lodged in her ears making everything muffled and faraway. The distant yellow happiness, a brief time ago, disappeared in a gurgling rush as unwillingly she dipped into yet another wave, her face screwed up tight, while he stood and watched, ordered and chivvied.

'Can't I have a rubber ring,' she panted, paddling furiously to keep her chin above water, 'please?'

He answered in the familiar, brisk tone she already understood well; a tone which flattened any possibility of further discussion.

'Quite unnecessary. Everyone can float.'

He had been leading her round and round, one hand under her chest, but she had not noticed they had moved farther from the shore. He took his hand away abruptly with a sly chuckle.

'Go on. You can do it.'

The sudden absence of support, knowing there was nothing beneath her, made her body fold in terror. Her feet flailed wildly searching for the seabed and her frantic paddling had less and less effect. The sea was in her nose, her throat and ears. She thought she would fill up with sea, fill up with it and drown. Then unexpectedly she popped to the surface, gasping, straining up to the sun and, without any conscious intent except to escape, paddled briskly like a small, nervous dog towards land and safety.

Behind she could hear his triumphant shout rise up like a fisherman's net, sailing high in the air to trap and haul her in again. She felt for the bottom with an anxious foot and found it, rock and sand, something long and slippery trailing past her ankle, but at last it was there. She stood unsteadily, coughing and blinking through sea-heavy lashes.

'I said you could do it. Nothing to it is there. Just have to keep your nerve that's all.'

He had caught up and was grinning broadly but not with her or even at her. It was his victory not hers. She was simply its instrument. She coughed up at him, felt a string of saliva stick to her chin. Her face felt sore, salt-baked from the sunshine.

'Come on,' he said energetically, heading for the beach, 'one last thing and then it'll be tea-time.'

She had no idea what the one last thing was but his enthusiasm made her instantly wary. She trudged up the sand behind him, dabbing briefly at her red eyes with a sandy towel. But he was impatient and she trotted obediently alongside as he stumped off towards the pier. She hadn't taken in the fact that she had swum, of sorts, all by herself. Instead she had a blank sense of relief. She had obeyed, done what the grown-ups wanted and it was over, all over. For one hopeful moment, she thought she might get some reward. An ice-cream perhaps or some of those little paper flags for sand castles. But a dull anxiety grew in her stomach as they passed the arcade where the shops were and carried on to the end of the pier.

He told her to wait, an upraised finger reinforcing the terse instruction. Then he dived in, a graceless plummet. She watched the water smooth over behind his leaden entry and saw him emerge some way off. A cold disbelief came over her as he bellowed that short, impossible demand.

'Jump!'

And now, it seemed, she had been poised there forever, shrinking from the imagined curve and cold of that leap. Daddy had been going to teach her not Uncle Richard. It wouldn't be like this if Daddy was here. He would be home soon too. They had written and told him about the bombs and her being wounded and he had written back and said she was very brave. Brave, she thought, be brave Jenny.

She glanced secretly out again. She could picture Uncle Richard's mouth opening, fish-like and relentlessly demanding, clubbing her with that single, weighted verb until she fell stunned into the dark sea, completing his triumph over her. It was the unbearable thought of his smug gloating that decided her. She would jump now, and before he could say another word.

A straggle of cloud moved slowly on the faint breeze and there was a babble of squabbling gulls. She would count to three again and really jump this time. She would not look down at the impenetrable sea nor at him but at the faraway cloud.

'One.....two....'

To her own huge surprise she felt her body spring up into nothingness, held momentarily in mid-air, long enough to feel the strangeness of a self still, in her mind, rooted to the pier, waiting to complete the count. A swallowing plunge as the bottom of the world was whipped away like a magician's tablecloth and she rushed downward, far faster than she thought possible, a cold whistling in her ears, a billowing gale trapped inside the borrowed cap, not even time to think about monsters. She brought her knees up involuntarily and hit the waiting green with a cascading splash. Then tumbling down and down, limbs thrashing as she swirled and spiralled in a tunnel of sea. She knew there would be a deadening bump as her head hit the bottom but it never came. Inside was a terrified scream that could not escape through her clamped mouth. Then suddenly she was rising, the bubbling tumult beneath her. Rising surely, floating up. She opened her eyes and glimpsed a powdery fog before squeezing them tightly shut again. She began instinctively to kick out and paddle and, as she felt the little sliver of power those small, scrabbling movements gave her, pushed and kicked harder, more determinedly. She broke through the gleaming surface into the warm air, everything suddenly loud but distorted by the water in her ears. The sun made her blink and she gasped deep breaths of salt air, coughing and spitting. Immediately she began a scurrying paddle towards the distant beach.

'Well done! Now you'll never be frightened of it again!'

He was shouting even though he had swum close to her. He reached out as if to catch hold of her and pull her back into the controlling orbit of his voice, the voice she had silenced. The girl kicked out for shore and felt her foot connect beneath the water with the soft bulk of his body.

He let out a surprised groan then grunted into the sea, swallowing and choking.

'Sorry. Accident,' she sang. He grunted again, suspiciously.

'Come on,' he said, 'let's get back.' He swam at a cautious distance from her, yet easily keeping pace.

As the beach grew closer, the little trill that had begun inside her grew into a hesitant but proud birdsong of a triumph snatched back, a triumph of her own. And she did not really feel sorry at all. Her feet touched bottom and she scrambled through the shallows, beaming up at the sun and wallowing in its warmth.

Back amongst their clothes and belongings, she began to shiver and wrapped herself in a towel. She sat on the sand, looking out at the pier and could hardly believe how far away it was, how far she had swum. Uncle Richard stood and rubbed at his arms and chest vigorously, drying himself like a plump, preening bird. The weathered canvas of the deck-chair billowed behind him, echoing his shape as it bellied out, swollen by the breeze.

He dressed awkwardly, clutching the towel carefully around his waist, then rubbed energetically at his hair and combed it into place with quick, sweeping motions.

'Come on young lady, get yourself properly dry.'

She dragged the wet lump of towel across her back and up and down her legs, then wrapped it round her and peeled off the sodden costume. She still felt damp and sandy but her shivering subsided when she put on her dress and the thin cardigan Uncle Richard insisted on. He made her stand in front of him while he rubbed her hair dry with his towel and tried to comb it. It was still quite wet and tangled and his inexperienced combing pulled at it painfully. He wrung out their costumes, rolled them neatly into the towels and bundled them under his arm.

'All ready?' he asked cheerfully, 'Let's find some tea.'

They were staying at a guesthouse for the weekend. He called it 'our adventure'. It was a small south coast resort, the town backing up from the original, ornate Victorian seafront houses around a featureless bay. The newer houses had pebbledash facades painted drab cream or a tired pink. Many of them were hotels or boarding houses with elaborate verandas furnished with old cane chairs. She had noticed shadowy old people sitting there, peering out to the young world of sunshine beyond.

As they walked his shoes tapped out a resolute tattoo against the pavement. She wanted an ice lolly from the Italian parlour but would not ask for one and tried not to look at the bright canopy as they passed. They marched at his pace and she felt herself dragged in his wake. The backs of her knees were sticky and sore and it was hard to keep up. She was trying to keep her little triumph safe in a secret place inside where it would not be drowned out by his clicking strides. She was beginning to understand that to keep it she would have to keep winning over and over, just to hold on to it, to be sure of it. It was an awesome prospect.

'I've left my spade behind!' She stopped dead, aghast.

'Well,' he said shortly, 'that was a very silly thing to do wasn't it.' He paused, frowning, 'You'll have to look for it in the morning.' He stopped as if that was it, final, the last word. But it was also as though he was waiting, leaning almost imperceptibly closer to her. She looked up at him imploringly.

'But it won't be there tomorrow, I know it won't, someone else will take it. Please let me get it, please. I'll run all the way there and all the way back, please…' She trailed off, out of breath and words. He still looked disgruntled, but there was a faint softening in his face.

'Well……' he hesitated.

'Please!' she pleaded, bouncing urgently. She had spent all her money just on the beautiful spade, 'please!'

'Well……' he said again, with a slowness that made her spade seem farther and farther away by the minute, 'all right then. But be quick.' He pulled a packet of cigarettes from his pocket and lit one, giving a long-suffering sigh as he blew out the match.

'Thanks!' She raced off back round the small promenade, past the ice-cream parlour and towards the pier.

She couldn't see it anywhere. A flutter of tearful dismay claimed her. She scanned the wet sand and sizzling backwash anxiously. There was no sign of it. Someone must have found it and taken it. A surge of bitter resentment against the unknown thief welled up inside her. Quickly she wiped her eyes with the sleeve of her cardigan and looked again. The sun glinted on something bright moving sluggishly in the shallows. She pulled off her shoes and socks and tiptoed in, holding her dress up out of the water. Her hand darted down like a heron's bill as the spade floated at her feet. She grabbed it and held it aloft, felt the drips splash softly onto her. A surging wave rose past her knees and spluttered against the sand, angry at this child's trophy it had been denied.

'Got it!' she said exultantly, 'Got it!'

She ran back barefoot, the precious spade in one hand, her shoes and socks in the other. He was standing impatiently where she had left him. As she approached he began to pace round in a stiff, irritable circle. There was no trace of that brief softening in his face.

'Well come on then,' he snapped, 'now that you've got the damn thing.' He began to stalk off then stopped abruptly and rounded on her. 'Where are your shoes for goodness sake?' Silently she held them out, the spade gripped tightly in her other hand. 'Well don't just stand there, put them on. Sharpish!'

She rubbed hurriedly at her feet with one of the damp towels and hopped awkwardly from foot to foot trying to be quick. A ribbon of pale green seaweed was stuck to her ankle. She picked at it in vain then gave up and pulled her sock on over it. He looked at his watch irascibly as she buckled her sandal and stood for inspection.

'Come along,' he said, striding off quickly, 'and hurry up or we'll be late for tea.'

She couldn't understand why. It wasn't like at home where tea was always at half past five. Uncle Richard's life seemed to be organised around some inviolate timetable that was a baffling mystery to her.

The place he took her to was the faded remnant of a once grand hotel. It was dreary and still inside as if its heavy wood panelling had, over the years, imposed a sombre solidity that squashed out any hope of gaiety or lightness. The only other customers were two elderly women each silently confronting a large slab of fruit cake as they sat together in a corner. A big clock ticked wearily and echoed round the uninviting interior.

Their order was taken by a bored young woman with garishly blonde hair who wore her frilled apron like a girdle of contempt. Jenny asked for tomato soup and ham salad. She always asked for the same thing.

'Don't you want something different, for a change?' Uncle Richard whispered gruffly.

'No thank you,' she said quietly from behind a large cardboard menu.

The waitress brought a metal tray of tea things and rattled them noisily onto the table. Deliberately noisy, the girl thought, as the two old women turned waxen, disapproving faces towards them.

Uncle Richard waited for the waitress to go before pouring the tea, slopping some into her saucer as he slid it across the table to her. Furtively she dunked eight sugar cubes into her cup and stirred it solemnly while he was pouring his own.

She sipped the warm, sweet tea and stared down at the tablecloth. It was white with a border of little yellow, blue and pink flowers. Putting down her cup she absently stroked the curved scar in the soft skin of her forearm. She had picked at it when it was still a scab, even though she'd been told off, but she couldn't help picking at it and now it was a scar, just as she had been warned. She cast glumly round the drab room. They never went to places she liked and there were lots of them on the seafront, bright with sunshine and full of people. Places where children ate ice-cream sundaes in tall glasses just like the glossy pictures in the windows. She wriggled in her seat trying to shift the gritty sand stuck inside her underwear and felt guiltily envious.

The soup, gracelessly presented, was a watery pink and did not taste of anything. The salad had one little piece of ham and lots of grated carrot which she did not like. She read the menu, chewing unenthusiastically. Right at the bottom it offered ice-cream. She looked up at Uncle

Richard. He was eating fried fish and his lips were shiny as he forked it into his mouth.

A young family bustled noisily into the café and found a table by a window. Undeterred by the inhospitable atmosphere and the offhand service, their unrestrained laughter provoked withering glares from the waitress and silent condemnation from Uncle Richard and the two old ladies. But for Jenny it was as though the sun had stolen boldly in with them and she found it hard not to stare and smile. They looked happy, full of fun. The woman was plump and pretty, the man always grinning. There were two girls who had spades like hers but they had beach buckets too. She hadn't had enough money for a bucket as well. They were all giggling behind the waitress's back, amused and not in the least intimidated by her petulance, and she liked them for it.

'I think we'll have the apple pie.' Uncle Richard's voice broke into her thoughts and she looked up at the frowning waitress busily scratching the order onto a small pad.

'Oh, but......' Jenny said, disappointed. She hadn't meant to say anything. At the other table they were eating pink and white ice-cream. Uncle Richard followed her gaze. There was an unfamiliar look on his face as he turned back, a thin shred of unease. 'Did you want something different?'

She paused. She would not ask and now did not want. She could hear the excited chatter from the distant table and shook her head silently.

On the way back to the guesthouse he stopped at a small shop and made her wait outside. He emerged a few minutes later with a bottle wrapped in brown paper but did not say what it was. Dusk was beginning to fall but there were still people on the beach, meandering on the sun-warmed sand.

He hurried her along, reminding her she was to have a bath. He had regained a stolid good-humour, almost teasing her.

'What would your mother say if I took you home grubby? I'd never hear the last of it!'

They had rooms on the second floor and shared a narrow, tiled bathroom at the end of a corridor. She had been in the bath for some time and was lying quite still in the grey, lukewarm suds, sucking water from the sponge. It was a chilly room, with a small window half covered by a yellow curtain, and beyond she could just see the blue-grey slope of an adjoining roof in the evening light. A stern notice hung behind the door warning guests not to wash sand down the waste pipe. She slid gently back and forth and with a mild prick of conscience felt sand rasping against her bottom. Her mind wandered back to the pier and her huge leap from it. Remembering made her shudder and she sank deeper into the water. She had done it though, she had shown him. She had been brave and now she could swim. The gleaming spade stood in the corner of the bathroom like a bright pennant of her victory. She was glad she had been allowed to go back for it. She had chosen it over all the other things in the shop and bought it with her own money. Money kept safe inside one of Daddy's blue and yellow cigarette tins which she had held on tightly to all the way here, the coins rattling and jangling inside. Best of all though, tomorrow they were going home, tomorrow in the morning. It was a wonderful thought.

She pulled out the plug and lay motionless in the bath as the water slurped out. Just before it gurgled away she jumped out and, shivering, wrapped the meagre towel around her. It wasn't at all like home here.

At home, in winter, she could run down to the big fireplace and lazily dry herself in front of it like a cat. And in summer she would sit by the enamelled range in the kitchen and soak up its gentle warmth. Here though, she had to get dry quickly and with a towel that was small and thin. There was a streak of pale, speckled sand in the bath, a sluggish procession that stopped short just before the plughole. She took a glass from the shelf above the wash basin and, filling it from the tap, shooed the sand away.

'I don't see how you can not get sand in the bath when you've been on the beach,' she thought and glared at the staid notice.

She put on her pyjamas and quietly opening the door, tiptoed down the corridor. She did not know why she tiptoed. It was the first time she had been away from home and it just seemed best to be especially quiet.

She could hear Uncle Richard whistling as she neared his door and remembered his instruction to say when she was out so he could have 'a bit of a wash and brush up.' Without thinking she pushed the door wide open and announced breezily, 'I've finished now!'

He was standing on one leg next to the bed, naked except for the white, flapping underpants he was struggling to remove from his raised foot. His mouth dropped open in mute astonishment and he lurched perilously, almost toppled off balance. She saw his huge sagging stomach and below was a strange, thick, wrinkled catkin. It was a dickie. It was called a dickie and only men had them and it was half-hidden in a forbidding crop of prickly-looking hair.

'Sorry!' she gasped and fled from the room. She dived into her own and flung herself down on the bed. It was dreadful, terrible. How could she have forgotten to knock, how could she? Yet creeping over her, as she hid her red face in the pillow, was a growing mischievous glee. It was funny. The dickie was funny. Imagine having something like that wobbling all over the place. And the look on his face. She giggled into the pillow, at the same time telling herself she shouldn't. But it was so funny, that dangly thing, and the huge tummy and his strangled expression, as if he had gulped something nasty. She could hear him through the thin wall, clearing his throat loudly, not whistling anymore. His door opened and he stepped out into the corridor. He would be furious with her. He had dressed and now he would march into her room and shout and bark at her for being so unforgivably rude. She braced herself for the door to crash open.

But it never came. Instead, out in the echoing corridor, he tentatively cleared his throat yet again.

'Um......I'll just be having my bath now, then I'll, ah, come and say goodnight.' There was a silence before he added quietly and for no reason, 'Yes......' He plumped softly down the corridor, closing the bathroom door behind him.

She sat bolt upright and stared at her door, still waiting for it to burst open and for the indignant tirade to erupt over her. Yet there was just the hollow clatter of his bath filling. She flopped back on the bed. So that was a dickie. And Uncle Richard had one.

Later her door clicked open and without coming in he asked in an abashed voice, 'Are you in bed?' The door opened slowly, he looked uncomfortable and gazed past her. She regarded him seriously and put on a face she hoped would look contrite.

'All fit?' he asked. 'Well goodnight then. I'll just be downstairs. Get a good night's sleep. Long journey tomorrow.'

He wasn't going to say anything at all about it. He wasn't going to tell her off one bit.

'Must I go to bed now?' It was still light outside. He stepped one pace into the room and nodded.

'Long journey tomorrow,' he repeated, then backed out and closed the door firmly.

To bed unfairly early, she lay awake as the last of the evening sun creamed lazily through the thin curtains shifting in the faint breeze. Other children's laughter floated up to her window and a lone gull mewled a doleful lament. She felt the weight of her spade on the bed and wiggled her toes under it. It would be the first thing she saw in the morning.

A woman's laughter came from downstairs, a shrill laugh that ended in a snort. Then a low and indistinct voice she thought was Uncle Richard's. A glassy chink, a dance band on the wireless, more laughter. She remembered then, with an uneasy combination of guilt and glee, how he had dipped his mouth in the water and blown bubbles, showing her what to do, while she, innocent face shining at him above, had peed furiously into the sea below. She couldn't help it. She had been desperate.

She began to drift. Tomorrow, tomorrow she would be home. She could picture Hadley and conjure up its familiar smells; sun warmth on wood, honeysuckle and rose, grass and nettles. She smiled drowsily to herself and fell asleep to the sound of the green sea still rushing in her ears, her arms still paddling through the waves. And, faraway, a ship boomed out its echoing warning through the gathering deep sea fog.

CHAPTER THREE

Her bare feet pattered urgently on the cold linoleum as she hurried to the bathroom. They had overslept. Uncle Richard's puffy face glowered at her as he fumbled back to his room clutching a sponge bag and towel.

'Be quick,' he snapped, 'we're late.' Again that mysterious, unseen schedule.

She had been jerked from sleep by his loud hammering on her door and a bellowed order to get up as quickly as she could. The bright spade clattered to the floor as she leapt from the bed. She stared down at it in a confused, sleepy stupor as he poked his head around the door to make sure she was awake. His remote, unintentional humility of the previous evening had gone, replaced by a crumpled face and red, narrowed eyes.

They ate a moody, silent breakfast. The landlady was uncharacteristically serious. There were none of the cheerful, 'Everything all right dears?' there had been on other mornings. Uncle Richard complained of headache and the woman solicitously brought aspirins. He had nicked himself shaving and had two little pieces of bloody paper stuck to his throat. Swilling down his tea he told Jenny to go and wait by the car.

She screwed her eyes up against the morning sun and watched him through the door as he settled the bill. He glanced over his shoulder at her then exchanged some hurried words with the landlady. The girl imagined it was about the bill. Then he bustled out to join her.

'Come along. Let's be off.'

She waved a secret goodbye to the sea as they drove away. He said she had to sit in the back so he could have the map open on the passenger seat.

It was a long, stiflingly hot journey. The sun quickly baked the car and she rolled down the windows. Uncle Richard concentrated grimly on the driving. She shouted against the noise of the engine to ask how long it would take and then, later, how far they had gone but eventually they settled into silence.

She sniffed appreciatively at the wind rushing in through the windows then sank into the cracked leather seats. It took all morning to reach Dorchester then on to Lyme Regis where they stopped and ate warm sandwiches and drank a flask of tea. Then on again through the spring countryside. She caught flashing glimpses of the glittering sea through gaps in straggling gorse as they sped along.

She was half-dozing in the stuffy heat when he spoke. His voice seemed dislocated, close to her, almost at her ear, yet still distant.

'Look. Down there. Nearly home.'

She sat up excitedly. They were poised on the brow of a hill. Below, a wide bay stretched into the distance, its sweeping curve shepherding in a sea full of brilliant crystals. Hadley was at the far side of the bay. If it was winter, she thought, and the big fire was crackling in the grate, she would be able to see the smoke. She bounced on the seat and gripped the spade tightly, full of anticipation.

Half an hour later the car shuddered to a halt outside the house. She jumped out, a tingling stiffness in her legs. Everything was still and deliciously quiet after the constant shaking of the car. And at last, home.

Uncle Richard climbed slowly from the driver's seat and let out a deep sigh. Liddy was already walking down the path to greet them and he came round the car and stood next to the girl, placing an arm protectively around her as if they were posing for a photograph. His arm was unpleasantly heavy and his closeness oppressive. An aura of sticky heat came from him and she wanted to shrink away. She looked up at him. His face was less bloated now but the little pieces of paper were still stuck fast.

Liddy's blonde hair was piled high and she was wearing a thin, flowered dress. For as long as she could remember the girl had called her mother by her name. She didn't know why. She was Liddy in private, Mummy if there were other people about. That was the rule. Jenny ran to her and the woman bent and hugged the chattering child, admired the spade thrust at her and serenely asked about 'your lovely adventure.' She kissed Uncle Richard lightly on the cheek, greeting him with the warm, graceful smile she so easily gave. It was a smile that set people at ease and made them feel singled out, especially chosen to receive its radiance.

'And did Jennifer really swim all by herself?'

'Just about,' the man said with a lop-sided smile, 'needs practice though.'

They had tea in the garden. A table had been set out under the cool, swishing willow. The girl ate quickly, scarcely able to contain herself, then darted off around the big garden, re-acquainting herself with the familiar and loved; hidden, nettled corners, the stone sundial, a small pile of smooth, round stones she had secretly made into a little cairn without knowing or asking herself why. She poked about in the shed and greenhouse, with their comforting tarry wood smells, amongst the jumble of tools and old, cracked pots. Sitting cross-legged on the grass, she blew at a dandelion clock and chanted in a whisper, 'I shan't ever, ever, ever go away again.'

She looked up at the house, at its solid white walls with their black-framed windows. Daddy said it was a special place because it made all the people who had ever lived in it happy and they loved it so much that, long ago, they made a special gate of elegant metal, painted white, with the name proudly across it in a sweeping crescent. And it didn't matter that it was a fib and that the gate wasn't old at all because she knew Daddy was right and that everyone who'd ever lived there had been happy, because she was. It was theirs and she loved it as she loved him. The blue sea was his place too. The same small waves that yesterday tickled her ankles might at this very moment, far away on the other side of the world, brush against the prow of his ship, slip past and bubble in its wake. Daddy said Hadley would be hers one day. It was to be the best gift. She would always stay. Always and forever. She had been born there. It was where she began.

Liddy's voice floated across the lawn to her. She was beckoning the girl from the cool shadows.

'He's going!' the girl exclaimed happily to herself. Everything would be as it should once more. She picked up the spade, trotted over to them and they walked slowly to the car. Uncle Richard paused and examined the sky thoughtfully.

'I do hope Jennifer hasn't been any trouble?' the woman asked. A hurried assurance was given and Liddy said, 'She's always been a good girl, such a good girl.'

'Goodbye!' Jenny said, too eagerly.

'And what do you say?' her mother asked pleasantly, beaming down at her from another world. The man looked at them, hooded and expectant. The girl felt her face contort into an uncomfortable smile; a moments pause, a squirming inside.

'Thank you.'

★   ★   ★

It was another sunny day when the news came. A choir of birds jostled noisily in the trees as Jenny pulled open her bedroom curtains and saw the postman cycling slowly along the lane, just like any other day.

She lingered at the window, then began to dress. She could hear the wireless below and the postman's knock on the door, a bright 'Good morning' from her mother and a low, male mumble in reply. The front door closed slowly.

'Today,' she thought, 'I'm going to play in the garden the whole day and be an Arctic explorer.'

She carried on dressing and was buttoning her blouse when footsteps drummed heavily up the stairs. She hurried herself up, expecting Liddy to call from the landing that breakfast was ready. But she didn't call out. Instead there were strange and unfamiliar sounds; long, shuddering moans, a loud gagging, something heavy and wet flopping into water. She rushed from her room. The lavatory door had been flung wide open and the ugly noises were coming from inside it. She peered apprehensively round the door. Liddy was being sick. Her face was a ghastly white and her eyes amber-flecked and wild. She was slumped on the floor, coughing and retching, her back rearing up in a quivering, straining arch.

The girl stood rooted with shock. Grown-ups weren't like this. Liddy wasn't like this. She had sick on her face and in her hair. Shiny strings of it dribbled from her chin and hung in trembling skeins. There was sick on the floor and it was yellow and smelt sour. Liddy struggled to raise her stricken face.

'Get away Jenny, get away!'

The words hung in the air as harsh and overpowering as the smell. The girl darted back to her room as though scalded. She sat stiffly on her bed, bewildered. The sun still shone outside, her toy monkey lay splay-legged on the pillow, the loose stitches that made up its mouth still unmended. Toys spilled out of the half open cupboard door. She sat in her room and felt it all differently. A trembling feeling in her stomach spread up her spine and gripped tightly at her shoulders and neck. She sat and could not move. The ugly, crushed look on Liddy's face hovered before her eyes. She had never seen her like that before and it frightened her. Everything had changed, something had stalked into Hadley, some animal thing that had no place there; it was horrible. The shrill birdsong outside subsided into the usual chirruping. Sunshine slipped over the windowsill and into the room making bright splashes over the floor.

The sound of vomiting slowed to a spitting cough. Then to nothing, silence. She heard Liddy shuffle unsteadily to her feet and flush the lavatory three times in succession, a smothered gurgling above her room as water bubbled from the roof tank to refill the cistern. Feet dragging slowly along the landing and down the stairs. Then returning, scrubbing and mopping noises and a sharp disinfectant smell that crept under her door. More flushing and the footsteps went downstairs again. After a while Liddy returned. A pause outside the girl's door then slowly to the bathroom where taps were turned full on and the bathroom door closed on the rumbling rush of water.

When later Liddy came into her room she looked if not normal then at least composed. She entered quietly and did not smile at the girl. Her eyes were still red-rimmed, her face pallid and drained; all of her usual grace had been stolen from her.

She came forward slowly and stood slightly bowed. Her strained eyes seemed to be struggling for expression, a way of looking. When finally she spoke it was an anguished whisper.

'It's very bad news Jenny. It's Daddy. He's gone.'

'Gone where?'

The woman sank to her knees, eyes downcast, her hands shaking.

'To heaven. He's gone to heaven. Daddy has died and we must be very brave.'

The girl struggled to comprehend, to interpret the unimaginable. Her eyes darted wildly around the room, clutching at the known. Dead. It was a church word, not a word for Daddy. As her mind gripped unwillingly at the meaning, there was a sound inside her head like a tin tray dropping to the floor; a faint whoosh as it fell, then a ringing chime that echoed again and again, spinning inside her brain and forcing hot stabs of intense light into her blurred eyes. Liddy's disembodied voice reached out to her across a vast distance, trying to catch her as the girl felt her body crumple and the white hand of unconsciousness pull her down and down.

'Jenny!'

CHAPTER FOUR

It was the middle of the afternoon when the car pulled up outside Hadley. It was old and immaculately polished. The man who got out of it was old too. He was wearing a dark suit but, when he turned, the girl saw a great slab of different colours, like postage stamps, pinned on his chest. He pulled a stick from the car and, leaning heavily on it, opened the gate and walked slowly up the path. He looked very tall and his face was gaunt and serious. Liddy joined her at the window where she was peering through curtains pulled in mourning.

'Go upstairs now Jenny,' she said in an expressionless voice. The girl went slowly into the hall. She still felt strange and scoured inside. Liddy had given her half a pink tablet to help make her feel better. The man's shadow loomed behind the glass of the door as she reached the foot of the stairs and the doorbell chimed, inappropriately cheerful, ringing through the silenced house. The sound and the man's shape at the door spurred her quickly to her room.

Her bed was still unmade, her hair and teeth unbrushed. All the usual rules had been broken. She pulled back the curtains a little so that some of the sunshine came in but was careful not to open them too far. Daddy was dead.

She never knew what the old man said or who he was. The voices from below were low and solemn. She picked absently at an unfinished jigsaw puzzle but soon got up again and went to the window. The black car was still there. She tussled with the stiff window catch and opened it, letting in the day. The warm breeze was soothing as it stroked her face. She put a small porcelain windmill Daddy had brought back for her on the sill and watched the sails float languidly round. The birds were still singing and a hum of insects filled the garden.

It must all be a mistake. Even if Daddy's boat had been sunk he could swim. She remembered now and clearly, he could swim for miles. She had seen him swim right out and then all the way back again without even being puffed out. He had come out of the sea grinning and all dripping wet and chased her around the beach, threatening to throw her in, and she had shrieked and shrieked and wanted him to keep doing it when he stopped. Afterwards he let her bury him in the sand and, when she had covered him up so that just his head was showing and he looked trapped and helpless, he just gave a great, laughing roar and heaved himself up out of the showering sand, chased and caught her and tossed her in the air as if she weighed nothing at all.

Daddy couldn't be dead. He hadn't seen her swim. The windmill whirred furiously in a quick warm gust and toppled over. She righted it and watched with satisfaction as it settled again into a smooth rhythm. Anyway the war was over. It had been for weeks. She had heard the King's stammer on the wireless saying so. Daddy couldn't be dead if it was over, he had to see her swim and see her new spade.

They had gone down to wave him off after his last leave. The ship looked tiny in the distance but when they were next to it the grey hull towered above them, blotting out a big piece of the sky. He had grinned and hugged her and she'd asked, as she always did, 'What will you bring me Daddy?' And in turn, completing the ritual, he reached out, ruffled her hair.

'I shall bring for you the treasure house of the world.'

Then, still grinning, he went up the gangplank and disappeared from sight. They waited at the quayside until two piercing hoots punctured the air and other men came down from the ship, their loud laughter abruptly dominated by a stern, booming voice.

'Language gentlemen. Ladies down below!'

She asked why the men weren't going too but Liddy didn't know and together they watched as the vast destroyer throbbed slowly away from the berth. Once or twice they thought they saw Daddy on deck and waved and waved even though they weren't sure it was him. He looked very busy. Then he turned and waved briefly before going below.

'It was him wasn't it?' she had said then.

How could he be dead? He always came home from the sea.

The front door opened and the old man made his way down the path. He paused before he got into the car, turned stiffly back to the house and saluted.

Hadley became an island, encircled by sorrow. It remained hushed and still despite the busy drone of summer outside. Their grieving could find no expression except in the mute continuation of routine. Liddy was a distant, slight figure who floated through the house, wan and rarely smiling. If she did smile it was a fleeting thing shaped from sadness. She was vague now about the everyday matters that once she had organised with cheerful precision; mealtimes, laundry, making sure Jenny brushed her hair one hundred times every night. Often the girl would come across her sitting alone in a silent room just looking out to the light and green of the garden and would know that she had been there, quite still, for hours.

Liddy did not cry nor did she share whatever thoughts filled her faraway mind. And because she didn't, the girl thought that this was how it must be with death, that it was something to be borne alone. Sometimes they would hug each other wordlessly but it seemed that they were each embracing a solitary emptiness and there was little comfort in it. The only thing Liddy did say was that they had to put a brave face on things because that's what Daddy would want. It was a phrase she would repeat on the day of the memorial service. So the girl cried alone in her room at night, remembering Daddy and his big voice that could fill the world outdoors, and learnt to keep her memories close, holding them inside like a precious breath. From then on she always kept his blue and yellow cigarette tin close by her, because once he had held it and it had belonged to him.

She could not remember what she did with the days. They had no plan anymore. She helped in the house, laying the table and clearing away afterwards. But meals were silent and unhappy, overshadowed by absence, a third place never again to be set. Sometimes she sat on the swing Daddy had made, swinging listlessly. He had scrambled up through the branches with a rope between his teeth, climbing so high that he seemed to disappear into the sun.

And just when she wanted to shout, 'Dad, Dad!', because it seemed he was lost and would never come down again, one end of the rope plummeted to the ground and he clambered down it, gleaming with sweat, a leaf in his hair.

Other days too when they had played hide and seek around the huge white sheets on the washing line, billowing like grounded clouds, so big they seemed to fill the garden and all of the sky. She had run and twirled in and out of them, no longer certain if it were clouds or flicking wet sheets that swept her up and made her giddy with the curve of the earth. He would talk to her about the stars as well because he was a navigator and knew all about them. He would point them out through her window when he tucked her up at night and recite their funny-sounding names.

The long summer, which had stretched enticingly ahead of her such a short time ago, was now a backdrop to a lonely bewilderment. She was in suspension, waiting for something to happen, the next piece of news. But there was no more. There would be no more news. It was at an end but felt unfinished. Liddy explained that the memorial service was for them to say goodbye properly to Daddy but it hadn't been like that. There was no coffin and no grave because he had been lost at sea. She couldn't understand all the words and was hot and uncomfortable in a thick, woollen dress; her only dark one. She didn't like the service. It was stiff and serious with lots of standing still. There were some men there from the Navy, all holding their caps. They looked uncomfortable too. One of them dropped his cap and she turned to watch as he fumbled to retrieve it, until Liddy's hand on her shoulder turned her firmly forward again to the mumbling voice and the round, bland face of the chaplain.

She didn't want to go to the party but Liddy said she must and that was that.

'We must all make an effort,' had been the phrase this time, as if effort alone could somehow erase the dull lament that was now part of the girl's everyday. Liddy had lately been making an effort, trying to return some ordinariness to their lives. She had subsumed her tragedy beneath a brittle veneer of her old self but it wasn't the same. They were still adrift.

'Must look our best,' Liddy mumbled through a mouthful of hairpins, as she tugged a brush through the girl's hair. Jenny hated the party frock with its puffy sleeves and satin sash.

They had walked to the village that morning and seen all the party preparations in full flurry. Shops were decked out with Union Jacks and bunting. A long row of trestle tables had been set up on the village green and a clutch of chattering women were placing cutlery that glinted in the sunshine.

'But why is there going to be a party?' the girl asked, a sullen resentment at all the fuss souring her voice.

'Because the war is over.'

'Why is it over?' Inside her, impossible to articulate, was the feeling that it couldn't really be over if there was no Daddy anymore.

'Because we've won.'

'What was it we won though?'

'Our freedom, for our country.'

'But we were already free weren't we?'

'Yes Jennifer, we were.' An edge of irritation crept into the woman's voice. Her pace quickened and there was a silencing tug at the girl's hand, 'But we wouldn't have stayed free unless we did win.'

Jennifer was quiet as they made their way to the post office. She still didn't understand it. They passed a small cottage with its curtains drawn against the bustle, a solitary reminder of another who had not returned.

When they got there she was allowed to reach up and drop the letter into the box.

'Who did you write to?'

But Liddy wasn't listening. She was looking up at the sky. Everyone else had stopped too and they were all staring into the blue distance at an insistent growl that was rapidly getting louder. Suddenly three Hurricanes blasted across the village, flying fast and low. A spontaneous ragged cheer went up as the planes shrank swiftly away, the snarl of their engines still hanging in the air. Jenny had ducked at the intense roar but now straightened quickly, not wanting to look foolish. The grown-ups were still beaming proudly at the sky.

'Them's the boys that did for 'im,' barked one old man, 'they did for that 'ole bugger all right!'

That afternoon, at the party, she was put in charge of a small, silent girl dressed in a cardboard crown and a long robe made from old blue satin. The toddler was an unwanted responsibility even though she sat quietly, ploughing through a bowl of red jelly. After a while she tugged at Jennifer's dress and made a solemn announcement.

'Queen needs a wee-wee.'

Jenny led her towards the church hall where her mother was helping but halfway there the toddler became tearful.

'Queen wee-wee now!'

They ducked into some bushes and Jennifer let her get on with it, while she peered out stonily at the party through a tangle of brambles. From a distance it looked small and sort of forlorn. The flags were hanging limply in the still afternoon. The vicar was holding forth to a small, attentive group, jabbing the air with a bun as a he spoke. One man in army uniform was sat with a squirming knot of children at one of the tables. He was doing magic tricks but she could see he was taking too long and the children were losing interest. It wasn't fair, she thought, all their Daddies were coming home.

A thin wail, like a siren, started up behind her. The little girl had peed on her satin robe.

'Oh come on,' Jenny said with exasperation, 'and for goodness sake shut up!' But the child continued to howl as they scrambled out and went back to the party, the wet robe dragging along the dusty ground. Jennifer wished she hadn't had to come. She wanted to go home.

CHAPTER FIVE

She couldn't quite get the proper grave shape. It was turning out to be more of a square but it was nearly right. She wasn't sure how deep it should be. Her seaside spade hacked resolutely through the soil but it was hard work. She stopped for a moment and wiped her brow. Dew dripped from new spring leaves; a pale, golden green shot through with morning light. The early sun was glowing and she could hear the daybreak incantation of fat woodpigeons. She was hidden away in a corner of the garden. A plump bee cruised noisily by and she set to again, the spade crunching into the earth, clanging on stones and flints.

Liddy was still asleep. The girl could see that the flowered curtains at her window were pulled across. Jenny had woken early thinking how it wasn't right that they didn't have a place, a special place, for Daddy. A place she could take flowers to. She had been shown the church wall where his name would go but it would be all jumbled up with lots of other names. It wasn't the same as a proper grave. She still didn't really believe it anyway. If the ship had been on fire, he would have jumped into the sea. She remembered the steep sides of the vessel and pictured him diving boldly from that sheer hull, flames leaping up behind him. Lying in bed she came to a decision. There would be a special place for him, a secret place she could look after.

Still in her pyjamas she crept out of bed and went downstairs. The spade was propped by the kitchen door where Liddy made her leave it now. Solid and shiny, it still proclaimed her conquest over Uncle Richard and over her own fear. Liddy had said it was kind of him to teach her to swim but he hadn't been kind. He hadn't been kind to her at all.

The hole looked deep enough now. She picked up the toy monkey she had brought. She'd loved it for a long time. It had to be something she loved very much. Liddy had mended its sewn mouth but it never quite regained the same guileless expression. She wrapped it carefully in a piece of blue cloth and placed it reverently in the hole. Then she doggedly shovelled the earth back in. Patting the mound she sat back on her heels to admire it. She had thought about making a little cross but then it might be discovered and wouldn't be a secret anymore.

She gave it a final satisfied pat and went back to the house, stopping to brush dirt from her pyjamas. She put the spade back in its place and went into the hall. An envelope lay on the front door mat and she put it on the hall table then quietly went upstairs, still thinking about the little grave. Later she would get some flowers and find a pot to put them in.

That morning, for the first time, she heard again a sound once familiar at Hadley but which had been silent since the news of Daddy; it was her mother singing; a clear resonant soprano that had once placed her at the front rank of the county's operatic society. People said she should have been a professional but Liddy would just smile, pleased but shy, like a young girl with her first cocktail at her first party.

And that night, as she would many times in the days to come, the girl stole from her bed and stealthily made her way through the darkness and down to the beach, her towel and swimming costume bundled under her arm, even though she wasn't allowed and would get a terrific telling off if she was caught. Uncle Richard had been right about one thing. She wasn't frightened of the water anymore. On the contrary, the sea had rolled dreamily into her soul, a new friend, unrecognised at first, who was always there and always would be. There had been another decision that day. She would show them, show them all. She would practise and practise until she was the best swimmer in all of England. In the whole world.

★ ★ ★

The long strange summer drifted on and the new school term began. In a way it was a relief to be subject again to another regime but still she yearned for the openness and lightness of life as it had been.

The relief did not last long. Everything at school had changed too. Friends, perhaps forewarned, were wary. One even pityingly called her an orphan. She began to envy the other children though could not put it into words. She both longed to be one of them again, yet stubbornly clung to her new and ill-defined status. She envied the easy, uncomplicated way they played and larked about. They had not been suddenly wrenched from the ordinary into a baffling world somewhere between child and adult; treated like the one but feeling more and more, in a faltering way, preternaturally like the other. She couldn't join in with the old games. She tried to but it was no good. The other children sensed it and sought her company less and less. She would watch them as if from a hilltop and knew there was no going back, no return. She took to solitary skipping at playtime, counting out loud to hurry, by ritual, the passage of time. Playtimes were loneliest. There was only one other child who had lost his father but the family had moved away before the term began.

Once, during morning break, she felt a light, insistent tap on her back and turned to find a bespectacled girl with blonde plaits.

'You 'avn't got a dad 'ave you, 'ees dead in'ee?' she asked flatly yet without the slightest hint of cruelty. She stared steadfastly through the round glasses waiting for an answer. Jenny wanted to scream into that pale inquiring face but stood transfixed by the shining spectacles and their wearer's wholly innocent insensitivity. Instead she ran off and hid by the dining hall, dabbing at her eyes with the sleeve of her cardigan. A grown-up must have overheard because nothing like it happened again.

The teachers treated her with discreet, clucking sympathy but she would not let them close. She didn't think Daddy would want that. It wouldn't be proper. Not brave.

Shirley, a girl she had been 'best' friends with, transferred her allegiance to another without a backward glance. In an odd, unstated way, her classmates began to regard her more as she herself felt, as somehow more grown-up, different. She was no longer privy to secrets or forbidden classroom giggles but, once or twice, was called upon to referee squabbles as though her distance now conferred upon her the power of arbitration. It was something the other children recognised without question. They too, knew she was now set apart from them.

The final severance came when she did not receive an invitation to Shirley's birthday party. She should have been crestfallen but wasn't. The snub without malice just reinforced her aloneness. And alone she would wander through the woods to the sea where she swam at dead of night, the beach long since cleared now except for a straggle of barbed wire and two faded signs, dimly warning of a danger no longer present.

It was a solitary world, filled with deliciously real and imagined terrors and freedoms. It somehow demanded her presence and held out in return a mysterious promise of something just over the next hill, coming in on the next tide. She did not know what it was but knew she had to be there for it, whatever it might be. She wanted to be nowhere else but here, with the silence of the green trees and the enticing blue sea. Not really a silence at all but suffused with a gentle rushing as the wind ruffled leaf and wave alike. She would lay down on the grass above the beach and feel herself become part of that sound, her breathing aligning itself to the same rhythm. Then, turning her head and opening one eye, was the sea, a blue plain stretching far beyond a child's imagination; unfolding, still concealing. This was the place she belonged. Always and forever.

★   ★   ★

She had posted Liddy's letter and bought a small bag of sweets in the post office. It was the day of Shirley's party and the village was emptied of children. It was good to be alone. She liked the feeling of not being where all the others were. She munched and skipped nonchalantly along the lane towards home, listening idly to the hedgerow buzz of the late summer. She broke into a trot, kicking up clouds of fine dust behind her. Home was a white blob in the distance but it was no longer Hadley, it was a glittering palace in a faraway land. The stallion beneath her was shiny with sweat as they raced towards it, bearing news of an advancing barbarian army gathering behind her, poised for attack. If only she could get there in time she could raise the alarm and save the Emperor. She ducked as a deadly arrow whistled past her head and spurred her proud steed as it pounded on, its brave heart still firm after their gruelling marathon. Then, just as they clattered into the imperial courtyard, Liddy came out of the back door, smiling.

'My, you look hot!'

They sat on the bench by the back door and drank lemonade. As the girl raised her glass the vivid white on white of the crescent scar shone in the sunlight and a trace of her game returned.

'An enemy arrow did it!' she thought grimly, connecting fiction to reality for a brief, satisfying moment that disappeared when Liddy spoke.

'What are you doing this afternoon?'

She hesitated; the ivy on the wall behind them shimmered and was still.

'I want to go to the beach for some shells. You can stick them all over a box and keep precious things in it. I've seen one in a book.'

'Have you got a box?' Liddy smiled.

'I'm sure I can find one,' Jenny said enthusiastically, 'or a tin or something.' She frowned thoughtfully. 'Have we got any glue?'

'I think so, somewhere. Well don't be late back.'

The girl gulped the last of her lemonade, darted into the kitchen for her spade and was off.

'Bye!' she called out to the slender, elegant figure still resting on the bench.

'Goodbye!' Liddy waved but Jenny was already leaping back onto her mount and racing down through the enchanted forest to the sea, the barbarians fleeing before her, scurrying for their lives like the cowards they were.

Her first glimpse of a sparkling triangle of pale sea, framed between green slopes, finally put to flight the scuttling enemy. She stopped, panting, and admired it. It was a wide curving bay, an untroubled sea shining like mercury and stretching away to a hazy horizon. She loved its sweeping curve. It was a place where anything at all could be just about to happen. A warm breeze stroked the sea holly and marram grass.

Far below, and disconcertingly, a man stood quite alone on the beach. He was delivering what sounded like a sermon.

'I told you. I warned you. The closer you come the farther away you are.' He spoke in a high, scolding voice and, as he did, hopped towards the retreating wash and then back again as the waves advanced. His feet were getting very wet. It sounded like he was saying the same thing over and over again. He was young, quite tall and very thin. He wore a thick tweed jacket that was much too big for him.

'He must be terribly hot,' she thought, still sticky herself. She squatted down and watched the peculiar ceremony. She knew he was unaware of her. Peeking at him, or anyone, was forbidden and therefore doubly satisfying. Not that she would have normally but his behaviour was so odd that it somehow gave her licence. She had never seen a grown-up do anything like this. It was like playing but it was a strange game, one she didn't understand. It was funny but at the same time it wasn't because he was so serious. He did look very silly though, hopping about in the waves, and he was getting very, very wet.

His strange, bony presence and inexplicable behaviour stopped her from going down. It wasn't that it was frightening. He was too thin and birdlike for that. Instead it was a reluctance to invade a weird privacy his bizarre ritual had thrown, like a conjurer's cloak, over the beach. Yet a curious feeling of mean culpability crept over her; his funny dance was certainly outlandish but it wasn't really right to be secretly watching him. She couldn't, though, just stroll down there while he was carrying on like that and pretend it was normal. It would be awfully embarrassing. She retreated a few yards into the trees then began to whistle loudly.

When she came out into the open he had stopped. He was standing completely still, not looking round at her but straight out to sea. His shoulders were hunched up and he looked even more like a frail bird. Her perky whistling seemed literally to have petrified him.

She would pretend he wasn't there. She wandered past him and down the beach, still whistling as though completely unconcerned, then sank down on her knees at the waters edge. She began to dig, piling up the beginnings of a castle, patting it into shape with her hands. She glanced at him sideways. Still he had not moved. When she finished the castle she dug a moat and a shallow trench to the sea. The foaming tide gurgled up the trench and slopped into the moat, brown and frothy. She looked about for shells to decorate the castle and wished she had a flag.

She did not hear him come up behind her. There was just a sudden coolness as he stood between her and the sun. She leapt to her feet.

'You made me jump!' she gasped, 'I nearly jumped out of my skin!' She started to brush the sand from her clothes. He was smiling down at her, a smile that hid his teeth, and holding a single grey, gull's feather in silent offering. Even though he was smiling she could read nothing at all in his white face. He was older than she had thought and his skin was like paper with fine lines traced on it. The tweed jacket smelt sour and hung on him, ludicrously big. She reached out for the feather but he bobbed down and planted it on top of the sandcastle, beaming at her. She smiled shyly back.

'Thanks. I hadn't thought of that.'

Then suddenly he was off, running over the sand in a gawky trot, stopping to pick up more feathers. When he returned he had a fistful which he proffered excitedly. She took them and added them to the fortress.

'I'm Jenny,' she said encouragingly, but he stayed silent. She couldn't say she had already heard him talking because then he would know she had spied on him.

'I've come for some shells really.'

The grin dropped from his face and he looked deeply serious. He gestured her to follow him and loped off, minutely examining the beach. Then he would pounce on some bright shell which he passed to her with infinite care. Soon she had more than she could hold. She pulled her blouse from her skirt and put the shells in it like a pouch.

'That's enough I think,' she said gently.

He gazed at her with his open, smiling face and dropped the shell he was holding into the outstretched blouse.

'Thanks. I ought to go home now or I'll be late.'

His face fell and he looked down. His hands dropped to his sides, the bony wrists disappearing into the too-long sleeves of the smelly coat. He turned slowly and began to trudge down the beach, away from her. She was glad of the shells even though there were probably too many. Even so she felt an awkward relief, awkward because she thought perhaps she should have been more grateful.

She began to make her own way back. She stopped to collect her spade and for a last look at her castle, her fragile Camelot. He was quite a distance away now and looked sadly alone. She had said thanks but perhaps she hadn't said it enough. He might be all alone in the world and want a friend. She might still be able to put it right, she might just be able to after all.

'Goodbye and thanks again!'

A handful of words flung hopefully against the wind, against the rush and crash of waves. And from the stranger in the far distance, came an unfamiliar word, happily bellowed in a deep, straining voice. She imagined he was grinning again and smiled herself.

'Fuck......fuck......f..uck!'

CHAPTER SIX

It was the first dull day for ages. A clutch of seagulls circled moodily against a greying sky and the sea was swollen and subdued. She had wanted to come earlier but the week had been consumed by school and helping Liddy. Now the sun had gone and the sand was cold and hard underfoot.

When she arrived home the previous week she had counted out the shells in her room. There were twenty-three and her blouse had smelt of the sea. She wondered whether she would see the thin man there again. Equally, she wanted the beach to herself once more. It wasn't that she minded other people there as long as they went away again at the end of the day. But he was different. He had talked to the sea as though he knew something she didn't.

She paused and scanned the length of the bay. It was deserted and she smiled to herself. The sea and the beach, though hardly welcoming, was still her special place and even today seemed to accept her, perhaps with a grumble but not sending her away. The dark waves still whispered their own hypnotic language and she felt a deep, still satisfaction, the same feeling she got from creeping out at night and seeing it when ordinary people didn't. Most people only knew the sea as sunlit and blue.

Except Dad of course. He knew all about the sea. She remembered his stories about stormy oceans and men swept overboard never to be seen again.

Dad. He was why she was here today. She drew the bottle from her pocket. It was a small whisky bottle with a red and cream cap. For a long time it had been on the sideboard with just a tiny bit in the bottom but last night Liddy poured it into a tumbler and settled into a comfortable chair. Jenny volunteered to wash up and took it into the kitchen. She washed it along with the supper things and hid it down the side of the range to dry. Later she cut out a neat rectangle of paper and, taking up a pen, began to write, silently mouthing the words, the tip of her tongue stuck out in concentration.

She wrote his name and rank, what his ship was called and the date. Then her own name and address and *In loving memory* which she had seen on lots of gravestones. She fetched the bottle from the kitchen and tucked it into her jumper, said goodnight to Liddy and went upstairs. There she rolled the piece of paper up, slid it into the bottle, and screwed on the cap.

Now, on the gloomy beach, she wondered if the sea would get in and spoil it. She wasn't entirely sure why she had done it but had a mental picture of it floating poignantly over just the spot in the ocean where Daddy's ship had gone down. She had got the idea from a shipwreck story and, even though it wasn't quite the same, still wanted to do it.

She wandered along to the far end of the bay where flat brown rocks straggled out into the sea. Behind her a ragged footpath disappeared up through a sprinkling of stunted trees. This was the path the bony man must have taken. She wondered briefly where he had come from.

The slabs of rock spread out seaward like a giant's hand, gnarled and festooned with brown weed like shoelaces. She took off her shoes and socks and left them on the sand then tossed a stick into the foam and watched as it floated and twirled, eventually drifting out. She had only just remembered about the tide and would have felt silly if the bottle had beached itself at her feet. It was meant to be dignified, like a ceremony.

She tottered carefully out. The rocks weren't too wet but she avoided the clumps of slippery looking weed. The sea hissed, slapping noisily against the stone. A solitary gull hung in the air, black hooded and much bigger than the ones that waddled away from her on the beach.

At the end of an outstretched finger of rock, where waves flicked against the slab, she hurled the bottle so hard it made her shoulder hurt. It curved out to sea, spinning over and over, before plopping into the water. For a moment it disappeared completely and she wondered anxiously if it had sunk for good. Then it came up and swirled in the eddying tide. For a while it seemed drawn back to the rock and she fretted that it might smash against it. Gradually though it moved out.

'Off on its mission,' she thought, disappointed that it wasn't bobbing upright like the illustration in the story. She watched until it vanished into the grey swell.

The light was starting to fade and she hopped back to the beach and retrieved her shoes and socks. It was done. She trailed homeward, unexpectedly deflated; a hollow tummy feeling of there being nothing left. A quick, sharp blast of wind whipped her hair across her face. It was the first warning of the storm to come. She stared at the dirty white horizon, impenetrable as curdled milk. A wave crashed and doused her with thin spray. She hurried herself as she felt the first of the drizzle; she'd get told off if she got all wet.

Back in the woods, where high branches swayed and lurched, she heard a low growl coming from the sea and the distant, doleful sound of a foghorn. The drizzle prickled against her skin and she wrapped her arms about her, cold in the gusting wind. It became rain and quickly plastered her hair, cold drips slithering down her neck. She stopped and peered hopefully up at the clouds, blinking against the heavy drops of rain. It wasn't going to let up. Dark clouds were massing in the small patch of sky she could see through the treetops. She scurried on, sandals wet and spattering underfoot. It wasn't too far, just down through the woods along the lane and then home. When she reached the lane, she saw the oily yellow of an early light in a downstairs window. She was soaked through and bound to get into trouble. But afterwards there would be a hot bath, luxuriously deep and fragrant. She huddled against the driving rain and ran up the lane. Flinging open the gate she hurtled down the path and at the back door heard the rising notes of a soprano voice from the gramophone.

That evening the late summer was split apart by a violent storm. It finally broke well into the night, after the anticipated telling off, after the hot bath, and long after her bedtime.

She lay with the blankets up under her chin as crackling flashes flooded her room and rolling thunder stalked the deep combe. Rain pinged like gravel thrown at her window and a buttressing wind blustered through trees and bushes. She heard flowerpots crash to the ground and there was a hollow rumble as the dustbin rolled across the yard. She wanted to peep through the curtains but was too frightened. The roaring wind and startling crashes filled the night and she dozed fitfully while convoluted dreams rode in on the gale: wild dreams of a racing wind like a booming voice rushing over the lawn and striking the roof, demanding to be heard while she swirled over and over in a suffocating eiderdown sea that tossed her like driftwood. When she woke she could remember none of it clearly yet felt herself struggling against a disturbing confusion, a feeling that slowly slipped away as she got up.

Morning, and still in their nightclothes, she and Liddy stood outside and surveyed the night's damage. Half a dozen roof slates were dislodged, the garden bench upturned and broken, a length of fence torn down. The contents of the dustbin and broken pottery were strewn across the yard.

The woman looked despairingly up at the roof and sighed.

'I'll have to telephone Mr. Martin and get him to fix it,' she said. She seemed dreamy, what Dad used to call 'head in the clouds' as she swept back a wisp of stray hair. The girl watched as she awkwardly righted the battered dustbin then began to pick up the spilt rubbish.

'Shall I fetch the broom?'

'Yes please dear. It's just inside the shed. On the left I think.'

'Yes, I know.'

The woman wearily pushed back the same strand of stray hair, 'Yes of course you do.' She looked at the broken fence with an air of hopeless defeat. 'Perhaps we should dress first, that would be best. Oh, look at my poor flowers!' Scattered petals and bedraggled plants moped in the flower border.

'I'm sorry about the flowers,' Jenny said regretfully, 'we could take them indoors and put them into pots though couldn't we? They wouldn't all be wasted then.' Her mother looked at her sadly.

'Yes, we could, we could rescue the survivors,' She glanced grimly around the ravaged garden. 'Let's get ourselves up first anyway.' Gloomily they went back inside.

Jenny was down first, still buttoning her blouse as she went back outside, furtively scooped up a handful of the battered flowers and ran hastily to the secret grave. She jammed them unceremoniously into the pot she had previously placed there, admired them for a second and ran quickly back to the house. Liddy was on the telephone sounding especially gracious.

'If you could Mr. Martin. That would be most kind.' She put down the receiver. 'He's coming straight over.' She made the 'he' sound like a knight on a white charger.

After breakfast they began to clear up. Jenny sorted gingerly through the rubbish for shards of broken flowerpots.

'Couldn't we make something with them, for the garden?' she asked, but this novel idea seemed only to flummox her mother.

'I'm sure we could dear, but just at the moment I can't imagine what.'

Regardless, Jenny collected the pieces and put them in the greenhouse. Perhaps she would think of something later.

Liddy swept down the yard with disinfectant that dried rapidly in the early sun.

'It smells like school,' the girl said, exaggeratedly holding her nose.

True to his word, Mr. Martin arrived soon after. A stout man in blue bib and brace he rang his bicycle bell outside in the lane before wheeling it, and the trailer mounted on pram wheels behind it, up the path. He puffed at a black pipe and squinted dubiously at the roof.

'You 'ad it bad then Missus?' he asked unnecessarily. He treated Liddy with a touch of deference. She wasn't quite gentry but was unmistakably a cut above. Her husband had been an officer too, a hero probably. Nonetheless, his respect for her as a widow and 'a lady' did not in the least limit the profanity with which he peppered the most ordinary of conversations. Every now and then he would catch himself at it and smile, abashed. Then he would mumble, 'pardon my French,' and proceed to swear even more, as if the token apology gave him absolution. They brought him out a cup of tea which he slurped unselfconsciously before unlashing the ladder roped elaborately to his trailer.

Mr. Martin was undertaker as well as local handyman. He was locally notorious for his unsurpassed grasp of village gossip. Yet he was well liked and always cheerful. The local wisdom, only whispered, was that he had 'suffered poor man'; that once there had been a wayward wife. Unusually for one who depended on death for his livelihood, he had a coyness about it and made no mention of their bereavement.

'Start on the roof eh?' he said, setting up the ladder and shaking it vigorously against the wall to make sure it was firm. He selected a handful of tools and started heavily upwards, the unlit pipe waggling in his mouth. They watched with fascination as he expertly re-set the loose tiles. Seizing on his audience he bellowed down at them while the ladder wobbled alarmingly.

'D'you 'ear about that Edie Hoskin?' He didn't wait for a reply but carried on, 'Ruddy German landed on 'er cabbages with a parachute. On'y 'e weren't no German, 'e were a Pole and on our side n'all. All dressed up like one of our'n too but 'es gabblin' away nineteen to ruddy dozen jus' like a German an ole Edie, she do call 'er 'usband.' He paused and hammered enthusiastically. 'Anyhow, on'y tramples 'alf 'er patch tryin' to un'itch this parachute doan'ee? Then ole Levi Hoskin do come out with bloody rabbit gun. 'Hands up,' says 'e like bloody Dick Turpin, 'hands up and doan'ee move!' But the poor bugger's all caught up with parachute and falls over an' ole Levi, silly sod, lets fly both barrels, misses this 'ere German and blasts the rest of they bloody cabbages. Then 'e do step back into bloody cold frame and buggers marrers n'all.' He began to laugh, a deep-throated chortle. 'All they cabbages shot or bloody trampled. An', ole Edie she were that mad. 'Win bloody war and starve to death is it?' she says. Oh dear me, ruined they was, bloody ruined......' He looked down at them. 'All they blessed vegetables ruined and not even a proper German were 'e.'

'How dreadful!' Liddy murmured but Jenny could tell she was trying desperately not to laugh; her eyes were moist, and her mouth was quivering. It was hopelessly infectious. The girl looked away, failed to stifle a snort.

'More tea Mr. Martin?' Liddy blurted, yanking the spluttering girl back into the house while an oblivious Mr. Martin struck a match and sucked on his pipe.

Inside they both collapsed at the kitchen table.

'I was going to offer him some cabbages too!' Liddy wailed, blinking back tears. She turned on the wireless to drown their laughter. 'Stop it!' she said to herself, smirking and wiping her eyes.

Together they brewed fresh tea and tried to calm down. After a while Jenny was sent out to call the man in.

'Right-o,' he shouted and, whistling, clambered down the juddering ladder.

Indoors, he was suddenly on best behaviour and sat stiffly at the table, surprisingly ill at ease. The girl gagged on a biscuit as she caught sight of two fat cabbages in the vegetable basket. Liddy, with a seasoned performer's presence of mind, rubbed her back soothingly.

'Careful dear. Little bites.'

Mr. Martin, solemnly stirring his tea, suddenly stopped. Slowly he stood up, his face alight with a strange expression. Without a word he walked past them into the hall. He stopped in front of the chair by the telephone and to their astonishment knelt down. Quite baffled they looked at each other then followed him. He was gently stroking the wood, oblivious to them.

'Is everything all right Mr. Martin?' the woman asked hesitantly. He looked round, misty-eyed and wistful.

'Oh dear me,' he said softly, 'look at that, just look at that.'

'It's only our old hall chair.' A reproachful glance from him made Jenny regret her piping dismissal.

'Oh no child,' he clucked, 'no. it's more than that ain't it Missus?'

Liddy seemed equally perplexed.

'Well, I don't know……' she faltered. 'It belonged to one of my aunts.' Her voice trailed off as Mr. Martin tenderly examined the chair.

'It ain't bad,' he said, 'not at all bad.'

'But what is it Mr. Martin?'

'Doan'ee know Missus?' he looked up at her with genuine surprise, 'Doan'ee know what you has 'ere?'

'Well, no. Not really. It's a nice chair……'

'It's a treasure my dear,' he said emphatically. It sounded funny to the girl, him calling Liddy my dear. 'It's a Gimson. Ain't it lovely though.' They began to look at the elegant chair in a new, if still uncomprehending, light.

'Gimson?' queried the woman.

'Ernest Gimson. Made chairs, cabinets, all sorts.' He buffed one of its satiny arms with his sleeve. 'Wonder who's sat on this in its time.'

'Was he famous this……Gimp……?' Jenny asked.

'Gimson. Ay, you could say.'

'Is it worth a lot then?' the girl asked candidly.

'A bob or two I reckon,' he smiled, 'but it's a beauty, you wants keep 'un in family.' He sighed and returned to the kitchen. Jenny trotted after him and lounged thoughtfully across the table.

'Are we rich then, I mean if we sell it?'

He put down the cup. Liddy came slowly into the kitchen and stood with her arms folded.

'You'd be the richer for keepin' hold of it.'

The woman poured herself more tea. The atmosphere of suppressed laughter had evaporated with the extraordinary revelation of Mr. Martin's secret passion. There was incredulity in her voice when she spoke.

'Well I would never have guessed. We might never have known if it hadn't been for you. Who would have thought it.'

'Sometimes never do know what you really 'ave Missus, till someone else do see it clear for you.'

'No, you don't. How should we look after it. Now that we know I mean?'

'You just keep on how you 'as been. No point in putting it behind glass. They were made for using, not gawpin' at.' Liddy looked mildly unnerved. She picked up the teapot.

'More tea Mr. Martin?'

'No Missus, though thank'ee for what I 'ave had.' He got to his feet. 'Well,' he said resolutely, 'this don't get the work done eh?' and he stumped back outside, lost in thought, absurdly wiping his boots on the doormat as he exited.

The fence was soon repaired and the broken arm of the garden bench carefully removed to be repaired in his workshop.

'Thank you so much,' Liddy smiled as they watched him load up the trailer, 'shall I settle up with you now?' The man removed the once more unlit pipe.

'When the job's all done eh?' he drawled, 'that'll be soon enough.' He gave a perfunctory wave and pushed the bicycle and trailer down the path. A ring on the bicycle bell signalled his farewell. The woman turned her attention to the garden and cast a critical eye over it, hands on hips. She went into the garden shed and armed herself with tools.

'Right. Plenty to be done.'

'Can I go exploring now?'

'If you like dear. Don't get lost.'

CHAPTER SEVEN

S he was a pirate. A willow cutlass in her hand hacked a path through the dense jungle. A giant snake hissed malevolently from a low oak branch. She fled from the slimy thing, slashing furiously left and right with her sword but the creature slithered after her. She could hear it crashing through the undergrowth as parrots shrieked and monkeys chattered anxiously. She stopped and, pulling out a pistol, shot the beast dead with a single bullet between the eyes. Keeping a sharp lookout she stumbled backwards out of the jungle and onto the beach. Idly she wrote her name in the sand with the cutlass then looked around for footprints. There were none. She was alone on the island, facing years and years of terrible solitude, perhaps a lifetime before some roving corsair found her bones in a cave and, if he had one kind corner left in his black heart, took them home for burial. She scanned the horizon but the limpid blue was empty. At her feet a piece of driftwood lay in the sand. She picked it up and wondered what stricken-man-of-war it came from and the wondering brought it all back again. Not Daddy's. His ship was made of iron.

She looked out to sea and felt alone. He wouldn't be coming back now, not ever. Her visits to the beach, especially at night, had allowed her to weave a hopeful fantasy that it was all a horrid mistake and that, one day, she would be here when he came swimming back, his grin gleaming at her over the waves. Yet as the days passed she began dismally to apprehend that this bewitching fancy was just plain wishful thinking. She swished the cutlass despondently, her imagination once again sea-encircled, marooned on a treasure island.

Marooned! What if he had been marooned? What if he had escaped to a real desert island? She was buoyed up by this tiny flicker of hope against the overwhelming black evidence of his absence. It could be true. It might just have happened. She thought of her message in a bottle. What if he got it, if it was washed up on his island and he read it? He would think he was dead.

But no. If he had been stranded somewhere he would've built a raft. He wouldn't just sit and wait for rescue. He knew all the navigation sums to do and would be able to get back to just this spot even if it was thousands and thousands of miles.

She looked out again, half expecting to see a raft bobbing pluckily out at sea. But there was no raft. It was still the same bright, empty sea. She sat on the sand, once more downcast. There were no desert islands anymore. All of the world had been explored. Perhaps they'd missed one though, just one tiny little one.

She closed her eyes against the sun, heard the hiss of soft waves, and dreamt of different shores. A flurry of sparrows sped across the sky, chattering frantically, bringing her back to the here and now.

Jabbing the cutlass into the sand she thought of the buried treasure. It wouldn't be here though. It would be hidden inland and marked by a special tree or a rock. She wished she had a map. Scrambling to her feet she turned to study the imposing jungle.

The X on the map would be deep in unknown regions. She spied a small opening in the gorse, just big enough for someone to crawl through. That would be the way a bloodthirsty crew would go, dragging an iron bound chest full of gold and jewels. Brambles caught on her sweater as she ducked down and went through the gap. Just yards from the beach but this was new territory, a dense, labyrinthine copse. She clambered up a steep slope. The trace of an old footpath stretched away over the brow and she followed but, towards the top, it got so steep she had to struggle on all fours and was quickly out of breath. She rested against a tree, then started down the other side, following the winding spoor of a path untrodden for years; pirates were probably the last people in the whole world who had ever used it. She could just glimpse the sea through the thick greenery and there were dull flashes of rock below. Something tugged at her ankle, a bramble clinging to her sock. She unpicked it then saw that the bush was bursting with fruit.

'Blackberries!' Taking out her handkerchief she held it by each corner to make a bag and began to pick them. The dark fruit quickly stained the white cotton. She ate some, relishing the sweet squish as her tongue pressed down on them. She was reaching up for the swollen bunches at the top of the bush when suddenly she stopped dead. Voices, a murmur, floated up mysteriously from below. Apprehension darted through her; she ducked down quickly and listened. There was nothing now. The voices, if they were voices, had gone. She wasn't even sure she had heard anything. She craned forward cautiously. There must be a little cove down there. She could just make out a horseshoe of tumbled rocks. Uneasily the spectre of long dead buccaneers loomed before her, ghostly sea-dogs endlessly repeating the evil deeds of centuries before in the secluded lagoon below.

'Silly,' she told herself sternly, 'you don't get ghosts in daytime.' Yet she felt only half-brave and the flimsy cutlass inadequate against whatever was down there.

Daddy would be brave, she thought, he wouldn't let himself down. Still clutching the dripping, makeshift bag of berries she took two steps away from the safety of the bush. Beneath her foot the quick snap of a twig sounded horribly loud. She stopped again and listened for the shadowy voices that inhabited the undiscovered domain below. Still there was nothing.

'There can't be anything really,' she reassured herself, 'not really, only in pretend.' Another two steps and still silence. Screwing up her courage she quietly made her way down the slope. All she could hear was the sea gently slopping in and out of the little cove. Stepping like a timid deer to avoid other twigs she reached the bottom and crouched down behind bushes, peering out apprehensively. The cove was shaped more like a question mark, edged round with a rough semi-circle of boulders. From her hiding place she could only see the far side, the rest was hidden behind a screen of the familiar stone, several yards high. There was no one there, no ghosts, no phantom owners of unearthly voices.

In a way it was a disappointment. She felt sheepish, being scared so easily by a silly, imagined voice.

'There could have been pirates,' she thought, struggling to bolster dented pride, 'but it would've been long ago. It is a sort of pirate bay, or a smuggler's one.'

She got to her feet, pushed through the bush and meandered towards the towering boulders. She wasn't scared now. She had been brave after all and not let herself down. The rock was warm and she trailed her hand slowly along its bulging surface as she wandered round it and into the cove. Idle waves shuffled languidly and a lone gull swooped low across the water.

'Hullo!'

It was a deep, male voice and very real.

She let out a startled yelp and, without looking, scurried to the trees like a frightened rabbit, still grasping the berries.

An eloquent laugh rose up behind her and the same voice again, but lighter, friendly.

'Sorry. I didn't mean to startle you. I got quite a shock too!' She turned, still poised for flight. Dry sand scrunched uncomfortably in her sandals.

He was a young man, just below medium height with a freshly tanned face and dark, curly hair. He was grinning, a boyish grin, edging at the mischievous. He wore a baggy pullover and trousers rolled up above his ankles. His feet were bare. Behind him, against the rocks, was a small boat, dipping in the effervescing swell. It had been holed at the stern and lurched wearily at anchor. He followed her gaze and grimaced good-naturedly.

'Bit of trouble with the old tub. Thought I could just creep round the coast. Should've known better really. Never was much of a sailor. Real stinker that storm though and no warning. You live round here?'

She barely heard the question. A castaway! A real, live castaway. Not pretending, not a game, but real! She went slowly towards him in awe, holding out the berries in offering to this stranded soul.

'Breakfast!' he exclaimed and scooped out a handful. Ravenous, she thought, days adrift at sea……

'Delicious,' he beamed, 'and very welcome. Well you must be Jenny Robin.' She looked at him in astonishment, eventually found her voice.

'How do you know that?'

'Obvious,' he grinned, gesturing at her red jersey.

'Well I'm Jenny anyway,' she answered shyly, too polite to point out it should have been Jenny Wren.

He gave a little bow, 'I'm very pleased indeed to meet you Jenny, Robin or not.' She quickly warmed to his easy attractiveness, this being talked to as if she was a grown-up.

'I thought I heard voices,' she said, 'when I was in the woods.' He pulled a face, repentant and funny at the same time.

'That was me I'm afraid. Hope you didn't hear it too well. I was, um, telling the old girl her fortune.' He jerked a thumb back towards the wrecked vessel.

'I thought it was ghosts. It was a bit scary.'

'Well I'm no ghost. Any more of those berries?' He wolfed the last of them gratefully.

'Haven't you got any food on the boat?'

'Did have but the sea got to it.'

He needs to shave, she thought, and have a hot bath probably. She was sure it would be all right with Liddy. He was shipwrecked after all.

'You could come to my house,' she blurted out, 'you could get cleaned up and have a proper meal.'

He looked suddenly weary and rubbed a hand over his stubble.

'That really would be......just the job. You sure it would be all right though?' She nodded vigorously and her assurance seemed to put new life in him.

'I'll just get my stuff.' He began to wade out to the boat, still talking. 'Took a real pasting last night. The tide was running out fast when the engine died on me and I thought, that's it, your number's up. Then the old girl shifts round all by herself and slides into this little hidey-hole. Came to grief a bit on the rocks though. Still can't have everything. At least I'm still sunny side up. Funny though, her doing that; lot of freak currents round here are there?' He heaved himself up over the gunwale and went below. She could hear him crashing about as he collected his belongings.

No, she thought, remembering a dream, a voice above the storm. Dad brought this boat here. Dad saved him and guided her in between the rocks. She was so certain that it filled her with an odd calmness as though she were floating. She was absolutely sure that somehow Dad had steered the boat to safety; his sure hand on the wheel, his keen eye piercing the night and the storm. There could be no question of it.

The boat looked like a bloated fish cast up and forlorn. An old tyre was slung over the side like a sightless eye. Daubed roughly across the bow was her name, *The Seventh Angel*. She thought he'd have a seaman's bag but when he emerged he was carrying a large suitcase with a jacket draped over it. He dragged it across the deck and, lowering himself back into the sea, hauled it onto his shoulder and started back to shore.

'Why's it called that?'

'Dunno.' He was puffing loudly and, reaching land, heaved down the suitcase with a grunt. 'Phew. Just take a breather for a moment.' He pulled a packet of cigarettes and matches from his pocket. The matches must have been damp for none of them would strike and he threw them down. He looked fed up and dolefully put the cigarette back in the packet.

'I could try rubbing some sticks together,' she offered willingly, 'I've read how to.'

'No, never mind. Thanks anyway.' He stood and looked up at the hill behind them, then dubiously at the suitcase. Picking up the jacket he slipped it on and, as he did so, a flash of colour caught her eye, something in his pocket; the neck of a bottle, a red and cream cap. She gaped at it in disbelief, taken aback. He looked down at her, brown eyes crinkling, as she tried not to stare at it. He had, she thought, a sort of neat face, neat and square. It wasn't like Daddy's big, open face but she decided she liked it.

'Well Tinker Bell, lead me to safety.'

'Tinker Bell?'

He cocked his head to one side. 'Not read *Peter Pan*? He was rescued from the perils of the deep by Tinker Bell, didn't you know?'

'No,' she answered meekly, eyes downcast, and felt hopelessly naïve before all the bright things he must know, 'sorry.'

'Come on then,' his voice was kindly, as if apprehending, 'I do envy you living here. '*Et in Arcadia Ego* eh?'

Her brow furrowed, 'What?'

'*Et in Arcadia Ego*. It means, um, I too am in Arcadia.'

'No,' she shook her head firmly, sure of her ground this time, 'this is Devonshire.'

It was a long trudge back up the hill. He struggled with the case as it bumped against his legs. She thought he really should have had a seaman's bag. It was hard not to leave him trailing behind. She kept hopping back down the slope to him. He was red in the face, the dark curls damp with perspiration.

'This is the worst bit,' she called as once again she found herself well ahead. He rested the case and sat on the ground. She bounded down and squatted in front of him.

'Little break for a minute eh?' He smiled wearily and closed his eyes. The still of the woods descended on them. 'I'd give my eye teeth for a long, cold drink,' he muttered. For a moment she was tempted to remind him about the bottle in his pocket, in case he had forgotten it, but it was private and her curiosity too impolite.

'It really isn't very far. I could help,' she reassured and when they continued he awkwardly pulled the case while she pushed from behind, ineffectually but enthusiastically. As they neared the summit he caught her eye and winked.

'Suppose I should've left the kitchen sink behind after all.'

She grinned, and again tried not to look at the bottle jutting from his pocket and the familiar colours of its cap.

They stopped at the top for another rest and he picked off the high berries she couldn't reach. They munched them greedily and laughed at each others purple-tinged lips. While he rested again she wandered round the little peak. Far down the slope she noticed for the first time a long ribbon of vivid orange peel, draped over a bush. Perhaps, she thought, there had been someone else there as well.

He seemed a little more jaunty, restored, when they pressed on, bumping down the other side of the hill, whooping like red Indians. As they neared the bottom he lost his grip and the suitcase tumbled end over end, crashing spectacularly into a bank of thick gorse. Laughing, they rescued it and struggled through the tiny gap out into the sunlit beach. She wanted to say that it was her special place but didn't, too daunted by the hugeness of it to explain.

'Why are you hanging on to that stick?'

'It's a cutlass,' she said guilelessly, waving it in the air, 'I was being a pirate until……'

He thrust his arms in the air and assumed an abject expression. 'Give quarter!' he pleaded, 'and spare me the plank.' Then he dropped his hands, and the funny face, and said gloomily, 'Well I'm marooned all right.'

'But you're rescued, and it's not a desert island after all.'

He nodded, 'How far is it now?'

'We're nearly there. Just through the woods and up the lane.'

'Up the lane?' he questioned suspiciously.

'It's not steep though, not like before.'

'Come on then,' he groaned, then winked at her again, cementing their conspiracy.

Soon they were in the dusty lane. She pointed excitedly at the lone white house as it came into view.

'There it is! I said it wasn't far didn't I?' She skipped around him while he struggled with the lumbering case. As they drew closer, she pointed out the little parts of her world.

'That's the tree where Dad put up my swing. Over there is my flower patch. I'm growing sweet peas and love-in-a-mist and, last year, I made a huge snowman and put a real hat and scarf on him and that's the only time in my whole life we've ever had snow. And that……' she jumped up and pointed eagerly over the hedge, 'that's where Li……Mum grows special flowers. She's won prizes, well once she did.'

'Hope they won't mind, your Mum and Dad. Bit of a cheek really.'

The girl looked down, shuffled. 'Actually it's just my Mum, just me and Mum.'

'Oh……I see.' He sounded surprised but did not pursue it. Overcome with the thrill of having saved a castaway, she raced ahead, clanked open the white gate and rushed down the path. Liddy was drifting slowly round the garden, humming, a shallow basket of flowers in the crook of her arm.

'Liddy!'

The woman looked up and smiled. The girl stopped, suddenly tongue-tied, and pointed down the path to where the man, whose name she still did not know, was standing quite motionless, as he stared at the gate. For a moment Liddy appeared to sway in the hot sun. She put the back of her hand to her brow. Jenny's voice returned in a garbled rush.

'Look! I found him on the beach. His boat's all wrecked from the storm and he hasn't eaten in ages……' the gentle smile faded from the woman's face and the girl did not hear her slow, incredulous whisper.

'You'll never guess what,' Jenny chattered gaily, 'I thought he was a ghost. He's not though is he, not a bit!'

CHAPTER EIGHT

'Is he up yet, is he awake?'

'No. He's still fast asleep.'

Liddy still didn't look quite right. Perhaps she had one of her headaches coming on. It had all been a bit of a shock. That must be it. She wasn't usually so shy. Anyway, Jenny herself had been shy of him at first and he did look pretty terrible when they got home, his trousers wet and bits of bush stuck all over his jumper.

He had been pensive when the woman walked slowly down the path to him, deserted by his blithe good humour.

'Mummy this is......' but then Jenny had stopped, giggled and turned to him, 'I don't know your name!' The stranger from the beach gave a fragile smile.

'Kit. Kit Fallon. Sorry.'

'He was shipwrecked in the storm and I thought he was a ghost and he gave me a fright but he didn't mean to and his boat's all broken up and we ate some berries but I expect he's really hungry......' she gabbled on as it tumbled out. The woman looked pale and unsure, her voice wavered as she reached out hesitantly to shake his hand.

'How do you do,' she said at last in a frail voice.

'Sorry,' he repeated with an air of hopelessness, eyes downcast as if in minute examination of the gravel. The three of them stood for a long, silent moment finally broken by Jenny's voice.

'Mum, I think he should come indoors now.' The girl's words seemed to jerk Liddy from her odd abstractedness.

'Yes of course, of course he must.' It was as though she had forgotten her manners and was now embarrassed, anxious to make amends. They struggled up the path with the case and Jenny bustled the dishevelled figure into the house.

'Come on Mr. Fallon,' she fussed as he collapsed gratefully onto the sofa.

'Sorry,' he said again, but this time with a touch of wryness 'what a bother I am.' He gazed wearily around the room. 'All these books. Never seen so many.'

'They're Dad's,' the girl said proudly, then corrected herself, 'were his I mean.' He sank back onto the cushions and while they made tea in the kitchen fell heavily and noisily asleep. They closed the curtains and Liddy made the girl tell her all about it while they drank the tea intended for the unexpected guest.

But that had been hours ago. A ponderous chime from the hall clock announced the hour as Jenny lolled and fidgeted in the dining room, not knowing what to do, not liking doing nothing. She wanted him to wake up and be fun again.

Liddy had listened gravely as they sipped their tea. The girl wanted her to be won over by him too. When the tale was told she leant forward, peered at the woman with searching seriousness, 'I like him don't you. What are we going to do with him?'

'I really don't know.' The woman looked away then added, almost to herself, 'It all depends.'

The chimes of the clock died away and the girl sighed, bored with herself and the waiting.

'Darling, would you go to the shop for me?' Liddy had glided quietly into the room and spoke in a theatrical whisper. She took a note from her purse and gave it to the girl together with a list and ration book.

Jenny set off quickly to the village. At first she counted steps but lost count when a woman rode by on a big snorting horse that shook its head irritably. She waved and the rider waved back; more of a salute than a proper wave, the girl thought.

The grocer's shop was long and narrow, fronted by half-glazed doors. The floorboards were bare and scrubbed white. On one counter there was a shiny machine for slicing that whirred and slid dangerously when it was used. The shop smelt of coffee, washing soda and bacon.

She didn't like the grocer. Once she had come in with Daddy and he had fussed and bustled, saying, 'Yes Sir' all the time with a funny smile on his face which he didn't usually have. He did it with Liddy too. When Jenny went in on her own, he wasn't like that. He was quite fierce and glowered over the counter. And he had hair in his nostrils and ears and always wore a blue work coat that was too tight around his middle so that it looked as if the buttons might pop off at any minute.

The shop bell tinkled behind her and the man looked up from behind the counter. He always seemed put out and cross, as if she had stopped him from doing something else, something important.

'Sweets is it?' he asked impatiently.

'No……' she faltered, 'well yes……but other things too.' She held out the list. Leaning on the counter he sighed heavily and scrutinised it. Jenny stood uncomfortably, hands clasped behind her back.

'Beef!' he snorted, making her jump. 'A'int got no beef. Weekend innit?' The length of the list though, seemed to mollify him a little as he continued to read.

'Got a bit o' pork you can 'ave.' She blinked and nodded a quick acceptance. He made every movement a long-suffering one as he went round the shelves, collecting the items together in a pile by the till.

'Right,' he said, looking at the heap, 'got your book then?' She handed it to him with the money and he clipped out some coupons and rang up the till.

'We've got a visitor,' she announced importantly, wanting to put her exotic guest on display, show him off like a fan of peacock feathers. He grunted disinterestedly.

'Give us your bag then.' Caught out she squirmed and confessed,

'I forgot to bring one.' He glared at her and rummaged under the counter, reluctantly producing a string bag.

'I want it back mind. Make sure your Mum brings it back.' She nodded again, remembered the sweets and decided to forgo them rather than prolong the encounter.

The bag was heavy. She clutched it with both hands as she hurried back in the late afternoon sunshine, struggling with the awkward load. The pork, wrapped in greaseproof paper, smelt unpleasant and she wrinkled her nose up in distaste. Blood was beginning to seep through the wrapping. It was all right when it was cooked. Liddy was a good cook. She had learnt from their cook at home when she had been a little girl. She could remember asking about it.

'Did you have servants?'

'Well yes, only two though.'

'Were you rich then?'

'Oh no. Not at all. There were rich people where we lived though.' Liddy was the only child of a doctor who yearned with simmering rage for a son and heir. Years later he yearned just as fruitlessly for a grandson, which soured him even more.

'How many servants did the rich people have?'

'One house had nine, including the grooms and gardeners.'

'Grandad wasn't rich then?' Jenny could barely remember the grandparents who had perished early in the war after a direct hit on the large unhappy house where they lived in silent, mutual denunciation. All she could recall of her grandmother – who had also yearned but for another and better reason; a longed for re-emergence of that brief flicker of passion just after their marriage – was the fascinating, tight, grey knot of hair at the back of her head and the laced-up boots she always wore.

'We were comfortable. Not rich though.'

'Why haven't we got servants? We're comfortable aren't we?'

'People just don't have them these days.'

'Except rich people.'

'Except very rich people.'

The girl put the bag down on the grass verge, emptied it then re-packaged the purchases with the damp parcel of meat at the bottom. That was better. She couldn't smell the dead pig anymore.

She bumped open the gate and skipped happily up the path. He'd probably be up soon and Liddy would be able to get to know him. Discovering him first had given her a rescuer's pride and a proprietary claim. She hadn't exactly saved him from certain death but who was to know what might have happened. She had to be there when he woke.

As she reached the back door she heard peals of laughter. He was up already, he was awake! The laughter rose up again, mostly Liddy this time, trickling and carefree. But he shouldn't have woken up before she got home. That wasn't how it was supposed to be. She pushed open the back door. They were sitting at the kitchen table. On it was the bottle with the red and cream cap, half-empty and not, after all, a mystery. They each had a glass and turned, still laughing, as she entered. The girl fumbled with the shopping; she was interrupting, a flush rose in her cheeks and she looked anxiously at them.

'Sorry!' she blurted out.

'Hello dear,' Liddy's smile was wide and she was giggling, 'he is funny, your Robinson Crusoe.'

CHAPTER NINE

For Jenny that first evening swept past in a blur. Unused to conversation, adult conversation, she found it both compelling and puzzling. But the thing which flattened her was the realisation that her self-appointed role as go-between wasn't needed. He and Liddy were getting on like a house on fire. Instead it was she who was all at sea in the swirl of their conversation. He was still funny. She could tell from his arch expressions, sidelong glances and from Liddy's reaction. But it was a different sort of funny, one she couldn't quite grasp.

Liddy was clearly captivated. She wasn't at all frosty with him now. She had a sparkle about her and covered her laughing mouth with her hand, eyes twinkling at the endless stream from this curious man. He didn't make jokes really. He just had a funny way of looking at things and lots of tales about people he had known. He played out little scenarios, putting on voices and faces. Jenny laughed when they did, not always comprehending.

Liddy excelled herself with the supper. Nevertheless, the girl could not forget the smell of the meat and prodded it around her plate. Guiltily she ate all of the vegetables, even the brussel sprouts.

The grown-ups finished the little bottle of whisky and Jenny was sent to fetch another, bigger one from the sideboard. She was quiet during the meal, unable to break into the glittering chatter. During one brief pause she said perkily,

'I told the grocer we had a visitor.'

A silence fell across the table. The two adults looked away from her and at each other. Without knowing why the girl felt she had punctured all the fun, the flashing brilliance of the evening.

'What did you say to him Jenny?' Liddy's voice was serious, gently questioning.

'Only that we had a visitor, that was all.'

'Did you say who our visitor was?'

'No.'

The woman pursed her lips and then said simply,

'Well, in future, if anyone asks we'll say that Mr. Fallon is a relative, come to stay for a while. It'll be easier that way. We'll say he's my cousin.'

'Can't we say who he really is then?'

The man chuckled indulgently and it made her feel silly because she couldn't see why it would be easier.

'It's only a little fib,' he smiled, 'won't do any harm. Just stop people getting the wrong idea that's all.'

A hot prickle came to the girl's cheeks. She looked down, ill at ease. A chair scraped as Liddy rose and began to clear away.

'Jenny.' His voice was soft, kind. She looked up slowly. It was the voice she had first known, the voice she had let shore up the conspiracy between them. He reached forward and touched her ear, just brushed it with his hand. When he withdrew it he was holding an egg and grinning at her, 'Hey presto!'

Her eyes opened wide, 'How did you do that?'

'Ah ha,' he said exaggeratedly, 'trade secret.' Leaning forward again he tickled her ear and held up a now empty hand. She clapped her own to the side of her head. 'Careful,' he warned. But there was nothing there, no egg. She knew there wouldn't be, but had to check and giggled despite herself. It was all right again. The little bit of magic had eased her disquiet. Liddy was smiling at them, hands in the sink, the cosy smell and sound of soapy dishes jostling in the water filled the kitchen.

'Are you going to stay with us then?' the girl piped, trying not to sound too excited. It was Liddy who answered.

'Just for a little while. Until Mr. Fallon......'

'Kit' he interrupted warmly.

'Until Kit, she continued, 'can get things sorted out. After all it isn't every day one gets shipwrecked.'

Later Jenny helped as they made up a bed for him in the spare room.

'Where were you going?' she quizzed, pummelling a pillow into its case. He slipped again into the way he had of talking to her as if she too were grown-up.

'Just along from here a bit. Had a two-nighter all fixed up.' He pulled a face. 'I've lost that now.' She didn't know what a two-nighter was but nodded as if she did. 'Thought I'd make it round easy enough, didn't think there was a big blow like that one coming.'

'Aren't you a very good sailor?' she asked seriously. He laughed.

'No, not me. Not much sailing in the army. Good at knots though.'

'Were you a soldier?' she was enraptured by his fragmented biography.

He saluted solemnly, 'Captain Kit Fallon at your service.' Captain! He'd been a captain.

Liddy finished smoothing down the bedspread.

'Come along Jenny. That's enough questions for one day and……' the conjunction was heavily weighted and familiar, 'it's bedtime.'

'It's still early,' the girl pleaded, knowing it would be in vain.

'And it's been a very long day. For all of us.'

'Oh, it's not fair,' Jenny whined. She hated being packed off, there was so much to ask. She had a last stab. 'But what about your boat?'

'Well,' he said slowly, 'it's not strictly mine. Have to see about it in the morning.'

Liddy fixed her with a stern eye, implacably steadfast.

'Bed, young lady.'

★   ★   ★

Early next morning, she saw Kit from her window astride her mother's bicycle, pedalling furiously down the lane. When she got downstairs she discovered he had gone to 'sort out' the damaged boat.

'He did look funny on your old bicycle.' Liddy looked tired but she smiled.

'Yes he did rather. It is a bit small for him.'

He returned, out of breath but chipper, within the hour. It had all, he assured them brightly, been 'fixed up'. Later Jenny went with him to the cove. By the time they arrived the little boat was already underway, in tow to a local fishing lugger. *The Seventh Angel* sat heavily in the water, a rough patch of planking and oilskin across the gashed side.

She looked lost and woeful as she was dragged unceremoniously through the flat sea, limping home to port.

'Will they mend it?' Jenny asked, hopping up onto a rock for a better look. He shrugged and lit a cigarette.

'Perhaps. Don't know how bad the damage is really.'

'I hope they do.'

They trudged back through the woods to Hadley. The high spirits of the evening before had given way to listless weariness in them all and a descent from yesterday's headiness. It was no longer a brief adventure, but something else, and already, because of his presence, there was a new, unfamiliar routine in the house.

When Kit suggested a picnic in the garden they all jumped at it. 'After all there won't be many more sunny days,' he said matter-of-factly.

They lounged in contented silence on the lawn, the remains of the picnic strewn about them in lazy disarray. A pot of tea had been made but after a while Kit went indoors for a bottle of wine. Clouds moved in gentle procession and the afternoon sun flickered through the treetops as sleepy pigeons called out across the garden.

'We thought you looked funny on Liddy's bike,' Jenny baited, giving her mother a secret, sly look. He looked up and pretended to be affronted.

'Me? Funny? Can't believe that!' He took a deep swallow from his tumbler. 'What was funny though, now I come to think of it, was the sight of you gawping out of the window with your chin around your knees. Very funny that was.'

'You could've used the car…' the girl said nonchalantly, pecking at a slice of cake. He sat up abruptly.

'A car! You've got a car! Where? Where is it?'

'In the garage of course,' Jenny giggled.

'Well you might have said……'

'And you might have asked young man, if you hadn't been in such a tearing hurry.' Liddy's mild bantering left him, briefly, speechless. He eyed them both with playful suspicion.

'I can see I'm going to have to keep an eye on you two.'

The car was a black Alvis, highly polished and wheelless. Jenny could not remember Daddy taking the wheels off and standing it on bricks. It must have been a long time ago. It was strange now to see someone else, another man, with it.

'It's a beaut.!' Kit said admiringly, running a hand along the gleaming contours.

'It was Dad's. He used to call it Tin Lizzie. Do you know about Dad?' she asked, lowering her voice.

'A bit,' he said, already tinkering.

Half an hour later, as the last of the dishes were being put away, a roar from the garage announced the vehicle's noisy rebirth. They hurried outside as the long saloon rolled slowly out of the garage. Kit was beaming from ear to ear. A furious belch of smoke erupted from the exhaust as he wound down the window.

'Right then ladies,' he yelled above the din, 'we're off!'

But a week was to pass before they were, finally, off. He insisted on keeping the destination secret. If Jenny pressed him he put his hands over his ears or, even more annoyingly, tapped his forefinger against the side of his nose.

'That's for me to know and you to find out.'

For Jenny it was the first week of a new term and a new double life, by day enduring the bustling, solitary drudge of school, anxiously counting the minutes until she could be with her new and mysterious friend again. She hurried home now. She didn't want to miss anything.

It was funny having someone else around the house, funnier still to have someone like him. In the evenings he brought the late summer garden to life, making it a magical playground. He did silly things like squirting her with the hose and getting her clothes sopping wet but even then Liddy didn't seem to mind. Sometimes he turned the wireless up loud and waltzed Jenny round and round, giddyingly fast, across the lawn. Or he would recite bits from plays, talking in funny accents and wearing hats from the hall stand. She couldn't imagine Daddy doing half the things he did. They were silly but it was fun. It was all such fun.

'You could be in a show or on the B.B.C.'

Again the low, somehow mocking bow sweeping down in front of her.

'Very astute young lady.'

'Do you mean……?'

'Indeed I do. Kit Fallon, strolling thespian, at your service.'

She laughed, 'I meant an actor.' He raised a disdainful eyebrow and rolled his eyes.

'A thespian, for your information, is an actor. Oh, the pitiful shortcomings of a provincial education……'

'You're an actor? Really? Are you famous?' She looked at him in amazement.

'Fame has yet to truly beckon but……' he winked, 'there have been moments.'

'But really an actor?'

'Yes, Really.' He sounded slightly put out that she should doubt it.

'Is that how you know all those things from plays?'

'Mostly. Some of them are just improvised.'

'What's improvised?'

'Make believe.'

She wrinkled her brow thoughtfully, 'I thought only children played make believe.'

'Not always,' he said enigmatically.

Early one evening, Mr. Martin telephoned. The bench repairs were done and he arranged to come the following afternoon. He was still there when Jenny arrived home from school, sticky and dishevelled in her grey uniform. The bench was in one piece again and Mr. Martin was carefully brushing on a tarry liquid. Kit and Liddy greeted her as she came up the path and Mr. Martin turned and waved his pipe.

'Been looking after my chair young Miss?'

'Well,' she hesitated shyly, 'I haven't sat on it.'

He gave a short laugh and carried on brushing.

'Chair? What's all this Liddy?' Kit asked, turning to the woman. She gave a light, trickling laugh.

'My cousin doesn't know about our find, Mr. Martin.' It was the first time Jenny heard her say the fib out loud. 'According to Mr. Martin,' she continued, 'what we thought was a perfectly ordinary hall chair was, in fact, made by......who was it now?'

'Gimson.' The workman answered without interrupting his steady brush strokes. 'Ernest Gimson.'

'That's it. And all the time I thought it was just an old chair. I think it came originally from Aunt Harriet, your Great Aunt, Jenny.' The girl had never heard of Great Aunt Harriet. It was the second fib, the next stitch in a tapestry of sham. Kit looked unusually interested.

'What's so special about it?'

'Means there's plenty o' folk like me as would like to get their 'ands on one.'

'It's worth something then?'

'Worth something?' The old man scraped his chin, 'few bob I daresay, good few. But I says hold on to 'un, young fella.'

'I'd sell it.' Kit said flatly with an uncomprehending shrug. Mr. Martin looked slowly round at him, an age-old appraising look.

'I reckon as 'ow you would,' he said at length, jamming the pipe back in his mouth and resuming his work, his back turned towards them in square repudiation.

CHAPTER TEN

Exeter Cathedral. She saw the twin stone towers and remembered.

'I've been here before,' she mused, uncertainly, 'I think I have anyway.' Liddy turned from the front seat.

'Quite right. We came with Daddy. Long time ago though.'

'Spot of shopping and a special treat,' Kit drummed his palms airily against the steering wheel, 'lunch on me, a thank you for the timely rescue.'

The drive had been happy. He regaled them with tales about the theatre; snippets from what sounded a hectic life lived at breakneck speed. But now the girl felt a tinge of disappointment. She had imagined, against hope and reason, somewhere and something more exciting. The long week had allowed her to build up unfulfillable expectations. She should be grateful though; a special treat because she had rescued him. He hadn't forgotten it.

They traipsed round the shops. Liddy bought lots of new clothes for them both. Kit disappeared for a while and met them later with several brown paper bundles under his arm.

The special lunch fell short as well. It was in a department store restaurant and its gloominess reminded her too much of the dreary meals she had endured with Uncle Richard. This time at least she got ice-cream and in a tall glass.

As they finished, Kit produced a square parcel, neatly wrapped and tied with string. He twinkled and passed it to the girl.

'What is it?'

'It's for you.'

She picked at the knot but couldn't untie it. Kit took out a penknife and sawed at the string until it pinged asunder. She unwrapped the brown paper, liking the crinkly sound it made. It was a book, pleasingly heavy.

'*Peter Pan*!' It had pictures and everything and inside he had written *To Jenny Tinker Bell* with his name and the date.

'A thank you,' he said, 'for answering my S.O.S.'

She leafed eagerly through, pausing at the illustrations.

'Well……?' Liddy said quietly.

'It's jolly good,' she said, head buried in it.

'What do you say then?'

'Oh, sorry. Thank you.' She became aware of them looking at her and felt uncomfortable, didn't quite know how to respond, what it was they wanted. Shadowed by guilt about her niggardliness with Exeter she was caught out by his generosity and embarrassed.

'Thank you very much,' she said again, swallowing the reproachful lump in her throat.

'You like it then?' he questioned gently.

'Oh yes it's lovely,' she clasped the book to her chest, 'it's really lovely.'

'Good,' he tipped back his drink, 'time to go?' The woman nodded and drained her glass. Kit paid and left a handful of coins on the table.

It was overcast outside and an uneasy simmering breeze snaked ahead of them. They were peering into shop windows when the sudden clamour of an angry crowd erupted from a side street. They looked down it and saw a jeering sprawl of people milling around in front of a row of shabby, terraced houses. A police car was parked outside one of them.

'What's going on?' the girl asked.

'I'm not at all sure……' Liddy's voice was nervous. Kit though, like a schoolboy sensing a playground scrap in the making, urged them eagerly down the dingy street.

'Come on!'

They joined the fringes of the surging mob, Liddy's hands clutching the girl's shoulders protectively. The atmosphere growled with barely contained menace. A thin drizzle started, spotting the pavement and the shiny black vehicle.

'What's going on?' Kit shouted to a man in front. The man turned brusquely, red-faced.

' 'Ees bloody barmy 'ee is! Not right in bloody 'ead!'

Liddy fidgeted uncomfortably and coughed. The man looked past Kit, touched the brim of his hat. 'Sorry Missus, didn't see you there,' then added angrily, 'I'm right though, 'bout 'im. I'm right with what I do say!' He grunted and turned away from them. The girl felt Liddy recoil from the man but Kit was grinning broadly. He raised a finger to his temple and described circles with it. 'Loony,' he mouthed silently. He ushered them closer to the police car and Jenny heard him mutter 'bloody bumpkin' under his breath, but he was grinning still, enjoying the unfolding drama.

It was then the girl caught a glimpse, so fleeting she wasn't sure it was him at all. The crowd roared, moved forward and closed up as one. She ducked and squeezed through the thick hedge of baying onlookers. It was him! The man from the beach, the bony man. But now his thin wrists were handcuffed and he was standing in the doorway, flanked by two grim-faced policemen holding his arms, and he was smiling, angelically.

'What's he done?' she shrieked to a wiry man with cropped hair. He glared down at her.

' 'Im? 'Ees doolally 'ee is. Not the full shillin'. Killed 'is auntie with a bloody brick. Bashed 'er 'ead in!' He pointed to an upper window, 'Up there, with a brick!'

'Jenny!' Liddy reached through the crowd and yanked the girl back. One of the policemen said firmly, 'Come on now, give us some room. Let's all calm down a bit shall we.' The crowd backed away grudgingly as the man was led down the steps and towards the car. She could see him clearly now. He was still smiling, a shy smile like a boy, oblivious to the bristling crowd. He glanced up timidly and beamed at the mob. Jenny's head was reeling. He had killed someone, killed his auntie. It couldn't be true, not him. What was it that man had called him, Lally? Then he saw her and flashed a winning grin of crooked yellow teeth and black gaps at her. He was gone in a moment, ushered quickly into the back of the dark car. The engine roared and the police bell rang out, drowning the ugly jeers. The crowd began to disperse, grumbling and disappointed. She felt saddened and wanted to cry. He couldn't really be a murderer. They were only in newspapers. It must be a mistake. She heard the strident bell ringing in the distance.

'Goodbye Lally, goodbye,' she whispered.

★   ★   ★

'I've told you, you must never, ever disappear like that. I'm very cross with you!' Liddy scolded, jerking at the girl's hand as they hurried along. The drizzle had become sluggish rain and they were damp and miserable by the time they got to the car. 'You must never do it again Jennifer!' The girl's eyes began to fill with tears and she sat unhappily in the back seat, holding on to her new book.

'Come on Liddy, no harm done.' Kit's voice was calm, soothing. 'Wonder what they nabbed him for? All those people baying for his blood?' It was an idle question but for a moment the girl wanted to answer, as if it might redeem her, take away the telling off. Yet she stayed silent. If she said anything it would lead inevitably to telling about the beach too. And a disquiet about that day had remained with her. That was why she had kept it to herself. But murder, killing someone. It just seemed……not possible. Alone in a bubble of bewilderment she jolted along in the back of the car.

Kit began humming a breezy tune. He glanced at Liddy. She was sitting rigidly beside him.

'Cheer up!' It was a passable impression of a famous cockney comedian. 'It might never 'appen!' He pulled a hip flask from the glove compartment, casually took his hands off the steering wheel to unstopper it and winked hugely at Jenny in the rear view mirror, 'Look, no 'ands!' Taking a deep swig from the flask he passed it to the woman; 'Go on,' he urged, 'that'll perk you up a bit,' and he began to sing, still in the same broad, swaggering accent.

Liddy took the flask and sipped then, unexpectedly, began to sing along. Jenny didn't know she sang funny songs like this one. She couldn't do the accent though. When the song came to an end Kit, still in character, launched into a music hall routine.

'So this geezer says to me, 'ee says wot's the difference between a buffalo and a bison and I says to 'im: I don't know, wot is the difference between a buffalo and a bison? And 'ee says yer can't wash yer 'ands in a buffalo......' The stories came so fast Jenny couldn't keep up. Some of them he whispered to Liddy and she would giggle and look back to make sure the girl hadn't overheard.

He took another gulp from the flask, relishing the laughter. For Jenny the smell of leather, wood and polish in the car, together with the faint but evocative trace of Daddy's tobacco, called up half-remembered, distant times when he himself had been at the wheel and in charge.

Kit drove fast through the narrow lanes, the green hedges outside just a flickering blur. She bounced on the smooth seat, exhilarated by the speed and the noise. Suddenly the car lurched wildly and seemed to jump across the road. She was thrown across the seat and felt a cold crack as her forehead struck a door handle. The engine whined and roared and she heard the soft, jostling collision of the grown-ups in the front, Kit's voice abruptly spitting out the single word, 'Christ!' The car screeched, stopped and, hurled back again, she banged her head a second time against the shiny, walnut door trim. The big Alvis shuddered and the engine died, enveloping them in a silence broken by the familiar creak of the handbrake as Kit automatically yanked it on. Something outside of the car tumbled onto the road, spinning round until it clattered to a halt, completing the silence.

'Bloody hell!' It was Kit's voice. He turned to the girl, 'You all right love?' Liddy too had struggled upright and was looking back with a dazed, pale expression. She had a hand to her chest and was breathing hard. 'Jenny?' The girl pushed herself up in the seat. Her new book was on the floor of the car, as though thrown down in a tantrum. She struggled to clear her head. 'Oh, my book......' It was only then she felt the warm trickle on her brow and looked up at them in disbelief. 'Am I bleeding?'

It was just a scratch, Liddy said, but it would probably leave a nasty bruise for a few days. The woman mopped it with an embroidered handkerchief, its pattern slowly obliterated by the blood. The girl's head ached and for a while she found it hard to see properly. Kit got out of the car and was pacing around it, drawing pensively on a cigarette. He looked tight-lipped and brooding when he climbed back in. He turned to Liddy, sighed, 'Well, not as bad as I thought. Bit of a dent though.' He took a deep breath, 'Sorry about that, girls,' he announced, 'got a bit close to the verge.' Then, and oddly out of character, he implored, 'Forgiven?'

They forgave him, in a numbed, half-hearted way but as he fired up the engine Liddy said, with more hope than reproach, 'Let's just get home in one piece now shall we?' Her breathing was still quick and spasmodic and she was clearly shaken.

Kit drove the rest of the way home with inordinate care. When Hadley came into view the girl felt returned once more, and thankfully, to safe harbour. The damage to the car was mechanically superficial but she gasped when she saw the great buckled dent where the front wing had crumpled. The number plate was twisted too and part of the bumper stuck out at an odd angle. She stood looking at it with Liddy, not knowing what to say.

'It's not too bad really,' Kit spoke quickly, persuasively, 'looks worse than it is. I'll get it fixed, don't worry. Be as good as new.' They were silent and his glance flicked anxiously between them. 'It will, believe me. I promise.'

But the girl hardly heard him. The ache in her head muffled his assurances. All she could think was how angry Daddy would be.

★　★　★

She was given an aspirin and put to bed. Liddy said a little sleep would make the headache go away. Indulgently, the girl was allowed the luxury of her mother's big bed. Whichever way she stretched she could not reach the edges of it. The room was pleasantly shadowed. A small photograph of Dad was on the bedside table. He was smiling, his cap pushed casually back. She fell into a doze, smiling at his smile, riding on the soft, caressing wave of the big bed.

When she woke she lay still on the satin bedspread, the blanket over her pleasantly ticklish under her chin. She felt cocooned in a cool, comfortable warmth that was attractively unfamiliar. The room was darker now, late afternoon slipping into evening. The door opened quietly, a faint click of the latch, a tousled head peering tentatively in. Kit smiled and sat on the bed.

'How's the old head?'

'All right really.'

'Sure?'

She nodded, 'I'm sure.'

'Look, I really am sorry……I just didn't……' his voice tailed off and for once he was lost for words. His face was full of weary contrition. 'Liddy's a bit jittery too, got a touch of the trembles,' he added absently.

She was sorry for him. 'I am all right really, look,' and she pulled up her fringe, wincing as she brushed the tender bruise. He bent forward solicitously and examined it.

'Hmm……I think some special medicine is called for.'

'Special medicine?' she echoed anxiously. Medicine usually meant something nasty. He smiled.

'Very special, very secret medicine.' He pulled a paper bag out of his pocket and rustled it temptingly. She dipped in, took one of the sweets it contained and sucked happily.

'A bigger dose than that I'm afraid,' he said, pretending to be serious and tucking the bag into her hand. Yet he still looked dejected, like a lost boy, and she felt a wave of sympathy.

'I am okay,' she insisted, 'I've had a worse accident than that you know.'

'Have you?' he asked curiously, 'When?'

'Oh ages ago now,' she replied airily, 'look at this.' She lifted her arm out from under the blanket and thrust the pale arc scar under his nose.

'Good God!' he exclaimed, genuinely surprised. 'How did you come by that, fall out of a tree or something?' He was again talking in the way she liked and she had his full attention. She shook her head.

'No, in the war.'

'The war?'

'In an air raid,' she hissed, 'a bit of an aeroplane came whizzing through the roof of the shelter. Whoosh!' She sliced her arm down on the bedspread. 'Like that, straight through. Liddy says I was really lucky it didn't hit me on the head.' Warming to her own story-telling she added darkly, 'I could've been chopped in half.'

He gulped, apparently spellbound, 'What a lucky escape......' A small smile played at the corners of his mouth.

'Did you get shot or anything?'

'Shot?' he asked in surprise.

'You know, in the army.'

'Oh I see. No, no I didn't,' he gave an ironic snort, 'I was lucky. Came through the whole show without so much as a scratch.' He chuckled, then added enticingly, 'Well, nearly.'

'What?' she asked, goggle-eyed, 'What happened?'

He switched on the small bedside lamp, then with deliberate slowness rolled up his shirtsleeve.

'I did get this though……' On his forearm, emblazoned in deep indigo, was a bird poised in full flight and below a scroll with the word 'Mother' tattooed ornately inside it.

She gaped at the bird, 'It's lovely.'

'The old blue bird of happiness,' he said wryly.

'I expect your mum was pleased wasn't she?'

He threw back his head and laughed, 'Oh no! She didn't like it a bit. Not one bit!'

★　★　★

When she came downstairs a fire had been lit in the front room even though it wasn't cold, and she was given a second aspirin. She felt pampered and pleasantly woozy. She could see Kit through the French windows, lying underneath the car. When he clambered out he spied her and pulled a face. Dreamily she poked her tongue out at him.

She settled with her new book in front of the soothing glow of the fire and turned the pages. The special day hadn't all been spoilt by Liddy being cross and by the accident. She thought about the man from the beach. He'd be in a dark dungeon now and probably very frightened.

Kit waved from outside, holding up hands blackened with grease. A thick streak of it was smeared down his face. It seemed he had been at Hadley much longer than just a week. He and Liddy were getting on famously, just like old friends and that, after all, was what she had wanted.

She flicked through the book, unable to concentrate on the story but enjoying the pictures. Tinker Bell was very beautiful, a starburst shimmer across the page, and she liked Captain Hook's twirling moustache and gold ear-ring. Peter looked spoilt and petulant. There was something in the way his face had been drawn. It was more than just mischievous, it was crafty and cunning. He didn't look like a hero. She liked the crocodile though. It was a sleepy looking, well-fed crocodile and it had *TICK TICK TOCK* written in big black letters around its snapping jaws.

After a while Liddy elbowed open the door. She was carrying a tray piled high with muffins to be toasted in front of the fire, then spread with butter that would melt to a golden liquid. Kit joined them soon afterwards, his hands washed clean of engine oil but the black smudge still on his cheek. Liddy moistened a corner of handkerchief between her lips and wiped ineffectually at it. Eventually he was sent to the bathroom, grumbling cheerfully, to wash it off properly. By the time he returned the muffins were toasted and they began to eat.

'Do you like your book?' Liddy asked.

'I haven't read it all yet,' she fibbed, 'but I do like it, and the pictures.' Turning to Kit she said artlessly, 'How long are you staying for?'

'Miss Jennifer Hawker!' Liddy exclaimed. 'You mustn't ask things like that, it isn't polite. Kit is our house guest!' The girl bit her lip, chastened, but Kit waved a placatory hand.

'That's all right. It's a fair question. Um, a little while longer, if you'll have me.'

'Oh yes!' Jenny said, then looked at her mother and added quickly, 'at least, I think it is.'

'Yes of course, you must stay as long as you like. We can't have our Crusoe roving off and getting lost again, can we?'

'It's very good of you.' Kit got up and turned on the wireless. Gentle, frothy music filled the room and he waltzed an invisible partner back to his chair. 'Tell you what, let's listen out for the weather forecast, if it sounds promising we could take ourselves off to the beach tomorrow. Last swim of the year, eh?'

Jenny clapped her hands jubilantly then, remembering his self-confessed shortcomings at sea, asked gravely, 'You can swim can't you?'

'Swim!' he blustered, aping outrage, 'like a fish young lady, you'll be floundering in my wake.'

She rose to it knowingly, 'Bet I won't, bet I can beat you. Bet anything you like I can.' He leapt to his feet, full of mock indignation.

'A race then, to settle it. This is a matter of honour!' he glowered theatrically, flared his nostrils.

'And I'll be lumbered with stopwatch and towels I suppose?' Liddy frowned teasingly. Kit swept low in grandiose supplication like a medieval courtier.

'Madam, pray will you do us the great honour of awarding a magnificent trophy to the winner of this tournament?' They giggled and he arched first one eyebrow then the other in disapproval.

'And what trophy might that be, my lord?' Liddy asked, going along with it. He became Kit again, pressed a finger to his lips thoughtfully.

'I've got just the thing.' He rushed from the room and banged up the stairs. He was back in a moment and stood before them holding something behind his back. A measured pause then, tantalisingly slow, he produced a bottle. Inside was a magnificent ship, a clipper in full sail. Jenny looked at it admiringly, 'Where did you get it?'

'Oh, picked it up on my travels.'

'It'll be a wonderful trophy,' Liddy said.

The girl nodded, soaking in every tiny detail, 'I've always wanted a ship in a bottle. It's beautiful.'

'Well you've got to win it yet.' Kit laughed as he placed it carefully on the sideboard. He glanced at his watch, murmured, 'What a good idea,' and picking up another bottle from the tray, said, 'drink Liddy?'

The girl listened to the jaunty music from the wireless. She was determined to win and wondered how good he really was. She tried to imagine the race, Kit in a bathing costume, and remembered his tattoo.

'Has Liddy seen your blue bird of happiness?'

He hesitated, opened his mouth to speak but it was her mother, radiant in the firelight, who answered quickly.

'No dear. I haven't.'

CHAPTER ELEVEN

The following morning was bright and clear. Jenny could hardly contain herself. The making of sandwiches, the finding of towels and sweaters in case, improbably, it should 'turn chilly later,' all seemed never ending. She kept glancing anxiously out of the window as if the glorious day might be whisked off to another, more deserving, part of the world.

Finally they were off, loaded down with bags and provisions. Jenny marched ahead whistling, leading the way to what they called, 'Jenny's beach.'

'But it's not mine at all,' she protested, 'it belongs to all the pirates and buccaneers from hundreds of years ago.'

Liddy was shown the bay where Kit had come to grief. He leapt on a rock and regaled her with a hair-raising account of how he fought for his life on the deck of the sinking vessel, surrounded by sharks and sea monsters when, out of nowhere and armed to the teeth, came a fearless Jenny who single-handedly saw them off and rescued him.

The girl grinned and squirmed. 'It wasn't really like that,' she explained, 'he's pretending again.'

They made their way leisurely to the bigger, adjoining bay. Sunlight glittered across the wide stretch of water lapping contentedly at the deserted beach. Jenny slipped quickly into her bathing costume and stretched happily up to the sun, her skin tingling. Kit looked slightly abashed in his costume. He wasn't big like Daddy but wiry and his skin was very white. She pointed to his forearm.

'Look Liddy, isn't it a lovely bird, just about to fly away across the sea.'

The woman glanced briefly at the tattoo. 'Perfectly lovely,' she murmured coolly.

'Last one in's a cissy!' Kit yelled, scrambling to his feet and rushing down the beach. The girl leapt up and sprinted after him.

'Not fair!' she gasped. 'You started before you said.' She felt brilliantly alive; the hot sand under her feet, the inviting sea beyond. She overtook him and splashed noisily in, plunged forward and swam out. When she stopped and looked back he was still only in up to his knees, lifting himself up as each wave passed.

'Come on!' she shouted.

'It's freezing!'

'No it isn't. It's lovely and warm.' She floated on her back, kicking up a frothing ball of foam and spray. It was good to be in the tangy water, to have mastered it. She turned over and did the racing stroke she had practised, moving smoothly, powerfully, through the velvety water, a stream of bubbles gleaming from her.

'I didn't think you were that good!' He was in up to his waist now but he looked as though he was on tiptoe.

'Nor did I.' Liddy was at the edge, tentatively dibbling her toes in the shallows. 'Did you learn all that from Uncle Richard?'

'Yes!' Jenny lied cheerfully. She basked in their attention, their admiration and pushed back her hair, the water streaming from it. 'Come on!' she urged.

Kit looked at her dubiously, put on an expression of alarm, clutched his nose and sank. For a few seconds there was nothing, then a flurry of bubbles and he burst up again with a squawk. A quicksilver shower pattered around him. 'It is cold you fibber!' He dived forward and swam out to her. She eyed him critically. He wasn't a bad swimmer, quite fast, but he looked a bit out of practice and he was puffing loudly. He rubbed the salt from his eyes and squinted at the beach.

'Come on Liddy.'

'Too cold,' the distant figure was still standing at the edge, 'think I'll wait for it to warm up a bit.'

'It's lovely once you're in.'

Liddy, though, shook her head and waved a dainty refusal.

'She doesn't like the cold,' the girl floated up on her back again and looked at her toes, 'she says she's got thin blood.'

'Does she?'

'Dad used to say her feet were like blocks of ice in bed.'

'Did he?'

'And that her fingers were like icicles.' The girl glanced sideways at the beach. 'Liddy's very beautiful isn't she?'

'Yes, she is, very.'

'Do you think I will be, when I grow up?'

He scrutinised her solemnly. 'Not a hope' he laughed, swimming quickly away.

'Well at least I was first in!' she shouted, splashing water after him, 'anyway what about our race?'

He stopped and surveyed the bay, 'How about from here to those rocks?'

It was a distance of some fifty yards. Having just settled herself, Liddy was pressed into service as starter, judge and, not least, audience. She walked down the beach and climbed awkwardly onto the rust coloured promontory; her distant voice floated like a fragile bubble across the water.

'I'll shout ready, steady then go, all right?'

The girl's thin muscles clenched in anticipation. A thrill fluttered through her as she crouched down, chin brushing the water. Kit stood silently beside her, staring fixedly at the rock. She noticed goose bumps on his torso and dark, wet tufts of hair in his armpits. On the beach he looked slender, almost slight, but now there was a subtle shift in the set of his body and he seemed lean, full of raw, male certitude, an unexpected determination.

'I'll win,' he said knowingly, 'you see if I don't.'

'Ready?' Liddy's voice quavered thinly. The girl stiffened.

'Steady?'

She rose up on tiptoe, locked in concentration. The longest of pauses, punctuated only by the lazy hiss and wash of the sea and the distant call of a gull. Kit made a movement at the edge of her vision; she flicked a swift look at him. He was grinning, a wide, disarming grin and rubbing his hands together gleefully. He chuckled at her as she returned the smile, weakly, unresistingly, and as she did her poised muscles relaxed and her attention faltered.

'Go!'

She lunged forward but already he was ahead. She had been caught off guard, unready. She flailed and splashed, forgetting all she had taught herself. Her body was all wrong in the water, clumsy and uncoordinated. She gulped and the bitter sea burned her throat. He was pulling effortlessly away, a humiliating reproof to her showing off. He was streaking ahead, would win easily and she would feel silly and ashamed. She ploughed on in despair, regretting she had ever thrown down such a stupid challenge. She wanted to be back on the beach, to slip gently back into being a child, playing with her spade and making castles.

Her spade. She remembered how she had nearly lost it that day. She remembered too the taste of winning. She had won then. She had beaten Uncle Richard and his ordering her about, not in a race like this but still a contest. Daddy said never give up until you were well and truly beaten, not ever, and in a flash she understood. If she gave up now she would condemn herself to hiding shame-faced on the beach and the admiration the grown-ups had shown would count for nothing, nothing at all. Seized with a new determination, she forced herself to calm down and concentrate. Her breathing became steady and her body stopped rolling ineffectually. She struck out resolutely and felt a powerful rhythm re-assert itself. Peering forward through his splashes, she saw he was closer than she thought. Even though she had been put off at the start and done it all wrong, he still wasn't that far ahead. He was gasping for air too and she wasn't at all tired. She was an arrow skimming the waves. Entranced and electrified by this potent image of herself, she piled on the pressure. Ahead he was beginning to flag, she could hear his gulping as he fought for breath. He was sending up sheaves of spray trying to keep up the pace. The gap between them was closing; she wasn't just wishing it, it really was closing. She buried her face in the sea and swam for all she was worth. When she looked up she was alongside him and saw the wild look as he flung his head from side to side. Then, as though nudged by a partial trade wind, she slid smoothly past. She could hear Liddy's voice, shouting excitedly. For the merest second, through the rush of water flashing over and past her, trailing down to her feet and away, there was something else; a flickering like fingers at her ankles, encircling, snake-like. She kicked away from it, fuelled by ancient, instinctive repugnance and glanced fleetingly back at Kit. All she could see was his gasping face and the white thrashing arms. When her head bumped the rock it was still his desperate look that filled her mind.

'Well done Jenny, well done!' Her mother was clapping, hopping up and down. The girl looked up through salt-misted eyes. Liddy seemed to merge with the faint, white clouds drifting way up in the sky above her.

'Yes well done. Jolly good,' his hand touched her shoulder and she turned. He was panting, 'beat me fair and square.'

'Sorry,' she spluttered, a husky, sea water whisper. Fair and square. It echoed, ringing, inside her head.

Liddy was bending down to them, girlishly excited. 'Well you certainly are a surprise. And you learnt that from Uncle Richard?'

'Oh yes!' the girl said eagerly, smothering the fib with her own dazed brightness. She was floating in more than just the sea and allowed herself to loll languidly in the warm, reaffirming triumph.

After they had recovered they went back to the beach. Her spade was stuck in the sand. She wished that, somehow, there could be a winner's pennant fluttering brightly from it. Kit burrowed in a bag and brought out the prize, the wonderful ship caught forever in its glass bottle.

It shone in the sun, surrounded by the sound of the infinitely larger, real sea.

She thought there might be a presentation, a ceremony of sorts; one of his jokey, sweeping bows, a funny speech in a funny voice, but he seemed to have run out of steam.

'Here you are then. All yours.'

It was unexpectedly heavy, more solid than it appeared. She put it carefully beside her on the blanket while they ate. Liddy and Kit toasted her success with tumblers of wine but the conversation quickly went back to the adult and obscure. She had a growing, unclear sense of pique. She had won but they didn't seem to realise how important it was. She wanted to be cheered and carried shoulder-high, wanted it to seal something. Yet she wasn't at all sure; perhaps he had let her win. Grown-ups sometimes did that sort of thing and she wanted to have really won, not have them pretending and knowing all along it wasn't true. Paradoxically, she had a faint suspicion, one she tried to push away, that it might have been him trying to grab at her feet. It might have been an accident, or one of his jokes. She was proud of winning but chary that it might not have been a proper race nor properly won. At the same time she thought she was being churlish; ungrateful, ungenerous emotions she had been taught not to have, and they shamed her.

Lunch over, the grown-ups stretched out on the blanket and closed their eyes. Jenny meandered along the bay, ostensibly beachcombing. She climbed up and away from the beach to a flat hilltop close to the path that lead home. It was strewn with stones all roughly the same size. They looked as if they might have been dug up and left there for some unknown purpose, years before. She began to arrange them in a large circle. It absorbed her completely and it was only when the circle was almost complete did she fancy that it was magic, a protection from bad pirates. When it was finished she stepped daintily inside, picked up a handful of earth and sprinkled it like dust. 'I did win,' she said aloud to the circle and the distant wind-riffled water, 'I did.'

Below she could see them lying motionless in the sun. She trailed down to the beach and slipped back into the sea, then swam steadily across the bay. It was calm, peaceful. She looked back to the beach and saw Kit sit up, scratch and lie down again.

She broke easily into a lazy crawl, arms arcing through the air and plunging deep as she cleaved smoothly through the shimmering liquid. She had only gone a few yards when she was jerked violently to an abrupt halt. Something had seized her wrist, something under the sea. It was holding her, dragging her down. She thrashed in panic, the dread vision in her mind again of a dark, uncoiling snake, gliding around her body, weaving through her legs, pressing its sliminess against her. It must have been there all the time. It hadn't been Kit at all. In terror she jerked her arm up and felt it snap horribly tight around her wrist. She pulled again: a searing pain this time as if her flesh had ripped. Her arm was trapped so deep that her chin was only just above water. She glanced wildly at the beach. She could see them asleep in the sun and started to call out but a slapping wave filled her mouth making her cough and splutter. She spat and white froth drifted idly away. Any second the beast would rise up seething for the kill. She was helpless, fixed by numb fear, and her heart thudded as she waited for the inevitable. But the churning thrash of the serpent's tail in the sea around her did not appear. The water was calm, untroubled. Tentatively she explored the snared limb with her free hand. It was wire, thin wire caught in a loop around her wrist. She followed it down. It was attached to something square-shaped and slippery stuck into the sandy bottom. Ducking under she peered into the pea-green gloom and recognised a familiar, distinctly man-made shape. It was a piece of fence. She shook it vigorously. A cloud of milky sand rose up and she could no longer see. Her nails dug into the rotting wood as she wrestled with it. There was a dull crack as it began to give way. She bobbed up, sucked in lungfuls of salt air, then slipped down again, planted her feet firmly and heaved. It gave a splintering wrench as it broke and she surfaced triumphantly, tethered but no longer trapped. The wire was rusted and had left a red mark on her wrist. She untangled the loop and got it off. It was a remnant of the old wartime defences that had once kept the beach out of bounds. She was trembling but defiant and began to make her way to the shore, taking the snare with her. No monsters then after all, just the harsh keening of hungry gulls against languid clouds. She studied the beach. They were still asleep. But high on the distant hills, a lone figure looked down on her, strangely enshrouded in an overcoat as though it were already winter. She raised her arm and waved hesitantly but there was no answering salutation. Shivering, she dipped her shoulders back under and carried on. When she looked again the figure had gone.

Kit and Liddy hadn't moved. Kit was gently snoring and making a clicking sound in his half-open mouth. She wrapped a towel round herself and sat on the sand. The sea was just the same as ever, no trace of her struggle showed, everything smoothed over and disguised by the gentle waves.

She got up and, with her spade, scraped out a shallow hole and buried the wood and wire. Farther down, by the water's edge, she searched for flat pebbles to bounce over the waves. She wasn't very good at it. None of them would bounce more than three times. Alone on the beach she felt peculiarly empty and didn't know why. She ought to be pleased. She had won the race. The sea snake had just been a silly old piece of wire after all and the grown-ups hadn't seen her frightened and panicky. She regarded them and felt dejected. She wanted to be included in the world they shared after her bedtime, the laughter she could hear when she'd been shooed upstairs. She envied it and felt resentful and all wrong inside because she did. She wouldn't tell them about getting caught by the wire, to get back at them. It would be a secret of her own.

She picked up a big stone and heaved it into the sea. It plopped loudly, interrupting the solitude of the beach. She threw another, then another, making them splash noisily. Behind she heard them stirring.

'Have I been asleep?' Liddy asked drowsily.

'Sorry,' she answered, 'I didn't mean to wake you.'

'Are you all right dear?'

A sullen 'Yes.' She gazes out across the calm water. Inside a voice is intoning, 'I did win. I did win,' as the waves lap and curl to shore. Kit rouses, yawns, lobs the empty wine bottle end over end into the sea, asks brightly, 'One last swim?'

She does not look round, is unvanquished by them or hidden traps.

'No, I don't think so.'

★   ★   ★

Back home, after a subdued hike, Jenny was pronounced 'tired.'

'All that swimming eh, old girl,' Kit ruffled her hair amiably.

She had a bath before supper then ate it alone in pyjamas and dressing gown while they were busy in the kitchen. Afterwards she was packed firmly off to bed before it was dark.

'You can read for a little while but lights out by half past seven.' The door closed and she lay in bed listening to the late calling birds in the garden. She could hear Kit on the telephone downstairs. He made a lot of calls though she never knew who to or what about. Perhaps it was about getting the car fixed.

She was put out by the genial interpretation of her sulk even though she was herself confused by it. The ship, forever at full sail, was displayed on her bookcase next to Daddy's cigarette tin; less proudly than she would have thought or liked but still magnificent.

Music from the wireless floated dreamily through the house. The last of the sun glowed orange through the curtains and she clicked on her bedside lamp and opened *Peter Pan*.

"They flew away,' Wendy continued, 'to the Neverland, where the lost children are.' A wisp of breeze entered the room and fluttered the curtains. From downstairs a soft, trickling laugh and Kit's deeper, answering chuckle. She wondered what they were doing, tried to put it out of her mind and continued reading. She wasn't sure yet whether she liked the story or not. Her weary eyes began to drift and slide across the page, no longer able to concentrate.

The music from below became clearer, closer. She listened sleepily for a moment then, with an effort, put down the book and slipped from her bed. It sounded as if it was in the garden. Curiosity overcame tiredness and she padded to the window. It was dusk, hard to see anything. She crossed the room and turned off the lamp. Better now, more distinct. She could see the lawn and the dark shapes of trees surrounding the garden. Below was a rectangle of yellow light from the opened French windows. That's why it's louder, she thought. And there, just out of the light, were Liddy and Kit. They were sat on a bench, a bottle on the garden table in front of them. She couldn't hear what they were saying but they held their glasses up to touch them together. Then they stood and began to dance, swaying together across the lawn, not the way he had whizzed her around but slowly, hardly moving at all. Kit's arms were round Liddy and she had her head on his shoulder. The girl blinked, told herself that it was nice they were friendly. Yet it didn't seem entirely right. It wasn't the proper thing.

Troubled for a reason she could not name, she turned slowly away and got back into bed. She turned on the lamp and read.

'*No one ever gets over the first unfairness; no one except Peter. He often met it, but he always forgot it.*' Her eyes, though, were scratchy and she turned off the light once more and lay unhappily in the darkness. She could hear them laughing again, the music still sparkling in the shadowed garden. But then another sound swept it away in an instant; a heavy, purposeful tread on the stairs beyond her door, familiar, remembered and unmistakable, abruptly snatching her back from the edge of sleep.

'Dad?' she whispered hoarsely.

CHAPTER TWELVE

'You must have been dreaming darling,' Liddy crooned, hugging her.

'Nightmare more like,' Kit said irritably, turning away.

'He won't come back now!' Jenny wailed, tears streaming down her red face. 'He won't, not ever again!'

'Who won't dear?' Liddy quizzed gently. 'Who do you mean?'

The girl blubbed, a bubble of saliva kept popping in her mouth and her nose was running. 'Him,' she lamented, sobbing.

'Who dear?' The woman's voice rose in tender exasperation, 'do you mean Kit? Oh silly, he hasn't gone anywhere, he's here, look. What a terrible dream you must have been having.' She gestured across the room to the man standing by the window, half in shadow.

'N......n......not him, not Kit.'

'Well, who then, who?'

'Dad.'

A weighted silence filled the room. Liddy stiffened. Her voice was low, urgent. 'What do you mean, what are you talking about?' When Jenny did not answer she grasped her shoulders and forced the girl to meet her gaze. 'Tell me' she demanded.

Jenny looked down. A tear splashed from her chin onto her hand. 'It was Dad,' she murmured, 'outside my door. He came home.'

'That's nonsense Jennifer. You were having a bad dream that's all. A very bad and upsetting dream but that's all it was, do you understand?'

'But I wasn't asleep!'

'Yes you were. You were asleep and it was a dream. You cried out in your sleep and we came to see what the matter was.'

The girl felt sheepish, beaten. 'Did I?'

'One hell of a yell,' Kit was trying to make light of it. Jenny looked at them. Their faces were blurred and indistinct through her watery eyes but they seemed poised for something, on edge. A glass of water was brought and she drank it down in the dark, holding it in both hands. It tasted warm and salty.

'Now settle down and back to sleep with you. Bad dreams never come back, not twice in one night.'

'How do you know?' The sides of the bed lifted and fell as she was firmly tucked in.

'Because my mother told me and it always was so. Now go back to sleep. You're probably over-tired from the swimming.'

'Try counting galleons in bottles!' It was Kit's jokey voice. She heard him quietly whistling as he went downstairs. She would tell him, in the morning, that it wasn't a galleon.

'Goodnight Jenny. I'll leave the door ajar, just for tonight.' Liddy began to disappear into the thinning crack of pale light from the landing.

'Liddy?' she called softly.

The crack widened slightly, 'Yes?'

'What if it was Dad?'

The door froze, a snap of anger. 'Stop it right now, young lady. Right now or you'll get a smack!'

★   ★   ★

A creeping moss of orange rust had quietly established itself on the still unrepaired wing of Daddy's car. Jenny noted its slow spread as she returned from school each day. The bent bumper had been pulled more or less straight and a hand-painted cardboard number plate was tied over the damaged original.

Up in her room she would sit and watch from the window. The trees had begun to dip and nod towards autumn. The linden tree she had watched fill and spread in the spring was beginning to thin and a scattering of leaves lay on the ground beneath it. Through the gentle exfoliation a new, distant view was revealed and looking into it she thought that if a horse and rider appeared over the farthest hill it would take them an hour to reach Hadley, a whole hour.

There was a stillness to those early autumn days. But it wasn't a comfortable peace. It was edgy and fragile. Gone were the shining summer mornings ripe with hazy promise, replaced by limpid blue-washed mists and a melancholy chill in the air. Gone too, were the endless glittering days, azure canopied and shimmering with heat. It had all slipped quietly away and, it seemed, without a proper farewell.

At the first whisper of impending autumn she had hastened down to the beach on her own one Saturday afternoon. She wanted to see it as it had been all summer and store the memory, shore it up against the coming winter. But it had already begun to change. The thin, passionless sun no longer sparked off the sand making it glow vivid and yellow. Instead it all looked grey and tired. The trees were drab in dull ochre, fading green and brown. She wanted the vibrancy, the light of summer, and it was no more. A silver-winged gull glided over a despondent sea that swashed lamely against the shore. She ambled listlessly to the rocks, saddened and cheated. There, half-buried in the wet sand, were the jagged, shattered remains of a bottle. She could not tell if it was her bottle but gloomily thought it probably was. She scooped up a handful of pebbles and threw them disconsolately at the sea. One though she kept; a perfectly round, smooth speckled stone that, together with a shell, she put in her pocket to remember the summer by. She thought back to the night when Daddy came home and Kit and Liddy danced on the lawn. She wanted desperately to believe he had returned but wavered hopelessly. By day she told herself not to be silly, that Liddy was right and it had been a dream. But at night, reason and logic were ousted by the darkness and she would struggle to stay awake, listening and ascribing to him, with a singing leap of hope, the merest crack or bump in the heart of Hadley. She knew then, and absolutely, that it hadn't been a dream, that in some way, some form, he had come back. She had been dismayed by Liddy's anger and hadn't understood why she had been so cross. It seemed that Liddy was prepared to let go of Daddy and she, Jenny, must hold on to him alone. The day afterwards the grown-ups had been all right again and nice to her. They didn't mention the night before but the incident heralded a slow shift over the weeks and months ahead. Things seemed to change, or be changing. The grown-ups still played with her but increasingly less so. Kit still teased and joked. Yet when he noticed her new shell and held it to his ear, she announced loftily, 'It isn't the sound of the sea you know. It's the noise inside your head that's all,' and then wrestled with her petulance towards him. Often he was out 'on business' or making complicated arrangements on the telephone and he and Liddy seemed always busy with one thing or another and fended her off. Frequently she found herself eating a solitary supper with just the wireless for company while they dashed about or talked privately in urgent, low whispers. Once she asked what it was Kit did all the time, why he was out in the evening so much. Liddy had looked up, eyebrows raised in mild surprise.

'Well, what do you think dear. He has to earn a living.'

'At night-time? What job do you do at night-time?'

'Kit's an actor isn't he. He does shows.'

'What sort of shows?'

'Plays and things. You know.'

The girl paused, deflated at being made to feel dim-witted. 'What about the afternoons then?'

'Matinees of course. Now run along, there's a good girl.'

Some days later she asked Kit if she could come and see one of the shows but he just laughed.

'Good God no! That would really put me off my stride wouldn't it.'

Liddy though, said perhaps, one day, if she was good. One night, struggling through *Peter Pan*, she read:

'He often went out alone and when he came back you were never absolutely certain whether he had had an adventure or not' and she thought of Kit's rushing about, always racing to get somewhere on time, dashing back for a change of clothes and then out again, coming home late and sleeping in the

mornings while she and Liddy crept quietly downstairs, and she pondered what adventures he might have in his secret world.

In the meantime her world, at least the one she lived in from Monday to Friday, had taken on a new and wretched dimension. She had moved up to 'the big school.' It was on the outskirts of a small town two or three miles inland. A forbidding, red brick building that sprawled out from a rigid quadrangle, enclosed by a necklace of spiked iron railings. Here, formidable words like order, discipline and attention were rigorously upheld. Terrifying acts, only whispered about, were committed, like caning. She began to look back wistfully to the gentle, cardiganed ladies of the village school. Here it was another world, one of harsh, blunt authority and the expectation of complete obedience. Here there was angry shouting, ugly voices and piercing metal whistles that silenced the playground. And on her first day, two boys squatting against a wall,

'Do you know what fuck is?' they sniggered. That word again.

'What? What is it?'

They looked at each other knowingly. 'Go on, guess!' they chanted, but she walked away, their ribald laughter rising up behind her.

It was a place of unrelieved misery. She craved the bell at the end of each day signalling release from it. Within the atmosphere of harsh reprimands and ritual humiliations was a barely contained violence, the constant threat of which strutted the dingy corridors. It made her anxious and watchful. She wanted not to be noticed, to be invisible, and would walk the playground and corridors with her shoulders back, not looking left or right, completely, she thought, beyond attention, beyond criticism. In class her nervousness made her pause and take a secret, calming breath before speaking. Though she did not know it, outwardly her behaviour looked like cool self-possession. It had the opposite effect from the one she wanted. It got her noticed. Not so much by the teachers, who reacted with a tetchy puzzlement but could not fault her model behaviour. It was the outlaws who noticed.

They were a small knot of rebels who were always in trouble and didn't seem to care. There was a hard core of about five, all older girls in their final year, together with a sprinkling of younger hangers-on. At first there was an attractiveness about this little cell of insurrection, recklessly flaunting the rules. She had perceived them bathed in a Robin Hood glow, not cowed by the iron discipline. Yet the more she saw of them the more she realised that they weren't just against school but against anyone who got in their way or failed to observe a scraping deference. They were cruel and spiteful and boasted of stealing sweets and cigarettes. They subtly modified the regulation skirt, tie and blazer into their own tribal uniform. And they weren't at all fearless. Cornered, they treacherously blamed each other and faced punishment not with silent defiance and dignity but with craven pleading and loud protestations of innocence.

Jenny kept a distance but discreetly observed them. They both intrigued and repelled her. The outlaws didn't so much talk but snap at each other and they were always conniving, not just mischievously, but with a gleeful malevolence. There was a vindictiveness about them that took its cue from the teachers they sneered at.

It was November, several months into her new existence and she thought she had perfected being nobody. She would arrive at school and take on the mantle of compliant self-effacement. She was quiet and diligent but not so diligent that it made her stand out. At home she answered questions about the new school unenthusiastically. Kit and Liddy were, anyway, too busy to listen properly. They didn't notice the quick looking away, the uneasy biting at her lip. At night she would listen still but there was no step on the stair and the rushing winter winds outside seemed, after all, just that and prosaic. Nonetheless, she still fell asleep listening, waiting.

She cycled to and fro each day. The beginning of a school week was an unimaginable stretch of looming anxiety to be gotten through somehow, relieved only by small, private comforts she hoarded up; a comedy programme on the wireless, the relief she had on Wednesdays when there would be no more arithmetic for the week. She was sustained by these and other simple consolations, and by the thought of the weekend ahead. But then Sunday nights would be dark and unhappy. A bath followed by tea, only hymns on the B.B.C. She sat in her dressing gown, enduring the still, useless time before it all began again, a book unread on her lap, dulled into nervous inertia by the prospect of the next day, the coming week.

She started out for school especially early, sometimes even before Liddy was downstairs. She evolved particular rituals for the journey and always carried the stone from the beach in her coat pocket. It was a way of taking with her something of which she was also a part. There were things to look out for, places where she stopped briefly. If they were all in order, unchanged, everything would be all right. She always paused at a particular tree that had a smiling face where one of the big lower branches was missing and, farther on, at a sweeping view of the distant hills through a gap in the hedge. They were all markers on that unhappy journey to school, signing her closeness to the hated place and her farness from home. And at the end of the day, with a warm glow of relief in her stomach, she raced home, ticking off her secret landmarks as she flew past them until Hadley came into sight; still, and unalterably, the centre and focus of her existence.

It was Friday, mid-morning and cold. White frost peppered the tarmac playground and groups of raw-kneed, red-nosed children stamped, blew into their cupped hands and shouted to each other, leaving clouds of vapour trailing in the air. There was the merest trace, a butterfly's wing, of the sea in the wind and she sniffed appreciatively at this welcome visitor from her other life.

During break times she practised her invisibility by keeping on the move. It seemed to work. The less one was seen, she reasoned, the less one was noticed. It involved a carefully paced march around the entire perimeter of the school grounds. If she timed it right, a double circuit could be completed just as the summoning bell rang, although the only invisibility she really achieved was to mask the stiff nervousness she felt inside. In reality her calm-looking, measured pace, coupled with the two inches she had suddenly and recently added to her height, made her preternaturally graceful, fluid. Unknown to her she looked assured, feline, challenging.

The outlaws and their would-be imitators were in their usual place, huddled by the toilet block. She could hear the erratic hiss of the rusty cisterns echoing inside it. A bad-tempered ripple broke out amongst the lounging group and a smaller, younger member was cuffed, shoved and bundled between the three leaders for some unknown slight or indiscretion. She steadfastly avoided looking at them and loped past.

'Oi!' It was a thin, grating voice, 'You!' The beginnings of a red flush crept up from her collar and she felt suddenly feeble. She kept walking, not daring to look.

'There she goes,' the voice howled, 'Miss bloody snooty, stuck-up bitch!' The insult was spat at her venomously and an excited, whooping babble began. She heard the clatter of feet coming towards her.

'You!' A hand thumped into the middle of her back and sent her sprawling to the ground, scraping her knees painfully. She turned slowly, fearfully, and looked up at the ring of belligerent faces staring at her.

' 'Oo the 'ell do you think you are then, bloody fairy princess or summat?' Jennifer looked down at her bloodied knees. They no longer hurt. She was petrified, frozen into a dumb immobility.

'No......' she answered falteringly.

'We bin watchin' you, bloody stuck-up cow!' the biggest of them snarled. 'Think you're Lady Muck don't you?'

'No......no I don't......' she struggled to break free of the paralysis gripping her. Awkwardly she got to her feet. The leader of the outlaws towered over her.

'Teach you to be so bloody stuck-up we will.' An ugly cheer of encouragement went round the little mob. 'Stick 'er 'ead down the lavvy won't we eh? Won't look like a poxy princess then will she?' The girl laughed and pushed her face close to Jenny's. 'That'll teach you,' she scowled menacingly. Jenny stepped back involuntarily. The wind brought again the scent of the sea, her strange, salt-spiced ally. It washed and rippled through her, engulfed the fear and left in its place something shudderingly new; anger, sheer rage. It was alive in her, boiling up, urging her to strike out, not just once but again and again, to smash out of existence the thin, taunting face sneering into her own.

'No. It won't.' The firm voice surprised even Jennifer and it was her own.

'What?' the outlaw's voice bridled. Jennifer's hand closed tightly around the smooth, speckled stone in her pocket. She could feel grains of sand against her knuckles. 'No?' the girl repeated indignantly, 'you bloody little…' She lunged forward, the unfinished sentence crumpling between them. Jennifer stepped back quickly then rose up, suddenly light on her feet, an echo of the floating sensation she had before jumping from the pier. Galvanised, explosive and exuberant, she lashed out, the stone in her hand, and felt a soft, yielding scrunch as it connected. The big girl's scream pierced the jeering clamour around them. She sank to the ground, blood streaming down her face. It spattered onto the frosted tarmac and there was a silence like the pause of a great wave before it gathers itself and crashes down. The mob stood silenced, stunned faces staring down at their bawling, wounded leader.

'What the fuckin' 'ell d'yer do that for?' One of them rushed at her but she struck out again, quickly and with furious determination. The swinging blow caught the girl just by the ear. She dropped as if pole-axed and lay moaning, her face in her hands.

The angry trill of a teacher's whistle stabbed through the cold air and jerked to life the numbed little gathering staring silently at Jennifer and the two outlaws groaning at her feet.

'What's going on there?'

'Scarper!' The remaining outlaws scattered, pelting off in all directions. Jenny slipped the stone back in her pocket and stayed where she was. The teacher arrived red in the face and out of breath.

'Right then you two,' the man said sourly, 'what mayhem has gone on here then? Finally got around to beating the living daylights out of each other eh?' There was no disguising the sly satisfaction in his voice. 'Well you're both for it this time.' He turned to look at Jenny as if only now noticing her. 'Hawker isn't it? Well get along and stop gawping.' He waved her away testily. She looked down at the two girls. One was kneeling, face still hidden in her hands, hair streaked with blood and mucus. The other was lying motionless on the ground, sobbing. Jenny smiled to herself as she turned and walked away, her hand around the stone in her pocket.

During the rest of the day she barely took in a word. She felt darkly elated and self-contained in her victory. Her hand throbbed terribly and she nursed it beneath her desk. When the final bell rang she wrapped the bruised hand in her handkerchief and jammed it deep into her coat pocket. The two outlaws had not been seen since the fight but she was watchful and alert as she went for her bicycle, in case they were waiting there to ambush her. They weren't, and even the gaggle who usually hung around them shrank away from her as she strode impassively across the playground. She was quite certain the two girls wouldn't tell on her; the humiliation of being beaten by a first year would be bad enough. Anyway, even if they did, she doubted that the teachers would believe them.

As she cycled home, jaunty despite her hand, she counted off the markers as usual but especially cheerfully, with more than just relief at being homeward bound. The sky was overcast and a fragile drizzle began as she turned into the lane leading to Hadley. The bicycle juddered to a halt outside the white gate. She pushed it open and wheeled the bicycle noisily up the gravel path.

Kit was out as usual but Liddy was in the front room surrounded by official papers. She was wading through them with the earnest expression of someone trying to understand a foreign language. She put her hand to her mouth as Jenny appeared in the doorway and her eyes widened in dismay. Only then did the girl remember her badly grazed knees and the swollen hand wrapped in a now grubby, unravelling handkerchief.

'What on earth has happened?' Liddy asked, fussing round her.

'I came off my bike,' Jenny lied, mentally sinking into the warm bath of her mother's concern. 'I hit a stone on the road.'

'Oh you poor thing! Up to the bathroom quickly, we must get you cleaned up.'

The knees were bathed and anointed with a stinging yellow ointment. Her hand, mottled with bruises, was tenderly dabbed with witch-hazel from a brown bottle. She was given hot, sweet tea in the kitchen as she listened to the wireless, and then a supper of scrambled eggs before Liddy cleared away the pile of documents, putting them carefully into a shoebox and tying it up with string.

Kit was still not back by bedtime. She sat by the wireless and washed down an aspirin Liddy gave her with sips of warm milk. Later, tucked in solicitously, the girl could not sleep. Her hand ached insistently. The day had catapulted her into unknown territory. She had an unsettling sense of strange dislocation. Even though it was Friday night and two blissful days away from school shimmered ahead, she knew she would never again suffer the same anxiety. It was already receding, passing from her. She could win. She had proved it.

She was still awake when Kit got home. She heard the car pull up and his cheery whistle as he strode to the front door. Then the indistinct song of their talking, a chime of laughter and the touch of glass against glass. The voices dropped to a low mumble and she listened for steps on the stair but there were none. When at last she floated into a fitful sleep she could not tell if the sound outside her window was the distant sea or the gathering wind. And to the mysterious, absent ghost she murmured, 'I did it. I was brave.'

CHAPTER THIRTEEN

She came to with a start and sat up abruptly, pulling at the bedclothes. Already all she could remember of the dream was the single, disturbing image of a woman pulled from the sea, her dress streaming a silver shower, like a dripping wet sheet. It was a mesmerising vision and sent a shiver through her. The dream was slipping away even as she tried to recall it. The woman was young and beautiful. Jenny could see in her mind the long, wet hair and her arms, slender and white, held powerfully by someone unseen above her as she was hauled up into a brilliant light. She had no idea who the dream woman was or why she was in the water but the remembered fragment was startlingly real and it left her with an unaccountable feeling of alarm.

She looked at her clock. It was one-thirty in the morning. Gnawing spasms of pain gripped her bruised hand and she rubbed gently at it. The house was still. Outside she could hear the far sound of waves and thought hazily that it had been the sea after all. She wished that it was summer again and she could slip through the leafy sunshine to the welcoming beach. Already those days seemed distant. Then, decisively, she swung her feet out of bed and crept across the room. Gently pulling open a drawer, she took out a thick sweater and put it on over her pyjamas. The drawer let out a prolonged squeal as she closed it and she screwed up her face, poised to leap back into bed, but the house remained deaf and indifferent. Opening the door carefully she tiptoed out and down the stairs. Lifting her winter coat from the hall stand she went quietly into the kitchen, shutting the door with painstaking care. It was cosy and snug, filled with a comforting warmth from the slumbering, well-stocked range. A faint aroma of cooking was still in the air. She slipped into the heavy coat and buttoned it up. Then, pausing only to collect her spade, she went into the back porch and struggled into wellingtons. She strained at the heavy back door bolt with both hands. When it suddenly shot back with a loud bang she froze, certain that the jarring crash would wake Liddy and Kit, but the house and its occupants remained undisturbed and unaware.

She stepped out into a cold, immensely still night. It was a strange, wintry sky: a wisp of cloud against a full-ballooning moon and the faintest of breezes riffling the trees. The damp grass yielded beneath her boots as she crossed the lawn and clambered over the gate into the lane. Here the overhanging trees formed an ominous, dark canopy and she held the spade tightly like a weapon. Soon she was scrambling through the woods and down to the bay. As she emerged she gave a little squeak of astonishment. The flat sea was like a great stretch of luminous mercury reaching away to a clear horizon where thick streaks of cloud splashed obliquely across the illuminated sky. It was an extraordinary, uplifting vista. There was so much light that it seemed not like winter or night-time at all. She stared up in wonder, gasped with delight and the sea answered with a whispering backwash.

She stuck her spade into the sand and waded in. It felt strange, paddling in the cold, softly radiant water. She pushed up her sleeve, bent forward and let her hand slide into it, bathing the bruises. The cool sea slipped between her fingers, a silky bandage of green and foam and salt. This was what she had come for; to draw from the deep power. She raised her hand and watched the drops flow down her arm and back into the sea. Caught in the light, the curving scar inside her forearm shone with a translucence like the edge of the moon. The hand felt soothed and caressed. The bruising was still there but it felt that it shouldn't be anymore. The sea's magic had worked. There would, she reflected, be more days like today, days of conflict and fear. She knew though, that in finally striking out, she had been suddenly and acutely aware of not betraying something, something to do with Daddy and her own pride, and nothing remotely to do with being a good girl. She chafed, in an imprecise way, at what seemed to be her lot, and an embryonic sense of knowing that the future she wanted was very different took hold of her. If that person, that life, was to be, it would mean taking hold somehow and shaping it. The scar, that slender curve, was a permanent warning of what could happen if you didn't pay attention all the time. The piece of metal that caused it had come from nowhere, out of the blue. You had to stay on guard all the time because there were things in the grown-up world you couldn't see or hear or touch. You had to not let them take away hard won triumphs. People were sometimes different to how they pretended to be as well, like Lally. There would be other outlaws, and Daddy wasn't there to help her, at least she hadn't heard from him in a long time and then only once. Perhaps Liddy was right and it was a dream. Perhaps if she had tended the little grave under the tree better.........but that hadn't been the right thing even though it was a good idea then. She would have to find her own way.

She held back her fair hair and peered at the serious reflection in the sea, at the face she could never decide about. People said she was pretty but they might just be being kind. It was anyway a face that seemed to be changing, becoming more defined. Her hand felt much better and she dried it roughly against her coat. Without warning and from faraway came the long siren bellow of a lightship. She jumped, felt her heart thump and the sea slosh over the top of her boots. 'Silly,' she said to herself and stood gazing out at the sound. A thickening fog now obscured the horizon and a dead fatigue stole over her, as if all her energy had drained away with the tide. She went back to the beach and standing on one leg at a time emptied the wellingtons. The bottom edge of her coat was wet too. She waved solemnly, wearily at the sea, collected her spade, and began to find her way home. She was curiously dispirited as she trudged back, as if the blast from the lightship had brought her back to earth with an unwelcome jolt. It was easy to find answers alone at night, much harder to keep to them in daylight.

She clambered laboriously back up through the woods and into the lane. It seemed such a long haul home and her eyes were prickly with tiredness, making her blink. Hadley was still dark. It looked warm, welcoming. She could almost feel the soft, enveloping blankets and the plump cosiness of her bed.

Nearing the back door she looked over regretfully to the far corner where she had dug the little grave. Sea mist was curling slowly from the shadowed trees, billowing gently towards her, a pale blue, the colour of cigarette smoke. It too looked inviting, as if she could lie down upon it and, slumbering, float away to some Neverland of her own. She stood by the back door and leaning against the wall began to slip her feet out of the clammy boots. If was almost more effort than she could muster. She glanced longingly again at the velvety fleece unrolling over the lawn and stopped dead. There, in the distance, just under the trees, was the clear silhouette of a square, capable figure; a man, the collar of his coat turned up against the chill. She was completely unafraid. His face was hidden but she knew he would be smiling. There was no question, none at all. It was unmistakably him. As the warmth of recognition came over her it seemed wonderfully ordinary. He stood relaxed and motionless, then waved, and in that easy gesture she felt again his hand ruffle her hair and heard his true, undimmed voice. A ribbon of pale, fractured cloud passed across the moon and he was gone. She rubbed her heavy, stinging eyes and stared at the place where he had been. He was gone but her heart was full of him, flooded by his sure presence, not alone after all. She stared into the darkness, bound in new covenant, sealed by a trace of salt at her lips.

CHAPTER FOURTEEN

She wrestled with the lid of the cigarette tin and, when it finally came off, it clattered to the floor. Inside it was shiny and there were still a few black grains of tobacco stuck there. It smelt moist and musky, the same sort of smell as the inside of the greenhouse. She held the tin to her lips and whispered impetuously.

'I saw him, Daddy. I saw him last night. I was right all the time and it's true.' She clapped the lid on firmly, sealing it in. She wouldn't ever, ever tell the grown-ups. Not after the last time. A troupe of magpies descended swiftly and settled in the tree outside her bedroom window; seven for a secret never to be told.

A lolling mist still hung over the garden, softening its edges. The winter sun, low in the east, was struggling to break through.

Her still damp and discarded pyjama trousers lay in a heap on the floor. She hurried to the bathroom to rinse out the sea-soaked nightwear. She'd say she had splashed soapy water down herself while she was washing. Liddy and Kit were still sound asleep. When she had dressed, she left the screwed-up pyjama trousers on the kitchen draining board in readiness for her alibi, then stuffed her wellington boots with old newspaper to dry them. Pigeons cooed in the early morning as she opened the back door and glanced round it. The gossamer lawn, now webbed with mystery, was as it always had been. She half expected a shadowy figure to step out from behind a tree but everything was frustratingly normal. She inspected the ground looking for a trace, some evidence of what she had seen. By the time she thought to see if the grass had been crushed it was too late, she had already been over and over it, seeking something more tangible. She gave up and mooched back to the house, disappointed and crestfallen, her lips pressed together in bitter frustration. She wanted to cry but would not.

'I have to believe, I have to!' she told herself severely. 'If I don't believe he won't come or can't come. I have to believe. He didn't come for ages after I let them tell me it was just a dream. It's like a test.' And loitering in the back of her mind, unlucky to ask out loud, was when, when would he come?

Liddy was in the kitchen, sat at the big wooden table with her hands wrapped round a cup of tea. She was still in her dressing gown, hair wrapped in a white towel. She looked unusually pallid and dishevelled, stray wisps of hair drifting from the makeshift turban. There was a tautness in her face and creeping blue shadows around her eyes. Breakfast had been started but abandoned.

'I had to sit down for a moment,' she said. The girl casually explained away the pyjamas. Liddy listened, nodding, but it was as if she was far away. She smiled weakly but remained oddly unresponsive. After a while she went upstairs to dress and when she returned seemed herself again, poised to deal briskly with the day's chores.

'Liddy,' the girl asked with feigned indifference, 'have you ever seen a ghost?' The woman laughed, busy at the range.

'Goodness gracious, what a question. No, I never have and I don't think I ever will.'

'Why not?'

'Because there's no such thing.'

Just then the door of the kitchen creaked open and Kit, wearing an old dressing gown, his dark curls wildly out of control, stumbled in. His eyes were red-rimmed and his face shockingly white. He stared blankly, hopelessly, at them, winced and put a hand to his brow.

'On second thoughts dear,' the woman said dryly, 'I think one has just walked in.'

★   ★   ★

'It's up there somewhere, a brown box, but do be careful.' Liddy's voice floated up and echoed around the dark and musty attic. The girl made her way cautiously along the rafters, struggling to hold the heavy torch.

'Is it big or small?' she shouted down. The answering voice was flustered, aware of the unhelpfulness of the reply.

'Well......medium size really. It's tied up with string.'

The girl peered into the gloom at the jumbled heap of boxes and suitcases. She was hot, sticky and cross. Kit had promised for ages to get the box of Christmas decorations down but hadn't. Dust tickled her nose and cobwebby things brushed at her face as the beam of light wobbled in her unsteady hand.

She had not wanted to think about Christmas this year, but Kit was full of promises about it and, like a child, excitedly counted down the days. Despite herself she found it infectious, at least she did when he was around.

'Balloons, loads of 'em! And a tree, a proper one!' was his litany. 'And we mustn't forget to leave out a mince pie and a glass of sherry, eh Jenny?' But it had been Liddy who ordered the tree and organised things. As the day itself grew closer there were secrets in the house, cupboards and drawers that Jenny was forbidden to open. She was looking forward to the break from school although, as she had predicted, it was different now, or she was. Even the teachers seemed less monstrous. It had been, it was, so easy to fool them. The school climate was subtly changed too, as if the shock waves of her action had blunted the knife-edge of the place. The outlaws had been expelled and the mythology of the fight grew and was polished, embellished over the weeks.

Jenny didn't care about their fate. Instead she was wholly caught up with the appearance of the night visitor. Now she stayed wide awake late into the night, straining for a glimpse of him from her window. In the mornings she woke groggily, in bed, but not knowing, or remembering, how she got there.

They were glum, cheerless days; dark at Hadley by the time she got home, the countryside cold kissed by a winter that stripped the trees and blew away all the colours. The only lift to her spirit came with the salt smell of night breezes and the late turning landscape, delicately freckled with fallen copper-coloured leaves.

She had begun to suspect too, that there were other secrets, not at all connected with Christmas. Secrets between Liddy and Kit. Conversations that stopped when she entered a room, being shushed off to bed and then their muted voices talking far into the night. She didn't know what their secret was but her exclusion hurt and made her lonely. Kit's constant performance had also started to pall;

the jokes, catch-phrases and tall stories were now all too familiar, too often repeated. She had seen the whole repertoire and it had become jaded and tiresome. Another, creeping change had happened as well. He acted less like a guest at Hadley and more as though he had always been there. When he told her off for the first time, albeit mildly, for dallying with her food, she at last comprehended that, whatever she had hoped, he was firmly on the side of grown-ups. Head bowed, she stared sullenly at the rigid puddle of cold gravy on her plate and wished he had never been shipwrecked there. All that playing about and doing mad things had been to make her think well of him but it hadn't meant anything. It came in a rush, this new understanding about grown-ups. He wasn't, after all, what she had thought.

Liddy though, seemed completely and happily caught up with it. She thrived, became animated, when he was home, looked weary and diminished when he wasn't. Their lives, hers and Liddy's, were spinning in orbit around him, dumped on a rollercoaster in the middle of a gaudy carnival. It was his hectic schedule that dominated, dictated their own, yet Liddy didn't seem to mind at all, just as she didn't mind the ceaseless panic about clean shirts or costumes, the race to curtain up times or his things left carelessly about the house. Patiently she tidied up, cooked, washed and ironed. Sometimes, when Kit rushed off, Liddy would wave to him then turn back to the house and look wistfully at Jenny as though, if it weren't for the girl, she too would be off on the adventure with him.

Something which to Jenny had shimmered unclear and deceptive like a summer haze had now become transparent. She no longer had unquestioning trust in them. Not that she had recognised or understood the existence of that trust before. It had simply been there. But now, trickling away, its absence left a stark emptiness inside her. She wanted to trust them, wanted that uncomplicated wholeness, but she no longer did, not fully.

It was a Christmas overshadowed by doubts, yet her disquiet about Liddy and Kit was squashed and put to one side with the rush to get ready. She half-believed, without any reason to, that after Christmas everything might be better again and that she too would be different, no more ugly thoughts. There was a small, glistening bauble in her memory of what Christmas had been like and all these preparations seemed hollow in comparison. Yet she threw herself into them, not with gusto but with solemn determination, and allowed them to mask her unease.

In bed one night she asked God what she should do but got no answer and thought he must be busy somewhere else. It would all be so different if Daddy hadn't died. Her eyes sought out the cigarette tin nestling on the bookshelf. It was a small beacon of faith in the dim room. And in the darkness, closed in by the night and the season, she realised the blindingly obvious; he had been with her all the time. He had helped. He had given his power to her, his strength, the strength that helped her win. If only she could see him again, or hear his voice, just to be sure. A magic spell might make him appear, his big smile and handsome face lighting up the room. Spells though, were beyond her. Whatever combination of words and incantations she gleaned from books just sounded childish when spoken out loud. All she could do was be patient and wait for him to come home again.

But all through those weeks leading up to Christmas she simmered helplessly. Everything was so overwhelmingly wrong and muddled. It had been so simple before. When Kit first arrived it was new and exciting but he had eclipsed her somehow, in the house, and she had brought him there. She had been entranced by him and wanted him to stay. Now she was caught by the same petard she had so gaily hoisted. It was a bitter pill to swallow, and just herself to blame.

A glimmering thread of tinsel caught in the torch beam, a thin strand escaping from a box under the eaves.

'Found it,' she shouted unenthusiastically to the woman below and began to step precariously over the rafters towards it.

★   ★   ★

The Sunday before Christmas was soft and clear. Liddy had been working flat out all week and decided they should get some air. They took the cliff walk over Bathsheba Point where the local white rock stopped all at once and in the distance rose up the dramatic deep oxide of red sandstone.

Kit kept up a sparkling barrage about the celebrations to come and a twinkling tease at what Jenny might, or might not, find beneath the now decorated, and magnificent, Christmas tree. She found it hard not to be caught up with it and had a small stirring inside at the prospect of presents to give and get and carols to sing. She had bought bath cubes for Liddy, decorated with pictures of lilacs and irises, and a little pottery ashtray for Kit with *Souvenir of Devon* written around the rim. Both were wrapped and hidden in her room.

Kit's seductive burlesque alternated with quiet asides to Liddy. He was wearing a new camel hair coat which he paraded for them at breakfast.

'Got it for a quid,' he said, elated and faintly smug, 'look, silk lining and everything.' He flung it open to reveal an acreage of shiny scarlet.

They climbed leisurely up the steep, uneven path edged with straggling bush. Kit turned his attentions to Liddy and the girl lagged behind, engrossed in her own thoughts.

'Look out slowcoach!' He spun round and tossed something at her. She clapped her hands together but missed it and the object fell to the ground. It was a boiled sweet. She scooped it up, unwrapped it and popped it in her mouth, lemon flavoured, bittersweet and sharp.

'That better?' he grinned, sauntering backwards to look at her, 'had to do something about that long face.' He fished in his pocket and gently lobbed another at her. This time she caught it. 'Cheer up,' he implored, 'might never happen!' It was hard not to like him when he was like this. She found herself smiling.

'Thanks.'

It took them twenty minutes to reach the top. The view was familiar but still extraordinary; the curving bay, red cliffs in the distance surmounted by a pale purple sky. The sea was steely grey, untroubled. A bench had been installed on the exposed grassy clearing at the summit. A breathless Liddy sat down quickly and pulled her collar up round her as if she were cold, although the day was unusually mild.

'Oh it seems so much farther than I remember,' she sighed, 'I used to run up that path when.........when I was younger.'

'Take a breather,' Kit said genially, 'it'll be easier going down anyway.'

The mid-winter emptiness of the place suited Jenny. She liked the clearness and the warm red of the distant cliffs.

'There's just that one show on Christmas Eve and that's it!' He was back to his favourite theme and bubbling over with it. 'Then three whole days clear!' The woman nodded and smiled indulgently, 'It will be a lovely Christmas.'

They fell quiet and Kit scanned the view importantly. He pointed to the hills across the bay. 'What's that over there? Can you see it Liddy?'

'Don't know.' The woman's voice was muffled by the still clasped collar.

'Can you see it Jen?' The girl went and stood next to him, squinting into the distance.

'I can't see anything,' she said, peering earnestly 'there's a sort of white blob but I can't make out what it is, is it moving?'

'No,' he announced airily, 'houses can't move.'

She blinked, stared even harder, 'How do you know it's a......' she began, then warned by something in his voice, glanced up. He was looking through a small telescope, more like a toy than a proper one. He chuckled down at her.

'Had it in my pocket all along.'

'You sneak,' she said, without malice although she did feel a bit put out, or caught out, by him. 'Can I have a look please?' He handed her the telescope.

'Have a good gawp while I rest my feet.' He went and sat next to Liddy on the bench, chatting and waving his hands to emphasise some point.

She found it hard to aim the telescope and the little white house swooped in and out of her round tunnel of vision. When at last she steadied it on the target it was disappointingly unremarkable; a small stone cottage with a neat front garden. No one about at all.

She swung the telescope out to sea. The meagre sun cast the faintest sparkle across its gently heaving surface. There was nothing really to see but she was enjoying the novelty of seeing it close up. Then far out, a glimpse of red sail moving slowly towards land, an unlikely pyramid in a liquid desert. She couldn't see how many people were on board and stepped forward as if to shorten the distance. Turning into the wind the vivid red triangle eclipsed into a slim, elegant pencil of resistance. She stepped forward again. The boat was enticing, mesmerising in the dreariness of winter. She could see it more clearly as it came in. What from a distance seemed a slow, stately progress, through the telescope looked all of a rush, the sails straining and white foam breaking at the bow, an indistinct pennant fluttering wildly at the masthead.

She was smiling to herself as she stepped forward once more, smiling as her foot reached out for solid ground and, startlingly, found something else instead. It was thin air.

She screamed as she toppled over the edge and slithered down the steep, damp, grassy slope. Ancient rock scraped at her knees. The telescope was knocked from her hand as she tumbled, grabbing wildly around her for anything to arrest her fall. The scream stopped as she caught hold of a small bush and came to a bumping halt, the breath knocked from her. She was perched on a rock-strewn slope that plunged down towards the cliff edge. She hung on fearfully, staring at the sparse blades of grass inches from her nose.

Slowly she looked unwillingly down. The scrub covered incline terminated abruptly some twenty feet below then it was sheer cliff dropping away to sea. She couldn't see the telescope.

'Jenny!' It was Liddy, her voice cracking, almost hysterical. 'Oh my God, are you all right?'

The girl looked up cautiously. Liddy was peering over the edge. 'Yes,' she answered, 'but I can't climb up.' Kit was nowhere to be seen. She squirmed closer to the bush and dislodged a mossy stone. She watched with dread fascination as it fell away down the slope.

'Don't try!' the woman urged, 'Stay completely still. We'll get to you. Don't move!'

It was then that Kit's face appeared. She could see him quite clearly, it was a face of shrinking hesitation. As he looked down it turned to unconcealed horror and he quickly withdrew. Liddy called out, 'Just hold on!' Then she too disappeared.

The girl could hear their voices. It seemed to be taking an awfully long time. She felt curiously unafraid now and was coolly adamant that she would not fall, no matter how long she had to hang on.

There was a scramble above, a handful of pebbles clattered past her and, reassuringly, came to rest on the slope. She looked up. Liddy was climbing awkwardly down. She was holding Kit's hand as he knelt nervously at the edge, his face white and aghast. He opened his mouth but no sound came out. The woman was barefoot and in her free hand had the coat, his precious, new camel hair coat, by its sleeve. She shook it out before her as she descended. The other sleeve had been knotted. Soon it hung down just above Jenny's head. Liddy's face was screwed up in a frown of intense concentration.

'Can you reach it?' she panted. 'Can you get hold of it?'

'I'll try.' The girl heaved herself round with a grunt, one hand searching overhead. She made a wild grab and caught it.

'Well done! Now hold on tight.'

As the girl's weight transferred from the bush to the coat her sure calmness momentarily gave out. For a second she felt the smooth material stretch and give, imagined a gaping rent as it split, red lining billowing like a flag; too fast for her to save herself, too slow not to be agonisingly aware of her fate. But it was not to be. The coat held.

'Pull Kit, pull!' the woman cried vehemently, struggling up the slope, the coat a stretched umbilicus between them. Jenny fought to get her feet under her. She heard Kit's voice, urgent and strangled, 'For Christ's sake hurry up!' and looked upwards. His face was like a pale, frightened moon over her mother's shoulder.

When at last they scrambled over the brow the exhausted woman collapsed onto the grass. 'Thank God. Oh, thank God,' she murmured. She was breathing quickly and coughing. The girl knelt by her.

'Are you all right Liddy?'

The woman's eyes flickered open. She clasped Jenny's hand and held it to her cold cheek.

'I'll be fine. I'll be all right. Just let me get my breath back.' Again she closed her eyes.

Jenny stood and brushed herself down. She took out a handkerchief, spat on it and gingerly blotted her bloody knees. Kit was standing by, away from the edge, his hands shaking as he tried to light a cigarette. She walked slowly to him and smiled diffidently but he could not look at her. He pulled deeply on the cigarette and exhaled at the sky. His hands were still shaking. Finally he looked at her but with shamed eyes in an ashen face.

'Heights,' he shrugged, 'always give me the shivers.' He tried to laugh, to return himself, them all, to the everyday, then pulled an unconvincing wry face. 'Sticky few moments eh?'

But for Jenny, gazing quizzically up at him, it had seemed much more than a few moments. She had not felt in grave peril but was conscious of some sort of revelation far more subtle than just his fear of heights. She had a feeling too, that it might be dangerous, though in what way she could not tell.

'I'm sorry about the telescope,' she said. Below them, close as it now was to land, came a resonant crackle of canvas as the wind filled a swift, red sail.

CHAPTER FIFTEEN

She woke on Christmas morning to the sound of Liddy coughing. It wasn't a harsh noise but softly childlike and persistent, a distant cadence sounding much farther away than just along the passage.

She got out of bed, began to dress, and then remembered it was Christmas. Last thing on Christmas Eve she had wished and wished for the night visitor to appear but it had been in vain.

Sunshine was streaming in through the curtains. She looked out. It hadn't snowed either, she thought grumpily. It was just like any old day.

Downstairs she surreptitiously tweaked the present with her name on it. It was a box, quite heavy, more than that she couldn't tell. Nor, to her surprise, was she especially curious.

When Liddy came down she looked haggard, her face pinched, blue-smudged beneath the eyes. She brightened when she saw Jenny, flung open her arms and embraced her.

'Happy Christmas darling!' she exclaimed. 'Terribly exciting isn't it? I do so love Christmas.'

The girl wished her happy Christmas back. She could tell Liddy's gaiety was staged, the Christmas joy a shade too exaggerated. The woman made a great fuss of plugging in the Christmas tree lights and clapped like a schoolgirl as the tiny coloured bulbs gave their annual performance.

They breakfasted on toast and bramble jelly then began to prepare the dinner. There were carols and hymns on the wireless and Jenny liked the shared bustle in the kitchen. When the turkey was in the oven and saucepans gently bubbling she said, 'That lazybones still isn't up! He's the one whose been making all the fuss. Shall I go and wake him?'

Liddy was peeling vegetables in a colander, 'No……well……' She smoothed her hands down her apron. 'He's not here. He didn't get home last night.'

'What?' Jenny was incredulous.

'Oh it's all right,' the woman's voice was matter-of-fact, 'I expect the car broke down or something. You know how it's been playing up lately. He'll probably telephone in a minute. He'll turn up, don't worry.'

The day wore on and still there was no sign of him. The telephone remained obstinately silent. At one point during the afternoon Jenny said, 'What about our presents then, can't we open them?'

'Well it would be nicer dear to wait until we're all here wouldn't it? Let's lay the table.'

Later the girl prowled the house, looking for something to do. Out of boredom she made three paper crowns and, with her paints, put their names on them in elaborate scroll. When the paint dried though they looked dull and the paper wrinkled. She tried to read *Peter Pan*, to finish it off, but had been getting cross with it. Her mouth moved silently as she read the words:

'*Tink was saved. First her voice grew strong; then she popped out of bed; then she was flashing through the room more merry and impudent than ever. She never thought of thanking those who believed, but she would have liked to get at the ones who had hissed.*'

As she read on she decided it was Peter himself she didn't really like. He was actually quite silly and not very clever. She tossed the book aside impatiently and gazed at the fire popping and crackling in the grate.

The remembered aroma of Christmas dinners wafted through the house and she followed her nose to the kitchen. Liddy was standing at the sink, weeping in silence, her shoulders shaking.

'Oh Jenny,' she sobbed, 'it's not the Christmas I wanted for us.' And as if this admission, held back all day, had finally breached some inner sea wall, she sank onto a chair, and wailed.

Bewildered Jenny automatically stroked her back, in just the same way that her own was rubbed if she was hurt or upset, soothing and tender, yet also somehow imbued with a very English entreaty to pull oneself together.

'I bet the car has just broken down! I bet that's what it is. He'll be home soon. He'll be ever so upset if he sees you've been crying.'

She coaxed Liddy upstairs and to the bathroom where the woman washed her face and brushed her hair, still sniffing. Then Jenny looked on as she re-made her face from an array of jars and bottles in the bedroom. She liked watching Liddy put make-up on: the skilful, practised flick of her hands, the careful painting of eyelashes and the ritual of the bright red lipstick, from first pucker to her final smack of the lips.

'You'd never know,' she said encouragingly, sitting on the big bed.

'Never know what?'

'That you'd had a little weep.'

The woman smiled sheepishly, had a final check in the mirror and together they trooped downstairs.

'Would you like a cup of tea?' the girl offered, adding with helpful alacrity, 'I'll make it. You go and sit down.' Liddy nodded. She had regained her composure and gazed fondly at the child.

From the kitchen Jenny could hear a choir of children on the wireless. As she filled the kettle and set it to boil she thought back to her old school in the village. Things had been less complicated then. She could remember being in a Christmas play, the echoing plink of the school piano and the pervading smell of scrubbed wooden floorboards.

There was a gin bottle on the kitchen table and a half-empty tumbler next to it. She picked it up and sniffed. It made her shudder. She screwed the cap on the bottle and put it back in the cupboard.

The tea was drunk and another hour passed as they gazed hopefully through the window, but neither the familiar sound of the car engine nor the shrill ring of the telephone disturbed the silence. Eventually Liddy got up and gathered the tea things together on a tray. When she spoke her tone was one of prickly resignation.

'Well, we'll have to eat soon or it will be spoilt.' She carried the tray out to the kitchen and began to wash up. After a while Jenny followed. The gin bottle was back on the table and Liddy was banging pans about, coldly dry-eyed. She glanced up at the clock on the wall and filled her glass. A tiny spill left a viscous puddle on the wooden table. She raised the glass and drank, then said decisively, 'Right. Come on. Let's eat.'

The girl trotted back and forth with steaming dishes while Liddy heaved the turkey from the oven. She paraded it into the dining room where the waiting girl was already sat at the laden table. A quick, perfunctory grace was said then the woman began to carve the turkey.

'Oh dear,' she said apologetically, hacking at the white flesh, 'I'm making a dreadful hash of this. Oh well, it'll have to do.'

They ate in uneasy silence. Halfway through the meal, Jenny remembered the paper crowns and fetched them to the table. She put Kit's on his place mat. Liddy self-consciously perched hers carefully on her head.

The sound of a car pulling up as they were finishing Christmas pudding caught them both unawares. The woman peered out into the darkness. It hadn't come up the drive but was stopped in the lane, its engine idling. A door slammed and the vehicle moved off. Then quick, scrunching footsteps up the path, the back door flung open.

'Hello?' It was Kit.

He burst into the dining room, dishevelled and unshaven. His shirt collar was sticking up and there were grubby marks on the camel hair coat. There was too, a flourish of sweet alcohol around him as he whirled in. He was breathless and the words toppled out in a rush.

'Oh look, I am so sorry! This is awful! I've had the most rotten luck. What on earth must you think.'

'Well, where have you been?' the woman demanded, a spoonful of pudding still poised in mid-air.

'Bloody well stuck. Stuck good and proper.' He looked abject and distraught.

'But where?' Liddy's voice sounded cross and impatient.

'You won't believe it, just won't believe it. I did the show last night and that ran over a bit, then there was a bit of a do afterwards that I just couldn't get out of and when that finished the ruddy car wouldn't start and it was pouring with rain, absolutely chucking it down. I couldn't fix the damn thing and, of course, everyone had vamoosed so I ended up sleeping in the back seat, soaked to the bloody skin. Then this morning, Christmas morning,' he emphasised darkly, 'I had to hike miles to the nearest town to get help. Everything was closed up as you might expect. Not a soul about.' He paused for breath and sank into a chair. 'In the end the local bobby fixed me up with a lift. I had to stump up a small fortune to some bloody farm oik,' he rubbed his face wearily. 'What a Christmas.'

It was Jenny who broke the silence, her spoon clinked against her plate.

'Sorry,' she whispered, then, 'but why didn't you telephone?' He looked at the girl with a helpless expression and shrugged.

'All the lines were out. That's what the bobby said. To do with the weather.'

Liddy rose slowly to her feet. To the girl's astonishment, she laid an arm around Kit's shoulders.

'You poor, poor man,' she cooed, 'how perfectly dreadful. And your clothes are all damp. Come, come. It's all right.'

Kit's shoulders were shaking, his face hidden. When at length he spoke his voice was strained.

'I am so sorry. I've spoilt your Christmas.' His eyes were moist as he looked at them.

'Nonsense,' Liddy crooned, 'we've kept dinner for you and saved the presents till you got home.' She leant over him and filled his wine glass. 'Our Christmas will just begin a bit later, that's all. It can't be helped. Now come on everyone, let's have a toast.' Kit reached out for the glass and held it aloft. Liddy, face radiant, followed suit. Jenny picked up her lemonade.

'Merry Christmas, here's to health, long life and happiness. To us.'

'To us,' echoed Kit, smiling, though he looked as if he had a lump in his throat. Glasses were clinked together and they drank.

'Oh, that is better.' Kit looked appreciatively at his empty glass, reached out for the bottle and re-filled it. He turned to Jenny and grinned. 'He came then,' nodding towards the presents under the tree.

'Who?'

'Father Christmas of course.'

'Oh yes,' she said half-heartedly, 'I forgot to put out a drink and a mince pie though.'

'Better make it a double next year then.' He laughed, looked away and smiled at Liddy.

He was made to go up and change into dry clothes while his dinner was served. When he came down he looked himself again, the dark curls more or less under control, the boyish grin firmly back in place. After he had eaten and been pressed to two helpings of pudding, Liddy said, 'And now for the presents!' Kit got up and went over to the tree. He picked up the parcel she had secretly fingered and gave it to her.

'Something special for a little girl who has been more patient than I deserve,' he said affectionately.

She sat on the floor and ripped the paper off. Inside the box was a chubby, pasty-faced doll. She took an instant dislike to it. Dressed in a stiff yellow frock it had vacant eyes and its blonde hair was set in hard ringlets. She examined it with dismay, looked up at their eagerly expectant faces.

'It's very nice. Really it is.'

'It's from both of us,' Liddy said fondly.

The girl lifted the doll from its box and cradled it unwillingly, because she knew she had to, was supposed to. She didn't want it at all but she especially didn't want it to be from Kit too.

As she lay in bed that night, keeping watch not for the ghost of Christmas past but for an altogether more real and significant presence, she thought about Kit's story. Liddy believed it, but she didn't. Not a single word.

★   ★   ★

In the week following Christmas a letter arrived from Uncle Richard. It contained a postal order for Jenny and, to their surprise, the news that he was being transferred to Kenya.

'Kenya?' Jenny was incredulous. 'Kenya in Africa? But there are snakes and wild animals there.' As she pondered, she slid into a fit of giggles, inexplicable to the grown-ups, as the stumpy image of Uncle Richard, red of face and swamped in enveloping khaki shorts, rose up before her.

'Who is he exactly?' Kit asked.

'He isn't an uncle at all really,' Liddy explained, 'he knew my parents. We only see him every now and then. He taught Jenny to swim, didn't he darling?'

'What does he do then?'

Liddy thought for a moment, looked faintly puzzled. 'I'm not entirely sure. Something in the civil service though.' She read the letter again. 'Imagine,' she mused, 'Africa.'

For the rest of the holiday Jenny watched and listened for the night visitor with a new determination, willing him to return or even just make a sign. He was, paradoxically, the one thing she was sure of. Everything else, all her past certainties, were being slowly eroded. The doll, not played with and left in a corner of her room, compounded all that was wrong. She wished she could put it in a cupboard so she would never have to look at its silly face again. But she couldn't. It had to stay where it was. It was a present.

Often, she went down to the deserted shore, to walk along the cold sand and listen to the waves. There was little comfort to be found in the deadness of winter but it was familiar, a place where happiness could be. She wrote in the sand with driftwood. It began as idle play: her name, a rhyme. Then one day, without thinking, she wrote 'Come back soon' and stood looking down at the spidery letters. Hurriedly she added 'I love you Daddy' and squatted on the beach, watching as the tide crept up and over the words, stealing them away. It became a little ritual, during those solitary days, to leave a message and watch as the sea took it and smoothed over the place where it had been.

At home the 'three whole days' Kit had been so exultant about were eaten up in retrieving the car and his trying to fix it. When eventually it spluttered reluctantly into life he glared at it with a cold smile. 'Bloody old heap,' he muttered venomously, 'I'll sort you out.'

Ironically it was a relief to return to school. She worked hard, as much from lack of any other purpose as from conviction that she should. In the evenings she diligently completed her homework before doing anything else. To stay invisible she had to be just clever enough to keep out of trouble but not too clever. No one bothered you then. At the weekends she trooped off and carved wishes in the sand but the night visitor obstinately refused to appear. She thought he would never come again.

The dull days when Hadley was buffeted by cold winds and rain gave way almost imperceptibly to a shy lifting of the grey, to just discernible sea breezes that were still warm from their faraway origins, a promise of spring to come. It gave her a touch of hope, a fragile spider's yarn of optimism. It was as if she had shut down a part of herself since Christmas. She did everything that was asked of her, she complied willingly. Yet a piece of her was absent from the daily procession, withdrawn into herself. If Liddy noticed it she put it down to the new, more adult regime of school. Kit was, as ever, so busy that he had little time for her and during the week she hardly saw him. Liddy's life seemed to be spent trying to keep up with him. In the evenings though, however tired she looked, she would lay out a table for two, a proper dinner table with a clean tablecloth. A cocktail would be prepared, wine uncorked and set out on the sideboard awaiting his return. It seemed to Jenny a quiet last bastion against complete chaos. Late at night, her own supper now invariably taken alone at the kitchen table, the girl would drift reluctantly to sleep listening to the low hum of their voices and smooth ballads on the wireless.

One morning Kit was, unusually, up and dressed at breakfast time. When Jenny asked why, he winked and said he was off on a secret mission. She forgot about it during the day but as she got home from school saw a squat bottle-green van parked in the drive. Liddy and Kit were looking at it admiringly.

'Well, what do you think?' Kit beamed as she pushed her bicycle up the path.

'What do you mean?'

He spread his arms expansively, 'This of course, our new chariot!'

'Lovely colour isn't it?' Liddy smiled.

'And look, it's got seats in the back as well. Fitted out good and proper it is.' He opened a door, inviting her to look.

'But we've got a car,' Jenny said, baffled.

Kit thrust his hands in his pockets, 'Got a better one now,' he murmured impatiently.

'What do you mean?' The girl spoke anxiously, 'where's our car, Daddy's car?'

The woman took a step towards her, 'Well it wasn't really suitable......'

'I've traded it in,' Kit's voice was dryly and emphatically triumphant.

'But you can't! It isn't yours......you......you!' the girl struggled for words, grown-up words, to match her distress. 'You didn't have permission!' she said hotly.

'Jenny!' Liddy spoke sharply, warningly.

'But he didn't! It was Daddy's car not his. He can't just do whatever he likes. It isn't fair!'

The woman stepped in front of her, tight-lipped. 'Jennifer, that really is too rude! You've gone too far! Now go to your room at once and stay there!' And as the girl fled tearfully, Liddy quickly bent and delivered a swift, stinging slap to her leg.

Upstairs she flung herself on her bed and wept, salt-burning tears of hopelessness and frustration. She hated him. He had sold Daddy's car and she would never, ever forgive him. And Liddy had known, she'd taken his side. He'd just pretended to be nice and it was like telling lies. He'd been friendly just to get his own way, that was all. She was filled with self-reproach too, as if something she had failed to do, or act on, had allowed it. Not just the car but everything.

She sobbed herself into a fretful sleep. When she woke the house was unnaturally quiet. She clambered off the bed and gently opened the bedroom door. She stepped out and peered cautiously over the banister. There was no noise from downstairs, no lights. The house was still.

'Can I come down now?' Her voice floated, echoing down the stairs. 'Please can I come down?' a timid question drifting, without answer, in the empty house.

A brief, curt note was propped up on the kitchen table. In its tone there was not a single crumb of reconciliation. She was to take the supper tray, laid out on the table, to her room. Afterwards she was to do her homework and then go straight to bed. They had, apparently, taken the van for a run and would be back in an hour.

She ate the sandwich and apple in the silence of her room and drank the milk that had been left. Poring over her arithmetic homework, she tried to let the jungle of fractions calm her mind. She was obediently in bed when they returned, the different growl of the new engine followed by doors opening and voices below, voices that sounded normal and untroubled.

Alone, she summoned up the image of her dark visitor, standing beneath the tree as he had been on that night; his remembered square outline, the gentle hand through her hair that had not really happened. More than ever she wanted the reassurance of him, to know that he was watching over her and wouldn't let anything bad happen. The memory nudged away the rawness left by the telling off. She hadn't been wrong to say what she did, even if it was rude.

'Where are you?' she whispered to the night and to the distant, waiting sea, 'please, where are you?'

Laughter from downstairs, crashing into her small peace. First, Kit's unrestrained giggle, unusually coarse. Then Liddy's answering peal, less attractive than usual, almost indelicate. They were laughing about it, she thought. They were laughing at her.

★   ★   ★

'Jennifer Hawker you are in disgrace. That was an unforgivable outburst.'

The girl looked down, shame-faced and mute as Liddy carried on.

'I was so ashamed of you. There will be extra jobs to do in the house and you are not allowed out to play.' There was a deliberate, uncomfortable pause to allow the full weight of the punishment to sink in. Jenny stole a glance up.

'Until when am I not allowed out?'

'Until I say so,' a longer pause, 'and now you will apologise to Kit.'

The girl looked at him. He was lounging against the wall. He didn't look cross like Liddy but there was an unpleasant satisfaction in his face and in the way he slouched.

'Sorry,' she said quickly, eyes downcast.

'Properly!' Liddy's voice was like a second slap, matching the one of the day before.

'I am very sorry for being so rude,' she intoned mechanically to the floor.

'That's better. Now off to school with you and do not be late back.'

Kit had not moved or said anything. She rushed out past him, trembling with humiliation. She got on her bicycle and pedalled fiercely down the path, scattering gravel in all directions. His voice floated after her, a confident sing-song; friendly but just taunting, normal but just jubilant.

'See you later alligator.'

★　★　★

Something had been snatched away from her and she wanted it back. She leant dangerously from the bedroom window to catch a whiff of the sea, out of bounds but for how long she did not know.

Her outburst had heralded a change in them, in Kit and Liddy, a shift in the balance. Outwardly they were no different with her. It was rather that they were now even more bound up with each other or, more precisely, with Kit's carnival existence.

It was late on a Friday afternoon. They had gone into town to shop and for Liddy to see the doctor. Nothing had been said about the ban being lifted and Jenny had not asked. It seemed, unhappily, that a second weekend of confinement loomed. A silence shaped itself around her and weighed heavily. Proscribed as it was, the sea's bewitchment of her was all the more powerful. She longed to return to it.

When they returned there was a pile of shopping to be unloaded and put away. The girl struggled in with the bags and was especially careful with the ones that had bottles in them. As the last of it was stacked in the larder she said, 'I've finished. That's all of it.'

Liddy filled a glass with cold water and swallowed two pills from a small brown bottle.

'Thank you Jenny,' she said, a touch stiffly, 'now run along and do your homework.'

'I've done it,' the girl said proudly, 'while you were out.'

'All of it? Well find a book to read then.'

The girl drooped inside. She had been hoping against hope for a reprieve. She got her school reading book and sat in the front room. She had stopped reading *Peter Pan*; all that stuff about how terrible it was to grow up. She didn't want to fly away either. She wanted to be here, at Hadley, and have things back the way they had been.

She pretended to read but instead listened to the wireless which was on in the next room. It was like family now. She knew all the programmes and rolled her tongue silently, luxuriously, around the strange names on the shipping forecast. The wireless shared mealtimes with her and sent her off to sleep, cradled in a web of gentle melodies. It wasn't fair that she was being punished for so long and she hated the new van. It was boxy and ugly and inside it smelled of sacks and tools, not like the sweet mingling of wood, Virginia cigarettes and leather in Daddy's car.

Daddy. There had been no sign from him even though she had wished and wished. Yet it might be, she thought, suddenly alert, that he was somehow waiting for her. Perhaps it was, after all, up to her to seek him out.

She went to bed early and sat by her opened window. The night smell of the tide was heady and fed her anticipation. She remained quite still listening to the wind. When the house was finally quiet she slipped noiselessly out, disregarding of the ban and unrepentant, pausing just briefly at the back door to peer into the gloom, though knowing that tonight she would not find him there. Dark clouds brooded in the night sky, jostled by an ill-tempered wind.

As she made her way down through the woods, the sound of the sea and the wind blurred into an indistinguishable, racing roar. The waves snapped at the shore like an angry dog. She knew at once she should not have come. It did not want her here. She sat on a rock and shivered, her emotions veering as wildly as the wind. She wanted him and needed him and he wasn't there.

She stands, feels the sting of rain on her face and walks solemnly to the edge. She looks out across the threatening sea at the fragile spindrift driven relentlessly across its boiling surface, driven as surely as she herself was and by forces just as powerful and mysterious. From a well of despair she cries into the face of the coming storm.

'I know you're out there! I know you are! They don't believe it but I do. You mustn't desert me. Please hear me!'

The sea dashes against her, enticing, playing a deadly game. She waits wretchedly. All of a sudden a letting of the wind, a cool lull in both herself and the gale. The quick-tempered tide retreats and is still; a breath of hush as it gathers itself and a slow unfurling breaker, like a glittering scroll of ancient secrets, breaks at her feet.

'Daddy?' she whispers.

CHAPTER SIXTEEN

❛ 'Ee were born with the mark see, great red thing it were, on 'is face. No side to 'im mind……'

The old man, waiting for his prescription, looked absently at the floor for a moment before continuing, 'So 'ee never married see?' His companion, a large woman with a florid scarf knotted under her several chins, nodded sagely.

Jenny wondered idly who they were talking about. She could tell that the woman was wearing rollers under her scarf. Her head was all bumpy. The chemist bustled importantly from his back room and gave her the pills for Liddy. She thanked him and set straight off for home as instructed.

Halfway down the lane she saw the van coming toward her, or rather crawling uncertainly, not bowling along as it usually did with Kit at the wheel. It came to a jerky, shuddering halt. A flustered Liddy was at the wheel. Kit sat ill at ease in the passenger seat,

'I'm having my first driving lesson,' the woman said proudly through the wound down window.

'But you always said you were too frightened,' Jenny was taken aback by this new development.

'I was being a bit silly,' the woman replied, 'it'll be much better if I can drive too. Seems quite easy so far. Did you get my prescription?' The girl nodded. It was funny seeing Liddy driving. She wasn't really even very good on a bicycle.

'We'll be back soon. Don't wander too far.'

The girl leapt at it eagerly.

'Do you mean I can go out to play?'

Liddy looked at her, relenting, 'Yes all right. But not too far mind.' She crashed the van into first gear and waved delicately. 'Tally ho!' Kit grimaced and the vehicle wobbled off, engine whining in complaint as it was hacked mercilessly up another gear.

The driving lessons rapidly became a regular occurrence and they were often out when she returned from school. Liddy though, was not a fast learner and the vehicle's stuttering progress and frequent stalling fuelled Kit's exasperation.

'It's so simple a child could do it!' he would exclaim, helping himself to a drink from the sideboard while Liddy hovered appeasingly round him.

A few weeks later the girl cycled home through a fine net of steady drizzle to find Hadley locked and the van gone. Yet another lesson, she thought ruefully. The drizzle became rain and she took shelter in the greenhouse. Nose pressed to the cold glass she looked out at the downpour and felt damp and disgruntled. She could see the place under the tree where she had dug the little grave, the memorial, and where she had seen him that night. The grave had never been quite right. It hadn't felt right either. That was why she had neglected it. The musty tar, earth and wood smell of the greenhouse was unexpectedly comforting, like a warm, friendly blanket to nuzzle into. Outside an ebony lacquered crow, strutting like a pompous emperor in obscure exile, pecked at the ground.

And still they were not home. It seemed she had been there for ages, the beating rain insisting a different tempo, outside of ordinary time.

What if they had crashed? All at once she saw Liddy straining to see through struggling windscreen wipers, careering down a narrow road; a moment's loss of control, a deadly swerve, Kit grabbing for the wheel but too late......something looming up in front of them, a tree or a lorry.......

She shook her head to dislodge the notion. Of course they would be all right. They were just a bit late that's all, perhaps they had a puncture or run out of petrol. But what if they weren't all right, what would happen to her?

Cocooned in the greenhouse she did not hear the van as it swept easily up the drive. Nor did she see them as they clambered out, coats over their heads against the rain, Kit from the driver's side, Liddy happily from the passenger's, laughing as they scuttled to the house. It was only when Kit kicked the van door shut that she heard, turned and saw. Tapping forlornly on the glass she watched as, oblivious to her, they hurried inside.

★   ★   ★

'To be honest we lost track of time. I do hope you didn't have to wait too long dear, was it awful?'

Liddy was rubbing at her hair with a towel and inspecting her appearance in the mirror.

'It wasn't too bad. At least it was dry.'

Liddy started to rescue her make-up with a skilful hand. The girl watched fascinated as the face in the mirror was quickly transformed.

'I think,' the woman said as she leaned forward for even closer scrutiny, 'that you are quite old enough now to have your own key.' She turned briefly from her self-examination and regarded Jenny. 'Do you think you're grown-up enough?' she quizzed.

'Oh yes!'

'And you wouldn't lose it would you?'

'Oh no. I promise.'

'Very well then. We'll get one cut when we next go to town. Kit's got the only spare.'

Sure enough, the following week she was presented with a shiny new key, or rather it was dangling in front of her as the 'you-won't-lose-it-will-you' warning was repeated.

'Now this means you are very grown-up so make sure you act responsibly at all times.'

'I will,' she said, hands behind her back.

'And don't let me down.'

'I won't,' she assured, timorously earnest.

The key gave them more freedom that it gave Jenny. She was free to let herself in. They were free to be out. Often she returned from school to find the house deserted, a brief note on the kitchen table. But she no longer minded. She could pretend when they weren't there to spoil it, pretend that everything was like it used to be. She would take down Daddy's photograph from the hall and rest it against the little table in the front room. Then she would turn on the wireless and eat her supper from the tray Liddy left, sat in front of a cold, untended grate spilling over with soft ashes. They were amongst her happiest time. It was Hadley again then, and home.

CHAPTER SEVENTEEN

Through the window she could see a bare winter tree sprinkled with cold sparrows. She was ensconced at the dining room table struggling with English grammar and distracted by the beckoning outdoors.

'Hello Tink!' Kit breezed in, laid a bundle of stage costumes across the table, 'How's you?' She looked up at him reproachfully.

'Doing my homework,' she replied glumly.

'Oh yes......' he said without interest, patting the bundle fondly, 'better get the rest ready for tonight,' and went out again, whistling. His cheerfulness set her on edge. She found it even harder to concentrate on the wretched grammar. It wasn't that she couldn't do it but it was dull and she wanted to be outside. She dipped her pen into the ink bottle and tried to pay attention.

Suddenly there was a loud blast from the wireless in the next room. She leapt up, startled, and cracked her knees painfully against the table. Kit must have turned it on, she thought crossly, as a blare of jazz flooded the house. He was so thoughtless and it wasn't fair, especially while she was trying to do her homework.

Something dripped lightly onto her leg. She looked down. The bottle was on its side and a glistening blue pool of ink was spreading rapidly across the table. She stared in horror as it glided towards the precious costume. Quickly she snatched up the bundle only to feel the bottom of it flop down and slew across the table, dragging through the glossy puddle.

It was as if everything had stopped dead. She could no longer hear the jazz or feel the ink dripping. Her mouth went dry. She stood helplessly clutching the ink-stained bundle, unable to move or think except for the one piercing wish that a single moment had never happened.

'What the......!' Kit was in the doorway, another bundle in his arms, his face just comprehending. 'What the hell has happened here!'

'It was an accident!' she bawled, still rooted to the spot. 'The noise......I jumped......I'm sorry!'

He dropped the clothes, stepped quickly forward and struck her; a quivering blow across the face with the back of his hand.

'Bloody fool!' he spat, snatching the bundle from her. 'You stupid, careless little fool!' He stared at the stain, 'For Christ's sake it's ruined. Look at it. Ruined!' He was trembling with anger, beside himself. She began to apologise again but stopped. It hurt where he had hit her, her face was smarting. But the blow had also knocked from her the last remaining vestige of belief she might have had in him. Inside, simmering beneath the fear and shock, she was coldly resolute; he would have no power over her, even if he hit her again. She wouldn't let him.

'It was an accident,' she said coolly.

'What on earth is all this shouting about?' Liddy had entered the room and stood in the doorway. Jenny realised that the wireless had been switched off. 'Well?' the woman demanded. The girl did not know if she had seen Kit hit her but thought her burning red cheek must make it obvious.

'Look!' Kit held out the costume. 'She's mucked it up. It's wrecked.' He sounded now more sullen than irate. The woman seemed to crumple from some enormous, invisible burden. She sank into a chair, shut her eyes and sighed.

'Is that all?' she said witheringly. 'Is that what this is all about?'

Kit looked awkward. 'But just look at it,' he said weakly, still proffering the outfit.

'It was an accident,' Jenny said evenly to the woman, 'I jumped up and knocked the ink bottle over when the music came on so loudly.' Liddy put her face in her hands and spoke wearily through her fingers.

'So did I, jump I mean,' she rose slowly and held out her hand, 'give it to me, I'll see what I can do.' He passed it over sheepishly and she examined it, then fixed him with her pale grey eyes. 'Did you really think she did it on purpose?'

'No……but……' Kit looked uncomfortable, caught out.

'I nearly jumped out of my skin when that row came on. It's only by the grace of God I didn't drop a trayful of china.'

'I didn't know it was going to be so loud,' he entreated. The woman looked again at the stains.

'Well the sooner this is dealt with the better,' she said briskly, and turned as if to go but stopped. 'And I think you owe Jenny an apology.' She waited. He looked down at his feet, shuffled then spoke in a chastened, thoughtful mumble, head bowed.

'I suppose you're right. Sorry about that. I did cut up a bit rough didn't I?'

'Right,' Liddy sighed. 'But I want you both to listen. You must stop this bickering and squabbling. You mustn't do this to me.'

★   ★   ★

He had said a sort of sorry but it rankled and Jenny wanted to get him back for it. She didn't know how or when.

It had long been taboo to ask to see his performance but, as spring yawned and stretched itself into life, she overheard them in the kitchen.

'It's an early show, just down the road from here. We can have a run out afterwards. Make a night of it.'

'But what about Jenny?'

'She can come too,' Kit said expansively, 'we'll find a pub with a garden and a swing or something. She'll be happy enough.'

'It's only just spring. Do you think it'll be warm enough?'

'It'll be fine Liddy. Few snifters'll give us a glow won't they?'

It was presented as a special treat, put on for Jenny's benefit. She went along with it but, after school on the Friday of the outing, calmly told Liddy a fib about getting some sweets and cycled off towards the village, the direction Kit had previously gone in the van.

It wasn't hard to track him down. As she free-wheeled into the village she saw the van parked by the church hall. She hid her bicycle behind a hedge and crept up behind the vehicle, peering in through the small rear windows. It was empty except for the usual untidy muddle littering the back. There was a wave of thin, piping laughter from the hall. Then a piercing shriek and something crashing to the floor, a babble of demanding infant voices. She tiptoed around the side of the building. The windows were too high for her to see in. She got her bicycle and rested it gently against the wall under a stone mullioned window, then clambered onto it and hauled herself up as laughter, interspersed with shouts and cries, rang round the hall. Balancing precariously she could just see in.

A man, dressed like a tramp but with a clown's face beneath an orange mop wig, was feverishly trying to grab the attention of a group of twenty or so young children. He pulled a feathery confection from his sleeve and presented it with a flourish. One solemn toddler clapped, the others concentrated on paper plates full of trifle.

It was Kit. As plain as if there were no disguise at all. He juggled desperately with tennis balls but dropped one and it rolled away. Two boys were locked in combat next to a trestle table laden with food. A pallid girl in a frilly dress blubbed for no apparent reason and at full volume. Kit danced a little jig that culminated in an unnoticed, unapplauded pratfall. Climbing to his feet he threw his hands up in a gesture of despair that belied the red painted grin he wore.

Jenny stared at him and wobbled on the bicycle. A tight-lipped woman came into view and stilettos clicked across the hall towards the crying girl. He had lied. He was a cheat. He wasn't an actor at all. He was a clown, a clown for little children at parties and not even a proper circus one. Then, unexpectedly, she began to laugh to herself and at him. It was a retribution exacted and paid out more fully than she could ever have imagined.

Later that evening though, as she sat alone in the van, noisily sucking lemonade through a straw, rain tipping remorselessly down, it seemed an empty getting even. The pub was ablaze with welcoming light and, to one side of it, the promised but sodden garden, its solitary swing abandoned to the weather. They had said they wouldn't be long but when at last they returned, glowing and conspiratorial, they found her huddled on the back seat, still holding the now empty lemonade bottle, and fast asleep.

It was when the weather really leaned into spring that Jenny persuaded Liddy to come with her to the beach while Kit was working. At first she had been reluctant; so much to do around the house, she was too tired.

'Come on Liddy, please. It'll do you good. Sea air remember?' Eventually she gave in and they packed up a small picnic and set off.

The day was clear but cool and they were glad of the sweaters Liddy insisted on. Liddy too, had redeemed herself a little in Jenny's eyes by the ticking off she had given Kit and the new light of the spring day excited and elated the girl. She couldn't wait to see the glittering waves, the remembered fluid sparkle.

But when they came out of the new greening woods it was not the sea that commanded their attention. Almost directly below them, though some way off, was a buoy beached on the sand. Not until they were close did they realise how enormous it was. It towered over them, incongruously out of its element, a deep sea buoy capped with a caged bell. It bulged with stern purpose and they circled it in awe.

'Should we tell someone,' the girl asked quietly, 'like the lifeboat people?' The buoy's brooding presence made her want to whisper.

'I don't know,' Liddy mused, 'I suppose we ought to really, don't quite know who though.'

'The Admiralty?' Jenny hazarded. It was a word she always had troubled pronouncing. It seemed to squirm off her tongue at the end. She was also not entirely sure what it was except that it was to do with the Navy. The woman twinkled attractively at the suggestion.

'Possibly,' she said, amused. They went back up on to the grass for their picnic and found a dry spot.

'How do you think it got there?' Jenny asked.

'A storm I daresay. Very, very far out to sea. Perhaps even in an ocean or the sea of a distant land.' It was an agreeably romantic notion and they tried to out-do each other with exotic locations.

'The West Indies.'

'Or Panama.'

'The Baltic!'

But when Jenny cried triumphantly, 'Paraguay!' the woman dissolved with laughter.

'What?' the girl asked, crestfallen, 'what's wrong with that?'

'It's inland!' the woman giggled.

'What do you mean?'

'Hasn't got any water you duffer!'

'Oh,' Jenny felt put out but not badly. Liddy composed herself then said kindly.

'It's   probably   somewhere   like   that though……except……'

' 'cept what?'

The woman giggled again. 'It's got Harland and Wolff, Ireland, written across its great big bottom.'

'Has it?'

'Ireland's quite far anyway.'

The girl rummaged in a bag and produced two apples. She passed one to Liddy, polished hers on her sleeve and looked at it.

'A is for apple,' she said in a contented, sing-song way and bit into it. They ate in silence then tossed the cores into the undergrowth. Jenny studied the distant buoy and gave the woman a sideways look.

'Race you to it,' she challenged.

Liddy looked doubtful, 'I'm too old for running, and too tired.' Disappointed, the girl picked listlessly at the grass. The woman leaned back, closed her eyes and smiled. For a moment, she looked once again young and carefree, tempted by a simple delight. Suddenly she leapt up and raced down the beach.

'Come on then slowcoach!'

The girl scrambled to her feet streaking after her. 'Not fair, you've got a head start!'

Liddy's voice floated back as light and vivacious as the breeze.

'And your legs are a lot younger!'

Determined, the girl put on a spurt. She easily outstripped the cantering woman and tore ahead. The wind rushed in her ears as she entered the broad shadow of the buoy. Her hands slapped against it as she stopped herself and a dull clanging echoed inside. She bent double, panting, happy at the winning. It took a moment for her to realise she could no longer hear Liddy behind her. She looked back bemused, thinking she had given in and would be strolling down the beach. Instead Liddy was sitting awkwardly on the sand, a hand flat against her chest, and she was coughing harshly. The girl ran back up the beach and squatted next to her. Liddy's face was a ghostly white and her eyes stood out, unnaturally bright.

'It's all right,' she said, still rasping, 'just have to get my breath.' She laughed weakly, 'Told you I was too ancient for that sort of thing.' She was taking in great lungfuls of air, punctuated by a racking bark. Jenny looked on helplessly and told herself she shouldn't have suggested the silly race. She floundered, not knowing the right thing to do.

They sat for a while as Liddy recovered then she began to fret about getting back before Kit. Slowly they made their way home. Once or twice, the woman stumbled and put a hand on Jenny's shoulder for support. At Hadley, and to Jenny's dismay, the woman immediately put on an apron and began busying in the kitchen. When Kit returned the girl told him what had happened. He made a great fuss of making Liddy sit down and put her feet up. Then he announced that he would make supper.

'Now what you need,' he said, moving over to the sideboard, 'is a little pick-me-up.'

Jenny was doubtful about his skill in the kitchen but the food, when it came, was surprisingly good, even if it was served in a bit of a muddle, without Liddy's calm competence. Kit bolted his meal and, after making sure that the woman was 'really all right', tore off in his usual rush.

'You know I would stay if I could,' he said apologetically, 'but I just can't. Rest up and that's an order.' He turned to Jenny, 'Be a good girl and clear up for me will you?'

The kitchen was unrecognisable. Pots and pans, coated with the congealed remnants of the meal they had just eaten, were dumped all over the place. The floor was slippery with grease and the sink awash with cold suds, an oily scum caked around its enamel edge.

She gritted her teeth and set to. It took an hour to clean it all up and wash the floor. As she scrubbed and cleaned, she thought again about his lies and deception. She had held back from telling Liddy that he wasn't really an actor. She hadn't been sure she should. But now, and perhaps meanly triggered by the domestic havoc he had left in his wake, she wanted to. He shouldn't have gone out either. He would have stayed in if he really cared.

Proudly surveying the once again ship-shape kitchen she spotted a dish she had missed, perched improbably, and rakishly, on top of a cupboard. A cold, thick snail of leftovers dripped from it and down the woodwork. It was the final straw. She would tell. Liddy would have to understand then and Kit would be made to leave. The re-kindled closeness she had felt towards her mother, today on the beach, and Liddy taking her side over the spilt ink had, she was sure, affirmed them as family once again. Perhaps Liddy too now felt differently about him but wouldn't say because she thought Jenny still liked him. It would be funny if they were both thinking the same thing but not saying. A warm scenario presented itself; her telling about Kit, Liddy being shocked and upset at first but then hugging her like she used to and being on her side. And when Kit was sent packing she could tell her about Daddy too and she would believe it this time and they would be together. Keyed up by the prospect she wanted to rush in straight away and get it all sorted out. It would be a good summer after all.

Liddy was dozing peacefully by the fire. The flickering light softened the lines around her eyes and the shadows beneath them. The girl sat watching her impatiently. She had found the answer and it had been there all the time. She could change things and make them better again, make them happy.

The woman roused and smiled drowsily. 'Must've dropped off,' she apologised in a thick, sleep-honeyed voice, 'what time is it?'

'Quite late I think,' the girl craned her neck to look at the clock, 'quarter past eight.'

'My goodness,' Liddy exclaimed, 'you should be in bed.' She stretched, yawned, and wriggled her toes. 'Oh I do feel better for that.'

Jenny beamed optimistically, a new voice was singing inside her, sparkling. She leant forward with happy certitude.

'I want to tell you something. A secret.'

'Ooh good. I like secrets.' The woman's eyes crinkled.

'It's about Kit,' Jenny hissed, as though he were still in the house and within earshot. Liddy cocked her head quizzically to one side.

'Go on,' she said quietly.

'Well, you see……' for a moment the girl felt flustered and didn't know how to begin. She took a deep breath. 'He isn't an actor at all. He only says that and he…' she hesitated at the word liar, '…it's not true. He puts on clowns things for children at parties, that's what he does really.' It hung poised in the space between them, ugly and unpleasant, and in the telling she no longer felt sure. There was an uneasy pause and the girl fidgeted uncomfortably.

'How do you know this?'

The girl improvised wildly. 'Some children told me……at school. They said it.'

A second, much longer pause. Coals spat, crackled and collapsed in the fire. When at length the woman spoke, the tired face that regarded Jenny was without expression.

'He is an actor,' she said slowly, 'and I know exactly what he does.' There was a momentary weighted silence.

'Being spiteful is not at all nice.' The voice was precise, allowing the full weight of her censure to settle over the girl who, no longer warmed by the fire or by expectation, now sat in a chill huddle.

'There are,' Liddy continued, 'thousands of men looking for work in this country, good men who fought for us and were lucky to come back with their lives. Many have to take whatever they can until things get better. I would've expected you to have some understanding of that, in our situation. But now I see now that I was wrong. I hope one day you will.' The woman turned, stared at the fire as Jenny shrank into her chair, away from the shaming reproach. 'You will go to your room now and think about what I have said. I do not expect a daughter of mine to listen to childish tittle-tattle.'

'But it wasn't like that, it wasn't meant to be…' the girl was drowning, hopelessly misunderstood.

'I no longer wish to listen Jennifer. Go to bed.'

'But……!' She was scrabbling, searching desperately for something to connect them. The woman rose, stony-faced, went to the door and opened it.

'Bed,' she commanded flatly and, as Jenny trailed wretchedly past, Liddy looked down at her, unutterably weary, then slowly, finally, closed the door.

Alone and exiled, where she herself had sought to cast out, the girl weeps into a sodden pillow. She is dirty and tainted. Liddy hates her and nothing has changed. A bell is ringing unrelentingly in her ears: discordant, random, sea-tossed.

CHAPTER EIGHTEEN

The months that followed were spent uneasily on edge. The hot sun of the unfolding summer was a blinding searchlight, exposing the treachery she had been made to feel. She wanted Liddy's trust, wanted to be liked again. The rebuke administered, Liddy was, to all intents and purposes, the same as before with her. Yet something tiny but vital, something Jenny couldn't find words for, was missing. She never knew for certain if Kit had been told about it but an uncomfortable truce and prickliness developed between them. Once she asked him how to tie off a string plait she had made from twine. He fumbled with it and swore as it unravelled.

'You don't know how to tie knots at all you fibber!' she exclaimed indignantly.

'I never said I could!' he retorted and stalked off, tossing it to the ground. Another time she had been outside, making shadows with her hands against the white wall of the house, when a bigger shadow suddenly loomed, obliterating hers. It was Kit. He leaned casually to one side, revealing again the shape she had made, and looked puzzled.

'What's that meant to be then?'

'A fairy,' she said, 'like Tinker Bell.'

'Bit old for that sort of thing now aren't you?' He raised his eyebrows and started to stroll away.

'You were wrong anyway, about Peter Pan,' she said sullenly to his nonchalantly retreating back, 'it was poison Tinker Bell saved him from, not the sea. And you were wrong about Jenny Robin. It's Jenny WREN, not Robin!'

The disconnection, principally from Liddy but also, in another way, from Kit, was hard to bear. She felt and was more alone than before and plunged ever more deeply into the shrouding mystery of the sea. There was though, little comfort in her protracted walks along the shore. She was inconsolably miserable but would not allow it to show. When they were out she would, as before, sit with the wireless on and Daddy's photograph before her, minutely examining it for some hint of disapproval from him too. She could not resolve the paradox of her misplaced but gnawing guilt and the sense that the hearing itself had not been fair, had in some mysterious way been weighted against her from the outset.

Whenever Liddy or Kit mentioned something that even remotely alluded to fibs or falsehoods, she wriggled with confused embarrassment. She brooded endlessly during her secret, unauthorised and wholly unrepentant swims under cover of darkness. There seemed to be no way now, no means, of getting Liddy to see the truth, her truth. The night visitor had abandoned her too, perhaps because she had failed, hadn't been strong in some way.

When at last she found the words, or rather they came to her as she morosely lobbed pebbles into the pitch-black sea, the words for that baffling missing element between her and her mother, she cried in defeated silence. It wasn't something in Liddy after all. It was to do with her. She didn't think she loved Liddy anymore.

★ ★ ★

Sun again, after an unseasonably cold week. She set off at a rush, swimming costume already on beneath her dress, towel under one arm and carrying a bottle of lemon squash and a paper bag containing sandwiches, hastily cobbled together.

The buoy had long since gone but now a new and altogether more elegant interloper awaited her. Anchored squarely in the bay was a sleek blue and white sloop, gently bobbing in the calm water.

She wasn't sure she liked it being there. It changed her expectation of the day from the anticipated private communion with the sea to something altogether more public. People on board might be watching her, perhaps with binoculars. She kept a dubious eye on the boat as she slipped off her dress. There didn't seem to be anyone on it and her misgivings gave way to curiosity about this trim beauty.

She hopped down to the water's edge and dipped a toe in. It was, irritatingly as the grown-ups had predicted, bitingly cold. She waded out gingerly, then pushed off the bottom and swam, circumspectly, closer and closer to the vessel. It looked brand new. The paintwork still had a glossy sheen to it and the furled sails were a brilliant white. In blue scroll against the white hull she read the name, *Typhoon*.

'Must all be still asleep,' she thought, and then loftily, 'what lazybones!'

She dived like a cormorant and swam underwater. Turning smoothly beneath the sea she looked up at the fragmented image of the white hull. A shower of drops scattered across the water and the image shimmered. She turned again and pulled strongly to the surface, coming up with an undignified plop.

A woman was leaning over the side, a bucket in her hands. But there any resemblance to ordinary women stopped. Her head was haloed in a splash of extraordinary blonde-white hair and she was, like the boat itself, decked out in blue and white; white slacks, an azure blouse. Her hair was bobbed and swept back, when she moved it bounced and danced. She straightened up at the sound of Jenny surfacing. Slender and lithe, she stood with lissom ease and, shading her eyes, scanned the water.

'Ahoy!' It was a friendly, sure voice accompanied by energetic waving. 'Bet it's cold!'

'It is!' Jenny gasped, treading water.

'Come aboard and warm up.' The invitation was relaxed and easy. 'We're not pirates!'

To her surprise the girl found herself swimming without question to the boat and the attractive voice. As she drew closer the woman unravelled a short rope ladder. Like everything else it looked new.

'Thanks!' She scrambled up it, a cascade of water streaming from her. When she got on deck she began to shiver and felt embarrassed by the pool of water at her feet. The woman though was completely unperturbed. She fished out a huge white towel and draped it quickly around the girl's shoulders. It was more like a fluffy sheet and folds of it trailed on the deck.

'Thanks,' Jenny said again, this time through chattering teeth. The woman grinned. She was, Jenny thought, very beautiful and when she grinned her whole face joined in.

'Come on,' she said, 'let's get you warmed up' and without ceremony she began to dry the girl briskly. 'Should you be out there all on your own?'

'It is all right. I've got permission and I'm a strong swimmer.'

The woman made a small disapproving noise. 'I agree about the swimming anyway. You're like a little dolphin.' The compliment was as warming as the towelling and presently the girl's shivers subsided. She could not take her eyes from the woman's face and tried hard not to stare at her. It was a clear-skinned Nordic face with a strong jaw line and classically high cheek bones, yet there was something disconcertingly and irrepressibly urchin about it. But it was the eyes which held the attention. They were an arresting blue, accentuated by make-up, both luminescent and full of animated devilry.

'I'm Anne,' she said, 'but call me Annie. I hate that slightly less. Who are you?' Unaccustomed to such directness, the girl tried not to blush.

'Jenny. Jennifer Hawker. Thank you for asking me aboard ......' she could not bring herself to use this stranger's first name even though it had been so effortlessly offered. The woman smiled knowingly as if she understood the reserve. She stood lightly, hands on hips.

'My last name is Bonny but please call me Annie.' It was as if at last some recognisable formality, a familiar ground, had been introduced to their meeting. Jenny felt too that some of the woman's easy manner had rubbed off with the towelling and, like that physical touch, left her aglow and relaxed.

Jenny nodded shyly.

'You've got a lovely boat,' she volunteered, unsure quite what to say. The woman's face lit up, crinkled with pleasure.

'Smashing isn't she, want to explore?' she dared.

'Yes please!'

'Let's get you into some dry things first.' She disappeared into the cabin. The girl could hear lockers being opened and Annie muttering. 'Too big......and that......ugh, horrible!' before she emerged with a yellow silk blouse and a pair of white shorts. She tossed them to Jenny. 'Might be a bit on the baggy side,' she warned, 'try them.' Jenny looked at the blouse in horror, felt the smooth, expensive fabric.

'But I can't wear this,' she protested, desperately wanting to put it on, 'it's too......too much!'

'Course you can.' The woman laughed. 'Believe me, if it's not too good for me it isn't too good for you. Enjoy it,' she exhorted casually, 'it's only a thing.' The girl held the clothing to her but did not move, not knowing where to change and too shy to ask. Annie twinkled. 'Pop below,' she said, 'I promise not to look.' A relieved Jenny ducked into the cabin and stripped off her wet costume. The shorts were indeed spacious but the blouse, though roomy, felt exquisitely rich and soft. She did a little pirouette of delight and wished there was a mirror. It was unlike anything she had ever worn. She felt timidly proud as she stepped out to face Annie's scrutinising gaze.

'Hmm......' she seemed to approve. 'Like it?'

'Oh yes!'

'Something for the insides now I think,' Annie said, diving quickly below. Jenny could see the burst of golden hair as she flitted around the small galley. 'So Jennifer Hawker, are you on holiday too?'

'No, I live here.'

The woman emerged brandishing a mug enveloped in steam. 'Hot chocolate,' she announced, 'for a cold dolphin.' They sat on the long cushioned seats in the cockpit. Jenny had had cocoa before, lots of times, but this was creamy, as smooth as the blouse. She drank it carefully, on best behaviour, licking off the stickiness around her mouth when Annie wasn't looking.

'How long have you been on holiday?' she asked politely. The woman swung her feet up onto the seat and hugged her knees. She looked at Jenny, an alarmingly feline gaze, and smiled wickedly.

'A long time. It's all a wonderful, never-ending holiday really.' Then she jumped up, went to the open forward hatch and shouted down, 'Hi Jerry, come and see what I've caught,' and to the girl, 'high time he was up anyway.'

It had not occurred to Jenny that there was someone else on board although, of course, it was unlikely that this woman would be sailing such a big boat alone, or that a woman like this would be alone. She became apprehensive, a touch uncomfortable, that their snug, female duet was about to be interrupted.

There was a low rumbling from below then a bearded, heavy-set man appeared through the hatch.

'Hullo,' he exclaimed genially, catching sight of Jenny, 'what a strange fish!'

'Not a fish at all silly,' Annie said, 'though she swims like one. Miss Jennifer Hawker, this is Jerry.' He seemed amused by the formality and raised an eyebrow at her.

'Pleasure to have you aboard Miss Jennifer Hawker,' he emphasised the Miss and again looked mock-darkly at the woman. The beard was neatly trimmed and he wore shorts and deck shoes without socks, a crumpled green shirt, the sleeves rolled up over his thick forearms. He peered at her fixedly until Annie came to her rescue.

'Don't be put off Jenny. He can't really see without specs.' She got them from the cabin and passed them to the man who put them on and smiled.

'That's better,' he said, 'you are a pretty thing aren't you?'

The woman showed her excitedly over every inch of the boat as if she too were discovering it for the first time. There were hidden lockers, concealed washbasins, bunks that doubled as tables, and it was all presented with an infectious enthusiasm. The man, Jerry, followed in a shambling, beguiled way. It was as neat and new inside as it was out. To the girl's surprise the small forward cabin was crammed with canvases, paints and dappled oily rags.

'This is Jerry's bit,' the woman explained, 'and that,' she pointed skyward through the open hatch, 'is his studio. He paints, pictures not houses, and I sponge off him.' The man gave a deep, resonant laugh.

'Don't believe a word of it Miss Hawker, she's the captain.'

'Are you really?'

The woman grinned, 'And first mate and bosun and ship's cook. I let him navigate sometimes.'

As they talked and continued exploring Jenny whirled pleasurably between them. They had a thousand questions, a thousand things to say, and she found it captivating. Eventually they made their way back to the cockpit.

'And where's your house Jenny?'

She pointed to the green hill, 'Over there. You can't quite see it. It's called Hadley.' she said and, emboldened, asked, 'Where do you live?'

Annie looked surprised, 'Here.'

'On the boat, all the time?' Jenny was envious. It seemed so romantic.

'Well yes.'

'And you just sail off?'

The woman shrugged, brushed back a stray lock. 'Wherever we like really.'

'Until the money runs out,' the man warned, but Jenny could tell he wasn't being serious.

'We just got back from France this morning,' Annie said, ignoring him.

'France!' Jenny exclaimed. 'Finistère……' she added dreamily.

'Not likely. We went south. It was a scream wasn't it Jerry. A riot. Hob-nobbing with the fast set.'

A scream, a riot, the fast set? It was a new language, an unknown world, magical and a bit scary.

'What's the farthest you've been?'

The woman was thoughtful then said quickly, 'America. But not in a boat. On an aeroplane.' Jenny was deeply impressed even though it hadn't been said with that intention.

'How big is America?' she asked innocently.

'Far too big,' Jerry interposed.

Annie clapped her hands. 'Who's for lunch?' she asked brightly. 'You'll stay won't you Jenny.' It was an invitation she would not refuse, yet the grown-up way was, she knew, to put up a token resistance.

'Um……it would be lovely but you see I've got some sandwiches,' she piped apologetically, pointing back to the beach.

'You won't want dull old sandwiches when you see what we've got,' Jerry said without looking up, 'feed 'em to the fishes.' There was something of the schoolteacher about him, a faint austerity or discipline, coupled in an unlikely way with an almost eccentric waywardness, a disregard. He had taken up a pad and was sketching. She noticed that, unusually, he was wearing two gold rings, identical bands on the third finger of each hand.

'You will stay won't you?' Annie implored, as if the girl's company was the most important thing in the world. Jenny nodded happily and the woman took her hand saying, 'Come and help.'

Down in the galley, Annie piled strange cheeses and a long, thick sausage onto a tray, added olives, peaches and grapes and broke up a French loaf into a basket. Finally she brought out a bottle of champagne and three glasses.

When they went topside the man was still sketching and puffing at a pipe. He looked up enthusiastically, picked up the bottle from the tray and opened it expertly with a quick twist. It popped but did not come gushing out as Jenny had expected.

'Always turn the bottle, not the cork,' he said, then winked at her. 'French champagne. No snitching to the Revenue. We'll dispose of the evidence.' Without asking the girl if she wanted any, he poured three glasses and handed them out. Jenny, remembering the etiquette from home, asked uncertainly, 'A toast?'

'Hang the rich!' they chorused as if on cue and laughing. Jenny politely raised her glass, clinked it against each of theirs then, baffled, asked, 'But why, you must be very rich......?' and was even more puzzled by their uninhibited hoots of laughter.

'We're paupers!' Annie answered at last, 'real orphans!'

'But the boat,' Jenny said feebly, looking round at its splendour, 'it must have cost a fortune.'

'She did,' Jerry chuckled, 'and we haven't paid up yet.'

'If I had a boat it would be a he,' Jenny announced gravely and, swept up by them, joined their laughter.

They lingered over the simple lunch. The girl watched them secretly, took her lead from the way they ate the unfamiliar food. But there seemed to be no rules here, and no knives and forks. It was all wonderfully easygoing and they weren't like strangers at all. She tucked in, found she liked it except for the strong-tasting sausage. Again, as if reading her mind, Annie said calmly, 'Just leave it, or chuck it over the side.' She couldn't decide about the champagne. She liked the fizz but not the metallic taste it left afterwards. She drank it anyway.

'And your Dad, what does he do?' Annie asked. The girl looked down at the deck.

'He's dead actually,' she answered, trying not to sever the bright chain that seemed to link them.

'Oh I am so sorry,' Annie was effusive, wholly genuine, 'I didn't mean to......'

'No it's all right, really.'

The man pulled at his pipe, 'In the war?' he queried gently.

'Yes. He was in the Navy. An officer.'

Jerry looked away, across the sun-touched sea. 'So many of them,' he said wistfully, to himself. Jenny nodded.

'My mother says lots of men didn't come back and that they were all brave.'

'It was children I meant.' He looked sadly down at his pipe.

Jenny didn't understand but he looked very serious and she just said 'Oh.'

'So it's just you and your Mum?' Annie asked tentatively.

'No. There's Kit as well. He's……' she hesitated, began to wish she had just said yes. 'He's a cousin come to stay with us.' She paused. 'He works terribly hard. He's an actor,' she fibbed, hoping to impress them with something about her.

'Is he?' Jerry said, again raising an eyebrow, 'dodgy old profession that is. Worse than mine.'

The girl tried to copy his sage look and piled it on. 'He has to work all the time, to get enough money.'

'Oh my dear!' Annie looked appalled. 'You should never worry about money. Never!' She popped a grape into her mouth. 'Still, good to have someone watching over you.' She got up and, bending over, began to put the remains of the lunch on the tray. Then the man did something which should have made Jenny feel uncomfortable but which, curiously, didn't. He reached out and gently squeezed the woman's bottom. It wasn't a tweak or a pinch. It was something far more personal and affectionate. He sank back into his place with a half-smile and Annie carried on clearing away. Neither of them spoke or appeared to think anything unusual had happened. Annie disappeared with the tray and the man took up his pad again, became engrossed.

'Do you have to work hard too?' Jenny asked after a while.

'I should do,' he replied, 'but there are other concerns.'

'What……other concerns?'

'Well, the ills of today have their feet in the past. It's up to all of us to make it work this time, to get the damn thing right.'

'What thing?'

'Just the world,' he grinned. 'Don't take any notice of old fogeys like us. You follow your own voices.'

'I am not an old fogey!' an indignant protest arose from below.

'But you're happy aren't you?' Jenny persisted to the man. He tapped the side of the boat with his pipe.

'Do you mean this? This is just a bit of fun now all the soldiering's finished.' He became serious again, realising the question was meant. 'Yes, but I don't honestly know how you get it, if that's what you're asking. It's more to do with recognising it when it comes along......if you're lucky enough.' He peered myopically over his glasses to where Annie was still tidying and also, as they discovered, listening.

'Se déraciner!' Annie trilled up at them with gusto, 'uproot yourself! Change your life! Throw out everything you don't like, all the dead wood. That's what I did. It's probably different for everybody though.'

'The trouble is,' Jenny spoke thoughtfully, 'is that grown-ups don't say. You have to guess at things.'

'That's the trouble for grown-ups too,' Jerry said. The girl pondered as he sketched. It was like being in the presence of two wholly different, fantastically plumed creatures. They entranced her. They were like separate strands, distinct and individual, but plaited together. Annie re-joined them and sat watching the man draw as she smoked a cigarette.

'How d'you get that?' Jerry asked the girl, pointing at her scar with the stem of his pipe. Again, it was an almost uncomfortably direct question.

'Eagle eye isn't he?' Annie smiled, 'at least with his goggles on.' Then, to Jerry, 'You shouldn't ask anyway. Not polite.'

Jenny fingered the white crescent. 'In an air raid,' she answered, 'bit from a bomber did it.'

The man grunted, unbuttoned his shirt and pulled it off one shoulder. A great knotted scar, like twisted rope, ran over the shoulder and under his armpit. 'I got this,' he said simply, as if comparing trophies. 'Africa,' he added and resumed sketching.

Granted licence by his questioning the girl asked, 'Why have you got two wedding rings?'

Annie laughed. 'Flashy isn't it. That's the showy side to him.'

The man held up his left hand. 'That one's for love,' he said unselfconsciously, then raised the other hand, 'and that one's for honesty.' It was said plainly, without further explanation. After a while he carefully tore the drawing from the pad and showed it to them. 'There, what do you think?' It was a delicate sketch of Jenny. He had drawn her as a mermaid, gambolling with sea horses in a mythical underwater grotto. The girl smiled, pleased and embarrassed. She hadn't realised he was drawing her.

'It's lovely,' she said. A tiny hope formed that she might even be given it.

'Oh Jerry, what fun. Can I have it to remember my new friend?' Annie giggled and leant towards him. He smiled and handed it to her. Although Jenny wanted it for herself she was pleased and flattered that Annie should want to remember her.

'How did you learn to draw so well?' the girl asked. He started another drawing and did not raise head.

'Drawing's easy. The hard bit is learning how to look.'

'Oh don't start him off Jenny,' the woman smiled but the girl persevered.

'Does it take long, to learn I mean?'

He looked up, eyes crinkling with amusement, 'I don't know. I haven't finished yet,' and he returned to the sketch, his hand darting across the pad. Annie chattered gaily, reeling off places they had visited and what they had seen. The girl recognised some of the names and envied their unfettered, and seemingly unplanned, wandering.

'You and your husband are so lucky!' she said captivated.

'Oh we aren't married,' Annie's eyes were twinkling. 'He's my paramour is Mr. Gerald Hartland.' She looked at him fondly as he laboured, oblivious to the conversation. 'Thou salt-water thief,' she quoted, 'stole me away he did, from me and mine the wicked rogue.' She turned again to Jenny and winked slyly, 'Lucky me.'

As the afternoon drifted idly on, the girl found herself liking them more and more, Annie particularly. She wanted to be like her and emulate her assuredness, her easy grace. Eventually though she looked anxiously at the beach, sighed with regret.

'I ought to be going home now.' Across the water the shadow of a cloud was swiftly climbing the green hill, darkening it like wine spilt on a tablecloth.

'Mum'll be wondering will she?' Annie asked, 'I'm sure I would if I was her......and......Kit? Was that his name?'

'Yes Kit.'

It was agreed that Jerry would row her across. The girl got her swimming costume and fingered the collar of the blouse with a pang.

'Oh no,' Annie said firmly, 'you must keep it. It looks much better on you. And the shorts. You'll grow into those in no time.' Jenny did not argue but thanked her and said she would treasure them 'forever.'

Annie looked up at the blue sky. 'It'll be another lovely day tomorrow,' she announced and then, quite unexpectedly, she gently took the girl's face in her hands.

'One day you will be a very beautiful woman. I envy you, and wish you happiness of it.'

Jenny was speechless. It was unimaginable that this bewitching woman, this vivacious, gleaming spirit, could envy her anything. She did not know what to say.

At the last moment Annie pressed them to wait, went below and came back with a camera. 'I'm just beginning to get the hang of this,' she said and rapidly took several pictures of the embarrassed girl, and persuaded a reluctant Jerry to be photographed with her. 'He's camera shy,' she said, 'thinks it makes him look fat.' Then she got the man to take one of her and Jenny, slipping an arm unaffectedly round the girl's waist. 'Now write down your address and we'll send some to you from wherever we are,' Annie said, adding, 'in the post, not a message in a bottle or anything as unreliable as that.' She opened the sketch pad at a blank page.

It was irresistible. The girl carefully printed out her name and address, adding *England* as a cautious afterthought.

'Well, au revoir Jennifer Hawker,' Annie held out her hand and they shook, oddly formal after, what was to Jenny at least, a deluge of unaccustomed intimacies. 'I'm glad you came aboard.'

The girl clambered into the stern of the small rowing boat and the man ferried her ashore. Annie, diminishing with the distance, watched them, waving. As they closed on the beach Jenny hopped out and through the warm shallows. She waved and called as he hauled the boat back then found her towel, dress and the forgotten sandwiches. She would have to change in the woods so that Liddy and Kit didn't see the wonderful blouse and the shorts, and then she'd have to hide them. She wouldn't, couldn't, tell them about today and her new friends. It was something else she wanted to keep to herself. She would have to dash though. She was probably late already. She could still see Annie on deck, surrounded by her blonde-white aura. The rowing boat was tied up alongside and Jerry was climbing the rope ladder.

'Goodbye!' the girl shouted, waving furiously. 'Goodbye, come back soon!' And across the water a golden, answering voice.

'See you next time around!'

Almost exactly one month later an envelope arrived for her. It contained three photographs, smiling faces encapsulated by sunlight, memories of a day untrammelled by doubt, and a simple, thin ring of twisted gold. There was no address on the note but at the top, in a scrawled hand, was the word *Rimini* and then the date.

What a happy day we had Jennifer Hawker! Wear this ring for luck. Everybody should have a bit of gold. We hope you remember us. See you again one day.

Love from your friends,
Annie and Jerry.

She slipped the ring on and hid the letter and photographs away. And after she had wiped her eyes and blown her nose, she went to look up in her atlas exactly where Rimini was.

CHAPTER NINETEEN

It came in a rush as though they had been saving it up. She spent the summer more or less alone, left to her own devices. She swam daily, shrimped unsuccessfully in the low tide rock pools, played solitary games of pretend and made sandcastles. Not a single day passed when she didn't long to see again the perfect blue and white sloop in her bay. There had been no more envelopes and still no sight, or sound, of the night visitor.

Then, and without warning, another bomb fell from the blue and exploded in her life, hurling fragments in all directions.

'Kit has asked me to marry him and I've said yes!' They were in the front room, where she had been summoned. 'Isn't it perfectly wonderful!' Liddy was standing over her, hands clasped excitedly together.

A trap door opened abruptly in the girl's soul and she dropped down, spinning in a sickening vortex. She was struck dumb, inert. Then a flash of profound disillusionment pushed her back up into the oppressive midst of these familiar strangers and their now revealed secret scheming.

'And you can be bridesmaid,' Liddy gushed breathlessly, 'we'll buy you a pretty frock!' Kit shuffled restlessly in the background, smoking.

Everything fell into place. It was a hateful jigsaw. She wanted to break it up and smash it. All the secrecy, the whispers, had been about this. Liddy hadn't seen the truth because she hadn't wanted to. The girl was numbed by this terrible new understanding and stared at the woman helplessly, as a would-be rescuer might at a lost soul, too far out and in too high a sea. Fixated by the flashing carmine lips she listened, trance-like, as Liddy told how it had 'crept up on them' and taken them 'completely by surprise.' A second, slower understanding coldly enveloped the girl; this had all been practised, rehearsed, before she had entered the room.

'And……' the woman said tantalisingly, 'guess what? It'll be in London! Won't that be marvellous!' It was her over-rhapsodic inflexion that snapped the girl to herself and she uttered the one word she was to speak.

'Why?'

Liddy clapped her hands together joyfully. 'Because that's where we're going to live. Isn't it exciting!'

And, as it had years before, a fragment came after the bursting bombshell and cut savagely deep into her. The girl stands stiffly; cold-eyed, dry-eyed, chillingly still.

'Oh you'll love it darling. There's so much to see and do. We won't have a spare minute. Theatres, cinemas, Buckingham Palace,' the woman laughed, a chirruping peal. 'There'll never be a dull moment for us again! And there'll be proper work for Kit. Who knows he might even become really famous!' And there it was, slipped in like a sugared pill, the real reason, Kit. It was Kit behind this. It was all his idea.

'More money too,' he chimed in. He poured himself a drink, stood nursing it. 'Streets of gold and all that.'

The woman prattled on, hands fluttering. They do not notice Jenny's silence. The words swirl around her but she is clinging to the only scrap of salvage and rising with it through the nightmare depths of future exile. Yet it is scant comfort, meagre absolution from her own inappropriate guilt. Despite how they tried to make her feel, the treachery is not hers. She is the one betrayed.

★　★　★

She was abject, consumed by foreboding. It was unthinkable to leave Hadley. Unthinkable. Over and over she wished she had not found the secret cove that day, had not stumbled across the deceitful castaway turned stowaway and been taken in by him. A scraped-out feeling stayed with her, like the wrenching ache after tears, but she did not cry, not then or ever. She concealed everything, all emotion, from them and steadfastly maintained an unresponsive silence or was doggedly monosyllabic. It was to be their punishment. But Liddy and Kit chose not to notice. The flood of plans now took up their time and attention, dominating them completely. Much as she wished for her unsubtle manipulation to wreak some sort of revenge, it became increasingly clear that it didn't. It didn't change anything.

Now, everything she was about to lose, Hadley, the bay, the spell-casting sea, etched itself all the more deeply in her mind. She wanted to weep for a past where everything had been different, when promises had yet to be broken and deception just a word.

Standing above the beach, where once she had made a circle of stones, she felt already cast out, forbidden to step on the sand. An accusing sea hissed at her and ill-tempered gulls clamoured. At the last minute, before she turned away and went dejectedly home, she rushed down and stole a smooth, ivory shell; different to the one she already had, so that, whatever she knew was the truth of it, whatever she had told Kit about it just being the noise in your head, she would always be able to listen to the sea, this sea, wherever she was. It was a shell for the sound of oceans, for messages from a soon to be faraway shore.

If not a reprieve then it was at least a stay of execution when she realised how long the process of moving would take. She stood alone in a glade of unwilling quiescence, resentful and withdrawn as they scrambled to resolve all the practical details of uprooting. Hadley was placed in the hands of agents and Kit drove to London for a few days, 'Bit of a recce, sort a few things out.' Liddy meanwhile, embarked on her own diligent sort-out of their possessions, the sheer scale of which soon gave her a defeated, overwhelmed look.

'We simply must get rid of some things,' she said, despairingly surveying a room in which every drawer and cupboard had been turned out onto the floor. 'We can't take it all with us.'

It was unsettling enough to see Hadley turned upside down but worse when Jenny's own room became the next target for the increasingly fraught purge. She watched in horror as toys and games were hauled from the depths of her wardrobe and shrank into herself as verdict was passed on them. She wanted to keep everything, except the miserable Christmas doll, even though she had not played with much of it for years. She was consulted, just, but frequently over-ruled and a stealthy tug-of-war commenced between her and the strained, harassed woman. As her mother piled up what was to go, Jenny would sneak some away behind her back and put them with the much smaller pile of things she was allowed to keep. It continued like this, with Liddy becoming more and more agitated, naively unaware of why she seemed to be getting nowhere, until Kit stomped up the stairs. He threw his hands in the air and resolved it once and for all by insisting that the girl could only take what would fit into one small box.

'Look, you're going to have to be grown up about it, that's all, there just isn't room for all this stuff. You can have all the toys you want in London. I promise.'

So, stung as much by his reasonable tone as by the ultimatum, she was left alone to collect her allotted boxful. In a spirit of sulky retaliation that would pass unnoticed she packed neither toys nor games but just her spade and her precious things. That done she sat cross-legged on her bed, put a thumb in her mouth – something she had not done in years – held the shell to her ear and rocked slowly.

Ironically, in the midst of all this scouring, her mother decided that Jenny should have new clothes. Everything seemed suddenly too small, too short or too tight.

'And,' she added brightly, 'you'll be all brand new for London.' A rare Saturday when Kit wasn't working was set aside for a trip to Exeter and a neat list written out. Liddy had taken to writing out lists of things to be done. They hung in the kitchen and ruled her life as she fretted about her slow progress. They fluttered reprovingly as she rushed in and out, reminding her of her apparent inefficiency. For it had all been left to her. Kit continued working at the same frenetic pace. Yet now, when he returned, he was irked by the mess where before he had been oblivious to his own. If it was a dream the two of them were chasing, they were running too slow for Kit, too fast for her mother.

★   ★   ★

When she woke the curtains were billowing into the room and it was filled with sea dampness. By her window the sails of the little blue windmill were spinning urgently. She went over to it and put her face close, catching its tiny breeze.

She got herself up and went downstairs. It was early, too early for the others to be about yet. She took a piece of bread from the kitchen, filled a tea cup with milk, and went outside. Late summer. The wind had dropped and the trees were almost bursting with green velvet fullness. Everything was still, just a sawing grasshopper on the path at her feet. She sat on the bench, ate her breakfast and watched the sun filter through the elegant iron lettering of Hadley's gate.

It was the day of the shopping trip, a wasted day she thought tetchily as a green caterpillar hunched its way up the wall beside her. When Kit appeared, an hour later, he had a long-suffering expression. He lit a cigarette.

'You all set then?'

'Where's Liddy?'

'In bed. Had a bad night. Been overdoing it lately. It'll have to be just us.' She had noticed before that whenever he was up early, which wasn't often, he spoke in a chopped-off sort of way.

'Can't we go another day?' she asked hopefully. He looked at her with moody exasperation.

'There aren't any other days left. Come on.'

'I'll get my coat.'

'And the list, don't forget the list.' He let out a plume of smoke and strode off towards the van.

She pattered into the house, got the list and collected her coat. Peering up the stairs it was hushed and dark, the curtains unopened.

'Bye!' her voice echoed around the landing but there was no reply. She hurried out to the van, got in and closed the door. It bounced off the catch and swung open again. Irritably, Kit leant heavily across her and yanked it shut.

It was a silent journey. She was sullen and resigned but wore a face of unimpeachable indifference, and the absence of conversation between them, especially his blithe and now particularly inapt humour, suited her perfectly. She looked away and out of the side window at the flexing landscape.

Exeter was busy and it took some time for them to find a place to park. Kit circled the same streets drumming the steering wheel. He stopped when he thought a car was about to vacate a space. A lorry behind them hooted and he glared at it in the rear view mirror.

'And you!' he barked, gesticulating wildly. Worse, the parked car stayed where it was, its owner had only returned to put some packages in the boot.

'Oh bloody hell!' he exclaimed and the van shot off again until at last they found a place and he wrestled the vehicle quickly into it, backing up with a squeal of brakes.

They trudged along the high street, both ill-humoured.

'What are you doing?' he quizzed impatiently as she lagged behind.

'Stepping on the cracks,' she answered matter-of-factly.

'I thought the game was not to.'

'Well,' she said flatly, 'I am.'

He looked at her patronisingly, 'And what happens if you don't?'

'Nothing of course.'

Eventually they came to a large store. He propelled her through the glass doors and down into the children's department. It smelt of varnished wood and starched linen. An assistant greeted them politely. Kit thrust the list at him saying he would be back in half an hour. Then he turned to the girl, 'No point in us both hanging around here,' and made off. The girl's distinct, though not impolite, lack of enthusiasm puzzled the salesman. Whatever he suggested she accepted. She had no interest in the clothes, in being 'all brand new' for London. She tried on the suggested items, returned them to the man with an indifferent, 'Yes, they're all right,' and watched without interest as he carefully folded the clothes and wrapped them in brown paper.

The half-hour stretched to three-quarters and there was no sign of Kit. She sat on a chair by the counter and swung her legs dejectedly. Other customers came and went but when it was quiet again, the salesman reached under the counter and produced a glass jar of boiled sweets. He held it out to her and she took one, unsmiling, and thanked him.

'Your Dad's a long time,' he said.

'He isn't my Dad,' she said quickly, 'my Dad's away at the moment. He's a cousin, my mum's cousin.'

'Oh, I see,' the man raised his eyebrows almost imperceptibly and busied himself tidying shelves. When Kit arrived he made no apology or explanation. But when he said, 'Got it all then?' she could smell the drink. She nodded and watched as he paid, then hurried her back to the van.

'Let's go,' he said through gritted teeth, 'I've had enough of this.'

She sat primly in the passenger seat, not knowing if it was Exeter or her he'd had enough of. She hoped it was her. Her dumb unenthusiasm could not be criticised and she was glad he had found no pleasure in the trip, glad too that he hadn't suggested, albeit improbably, some 'special treat' as in the past.

The van swung quickly out of the town and back through the soft winding countryside. She could not remember much about the clothes chosen for her but knew she had everything on the list and if they were wrong she would be above reproach because Kit had absented himself.

They were little more than a third of the way home when he stamped repeatedly on the accelerator and then cruised to a bumpy halt on the verge.

'Christ!' he snapped, 'That's all I bloody need!' He pulled a lever under the dashboard, got out and flung up the bonnet, disappearing beneath it. After a while he stripped off his coat and bundled it through the window. He dived back under and continued to tap, goad and tinker. The countryside around them was peaceful. A small river purred nearby. Jenny clambered over the driver's seat, unwilling to open her door in case it wouldn't shut again, and half climbed out.

'Can you fix it?'

'Course I ruddy well can!' he bawled back from under the wobbling metal dome. She got out and meandered up and down the verge, picking daisies and making a chain. It was well past lunchtime and she was beginning to feel hungry.

'Come on,' Kit slammed the bonnet down and waved her back. She took her place, remembering unhappily about the door as she did so. Kit jabbed at the starter button. There was a click and then more fruitless clicks as he stabbed fiercely at it. He covered his face with his hands and groaned.

'Are you sure you've got enough petrol?' she asked innocently but he made no reply. Instead he yanked at the lever, threw open his door and heaved the creaking bonnet up again. For a full half-hour he prodded and poked the van's faulty innards, then he peered round the edge of the bonnet and bellowed at her, 'Jenny, press the button, the white one.' She leant over, found it and pressed. It clicked again.

'Go on then. Press it!'

'I am, I am!' she shouted. He rushed round muttering darkly and tried for himself. Still nothing. He took out a cigarette, lit it and stalked up and down by the van, scowling.

'Thought you said you could fix it,' she ventured, pushing her luck but quietly gloating.

'I could, I could!' he exploded. 'Just haven't got the right tools that's all!' A furious plume of cigarette smoke erupted from him and he lashed out at the vehicle with his foot. 'Bloody thing!'

She waited a few moments, 'What about lunch?' It sounded convincingly artless.

'Bugger lunch! We'll just have to walk that's all.'

'Walk?'

'Yes walk,' he imitated, sarcastically, 'how else are we going to get out of this damn fix eh?' She looked around, turned a little circle on the grass.

'But there's nothing for miles,' she protested.

'Then we'll have to walk for miles, won't we?' he grabbed the camel hair coat and slung it over his shoulder. 'With any luck someone will come along and give us a lift.' She got her own coat and fell in behind him. After a few yards she stopped.

'Shouldn't we go the same way as the river? There are always places by a river.'

He glared at her and, without a word, turned to follow her advice and the gently rilling stream.

Kit set off at a great pace but gradually began to slow up. She noticed he was wearing stylish town shoes and walking as though they pinched, not that he would ever admit it. They stopped twice to drink from the river, scooping the water up with their hands, and for Kit to smoke.

The road rose steeply before them and they began the long climb. Kit grumbled that not a single car, lorry or tractor had passed them.

'Back of bloody beyond,' he said crossly. She didn't answer but overtook him and strode ahead as he began to flag. When she reached the top and turned back he was sitting at the side of the road, resting.

'Houses!' she shouted, pointing ahead.

'What?'

'Houses.'

He got up quickly and hobbled up the hill. A village lay before them some two miles in the distance. But it was another half-hour before they arrived. Kit chafed at its rural remoteness; one closed shop, an inn, also closed, from which swung a dilapidated name-board with *Sign of the Angel* scarcely legible on it. A dozen or so cottages surrounding it looked equally desolate.

'Everything's ruddy well closed!' he exclaimed dismally.

'It's Saturday afternoon. Everything's shut everywhere.'

He looked at his watch, 'Good God it's nearly five!'

'Well we have been walking for ages,' she grumbled, 'and I'm famished.'

Kit went to the inn and peered in a window. 'Must open soon,' he said to himself, 'did you see a phone box?'

'No.' She plonked down wearily on a bench outside the inn, swung her legs crossly.

'Just have to wait I suppose,' he said dejectedly and sat at the other end of it. They must have dozed for they were both startled as bolts on the inn door were rattled open.

The innkeeper was heavy-bellied and suspicious. He looked at Kit as if at a new and dubious breed of livestock, unlikely to give much yield. As their predicament unfolded though, he became more helpful. He scratched his stubble thoughtfully; no, there wasn't a garage for several miles. Yes he did have a telephone, his own mind, but seeing as how they was in a jam.......

While Kit went to telephone, the innkeeper sat Jenny down and stumped off shaking his head. Soon he came back with a cheese sandwich which she wolfed gratefully as he opened a bottle of lemonade, popped a straw in it and set it down in front of her. A lop-sided grin spread across his face as she devoured the sandwich and sucked noisily at the lemonade. 'That better then?' His voice was a growling burr and there was an unhurried, bemused twinkle about him. When Kit returned he had tracked down a garage who had agreed to come out the following morning.

'Cost a packet I bet,' he said bitterly. There had been no answer from Hadley and he thought Liddy must have gone to the village, he'd try again later. Reluctant but resigned, Kit arranged a room for them. The innkeeper looked at him, his face crinkling.

'Don't you worry Sir, we'll make sure you're snug for the night,' he said contentedly, their custom safely ensnared. 'You'll be wanting supper of course Sir?' The unexpected windfall their arrival provided clearly delighted the man and he was slyly adding in extras like hot baths, 'a bit of a sponge and press for them clothes eh? I'll give the missus a shout.'

Jenny liked him. She understood that his playing the country bumpkin to Kit's obvious urbanite, was calculated to jemmy as much from Kit's wallet as possible.

'Tea Sir?'

'Drink more like.' For the first time that day Kit's expression approached cheerfulness.

'Right you are then,' the innkeeper pulled a pint of beer and put it down in front of him, beaming, 'your very good health Sir.' Jenny smirked to herself. She could read the innkeeper's pouchy face, his crafty, country knowingness; beer would ease the way, grease the jemmy, and the irony was that Kit, actor himself, should miss it so completely.

'One for yourself?' Kit offered hospitably, his own half drunk in one gulp.

'Don't mind if I do Sir. Don't mind at all.'

★ ★ ★

She'd had seconds of supper and sat back bloated. She hadn't needed seconds but was happily in collusion with their host's avarice. She nonchalantly eavesdropped on a conversation at the next table where three men were swathed in pipe smoke.

'So in they goes to lay out body like, up to the 'ole bugger's room when it do sit up in bed, a huffin' and a puffin' at 'em! Well they two fellas is out o' bloody 'ouse and down lane like a bloody shot! Turned out it were wind in the belly, see, 'appens a lot on'y they two cocky buggers weren't to know, was they,' the man paused, slurped at his ale, 'always said 'e were 'ole fart.'

The bar was filling up and getting noisy. Kit was holding court and was, she observed dryly, now being addressed as Captain. She sat at a corner table while Kit leant casually against the bar, chatting animatedly with the thronging customers. After a while she wormed her way across the crowded room, plucked at his sleeve and said she was going up to have a bath.

'Right,' he struggled to make himself heard, 'be up soon.' He was grinning, in his element, an unlit cigarette dangling from his bottom lip.

The innkeeper's wife showed her where the bathroom was. She was small and had a scrubbed, sour look.

'You'll be wanting towels I suppose?' she asked grudgingly. Jenny nodded. She felt rather afraid of this woman and her rancorous expression. When they came though, the towels were big and soft. She soaked contentedly. The day had not all been wasted after all. She had at least found some satisfaction in Kit's frustration. It had been a small paying out. It was spiteful of her but she didn't care.

From below the noise of the bar grew louder; a muffled bawdiness that cackled up and slid in under the door. The bed nearest the window looked the most comfortable and she climbed in.

It sounded more like a party downstairs, waves of raucous laughter, a babble of voices, including Kit's. She couldn't hear what he was saying but knew only too well the act, the voice, his own irresistible need to perform. She closed her eyes. More laughter and another, local voice.

'Go on Captain, do us another one then!' It was the last thing she heard before she fell asleep.

When she woke Kit was lying on his bed, curled up like a child and snoring. He was still dressed, the camel hair coat draped over him like a bedspread. She rolled over and lifted up a corner of curtain. Kit stirred and stared at her blankly, without recognition. Slowly he sat up, put the heels of his palms against his eyes and groaned.

'What's up?' she asked unsympathetically. There was a long pause before he answered.

'Headache. Oh God, the king of all headaches. Find us a cup of tea there's a good girl. Lots of sugar.' He flopped back onto the bed, one arm across his eyes.

She dressed, pulled back the curtains, and left him to it. Downstairs the innkeeper was stocking shelves and his wife sweeping the floor.

'Good morning young lady. You sleep all right?' It was plain that whatever ailed Kit did not trouble this man. 'You'll be needing a good breakfast inside you I daresay, start the day right eh?' He didn't actually rub his hands together but might as well have.

'Yes please. He only wants tea though.' She pointed to the ceiling, the room above, where lay the stricken player.

'Martha! Take the gentleman a pot of tea and a proper breakfast for the child here,' he ordered. The woman scowled and bustled away. ' 'Ees a character all right ain't 'ee, the Captain!' he was lifting bottles from a crate, three in each hand, and clouting them down on the shelves. 'We 'ad a proper do in 'ere last night. Proper laugh we had,' and he rocked mirthfully.

She had finished breakfast when Kit stumbled downstairs, his face a deathly white, clothes crumpled. The innkeeper looked at him sorrowfully.

'I knows just the thing for you Captain,' he announced, 'hair of the hound eh?' But even Kit blanched, this time at least preferring more tea.

The man from the garage had arranged to meet them at the inn and take them to the van. He arrived in what had once been an army lorry. Jenny clambered into it while Kit paid the innkeeper's bill. When he came out his expression, though still pasty, was tight-lipped and stony.

'Bloody cut-throat yokels,' he muttered vehemently, 'talk about being stung!' The mechanic gave him a slow and unrevealing look but said nothing.

They drove quickly to the van and within five minutes the engine coughed into life. She saw Kit open his wallet yet again and reluctantly. They got in, Kit slamming his door.

'Bloody robbers the lot of 'em!' he spluttered and set off at high speed.

★   ★   ★

The white house, itself unchanging, came into view. Kit was still fuming and raced up the drive, gravel pinging under the wheels. They unloaded the parcels and carried them indoors.

'Liddy!' he shouted impatiently, 'Liddy!' He left Jenny with the parcels and clumped upstairs without stopping to take his coat off. The clock ticked loudly on the kitchen wall. Only silence from above. She took off her coat, hung it up, and tiptoed up the stairs. Still silence. The door to the bedroom was open but no sound came out. She padded softly along the passage and stood in the yawning doorway. Soft fragrance of jasmine. Liddy stretched out asleep on the bed, Kit hunched at the foot of it. Uncertainly she tapped lightly on the door. He turned and she saw his face wet with tears, unutterably distraught.

'She's dead!' he said in a stricken, disbelieving voice, 'Liddy's dead!'

CHAPTER TWENTY

'It was her heart of course. She could have gone at any time. Frail as a sparrow I'm afraid.' The doctor looked embarrassed and avoided Kit's red, swollen eyes. 'You were, I'm sure, aware of her condition?' Kit nodded dumbly, remained silent. 'I'd say she has been dead for a day old chap. It was at least a peaceful end. I am sorry,' he reached out and patted Kit's arm consolingly, 'so very sorry.'

Already dead for a day. The girl turned slowly away and sat at the top of the stairs but the words stayed with her. Liddy had remained undisturbed in her big room all that time. The sun had moved round and slipped in through the open window. Flowers in the Chinese vase dropped pink and white petals onto the small, round table on which they stood. Downstairs the telephone rang and then stopped. The sun began its slow decline and darkness, coolness, crept in. Later, night noises from beyond the window and the light of a waning moon stroked the pages of an open book on the bed. And all the time, that afflicted face, weighed down with hoarded secrets, had gazed sightless and mindless across the room. She had lain there alone for a day, a whole day and then a night. Three tides would have passed and if her death had been peaceful there was little ease in those eyes staring from the pillow, eyes now gently closed by physician's hand.

Jenny, already beleaguered, already consumed by another inexpressible sorrow, stares within at a barren landscape. A soft footfall beside her, a gentle hand briefly stroking her hair but it is not his, not Daddy's. She watches as the doctor passes her and treads heavily down the creaking stairs.

★　★　★

In the days that followed he was like a child, vulnerable and trusting. She would notice him staring at an ornament or a book then reach out to touch it as though somehow the object might just retain a trace of warmth from the casual brush of her, Liddy's, fingertips. If Jenny was out of sight, he called anxiously for her. He ate whatever she put in front of him, slept when she told him to, bathed and shaved at her gentle suggestion. Everything had been stripped away from him and he was crushed. He would slump silently in a chair, wracked by desolate sorrow and the girl's anger at him, at the lies, was suspended by compassion.

She too felt herself caught in some unwelcome sorcerer's spell; it hadn't happened, wasn't true. There had been no death, no deceit, she had never thought she didn't love Liddy. A veil like a thin wet sheet hung before her eyes, preventing her from seeing clearly, obscuring what had been. At the same time she kept seeing Liddy's staring face, her golden hair spread across the pillow, rippling when the doctor closed the window, just as it would have in life.

A clergyman came and she and Kit sat in a dazed stupor as he drank tea, nibbled a biscuit and talked in a kindly, solemn voice. He brought with him an air of cinders and old dogs. By the end of his visit everything, it seemed, had been arranged. Then later, a brace of village ladies who fussed and clucked solicitously before marching up stairs to wash and lay out the body.

Ironically, their lives had more structure, more ordinariness, then than at any time since Kit's arrival. The girl took up the domestic mantle, and in a way, expurgated her grief quite literally by scouring, scrubbing it out. The mundane tasks helped to lift the spell and allowed her to start to see again. They reaffirmed too her possession of Hadley, its welcome hold over her.

Kit's open grief confused the expression of her own. In comparison hers seemed feeble. She was culpably aware that in keeping things going she had done it a touch too readily, that it had perhaps too easily swallowed up her mourning. Yet Kit was reliant on her. The dreams he shared with Liddy had ended and she had, again guiltily, the shadow of an unworthy thought; there will be no leaving, not now. Not with Liddy gone and Kit......changed. Whenever the thought spluttered into her mind she squashed it, felt ashamed, and wondered if she was, after all, selfish, wicked and bad.

At the funeral she felt remote from it all. It did not somehow connect with her. Even when Liddy came out of the house, out of Hadley for the last time, she did not cry. Only at the grave side did she begin to weep. The scattering of village mourners may have thought it triggered by Kit's inconsolable, unrestrained tears but it wasn't. She had stopped grieving. She was absolved. She was not crying for Liddy but for the unbearable but now inescapable truth, the certainty in reflection and bound with regret, that the love she once had for Liddy was already dead. She looked on as Mr. Martin, sombre maestro, her mother's final conductor, carefully guided the coffin and Liddy's silenced voice, into the earth.

Left alone with the mound of soil in the still of the graveyard, Kit turned and clutched her sleeve, eyes glittering.

'But I can't leave her here! Not here…….'

She took hold of his hand firmly. He was dangerously at the edge of some madness. She squeezed the hand and he blinked at her, retreated once more into child-self and she led him away. That night, from her own desperation, she set down in front of him a full bottle, an empty glass and he began to drink, intensely and methodically.

★　★　★

He drank solidly for a week and it was beginning to run out. He stared in dumb silence, collapsed in a chair, only moving to slop more drink into his glass. They hardly spoke and not at all about Liddy. At best he responded to her in a wide-eyed, scarcely comprehending whisper. By the end of the day she could only tell quite how drunk he was when he tried to stand and she had to help him up the stairs while he mumbled, only half recognising her, and collapsed unconscious on the bed. The next day it would be well into the afternoon before he appeared, his face drained, bereft. She would make him eat even though he did not want to and then it would start all over again, the same broken performance, a trembling, white-knuckled fist pouring the first drink.

She had been kind to him and patient, but on the sixth day, as he filled his glass, she confronted him.

'That's all there is. Just that bottle.'

He looked at her blankly.

'You've drunk it all and it isn't good for you. You've got to stop.' She clasped her hands anxiously. 'Anyway there isn't anymore and there's no money, nothing in the tin.'

He squinted, uncertain.

'No money?' His voice was barely audible.

'Just a few pennies, that's all.'

He fell silent, struggling to understand, and from behind the hollow eyes came a slow, growing comprehension.

'I'm not going to go under,' he said, 'am I?' She searched for words, a grown-up phrase.

'You've got to pull yourself together.'

'Have I?'

'If you don't you will go under, and Liddy wouldn't like all this.'

He stared into the fireplace, 'I didn't phone again that night. I didn't phone. I forgot.' He fell back into silence, withdrew from her. That evening he finished the remaining bottle but managed the stairs alone and her relief was not for him but from her own weariness. He had run away and hidden himself because he was ashamed.

★ ★ ★

He was in a suit and clean-shaven. Only white pouches beneath the eyes and a certain fragility about him betrayed the smart appearance. When he spoke it was nervously,

'Is my tie all right, is it straight?'

'It's fine,' she replied, 'you do seem much better.'

He looked embarrassed, 'Well you were right I suppose. Thanks for looking after me and all that. Went a bit off the rails didn't I?' It was her turn to feel a blush now and he looked away.

'I'm off into town,' he announced, 'get things sorted out.' He patted a bundle of brown envelopes on the table, 'all the loose ends.' She allowed him a small smile, pleased that he was acting responsibly.

'And I'll bring some food back,' he said, eager to please, 'I'll get some groceries in and……'

'No drink,' she said flatly.

He looked downcast, 'No,' he said deflated, 'no, that wouldn't do would it.'

She made a list of the things they needed, sucking thoughtfully at the end of her pencil. After he had gone she cleaned the house and tried to arrange some flowers in a vase. She was in charge now and things had to be kept up. The flowers flopped about wilfully in the too small vase but it was the best she could do. She was clearing the decks for whatever lay ahead, imposing her own order on the house. Later she gathered sweet peas, camomile and larkspur and cycled to the church. It was upsetting to think of Liddy in the ground, covered by earth, and she could only think about her in a passionless way that still, despite everything, disturbed her. She remembered Liddy's voice when she accused her of spitefulness and lack of understanding. But they had lied and deceived her as well and if two wrongs didn't make a right perhaps they cancelled each other out. She wondered if Liddy and her father were together now in heaven, even looking down at her this very minute. It might be that that was what Dad had been waiting for and he had known, like ghosts do, that she would follow him. He might have been at Hadley not for Jenny at all but just for Liddy and that was why she had been so upset when the girl said she saw him. This neat speculation though did not sit right with her, despite its attractive logic. Liddy had passed on, she was gone. Daddy's spirit was, she was sure, still free, still with her. If Daddy had died like a normal person and been buried she might believe that he was gone for good too. The pretty flowers danced on the grave. They had been a gesture, of what she was uncertain. It was the right thing to do but she had yet to forgive, and knew Daddy would have understood why.

★   ★   ★

He was being elusive and it made her wary. Elusive and mysterious. The unspecified sorting out of things took him to town several times over the next few weeks. When she asked about them he brushed it lightly aside mentioning 'the estate' or 'title deeds'; things she did not understand but which, he assured her, she was not to worry her head with. His dependence on her waned and a gentle bantering took its place. She had the uncomfortable feeling that he was, by degrees, gaining ground over her once more and she was losing control. It had just been temporary, an illusion that suited her. Each time he went into town he returned more sure of himself. There were hints again of the old bumptiousness, the cocky charm. He had tapped into something outside of them, outside of Hadley, and it was giving him strength, returning the old self.

He could not bring himself to visit the grave and shuddered when she did. It was then that a look of horror crossed his face and he would gaze at her, silently terrorised, as though she might command him to go. That dread was soon the only trace left of the Kit whose life had collapsed when her mother died. That, and the fact that he was still not drinking, 'on the wagon' as he called it, why, she didn't know.

For Jenny the visits to the grave were a sort of duty, the proper thing to do. Unlike Kit she had assimilated the reality of her mother's death. It left a hollowness in her, that once Liddy filled, but she herself was still complete around it. She didn't care to look too deeply for there was also a quiet relief that now there could be no more plotting, no more falseness. Whenever she was at the grave she thought more of her father, still not at rest, still absent. She was upset Daddy hadn't come back when things had been at their hardest. If she squinted at the sky she could conjure up a romantic vision of him leading Liddy up to heaven, both bathed in a celestial glow, his purpose achieved, walking away forever, not looking back or waving. But it was like a game and any bitterness she felt short-lived. There was still Hadley, her Hadley now, hers by right, and with it confusion, an invisible legacy, her stubborn belief that Daddy was there. He hadn't gone away. He was there with her, for some reason refusing to appear, but waiting.

★ ★ ★

'Right! It's all fixed up!' he was rubbing his hands together and ominously there were two bottles of champagne on the kitchen table before him. He stripped off his suit jacket and draped it carelessly over the back of a chair, then executed a smart click of the heels and an exaggerated waiter's gesture towards the champagne. 'A little celebration's in order!' he chuckled.

'Celebration, what for?'

He sat down, lit a cigarette and leant back. 'Finally got everything sorted out, right down to the last detail.' He grabbed one of the bottles, 'Try a drop?'

She recalled her first taste of champagne in such very different circumstances and shook her head. A dull warning was clanging behind her eyes, a growing alarm at his perky self-satisfaction. The cork popped suddenly and froth spewed from the bottle and spattered onto the floor. He filled a tumbler, carelessly, and held it up, 'The future!'

'What……what's going on?'

'We're off that's what,' he replied, 'off to the bright lights, tinseltown.'

It was his word for London.

She shook her head weakly. The future, a future at Hadley, slithered away from her. 'No……not now. That's all……finished. We can't…….'

'Why not?' he demanded, drawing deeply on his cigarette.

She began to babble. 'Because……because……I don't want it, I want to stay here, I must!' Her voice rose, a thin wail, 'I've got to stay here!'

'You'll get used to it,' he said flippantly, examining the label on the bottle.

'I won't, I won't!' A sullen insurrection emerged from her despair. 'And anyway, you can't make me. It's mine now. Hadley belongs to me.'

He looked up at her from under a darkening brow, 'You just listen to me. We're going and that's an end of it.'

'No!' she shouted, 'I won't and you can't make me!'

He got up slowly and leant on the table. 'This house and everything in it goes under the hammer next week and then we are off, got it?'

'Why?' It was a reedy howl. 'That was all before……Liddy and……we don't have to now, we mustn't!'

'There are debts that's why!' he exploded. 'Bloody money owing all over the place. How the hell do you think we can pay it off otherwise eh, answer me that!'

'Debts?' she echoed, shrinking from his voice, taken aback.

'Yes debts!' he held up a threatening finger, 'And if we're lucky, if we're very lucky, we might just have a bit left over to live off. And if you think I'm staying in this God forsaken backwater one minute longer than I have to then you've got another think coming. I've got to work for Christ's sake, get that through your head, and London is where the work is. Savvy!'

Debts. Owing money to people. Daddy would've hated that. She plunged in desperately, tried another tack.

'You go then, you go and let me stay……' She was nodding, imploring.

'For Christ's sake grow up and don't be so bloody stupid. You ought to be grateful. Not everyone wants to be saddled with a kid. Count your blessings you're not ending up in an orphanage.'

'I won't go.'

The muscles of his neck tensed. For a moment she thought he was going to smack her. Then he sank slowly back into the chair, half-smiled at her. There was an unpleasant smugness in his voice.

'Oh yes you are. You're not spoiling it all. And anyway……,' it was the unbearable pause of someone certain of their trump hand, 'you haven't got a choice. Nor have I.' He pulled a sheaf of documents from the pocket of the hanging jacket and brandished them triumphantly. 'I'm your guardian. It's all legal.'

Guardian. It was an authority word, incontrovertible, a word writ large in thick capital letters oozing power and the sanction of the outside world, a world that no longer felt real. She was battered by it. There was the sickening thud in her heart of a future door slamming quite finally in her face.

'What will happen to me then?' she whispered plaintively.

★   ★   ★

It was all a blur. She watched from the bottom of the garden, her spirit shrivelled like a fallen, withered apple, undiscovered in long grass.

Hadley was being scooped out. An invading wave of strangers had taken possession. Auctioneers had arrived early and by ten o'clock cars had started to appear, a few bicycles and a lone motorcycle. She would not go in though, would not watch as Hadley was laid waste.

Kit was at the front door, greeting people with a welcoming smile, playing the part of mine host. He had his suit on, the one he had worn to 'sort things out', a phrase she now grimly comprehended only too well. She glowered at him, ineffectually. It was hateful, all of these people trampling about in her house, taking bits of it away with them. Some of them were even laughing and joking. She despised them but not as much as she despised Kit, loathed the practised, fluent charm he used to win people over. The scene was more like a sunny garden party, humming with good-humour, as these unwanted guests strolled in and out, poking their noses into everything. She turned her back on it and silently summoned up imprecations upon Kit and the mob he had allowed through her gate. She felt hollowed, empty except for blind outrage at what was happening and her own inability to stop it or even dent its remorseless progress. Worse, she knew Kit was right, horribly right. She had no choice. The authority he now held over her was unchallengeable. She could not win, or even see how to fight.

At first she had wanted to escape from the horror of the auction, get to the sea and let its gentle rhythm still her anguish. But the anger churning inside made her remain and be a distant witness. Kit knew where she was. Earlier, and with sour determination, she had walked away from him, hard-faced, as he set up a table in the garden for tea and lemonade. Deprived of any means to oppose him she used the only expression of dissent left open to her: obstinate, defiant silence. She hadn't managed to get under his skin though and she reflected bitterly that her pity for him when Liddy died had been woefully misguided. He had used her and now was holding her captive with his pieces of paper, the flimsy bond that shackled her to him and let him hold sway over her existence.

She wanted to shout, cry, give some sound, a howl from the deep forest, yet remained silent, restrained by her own determination not to give him the smallest of satisfactions.

Lost now, abandoned even by her imagination, she can endure no more and follows the old trail down to the sea. In the lane she spies the squat figure of Mr. Martin, accompanied by another man, both winding towards the village. She had not seen him arrive. He does not see her now. His voice is borne back to her on a tumble of black pipe smoke, a weary voice that has lost the day.

'Ah well, t'were too rich for my blood. Fine old chair t'was too.' The two men trudge off, round the curving, tree-tunnelled way.

The sea, jewelled by sun. A purring creature indifferent to her and, she thinks, scornful of her puny resistance. Exposed before its drawling disdain, she picks up a stone and hurls it in a high arc through the air and into the water.

'It isn't like that!' she shouts, stung, and in the small sound of her own voice a balance is restored. It is still her ally, not standing in judgement of her.

She takes off her shoes and walks in the sand, squeezing the yellow folds of it between her toes, stares out at the glittering richness, feasting her eyes until they hurt. Then with a child's dull resignation, bowing to a fate decreed by strangers, she puts the shoes back on, climbs up and away from the sea, away from her dear beloved friend. She pauses before vanishing into the trees, a quick, final look filled with salt-stinging tears. Her own slight voice touching the stillness.

'Be seeing you.'

★   ★   ★

'Oh come on Jenny, buck up for goodness sake.'

She glared at him through swelling eyes, sniffed, hiccupped.

'You'll love it when we're there, you see,' he cajoled, 'come on, pull yourself together.' Still she did not move. He raised both hands in exasperation. It was early evening and they were alone. Hadley had been plundered. Its walls bore smudged outlines where pictures once hung, where furniture had been. A few pieces remained, out of place and somehow shrunken in the echoing rooms. Kit had already packed her things in the van, a small suitcase and her box, the spade sticking out of it. He was pleased with himself, it had all gone to plan, and in a softened mood he faced her quivering sobs with emollient coaxing. High white cloud straggled across the sky, pushing away the light, and flecks of rain spotted on his coat. He looked up.

'That's all we need,' he muttered, 'come on, let's get going.' There was growing impatience in his face as he confronted the still and stubbornly unyielding girl. A metallic patter of drizzle jingled on the van's dark roof. Suddenly he banged his hand down on it.

'Right that's it!' he barked, 'I've had enough.' He flung open the rear door, 'Get in the ruddy van and stop snivelling!' It was like a slap across the legs, jolting her to involuntary action. She scrambled quickly in, biting at her lip and fighting back the tears that welled unbidden and unwelcome. She had been determined not to cry, not to let him see her weak, but when the moment came, so swift and appallingly ordinary, she could no longer contain it. He slams the door, shutting her in with the smell and with the debris, the thin wreckage of her life at Hadley. He starts the van and his voice is brusque.

'There's a blanket back there somewhere. Get some sleep, we've a long way to go. And for God's sake pack it up!'

He guns up the engine, drowning out the dinning rain, and the van shudders. She scans anxiously through one of the small rear windows, a circumscribed view of the world she loves. The clutch slips, the van pulls away, a hangman's knot tightening as she sways and bounces down the familiar scrunching drive. Last glimpses she will return to time and time again, pore over and remember with brooding inner sight. No swooping last minute rescue by a shadowy, dreamed spectre, no mystery, just a tiny, insignificant leave-taking in a universe swirling with departures.

Gone now, the bend in the lane has been rounded. She turns away from the window, leavened changeling, as yet unaware of what has truly altered within her. Gone too are the tears. She catches sight of herself in the small driving mirror and is transfixed by her own image, no longer familiar, no longer, or ever again, the self she had been; it is the look of a wolf, unblinking, both baleful and timid, eternal shadowed outcast.

His eyes flicker across the silvered oblong of glass, meet hers for an instant and look away.

'And stop staring at me like that!'

CHAPTER TWENTY-ONE

'Jenny! Get my fags and matches.'

She got up from the kitchen table, found the cigarettes and the matchbox with the crocodile label, sighed and went out through the open back door. She counted the six steps across the high-walled backyard and poked them through the diamond-shaped hole in the lavatory door. It was always the same. He always forgot them. Every day.

'Ta.' Kit's voice was offhand as he scrabbled on the floor for them. She heard the rasp of a match as she returned to the kitchen and his long, slow, contented inhalation. In a few minutes he would fold up his newspaper and yank at the chain. Then, in the kitchen, would finish the mug of tea she had poured out and be off, leaving her to clear up before school. It was the same unrelieved routine every day of the week, as regular as the clock they had brought from Hadley and which now hung on this distant and different wall. She loathed the stifling monotony, wanted to scream but then silence was best, silence with him.

A sputtering hiss as the fag end was dropped down the lavatory, the rustle of his newspaper. She drank her own tea. It was cheap and tasted of pencil shavings. In a minute he would emerge and without looking at her say, 'Right I'm off then', take his camel hair coat from the hook behind the door, drain his mug and go.

She could remember their arrival, some two years before, with absolute clarity. They had driven through the night, hours of bumping and jolting through which she fitfully dozed. It was the stillness of the van when it stopped that woke her. Through the windscreen was the dawn, fading darkness beyond the rain spattered glass.

Blearily, she asked where they were.

'Whitechapel,' he answered, rubbing a hand over his face.

She felt muzzy and confused, 'But what about London?'

'It is London,' he said shortly, offering no explanation. She looked cautiously out expecting stately palaces and distant towers. Instead she found herself in a street lined with tall, careworn houses, hung over with an air of decay. Along its length were one or two warehouses, still shuttered in the early morning, and towards the end an open yard dotted with lorries. She could remember too that at first everything seemed startlingly close-up. There were no distant views. Now though, her once sea-stark eyes were used to it. It was an area of cheap boarding houses where people were in constant drift, in and out of jobs and of the shabby accommodation, sometimes furtively, at night. She couldn't hate it because it wasn't anything, had no sense of place. For months afterwards she counted time backwards. 'Three Fridays ago,' she would say to herself wretchedly, 'I was still there.'

Kit laughed that first morning when she climbed stiffly from the van and went to the front door of the house he had pointed to, laughed and then said, 'Not there, there......' indicating a short flight of steps, leading down to a basement. She noticed then that the upper windows of the house were boarded over.

'It'll do us until we get fixed up,' he said with tired cheerfulness and, as she now knew, absolutely misplaced confidence. He had laughed that first day, made her feel foolish, and she had wept that night, when she found sand in her shoes.

They had four meagre rooms, which she surveyed with distaste. Kit looked affronted.

'It's all right,' he said disgruntled. 'Anyway it's only for a bit.'

She looked round doubtfully at the seedy furnishings, the streaks of sepia grime running down the kitchen walls and at the squat, encrusted stove. Kit's bedroom was at the front, next to a small ill-lit place he described as a sitting room and which they would scarcely use. At the back was the kitchen and a tiny room formed by partitioning off part of it. This was to be hers. Beyond the kitchen, a square backyard and the lavatory, a clammy brick box with a slate roof. The yard had been roofed over with corrugated iron making it even more claustrophobic and cheerless. Inside, the so-called sitting room was crowded by a faded sofa and shelves containing an odd assortment of paperbacks, which in time to come she would read and lose herself in. There was an empty sideboard and, without a word, he brought in a box from the van, took from it the ship in a bottle she had knowingly left behind, and placed it carefully on the scratched surface. The kitchen had a table with three mismatched chairs and a glass fronted cupboard with drawers. A tin bath hung on the wall. The floor was laid with linoleum, an indistinct pattern in brown and fawn. It all had a cramped and dingy air that she never erased, despite buckets of carbolic and hot water.

This was London, her new and unwanted home. Every day she called up memories of her real home in rich, hill-folded Devon, and fed her hatred of him with the trampled but undiminished memories of the life before; the remembered swoop of a gull and the rush and crash of waves. She could only think of Hadley as empty and would not allow the thought of other people living there. Often she sat alone in her room clutching the yellow blouse Annie had given her, her own few precious things spread out on the bed, knowing it would be sunny at home and the sea would be swollen and sparkling. There would be green, the deep green of an enigmatic landscape saturated with dreams and secrets.

It took her a long time to understand quite how big London was and, when she did, she no longer cared for she had withdrawn into her own intensely protected past. She had no curiosity about it at all. The magical place once described to her was thin ink on cheap paper. She didn't see any palaces and the Thames was just a murky sluice that washed listlessly through the capital. Kit spoke excitedly of the West End but never took her there. He found work but it was intermittent and poorly paid. The dazzling theatre world he at first extolled to her gradually, as ambitious auditions led to nothing, became instead a bitterly resented square mile. He raged around the small basement after yet another rejection.

'That lot wouldn't know real talent if it smacked them in the kisser,' he ranted, 'well I'll bloody show them. Just one break that's all I need, just one and they'll be hammering on that door. And you know what? I'll make the buggers wait in the street and laugh in their faces, that's what I'll do.' Blustered out he slumped in a chair, drained by his own rancour. He believed beyond all doubt that he possessed a great talent that some mysterious 'they', a loose conspiracy of agents, impresarios and promoters, denied him the rightful expression of. For her part she maintained a habitual silence with him, never questioning, asking nothing. Silence was best, and she endured his frequent outbursts impassively. Besides, there was some satisfaction, albeit small, in his failure, in the crumbling of his own dream.

In the meantime much of the money they did have was traded over the counter of the public house at the end of the road. Whenever the housekeeping money ran out though, he always managed to dredge up a ten shilling note or a pound, sometimes even a fiver. Yet he always gloomily insisted that they were 'stony broke, skint'. On rent days he sometimes refused to go to the door and made her hide with him in the kitchen. Other times he would exclaim with mock dolefulness, 'The tallyman cometh, snatching the food from the mouths of babes,' and pay up with seeming cheerfulness.

She quickly assimilated the accent, the quick market-stall way of speaking that everyone had, as did Kit. She did it consciously, so as not to be noticed, but with him it seemed natural and not, for once, just an act.

The local school was a walk of some fifteen minutes from what Kit, without apparent irony, called 'the apartment.' Baited at first for her drawling country accent, her contemporaries soon backed off from the uncompromising air of quiet menace she could exude, a menace bolstered by the cool stone she still carried in her pocket and the knowledge of what it could do. After a few days the other children drew uneasily away from her, left in no doubt that she was different and unafraid. It helped too that she was taller, by a couple of inches, than most of them. She privately disdained their scrawny city paleness and inspired something like awe in them on their annual visit to the swimming baths. School was a world she had already become expert at. She resumed and refined her old way of being invisible, of staying one step ahead, wishing all the time that it was as easy in the other, grown-up world.

She existed, at home and at school, in a demi-twilight, warily circling the brittle reality she found herself in and slipping away whenever she could into the shadowy forest of memories and dreams, always yearning for a way back, an escape, the path home. When Kit was working, or just out, she would set out her icons: Daddy's cigarette tin, the stone and listening shell, the yellow silk blouse, Annie's letter and photographs, the little windmill and the twisted gold ring. There were two other photographs she had stolen away too; the one Daddy had taken of her, years before, at the picnic, and the one of him that had been at Liddy's bedside. Beside them, completing the ritual, was her spade. They looked smaller here, enshrined in the anaemic light, diminished by their distance from home. She gazed at the photograph of her father, at the square, handsome face, eyes confident and, attractively, a shade sardonic. He could never be here of course, no matter how hard she might wish it. He could only be there, at Hadley. She sank inside, downcast. She was alone, with no one to turn to. It was up to her, to find a way and to act. As time passed and childhood slipped by unnoticed, 'the finding', as she called it, became a consuming obsession. Running away was out of the question. She knew Kit's guardianship had the weight of the law behind it and people who broke the law were always caught. Less pragmatically, she felt if she did run she would be marked out somehow, policemen would chase her with their whistles and catch her. As she grew older her perspective on it changed. Running away would not make her free because Kit would know where to find her. And if she didn't go home but hid somewhere there was always the chance that somebody would recognise her. Worse, even if she was never found the fact of him would still be there, always hanging over her. She had to destroy the power of his piece of paper, break his hold over her forever. Severance, and then burning her boats for good. That was the only way, if she could but find it.

It was after an unremitting string of rejections that the real change in Kit began, slowly at first but gathering speed, inexorable. He became maudlin and desperate, at one moment tussling with and then shying away from some confrontation within himself. Baffled and angered by the rebuffs, his once undoubted self-confidence was being eaten away. He kept up a familiar jokiness in public but in the shadowed basement was immersed in uncomprehending exasperation, always on edge.

Often woefully short of money, he would rush to the letterbox each morning and return to the kitchen either empty-handed and dejected or, less often, smiling widely and brandishing a brown envelope. The cheque it contained would be held up and kissed.

'You little life-saver! Just in the nick of time!'

It was, he told her, money owed from past performances, staggered payments. Once he said it was a tax rebate. Yet the intervals between the brown envelopes saw them reduced to a spartan diet; cheap, soggy, end of the day vegetables from the market and butcher's scraps that she lied were for the dog. The pile of coke in the covered yard was agonisingly eked out and he no longer so easily found a stray note in his wallet. She knew why. He was drinking, and heavily. Sometimes the fire wasn't lit for days and she would sit in her coat or stay in bed. It was then that the musty dankness of the basement crept slyly back and its stained walls seemed even more depressingly drab, unrelieved by the glim of comfort the fire provided. Kit would be out then, and always late back, his return signalled by a crash in the dark, a muttered curse or a giggle as, fuddled and drunk, he stumbled to his bed. One morning she discovered him in a contorted stupor on the old sofa, dead drunk asleep with make-up smudged on his face. A guttural clicking sound was coming from his open mouth and on the tiled hearth was a congealing pool of acrid vomit like yellow porridge. Floating in it was a pink dental plate with two false front teeth, the essence of his once winning smile. He rolled into consciousness as she returned to the room with a clanking bucket of steaming water. She looked down at him unsympathetically.

'I could do it you know, all I need is a chance, just one, a proper chance!' he whispered desperately then slid back into oblivion.

It was a decline she witnessed with dry caution. If he was losing she must be winning, yet she must never let down her guard. She lived, in all senses, as distantly from him as the tiny accommodation would allow.

When, with simmering reluctance, he was forced to sell the van, its ragbag of contents were dumped unceremoniously in the narrow hallway. A battered box of tools, a filthy striped blanket and a dented jerrycan. Redundant now, they served as a reminder of what he had lost and he would look down and swear as he squeezed past them.

Then, in March, she experienced a jolt and, with it, a new understanding of the self she was becoming. It was a brown envelope day and Kit had left early, whistling. She had seen it often enough to know that by evening his good mood would have evaporated and he would again be miserable. Most of the cash would be gone too. As usual she was sitting at the back of the class. It was geography and, from the world map unfurled like a multi-coloured sail from above the blackboard, it seemed that half the world belonged to Great Britain. At first she thought the hollow ache in her stomach was hunger but it was low down and worsening. Then to her horror she thought she'd wet herself. She shot an anxious hand into the air, was excused and quickly dashed to the lavatory.

There, squatting over the bowl, she discovered it was blood, a thin pink trickle, and let out a squawk.

'Who's in there,' it was a grown-up voice, a woman's, 'who's that?'

'Jennifer Hawker,' she grimaced, clutching her stomach.

'What's up then?' It wasn't a teacher, she could tell from the voice.

'I'm bleeding!'

'Well come out and let's get you seen to. What you done, cut yourself 'ave you?'

'No! It's......' she struggled for a word and could not find it, 'it's in my knickers!' A gnawing ache gripped her stomach and a shuddering moan was wrung from her. There was silence outside then the same voice, calm and level, slowly comprehending.

'How old are you Jennifer?'

'Fourteen,' she writhed, overcome with nausea.

'You come out now, love.'

With difficulty the girl pulled her clothing together and unbolted the door. Standing there with a kettle in her hand was one of the dinner ladies. She was fat in a strong, solid way but her expression had a gentleness that surprised Jenny; the battalion of dinner ladies were notoriously fierce. The girl crept out, frightened and embarrassed and avoided the woman's eyes.

'That's just your monthly sweetheart.' The dinner lady came towards her and laid a heavy, solicitous arm around Jenny's shoulders.

'Monthly? But it's blood, I'm bleeding!'

The woman tut-tutted, 'Oh blimey, don't you know, first one is it? Oh Gawd, I remember, thought I was dyin' I did,' she chortled, the massive, marbled arm wobbling, making the girl shake.

'What is it, what's happening to me?'

The woman was taken aback, 'Don't you know nothing then love. What's your mum think she's up to, eh?' she shook her head. 'You come and sit down for a bit.'

What followed was short and blunt but by no means insensitive. Jenny listened in wide-eyed astonishment. The dinner lady made it sound so ordinary, so commonplace, yet it was shatteringly strange.

'......and you look after that little kipper of yours. There'll be plenty of fellas after it. Silly great buggers they are. Just don't get yourself knocked up like I did. You 'ang on to it till you finds a good 'un. Gawd knows there's few enough of them.' She scrutinised the girl's face. 'Plenty chasin' you all right,' then giggled 'but us girls gotta watch out!' The 'us girls' jangled incongruously. 'Go on now, you push off home. I'll tell them.......' she jerked a businesslike thumb towards the school, 'tell 'em you was took sick.'

Jenny had listened intently, her brow furrowed. She remembered the grinning boys in the playground and, from long ago, Lally on the beach. She leant forward and asked solemnly, 'Is that what fuck is?'

She dragged herself home deep in thought, searching for some trick in it all yet aware of the dinner lady's candour. It was so unlikely but then there was the blood, the dribble of evidence confirming what had been said. She had been admitted to adult secrets but it was intimidating knowledge. It both gave and took something from her. Looking up she realised she was nearly home. At her feet lay a dead cat in the gutter, the green eyes glazed and blank. She turned her nose up, looked away and walked on.

She had her key ready but the basement door was ajar. She pushed it open and went in. He must have come back for something.

'Kit?' There was no answer. A cool peace enclosed the dim interior. She struggled out of the coat that was now too small for her and hung it up. Passing down the hallway her foot banged against the jerrycan and a flat clank fractured the silence. She knew she had locked the door and was puzzled. Perhaps he had returned, gone out again and forgotten. It would be just like him.

She went into the kitchen and made a pot of tea. The dragging ache in her tummy was still there. Sipping from a brown mug she was glad of the soothing warmth of the tea.

Aspirin. That's what the dinner lady said. Aspirin would make it go away. She opened a drawer and rummaged for the small brown bottle. It wasn't there. Kit always had aspirins for when he felt bad in the mornings. There would be some in his room. She put a tea cosy on the pot, went to his door and opened it. It swung back and thumped noisily against the wall. Two prone figures in the bed sat bolt upright, jolted from sleep.

'Christ it's a kid!' The outraged voice belonged to a startled, white-faced woman. 'A bloody kid!' she screamed at Kit in a hard-edged voice, pulling the sheets up to cover her naked breasts, 'Brings me 'ere and you got a kid in the house? Never said nothing' bout a kid!' Then, modesty discarded, she lashed out at him. He put his arms up to protect himself and the girl saw that he too was naked. A wild fist caught him in the face and his nose began to bleed, dotting the sheets, but even then he didn't take his eyes from the girl, an unfocused but coldly venomous stare. The woman leapt from the bed and threw on her clothes, knocking a half-empty bottle of whisky to the floor.

Brusquely she plumped up her auburn hair and straightened her skirt. 'You ought to be ashamed, you drunken scum,' she lambasted him, 'brings me 'ere when you got a kid. Never mentioned that did you, what time does your missus get 'ome then you bloody swine, disgustin' you are!' she sneered and bristled past Jenny. 'Out of my way love.' Her absurdly high heels clicked along the passage and she cursed as she cracked an ankle against the van's jetsam, slamming the front door behind her.

A baleful silence then, suddenly, Kit's still slurred voice barking at her.

'What the hell are you doing here! You shouldn't be here!' It was as though the woman's anger had passed into him, coalesced with his own and emerged twice as virulent.

'I'm sick!' she shouted, pierced by his mad stare. 'They sent me home because I'm sick!'

He swung his legs out of bed and yanked on his trousers. 'Sick? You make me sick that's what! You're enough to give anyone the screamin' abdabs!'

She stood absolutely still. His thin pale chest was heaving and she saw as if for the first time his coarsened looks; the reddened face no longer fine-featured, the bleary eyes and mottled skin, and felt a shudder of revulsion.

'You weren't faithful,' she blurted, 'you weren't faithful to your promise, to Liddy.' For a second he was rocked by what she had said.

'Promise!' he bellowed, 'What promise? I never promised. I'll do what I flamin' well like!' He sprang across the room at her, both hands flailing in an explosive flurry of blows. 'Bitch, bitch, bloody little bitch!' he hissed as she crumpled under the onslaught and crashed to the hard, shiny floor. The fallen bottle bumped repeatedly against her and the overpowering smell of the spilt whisky, intolerably astringent, filled her head as she passed out.

★   ★   ★

There was only one mark on her face, a shallow red scrape along the line of her jaw. She mopped it gingerly with a damp flannel. Her arms and shoulders were heavily bruised and when she presented her back to the small mirror above the kitchen sink, and peered stiffly round to look, it too was smudged with purplish yellow bruises.

She was standing in the tin bath and shivering though it was not cold. She had bitten her bottom lip but couldn't remember doing it. The kettle began to bubble out a thin plume of steam and she stepped shakily from the bath and poured its contents into the milky bathwater. She swirled it round and sat down in the warm water with her knees hunched up. She was weighted down by a numb inertia and her mind could not think.

She did not know where Kit was. The basement had been empty when she came to, lying across her bed with no recollection of how she got there. After a while she struggled first to her knees and then, painfully, to her feet. That had been hours ago and it was dark now.

Climbing out of the bath she patted herself dry and got dressed, then emptied the tub with a saucepan, slowly scooping out the water and pouring it down the sink. The tea she had made when she first got back was still on the table, just as it had been, as though nothing had happened. She cleared it away, made a fresh pot, and dreamily took the mug into her room and lay down. She longed for the wireless, for the warm and friendly voices to wash cosily over her, take away the ache in her back and the bruises, take away the knowing. She wanted to be home, returned to a time and a place where none of this could have been. But there was only silence and what had happened loomed before her, all too real and impossible to ignore. She sat up with difficulty and sipped the warm tea. The little windmill was next to the bed. She picked it up, spun the sails and remembered her room at Hadley, the windmill in its place by the window, its sails touched by sea breezes. Green beyond the window, blue farther away still. Home. Her place. Blue and green.

That night, without warning, the past returned and with it an enigma. She dreamt again of the woman pulled from the sea, her dress like a white sheet shimmering with water and sunlight, and when she woke the vision was still with her and remained. It brought back the memory of Hadley even more vividly although it had not been in the dream and seemed unconnected with it. She lay in bed baffled by the identity of the rescued woman and of the rescuer, always out of view. It was curiously familiar, almost reassuring, yet it was really only a fragment, a moment from what she thought must be a much longer story.

When she tried to rise, her back and shoulders locked in a jigsaw of stiffness and pain. She fell back onto the bed with a groan. It was only by moving slowly, legs first, up to sitting then finally onto her feet, that she could get up. Faltering steps to the kitchen, shoulders tensed. It felt better when she moved, the muscles gradually unknotting. She had already decided to stay off school but was shocked to discover that it was already mid-morning. There was no sign of Kit. She peered apprehensively through his open door but the room was exactly as it had been. She crossed the yard to the lavatory and looked down into the bowl. No tell-tale cigarette end floating in the water. He had never stayed out all night before. She had been alone.

When he did return it was as though nothing had happened. He breezed into the kitchen munching a green apple, casually patted the teapot to see if it was warm and poured a mugful for himself. Whatever ideas she might have had, that he would return contrite and ashamed, disappeared. She could tell simply from the cocky way he stood that he was untroubled by remorse. All he did was look down at her in a half-challenging, half-dismissive way as if daring her to mention it. She felt anxious as he stood there, cowed by the violence she now knew was in him. Her mouth seemed to be twitching uncontrollably, giving away her fear of him, revealing weakness. Finally, and absurdly, she said, 'Where did you get that?'

'What?'

'The apple.'

'Scrounged it.' He shrugged nonchalantly and held it out to her, 'Go on. You can finish it off if you want.' It was not appeasement but rather a clumsy attempt to return them to the way they had been. She stared at the half-eaten apple and remembered his false front teeth. If she took it she would be accepting the pretence that nothing changed. She shook her head.

'I don't want it.'

'Suit yourself,' he said and bit again into the clean whiteness of it.

'I'm sick,' she offered, as if in explanation.

'With what?' he asked with a pointed lack of curiosity.

'Just sick.'

'Should be in bed then. Big enough to look after yourself now.'

'I don't want to go to bed. It's not that sort of sick.'

'Please yourself.' He was full of himself again and it was no surprise when he said he had an audition, just the fact of it had rekindled his own imagined celebrity and swept away the moodiness.

'I'm off down the 'dilly,' he called from his room, 'just slap on a bit of the old war paint. Be late back I expect. Might have some celebrating to do.'

She crept along the passage and looked in through the crack between door and frame. He was sitting in front of the mirror. Tubes of make-up, combs, brushes and cotton wool were strewn across the dressing table. He turned his face slowly from side to side, staring intently at the reflection. Then the eyes lightened and a small smile appeared. He looked straight at the mirror and slightly down, dramatically highlighting his expression. He was practising, she thought, rehearsing his appearance and she recoiled from the unhealthy self-absorption. Quietly, she returned to the kitchen and sat at the table.

Five minutes later he came back in, dressed in his suit and sweepingly assured. His face looked different, smoother and with elements of the old boyishness. It was the make-up. She had seen it often enough, this sudden transformation, and it no longer impressed her as it had when she was a child. Then she had thought it clever, like magic. Now she found it shabby. She looked sadly down at the table.

'Don't wait up,' he smirked in a voice sliding with conceit, 'keep the home fires burning.'

CHAPTER TWENTY-TWO

She was suffocated by the basement, trapped inside the stifling space that had witnessed her demeaning humiliation; a humiliation that blurred and confounded her thoughts of escape. There was no refuge here, no air to breathe. She couldn't win against his violence and would always be his prisoner. Yet it could not continue. She was frightened but not crushed. There had to be a way, the finding must be uncovered.

She examined the bruises again. They were less painful but the ugly yellow had spread across her skin. The graze on her face had tightened into a glassy red weal. It was a shameful badge of his hold over her, plain for all to see. It was unendurable to bear the mark of his fist. She could not allow herself to be seen like this. And from within her fierce frustration, quite coolly, she realised she didn't have to. She could mask the wound, conceal it, and she thought, acknowledging a kind of justice, by his own means.

Liddy's old vanity case was still on the dressing table in his room. She took it to her own and sat with it open on the bed. There was a mirror inside the lid and she scrutinised the gash again. When the case had been Liddy's, the girl wondered at the neat rows of matching silver-topped bottles, each containing some mysterious ingredient, and at the ranks of little tubes, their crimped ends carefully folded down as they were used up. It bore no resemblance to that now. The box was a sticky jumble of partly used creams and open tubes of congealing lotion, all shades of flesh. It looked and was dirty and uncared for with puffs of smeared cotton wool tossed casually, unthinkingly, into it. A small tin of talcum powder, not properly closed, had cast a fine sugared dusting over everything. There were tweezers and scissors, thick black waxy pencils and golden torpedoes of lipstick.

It had been the tubes she had seen him use most. She picked them out and read the names: Golden Skin, Rose Blush, Ivory Sheen. She arranged them in a line on the bedspread and tested them on her hand. She decided on Golden Skin, shyly squeezed the tube and the beige cream squiggled into her palm. She brushed it lightly along the red mark, wincing and imitating Liddy's quick, flickering fingers. Nothing had prepared her for the immediacy of it. It was like correcting a pencilled mistake with India rubber. The red line vanished under the cream. If she looked closely, pressed her face up to the mirror, she could just make out the rough surface of broken skin beneath it. But to all intents and purposes it had gone. She smiled with delight. It was so surprisingly simple. Quickly she rubbed the sticky stuff over the rest of her face, holding back her hair to smooth it across her forehead. It felt strange and stiff, this extra skin, a rigid disguise beneath which she could hide, breathe again. Encouraged, she swiftly drew in dark, arching eyebrows. They didn't quite work, looked too clumsy. She wiped them off and did them again more carefully. Finally she picked out a pale pearl lipstick and, puckering like Liddy had, applied the sweet, greasy colour to her mouth.

She sat back from the mirror and stared in awe at her reflection. Gone was the faint adolescent puffiness, gone too were all traces of her uncertain childhood. She felt she was holding a picture in front of her real face, a picture of a young woman who was quite different. This person had poise, grace, a sort of beauty. And she looked older. With a bit more practice she could pass for years older. This couldn't be her, but it was. She smiled. She liked herself. She had set out to conceal but the make-up had enhanced, brought out in her what was already there but hidden. It made her hopeful, irrationally optimistic. She began to dance around the tiny room, floating lightly to a lilting, remembered melody. She whirled happily, arms outstretched. It was such a wonderful discovery, that she could be someone else. The tune in her head became louder, more jubilant. She sang out loud to it, a triumphant lah, lah, lah, spinning round faster and faster until the room merged into a blur before her eyes and, hopelessly giddy, she collapsed onto the bed. The vanity case tumbled noisily to the floor. Its bottles and tubes rolled and clattered across the linoleum. She lay back and laughed, her ears were singing and the room was still waltzing around her. She didn't care about the mess on the floor. She would just shovel it all back into the case, he would never know. The giddiness began to slow and come to a halt. She liked the person she saw in the mirror, she liked her so much.

Still smiling to herself, she leant over to admire again her new reflection but the case was upside down. As she picked it up the remaining contents tumbled out, together with a piece of velvet covered card, the same oval shape as the case. Then, like butterflies, a handful of envelopes fluttered to the floor. She picked one up and turned it over. It was addressed to Liddy, to Hadley. Thoughtfully she examined the case. Inside, the bottom was ragged and unfinished. The piece of covered card fitted it exactly. She turned her attention to the white envelope. A moment of guilty hesitation. It would be sneaking to look. Nosy parker. Liddy's private things.......The envelope had been opened carefully, with a knife, and she remembered then her mother sat at the bureau, uncomfortably business-like and slightly prim, a silver paper knife in her hand. 'Just bills dear, as usual.' She could contain herself no longer and withdrew the single rustling sheet pensively, unfolded it and smoothed it on her lap.

Dearest Liddy,

Of course I feel the same way. You mustn't be so silly. You know how I've felt about you ever since Trial by Jury so just stop all this worrying. I'm going to try for the 10th, if everything goes according to plan, just need to get a few loose ends tied up here first but I'll be down no later than the 20th. Hold on till then my darling. Will telephone as soon as I arrive.

Can't wait but must dash now,
Love,
Kit

She read it again quickly, released and heedless now of the broken taboo, for at the head of the notepaper, beneath the scrawled London address she now lived at, the letter bore a simple, irredeemably treacherous cipher: *20th. May 1945.*

★   ★   ★

They knew each other. They'd known each other all along. Liddy hadn't just been swept off her feet or taken in by him. It had all been planned. The last secret was staring her in the face, hidden in a bundle of hoarded letters that might have stayed secret forever. It was all revealed now, out in the open. The shock of it sickened her, the sour collusion a tawdry mosaic of intrigue and deception. She recalled with a sinking rush Liddy's startled exclamation when Kit first arrived and how quickly they'd got on together, how famously. It was all set up and she had been piggy-in-the-middle. They must have planned it for ages, must have known each other even when Daddy was alive, and then when he died…….It was a shattering, chilling revelation that slithered and wound itself around her brain. How could they do it, how could they? She pounced on the remaining letters and devoured them with astounded, appalled fascination. She read them repeatedly, picking over the sketchy details they disclosed with intense revulsion. It was too horrible, hateful. She tried to sort them, to make it a coherent story, but some were undated and others missing. They refused order and sprawled at her feet. She couldn't pinpoint when it had all started but it seemed their plan had been for Kit to appear on the scene and gradually inveigle himself into Hadley and win the little girl over. He had done that all right, the only thing they hadn't planned for was the storm and Jenny's own unwitting role as rescuer. She raged at her naivety in believing Daddy had guided his boat through the storm and to her bay. It hadn't been that at all. It had been pure chance.

She cursed them both then, the little room echoing to that single, curt word heard so long ago and now spat out as she crushed the letters in her hands. They had double-deceived her, her and Daddy. They had lied and tricked and cheated without a thought for anyone but themselves and she had been ripped away from all she loved and dumped in this squalid, sunless slum a million miles from the sea, a million miles from home. She stared at the scrunched-up papers she had thrown down, at the ugly, half-revealed scenario, and a madness seized her. There had to be more, hidden somewhere. She kicked them away and hurled the vanity case into a corner. She must know all of it, the truth, however loathsome. She must, must know it all, the whole illusion they had ransacked her life with. In a frenzy, she dashed to his room and wrenched open drawers and cupboards, rummaging amongst his belongings and found nothing. She flung open the musty wardrobe, went through all of his pockets and still found nothing, no hidden evidence. Beneath his bed she unearthed a suitcase and yanked it out. It was locked. She scrabbled in the toolbox in the hall, took out a long screwdriver and angrily wrenched the skimpy clasps from the cheap fibreboard. It too was empty.

She stands with hands on hips in frustration, scours the room, and sees at once what in her haste she missed. There, in the open shelf of the bedside cabinet, a heap of papers jammed untidily in. It would be just like him not to care, not to bother to hide them. She swooped on them, pulled one out. It was screwed into a loose ball and she flattened it out impatiently but it was not a lover's letter. It was not from Kit or Liddy or anyone she knew. It was typed and had bold letters across the top.

Verney & Dampier, Solicitors
Yardarm Row
Exeter

Sir,
<u>*Mrs. Charlotte Elizabeth Hawker, deceased*</u>
In accordance with the terms of the trust fund established from the will of the above I enclose our quarterly cheque in the amount of £34 10s 0d made out to yourself as guardian of Miss Jennifer Hawker, daughter of the deceased, for the purpose of care and welfare as per the terms of the trust fund to which you are signatory.

It was signed with an illegible scrawl. She pulled out another. The date was different and this time it was for thirty-six pounds but otherwise it was the same. Exactly the same. They all were and went back to when they had first arrived in Whitechapel. She reads them all with cold comprehension and inside a part of her steals away between remembered trees to a secret lair in a cool woodland.

She stuffs the letters carelessly back, walks slowly to her room and in a stealthy, abstracted way sets out her little makeshift altar and waits for him, in darkness and in silence.

CHAPTER TWENTY-THREE

He was urinating in the kitchen sink, rocking on his heels and swaying drunkenly as a spluttering stream splashed against the enamel. She stood in the doorway, glaring at his back through the gloom.

'Where's all the money?' Her voice was low and blunt. It wasn't what she had planned to say.

'Wha......?' He looked back over his shoulder, unabashed, and fumbled with his trousers, 'Whassat?'

'Where's all that money gone?'

He thrust his face forward, squinting. 'Pissed it all away,' he sniggered then tottered to the kitchen table and clutched it. 'Whass'all this anyway? Should be in bed......not......not......creeping up like a, like a ......bloody spook. You jus' bugger off. S'bloody late.' He gulped as though about to retch. Jenny flicked on the light and he recoiled from it.

'I want to know what's happened to the money!' she demanded.

'Told j'er. Drunk it. Turn bloody light off.' He rubs his eyes and peers at her quizzically, 'Wass all that stuff on your face?' She had all but forgotten the painted layer but ignores him.

'I don't mean just tonight. I mean all of it, all the money you've robbed me of.'

'Wha' say?'

'The trust money! You stole it!'

He stared at her, a momentarily frozen look on his face, then mumbled, 'Dunno what'cher talkin'......'bout......' He was wobbling, still gripping the table. In the weak yellow light his face looked blotched and bloated. She stepped forward.

'Liar! I know all about it. You stole it from me. It should've been for me not you. You're a liar and a cheat and I hate you! That's why you got yourself made my guardian wasn't it? And you told me there wasn't any money. It was all lies!' To her astonishment she found herself jabbing an accusing finger at him. For a fleeting second he looked disconcerted, almost crestfallen, then the darkness on his face gathered and broke.

'Shuddup! You shuddup you! Mouthin' off at me......'

'No I won't! You tricked Liddy too because she was lonely. If she'd known what you were really like she'd never have wanted to marry you. It was all an act to get your own way and I've found you out!' Her eyes were clouded with tears as she slammed the letters down on the table. 'You can't trick me anymore. I know everything.'

He faltered, looked down at the envelopes then picked one up and read the address, holding it close to his face.

'Where d'you get these?'

'They fell out of the vanity case. They were hidden but I found them and now I know.'

He dropped the envelope back onto the table, gazed into the hollowness of the room and was silent.

'And I found the money letters in your room and I don't care because it was my money, meant for me,' she railed hotly, wiping her wet face with her hand. 'Liddy would never have trusted you if she'd known. I bet you twisted everything to persuade her. I bet you said you loved her when you didn't really just to get her away from me and Daddy. She'd never have trusted you because she was gentle and good and......'

'She never was!' he crowed suddenly, head thrown back. 'She wanted it as much as I did! She wanted to get away, she wanted to live!' He was staring at her, hands stiff and white on the table. 'And you're wrong, wrong. I loved her, I did truly!' It was a clumsy declaration, stripped bald of artifice. Tears dripped from his face as he confronted her. 'It wasn't supposed to happen like this. It was what she wanted, what she always wanted! You think I was the first do you? Well I wasn't! Grow up for Crissake, it's not bloody never-never land!'

She lunged across the space between them and leapt at him, clawing and gouging at his face and chest. The scraping of the table as it skids across the floor, his startled white face as he shields himself and above everything her own explosive howl of rage. She hardly hears his cursing, hardly feels the lurching, wild blow that smashes into her cheekbone, cracking the stiff mask and sending her sprawling backwards, insensible, the smooth, round, speckled stone, half-drawn from her pocket, rolling noisily from her hand.

★   ★   ★

Morning, and rain drums steadily on the corrugated roof over the backyard. She drags herself up from the hard, chill floor where she spent what remained of the night and automatically rights the upturned kitchen table. In her mind she hears once more familiar tunes from the wireless, scents the sea-spiked breezes of home and, curiously, there is an encouraging, gently prompting voice.

'Work to be done Jenny, work to be done.'

She collects up the scattered envelopes and puts them neatly on the table as if they are the morning post. There is no pain, just a floating sense of dislocation. She washes her face, rinsing off the smudged make-up. As always his cigarettes and matches are on the shelf above the sink, this time with a handful of small coins. She can hear him asleep in his room, not snoring but breathing out with a wheezing, whistling noise. Mechanically, she begins the daily round of chores, the familiar routine of clearing up and putting out the rubbish. Retrieving her stone from a corner of the kitchen she returns it, absently, to her pocket. For once it does not seem such a drudging grind and when the kitchen is once again ship-shape she opens the back door and looks up at the sound of rain before setting a kettle to boil for his tea. They are later than usual. Much later.

The tea is brewed and his mug put out ready for him. She fills the kettle again and while it boils fetches the heavy jerrycan from the hall, quietly so as not to wake him. Struggling to unscrew the brass cap she sniffs warily at the bitingly clean smell of petrol. She picks up the can with both hands and carries it out across the yard, opening the lavatory door with her foot. As always there is a dampness of crumbling brick inside the shadowed chamber and the door swings back on its hinges, creaking plaintively, as she rests the spout of the can against the porcelain bowl, its scrazed surface a network of brown threads. It makes a funny glugging noise as she tips it up and pours, a noise that makes her smile. Leaving the door open she returns to the basement, puts the now empty can back in the hall and fills a bucket with hot water from the kettle. Then, with a bar of carbolic and a scrubbing brush, scours the lavatory as she has so often before. She hums as she works and soon cannot smell the petrol at all, just the sharp, wood-like aroma of the disinfectant. Satisfied, she tips the grey water from the bucket down the sink and, pouring tea for herself, sits at the table. The clock on the wall shows nine-thirty but she will not be going to school today. She can still hear the music in her head and wishes it was a real wireless, like at home.

A cough from his room, the rustle of bedclothes. A creak as he struggles to sit up then a succession of heaving coughs followed by a low groggy moan. He shambles into the kitchen looking frail and spectral, his skin like mother-of-pearl. He is wearing just vest and trousers and holding his head in both hands, the tangled hair escaping over his fingers.

'Oh Christ!' he leans into a corner of the kitchen, face still cupped, 'Oh my Christ!'

'Tea?' she asks pleasantly, her hand hovering over the pot. Slowly he uncovers his face and squints at her through weak, raw eyes. Again, it is as though he does not remember, does not choose to remember. He nods tersely and watches as the thick, brown liquid splashes into his mug. She adds milk from a bottle, three heaped spoonfuls of sugar, stirs it for him and pushes it across the table. He steps forward, picks it up, withdraws again to his corner and sips noisily. He looks down into the mug, swirls it around and swigs again, his Adam's apple bobbing up and down as the hot, sweet liquid mingles with last night's gin and commences its habitual alchemy.

'More tea?'

He shakes his head, wrapped in his hangover, then slaps the mug down on the edge of the stove and makes quickly for the back door.

'No. Gotta go,' he says thickly, already fumbling with the top button of his trousers. She stares at the space where he stood, a tremble of expectation, of daring to do, shimmering through her. The lavatory door creaks behind him, the rattling latch snaps to. Silence between the long, slow ticking of the clock.

'Jenny! Bring my fags and box o' crocs.'

She leaps up at his voice, her chair grates back across the floor.

'Did you hear? C'mon, hurry up,' then irritably, 'bloody stinks in here.'

Quickly she scoops up the cigarettes and the matchbox with the crocodile label and, holding them out like an offering, stumbles into the covered yard, into the enveloping sound of rain. She blinks at the diamond-shaped hole in the door, hesitates, then stuffs them into the opening. A soft patter as they fall to the floor and he grunts as he leans forward, retrieves them. She steps back, cannot take her eyes from the black diamond as she retreats to the kitchen. The rasp of a match and his first slow inhalation of the day. Half closing the kitchen door she ducks down behind it, eyes tightly closed. The dull tick-tock of the clock and the beating rain combine in a jangling percussion. Nothing happens. Crouched and shivering, she opens her eyes again and hears the faint extinguishing hiss as he drops the cigarette into the bowl. Then a strangely soft, almost delicate sound: a crumpling, implosive flash blowing itself out almost as soon as it had begun and filling the yard with a blustering cloud of damp dust and caustic smoke. No loud bang, no explosion, it was more like a far rumble of thunder. She got up and peered round the door. The lavatory was still intact. It hadn't been blown to pieces. Even the door was still firmly shut. She knew she would never open it, never look. A charred stink like burnt wet leaves filled the yard as the cloud began to settle. He was dead. Beyond all doubt he was dead.

She shut the kitchen door against the smell and, quite calmly, like the sensible one in a children's adventure story, sat down at the table and composed a list of things to take. It was a brief manifest. Her few clothes, some food, her special things, wash bag, blanket and a clutch of tubes and bottles from the vanity case. She fetched them and packed them carefully in an old canvas bag Kit had kept in his room. Then she methodically cleaned the basement, even the already spruce kitchen. The letters were dropped in the stove before she went through his wardrobe and drawers until she found the document; the slender, legal notice that had bound her to him, and watched without expression as it too curled and blackened in the flames. Afterwards, she inspected each room with a charlady's ruthless eye for cleanliness and order. She discovered Kit's wallet on the floor by his bed. To her astonishment it was stuffed with notes. She counted them twice. It came to more than two hundred pounds. She folded the bundle, started to put it in her pocket then stopped, peeled off one of the five pound notes, slipped it back in the wallet and left it on the bedside cabinet. In the little sitting room she picked up the ship in a bottle, the trophy she had won all those years before, raised it above her head and hurled it ferociously against the wall. She turned, marched out and shut the door.

At last satisfied and with her things packed and ready, she returned to the kitchen and sat quietly, holding the special shell to her ear and letting the captured sound of a distant sea ebb her towards nightfall, all mystery finally laid to rest.

The rain had ceased and the early evening was still as she stepped out into the twilight. No remorse, no guilt. She had done it, found the way by herself without help from anyone or anything and was released. Above, the clap of a startled pigeon's wings as it rises from the rooftops. She looks up at the unpredictable sky and at a strange light emanating from behind a ragged bolt of black cloud straddling the heavens, a luminous glow shining through from the other side. An unexpected draught of wind swirled down the street, caught her hair, and, remembering, she starts off down it for the last time. In her pocket is the cool smoothness of the round stone. She is the outlaw now.

CHAPTER TWENTY-FOUR

She ducked down behind the ferns as the park keeper approached. He trod heavily across the trimmed grass, trailing puffs of vapour in the cold, misty, early morning. She felt safely hidden, cloistered within the dripping green of the spinney bordering the tailored lawns. Even though he was heading squarely in her direction she knew she was not his quarry. He was behaving in the way people do when they think they are alone.

When he reached the fountain, an inelegant cast-iron fish poised over an ornamental pond, he dug into his pocket and produced a spanner. Stretching up he tapped the fish's nose and waited, spanner held in mid-air, then clouted it impatiently.

'Come on you ugly sod.'

There was a subterranean gurgle and a clot of water erupted from the creature's gaping mouth and splattered into the pond below. The man watched as the trickle of water hiccupped then steadied into a tinkling cascade. He lit a cigarette, coughed vigorously, and spat at the ground before trudging off.

There was bracken in the little place and small clumps of primroses. It was a taste of old pleasures, an improbable field of green in the heart of the city. She breathed its smells and touched its earth, sensations so long withheld and now luxuriously indulged once more. The night had been spent concealed there, numbingly cold in the dark, only snatches of sleep.

When the park keeper was out of sight she bobbed up again and tentatively broke cover like a nervous deer, cantering to the fountain and drinking from it. She wiped her mouth with the back of her hand, looked round guardedly, and slipped back to the spinney.

The great shadowed building, shrouded in darkness the night before, was now revealed in the clearing mist; the massive sprawl of what she knew from pictures was Buckingham Palace, fronted by an elaborate stone confection of a dour Queen Victoria.

It had been a strange, dreamy journey through the night, across a city she lived in but hardly knew. Leaving Whitechapel she had been taken aback to find the Tower of London so close by. Somehow she'd always thought that the famous places were far away, concentrated together in another bit of the city that was forbidden her. From there she found and followed the hooting river, its winking lights and slapping wash lulling her into a restful languor as she dallied along the Embankment. If someone approached, or she heard footsteps, she dropped out of sight into the shadows in case they were already looking for her. She did not know where she was going, and had no clear destination except flight itself, but followed the lights along the river to Westminster Bridge, where, suddenly tired, she turned off and found the park.

And now, in the morning light, she had no thought except to leave and to leave forever. In the distance, behind tall railings, a troop of Horse Guards clattered past the front of the palace. It all seemed so ordered and safe at the Queen's house. And her home, Hadley, was singing a bright siren song. She could return. She was free and she had all his money, her money. Yet even as the temptation welled, she knew it was impossible. It would be the first place the police looked when they found Kit. She couldn't go back, at least not for a long time, not until it had all blown over and they had forgotten her. It had to be thought through carefully and planned. She could choose now, she was no longer bound to Kit or to anyone and her first decision, a quiet, implacable resolve, was to always, from now on, stay free.

During that day she lay low and watched the city wake, come to life and wind itself up like a vast and reluctant machine. She pitied those whose lives were spent in this wretched place, people who did not know what it was to gaze at the sea or a green combe. The palaces and towers, the stately courts and offices were not, to her, great or glorious. They were forbidding slabs of anonymous authority she viewed with deep mistrust. It must have been from just such a building that the hated document, Kit's guardianship, had come. She remembered watching it burn, become frail ashes. It no longer existed, no longer was, and she had snatched back, in part at least, something of what was due her.

Late that night she took one of the bottles she'd brought from the vanity case and dyed her yellow hair black in the ornamental pond. The following morning, having dressed carefully in her least crumpled clothes and made herself presentable, she emerged from the spinney and confidently followed the signs to the railway station at Victoria. She still had no idea quite where she was going but a poster by the ticket office decided her. It showed bright yellow sand, a blue sea beyond with a sailing boat on it, the sun glittering above and below, in the foreground, a sandcastle.

She stepped boldly up to the little window and, putting into practice the self she had invented, smiled gaily at the man with rheumy eyes incarcerated within.

'A ticket to Brighton please.'

CHAPTER TWENTY-FIVE

There was a sort of doughty flamboyance about the woman, the hint of a racy past in the ostentatious jewellery and tinted hair. Something in the eyes too, the glint of several lifetimes' experience.

'You're not a tart are you dear?' she asked, matter-of-factly.

'No……of course not!' Jenny stammered, shocked. Though not nearly as tall the woman seemed to tower over her.

'Only they do try it on,' she continued, 'and you can't be too careful. I've had to sort a couple out in my time I can tell you.'

Jenny reflected on the nature of such a sorting out. She had little doubt that it would have been thorough.

'Mmm……' the woman crossed her arms, looked Jenny up and down critically, 'bit of a looker though aren't you. I don't allow men in the rooms, or drinking.'

'Oh no,' Jenny quickly nodded her agreement.

'And a month's rent in advance.'

'That's quite all right.'

The woman sucked in her cheeks and thought for a moment.

'Well, all right then. You can have the top room. Keep it clean and mind the house rules.'

'Oh thanks!' Her own room, her very own.

'And you call me Mollie, dear, everyone else does.' She was quietly chuckling now, 'Let's put the kettle on and I'll show you the room.' She glanced down at the by now careworn canvas bag at Jenny's feet.

'That all you got is it?'

'Yes, well the rest of my things are being sent on. Soon as I'm settled.'

Mollie raised her eyebrows, sighed unaccountably and marched them off to the kitchen.

It was a small but, to Jenny, wonderful room in the attic of a tall Victorian house. There was even a little washbasin in one corner. The ceiling sloped almost to the floor on one side and through the open window came a trickle of familiar sounds and scents, a fresh breeze touched by the sea that sent a delicious frisson through her. And birdsong, the chirrup of sparrows. She looked out across a patchwork of rooftops, aware that the sea was just beyond them. She was burning with impatience to get to it. She'd returned and this would be home until it was safe to go back to Hadley. To think that just this morning she had been in London and just a few days ago she had been......what? What would she call it: a prisoner, a captive? Someone else, she decided finally. A few days ago she had been someone else and that person had gone too and a new and better one now stood in this room, breathing in an air like nectar. A person who was brave after all and who wouldn't look back on those bitter, wasted years. They were all past and gone. Standing at the window she made her second resolution;

she would hide here until the time was right, be anonymous and not live under any illusions, ever again.

She had told enormous whoppers, of course, but the woman, Mollie, had apparently believed her. When she first arrived at Brighton railway station she nipped straight into the ladies and spent an age with the make-up, putting on her other face. It had worked. She'd told Mollie she was 'almost' seventeen and that both her parents had been killed during the war. She invented a childhood spent in a home run by the council. No, she had no other family and, now she was old enough, wanted to make a life for herself in a new place away from all the unhappy memories that London held for her. She was looking for work and was sure she would find it because she could do all sorts of things and was very willing. In the meantime, of course, there was the money from her parents which she had recently become entitled to; 'my legacy' she had called it because it sounded more substantial. It had been a winning performance, calculated to elicit just enough sympathy without inviting too many questions. There had been just one panic, one thing she hadn't thought of, and when Mollie asked her name she blurted out, after the briefest of bewildered hesitations, 'Robin. Jennifer Robin.'

She sat on the bed, happily adrift. After Whitechapel the small and simple room was almost extravagant. She loved its peace and light, the fresh curtains teased by a playful breeze, carpet underfoot instead of cold linoleum, the yellow candlewick bedspread imbued with the clean aroma of washing powder and, most of all, the shiny gold-coloured key that lay just next to her hand.

The change, the dramatic shift in circumstances and in who and what she was, so swift and complete, at last overwhelmed her and she began to tremble and feel faint.

'This won't do,' she said quietly and shook herself. 'This won't do at all.' She went to the washbasin, splashed cold water on her face and thought of the sea, for so long absent from her life and now just a mere stone's throw away. She wanted to rush down to it but held back, timid and apprehensive. It might be different. 'Well it will be,' she told herself firmly, 'it's here and not at home......but it is the sea.' Nonetheless, she was guarded, superstitious about the reunion, that if she hurried it would inevitably be a disappointment. She wandered the town first buying new, adult clothes and shoes, pretty things that made her look the part. The shoes, fashionable and with her first modest heels, she wore while the clothes were folded and put in a bag.

Then out in the street she saw the first of the magical signs and could hold back no longer. It read simply *To the seafront.* She followed with assumed indifference, not wanting to look like an excited child and give herself away, but her pace quickened as the pulse of the sea, invisible and omnipresent, began to overwhelm her.

She rounded a corner and it was suddenly there, calm and silvered, a broad, flat gun-metal sea, breathing in and out like a woman gently asleep. She stopped dead in her tracks and absorbed it hungrily, found herself grinning, almost crying. Casting off the years she let out a whoop of joy and raced down across the scrunching pebbles. A heel on one of her new shoes snapped. She stopped breathlessly at the water's edge, dropped her bag and kicked the shoes off. Wryly, she examined the broken heel then with glee lobbed the shoe in an exuberant arc, followed swiftly by the other, far out into the creaming rollers. She stood and gazed, once again salt-gilded. The sea hadn't changed and neither had she. Whatever else was different they were the same, and together once more.

Quietly exhilarated she sat clinking pebbles. If she closed her eyes she could imagine the green woods leading down to her sea at home. It was wonderful and everything was ahead of her. She was Jenny Robin. She would be happy here.

Dreamily, she contemplated the bay and watched the mewling gulls floating effortlessly aloft. A great pier in the distance jutted out into the sea like an arm from the shoulder of land. It was quite different to the one she had jumped from, so big it had buildings on it, proper buildings with white domes. Yet as she looked more closely, she saw it had been raggedly cut in half, bisected for some reason, and the seaward end of it was effectively an island of iron and wood. It was a shame, she thought, it was like one of the wonders of the world.

For a while she tossed pebbles into the shallows and then, like anyone else might, got up, walked to the water and paddled. It was only much later, as she returned happily to her room, her new home, that she remembered the poster at the railway station and the enticing yellow sand it had promised.

★   ★   ★

'Crafty so and so knew you'd be good for business,' the woman called Frankie cackled amiably as a flustered Jenny returned to the kitchens with her third wrong order that morning. 'Knew it was a fib about you being experienced too, we all did.' She leant towards Jenny until their shoulders met. 'You ain't done this before have you? Don't matter though dearie. Nothing like a pretty face for pulling in the trade. He knows that. That's why you've been out front all morning. Now you listen to me……'

It had been a harrowing first few hours. She'd seen the card in a newsagent's window: *Waitress required for busy restaurant. Must be experienced……* and gone straight round. She went in and was seen by the owner, a Mr. McDermot, 'Mac the knife and fork we calls 'im,' Frankie told her later. After just five minutes he offered her the job. It looked so easy, being a waitress. She was sure she'd get away with it. He hadn't asked her much even though she was ready with a sprinkling of fictitious London restaurants to trot out in confirmation of her claim to experience. He just looked her up and down, smiled in a gentlemanly way and shook her hand. He was, she guessed, in his mid-fifties but still had a full head of astonishingly black hair. When he spoke it was with a thick Scots accent.

'Wouldn't think he's been down here a good twenty years would you love, eh?' Frankie remarked. 'He's all right though.'

Jenny emerged from his small, cramped office congratulating herself on the success of another necessary fraud, but now it had backfired on her. They had all known from the outset that she had hardly been in a restaurant let alone worked in one and she was shamed, publicly caught out.

But no one seemed to mind. They treated it like a game and, as Frankie explained, more trade meant each of them had a bigger slice from the pool of tips.

Under Frankie's wing she quickly developed the skills and the fleetness of foot the busy place required. It was just off the seafront and called, with unimaginative simplicity, 'Macs'. There were two other waitresses, Alison and Julia, both in their thirties and with families. Brighton born and bred, they had been through school together and were like sisters. Every now and then their normally affectionate relationship would erupt, for no apparent reason, into an explosive, seething row, where every other screamed word would be the one Jenny had first heard bellowed into the wind by Lally. There were other words too, as she quickly discovered, ones she had not even heard Kit use. They stopped short of blows, but only just. There would follow two, sometimes three, days of silent sulking. Then a tearful reconciliation, again sparked by some signal between them too tiny or obscure to be recognised by anyone else. Jenny liked them, the outrageousness of their squabbles and the uninhibited sweet emotion of their patching up. They were known as the twins and although they shared no physical resemblance it seemed curiously apposite. When the rows broke out the burly Scotsman quietly closed the door to his office and hid.

'Daren't sack 'em,' Frankie said, 'too good at the job. Just tells them to keep it out back.'

Out back, the kitchens were run by a self-effacing widow of fifty or so called Mrs. Norman. None of them called her by her first name or seemed to know it. She spoke very quietly, and was almost coquettishly embarrassed if a customer passed back a compliment. She had a knack of good-natured indirectness, of sliding the conversation away from herself.

'Used to be the tops in London, worked at the Savoy,' Frankie told her, adding in a hushed whisper, 'liked the bottle though. Never talks about it. Old Mac gave her a chance. Told her if he ever caught her with more than a glass of shandy she'd be out on 'er ear. Been good as gold……so far.' Later Jenny learnt that the woman had been there ten years.

It was Frankie Jenny took to most. She was tall and gaunt with deep hollows around her eyes and must once, Jenny thought, have been very handsome.

'Me?' she would say with mock incredulity, 'you don't want to hear about me,' and with no further prompting would unleash her life story. Or at least a version of it, for as Jenny quickly and delightedly discovered, there were several, all of them entertaining and each with a kernel of similarity but often ambiguous or contradictory. Part of the delight was that Frankie was completely bare-faced about it. The consistent facts seemed to be that she was born on the coast where her parents owned a hotel, sometimes elaborately grand though more often described as 'for quality people, you know.' She had wanted to be a dancer but was forbidden to and ran away to Paris. There she entertained at nightclubs and bars, always to rapturous applause. She got involved with a Dutchman who mysteriously let her down and later got himself killed in the war. When war broke out she returned home and found work wherever she could along the south coast, still entertaining.

'But what sort of entertaining Frankie?'

'Oh you know dear. Bit of singing and kicking up yer legs. Course I've lost me voice now, too many of these,' and energetically she would stub out the ever present cigarette, lighting up a fresh one a few minutes later.

'And what then?'

'Well, I got meself married.' She slapped her hands down on the table, spread out her thin red fingers. 'But I don't want to talk about that today. No offence but it gets me all worked up. It's best left.'

'Did you have any children?'

A silence; part melodrama, part not, and an almost imperceptible, unspecified wistfulness couched in a voice that sternly would not admit to it.

'Nope. Never did. No kids.' But there would be a distant soft look in the sunken eyes that belied her flintly tone. 'Course I was chased by a duke once you know......'

For the first ten days Jenny arrived home as wrung-out as one of the restaurant's dishcloths, completely exhausted. With Frankie's help though she adapted, learned how to pace herself and not panic, even though she often wanted to.

Mac himself remained something of a mystery, more often than not secreted in his little office. She soon found out why. If he had a weakness it was not for women or wine. It was not so much a weakness either but a passion, and a consuming one, for anything with legs that could race round a track. It didn't matter what as long as he could bet on it.

'If they put blindfolds on 'awstriches and made 'em run backwards he'd put a dollar down,' Frankie said, adding secretly, 'but don't you have nothing to do with it, you hear?'

The twins showed her the gamut of ploys that would virtually guarantee a tip, as well as the particular ones which would appeal to lone men; a coy wiggle in the walk, smile and then smile again, make them think they were getting special treatment. And keep smiling.

'Specially you,' Julia advised admiringly, 'lovely smile you got, and legs. I used to be just like you, pert little bum and everything, but since the kids......'

There was no envy or rivalry. It was a chirpy conspiracy, a bit of daring. At first she was too hopelessly shy but eventually screwed up her courage, and wiggled, and smiled. They all but clapped when she got her first substantial tip from a solitary, middle-aged businessman.

'You left him bloody well smouldering!' they giggled in the kitchens afterwards. 'Thought the tablecloth was going to catch fire!' But it was Frankie's laconic, smoke-cradled drawl that reduced them to hopeless laughter.

'Plain clothes copper he was. Bugger 'ad a truncheon in his pocket. Saw it when he stood up.'

Jenny slid easily into the comfort of it all, the quite new feeling of making friendships and allegiances. She relished the banter, the fun, and threw herself into the work. Inside she was uncoiling, poking a nose cautiously out from her inner woodland refuge and slowly, by degrees, beginning to become something that had nothing at all to do with serving at table.

CHAPTER TWENTY-SIX

It was weeks before she saw anything about his death and then only by chance. She had put him out of her mind, almost managed to convince herself he'd never existed, that it was a story she'd read somewhere. It was a sudden and unwelcome shock to see his name in the newspaper she was wrapping scraps in.

She read compulsively, a hand raised to her mouth against a nausea inside her: *Discovered by landlord.........authorities suspect a build up of methane gas in the drainage system and have warned other residents....... police still searching for young girl believed to be his daughter...... tragic misfortune.......* The black typeface blurred, rose up and filled her vision. She scuttled blindly to the lavatory and was violently sick, retching over and over until her insides were twisted and mouth sour.

She washed her face slowly in the small washbasin, rinsed her mouth with cool, fresh water. She was angry with herself for not being on guard, not expecting it. She looked in the mirror and straightened her hair, still unused to the jet darkness. Her eyes looked puffy and her face drained of colour. She must, must stay ahead or risk giving herself away. Determinedly, she unbolted the door, strode back to the kitchen and dumped the remaining scraps of peelings, fish carcass and bone onto the newspaper, wrapped it up tightly and dumped it in the bin.

The salt-scoured light of spring, and then summer, returned the smile to her face. She was confident that with her changed appearance she wouldn't be found, yet instinctively shied away if a policeman approached. Anyway, the paper said they were looking for a young girl and increasingly she felt and was more and more a young woman and, if the tips were anything to go by, an attractive one. It was Frankie who mildly scolded her for innocently looking round at wolf-whistling in the street. 'Well they aren't whistlin' at an old hen like me are they!'

Hungry to consolidate her burgeoning adulthood, she pored over fashion magazines, saving her wages and the money from tips to expand her initially meagre wardrobe. She developed an unerring eye for what would look good. Her dress sense was envied at work, especially by the twins.

'Don't know where you find them lovely things. Me, I spends a fortune and still ends up looking like a sack of spuds.'

But it was the simplest, cheapest and smallest thing she bought which astounded them most: a bikini.

'You can't wear that!' they sniggered, elbowing each other. Frankie held up the lower half in horror.

'Good Gawd, it's smaller than me hankie! People'll be able to see all yer doings.' Yet their amazement, both at the costume and at Jenny's nerve, turned to sheer incredulity when they realised the bikini had been bought for an altogether more practical purpose that its skimpy chic led them to believe.

'Going swimming, in the sea?' Frankie shuddered, appalled at the idea. The twins flinched visibly and gaped at her. It transpired that none of them so much as put a toe in, ever. Yet they all trooped loyally down to the beach to witness her first plunge.

'Bet it's bloody freezing!' they laughed, shivering on her behalf, huddled together on the pebbles.

If it was she didn't care. The taste of the sea and the silky rush as she raced through it, cleansed her finally of whatever traces of those city years remained, cupped her in an uplifting promise of a past defeated and a future wide open.

She swam far out, easily and with all the old power. It caused consternation on the beach as Frankie and the twins jumped up and down, waving her back. She laughed affectionately at them then, turning on her back, executed a graceful, rhythmic backstroke to shore.

Frankie was at the water's edge holding out a towel.

'Where d'you learn to swim like that?' she spluttered, a cigarette with a drooping inch of ash clamped in her mouth. 'Worried sick we was, miles out you were.'

'My Dad taught me,' Jenny said cheerfully then, remembering, added quickly, 'when I was very little.'

'Well get yourself dry.' Frankie gave her a grave look and fussed with the towel. 'You'll look like a ruddy prune if you stay in any longer.'

Throughout that summer she swam almost every day. Sometimes the others came with her and sat chattering on the beach but more often she was alone. It was then there would be a tantalising whisper from home, in the beat of a gull's wings and the tempo of the sea, a touch of wilder, more ancient coasts and an intense green landscape concealing myths and secrets.

In the evenings, she walked the seafront before returning to her room to listen to the small radio she had bought, a little guiltily for it was a luxury and expensive. But really, she told herself, it was a trifle compared to the luxury of a freedom she would never take for granted again.

★   ★   ★

It was almost three years; three comfortable, lulled and tranquil years, before the yellow silk blouse, Annie's extravagantly casual gift, fitted her properly. When it did she dressed up proudly, teaming it with a pleated, white skirt, and looked at her reflection. She remembered Annie's firm declaration that one day she would be beautiful.

'Not bad,' she said out loud. Privately she was more pleased than she thought it proper to admit.

'Party is it?' Mollie asked as Jenny came down the stairs, swinging her handbag.

'No, just off for a walk.'

'Ah,' the woman said knowingly, 'promenading. Good for you. Turn some heads for me.'

The entrance to the defunct pier was clogged with the usual stalls and barrows selling ice-cream, Brighton rock in a myriad shapes and colours, as well as fruit, vegetables, cockles, crabs and whelks. She bends from the waist, straight-legged, examining the apples. A covetous gasp of sea breeze suddenly billows the full skirt and underlying confection of petticoats, traces the curve of stockinged legs and a rear end briefly, unwittingly, revealed.

'Miss!'

She turns, still bending, narrow-eyed, mistrustful, all at once alert to it. An almost inaudible click, the slow sprung shutter of a camera.

'You cheeky sod! You've just taken a picture of my backside!' She straightens quickly, smoothes down the wayward skirt.

He is pale-faced, a face like a schoolboy's, badly cut light brown hair sticking up in tufts, and he is panic-stricken.

'No! It's not like that! I was just about to when......the......the wind......' He rushes forward aghast, hands up as though surrendering. She could see then he was older than he at first looked, perhaps twenty-three or four, but he had about him an adolescent's awkwardness, not helped by round, wire-rimmed glasses and a clumsy, gangling walk as if his shoes were too big.

'You did, you took a photo!' she snorted. 'You dirty little sod!' It was the language of the kitchens and she had learnt it well. He swallowed and looked round in acute embarrassment.

'Oh look I didn't mean to. It was accidental. It wasn't......it was the wind. I didn't do it on purpose. Honestly,' he implored, peering through the glasses. Something about him, the goggle-eyed desperation and white hands held up submissively, disarmed her. Nonetheless, she found herself quite enjoying his wriggling.

'Well?' she insisted.

'Look, honestly,' he pleaded, clumsily earnest, 'I just wouldn't do that. Please understand. I'm not like that, really I'm not.' He stared anxiously at her, searching her eyes for the smallest hint of a pardon. Then abruptly he pulled the camera from his neck, opened it and dramatically unfurled the roll of film, exposing it to the sun. 'There, see?' he said, blinking at her.

She gave an arch, sideways look. 'Well all right then,' she conceded, adding sternly, 'you'd better not have been though.' She began to walk away but he hurried after her. When she stopped his hand hovered at her arm, not daring to touch.

'Look,' he blurted, 'it really was an accident. It just happened. I'd hate you to think it was deliberate. Please let me buy you a cup of tea or something, to make up for it. I'm not that sort of person at all.' The words tumbled out in a rush. 'There's a nice place just over the road,' he said hopefully, with an imprecise wave. She studied him coolly. Waitressing had taught her all about propositions but his curiously artless manner convinced her this wasn't one. She looked at her watch.

'OK,' she agreed, unsure quite why she did, 'meeting a friend soon though.' It was a calculated fib, a marker set down should she need to extricate herself from this odd, birdlike creature.

He proved though a gentle, if agitated, host, anxious to redeem himself. In the rather stuffy tea-room he tried to impress by asking the waiter for the 'very best' selection of cakes they had, a flourish that fell flat when the man replied stonily, 'They all are Sir.' Crushed by the rebuke he looked down at the tablecloth, a meek waif. She wanted to giggle then but quashed it. She was enjoying the attention, albeit from this unlikely source, and was wallowing, unkindly she knew, in his continuing discomfort. Yet when the tea was brought, and a plate of hideously pink and white fancies put on the table between them, her indignation swiftly returned.

'Just a minute, why were you taking a picture of me at all?'

A strangled look came over his face and he avoided her eyes.

'It's what I do for a living. It's my job.'

'But I didn't ask you to, did I?'

'Well……you see…… you just go round snapping people, holidaymakers, and then give them one of these cards,' he fumbled in his pocket, took one out and passed it to her, 'and the next day they can buy the photo. Lots of people want to, specially couples.' His voice trailed off and he fell silent. She leant forward.

'But I'm not on holiday, or a couple. I live here.'

His eyes met hers for a moment then looked away. He nibbled his bottom lip, sighed and then spoke with a directness which surprised her.

'I know. I know you do.'

'Well what are you playing at then?' she hissed across the table at him.

'Look, don't get the wrong idea, please. It's just……I have seen you before, on the seafront and, well, I don't just take holiday snaps. What I mean is, oh help, this is going to sound strange but really I am a genuine photographer. I've even got my own studio, sort of……' he was becoming hopelessly enmeshed and defensive.

'Spit it out for goodness sake!' she whispered urgently. His voice had been getting steadily louder and higher, people were beginning to look. He glanced at her and spluttered edgily.

'I like to photograph beautiful women.' For a second he looked almost shocked at himself then, anticipating her, again held out his hands in a pacifying gesture and rushed on. 'No, look. It isn't what you're thinking. It isn't really. It's portraits, you know, like in magazines. Proper photography, faces……'

He had anticipated her wrongly. It was the comic gabble, the face contorted by his struggle to express himself and his absolute seriousness that finally set off her giggles.

It shouldn't have been funny but it was. She couldn't be cross with him. She put a hand to her mouth and tried to stifle her laughter. There were tears on her cheeks when she was finally able to speak.

'Faces? Got more than you bargained for this time then!'

He smiled, unsure, and a spreading blush crept up from his collar. She picked up one of the cakes and bit into it. It was cloyingly sweet and she put it down on her plate with distaste. She didn't know what to make of him but was basking in what he had said. He was looking at her in awe, as though expecting to be dismissed. She could not help milking it and said with a grin,

'So I'm beautiful am I?'

The reply was wrung out of him, a final submission.

'Yes……you are.' There was an intensity about him now, in the pale eyes and hunched shoulders, an intensity that made her wary and regret having pushed her luck. She looked at the time.

'Have to go now. My friend……'

'Oh yes!' He stood up sharply and looked sheepish. 'Of course. Um, it would be a privilege if……if I could take some of you. Portraits that is.' He shuffled uncomfortably, 'Only I think that……you'd be ideal.'

It was her turn to be flustered. She waved his calling card self-consciously.

'I don't know. I'll have to think about it and let you know. Yes that's what I'll do.' She turned to go, unwilling to leave with her composure faintly askew. She collected herself, faced him.

'Thanks for the tea,' she said with exaggerated breeziness, 'but don't leave a tip.' And, swinging her handbag, marched out to meet her waiting friend, the sea.

CHAPTER TWENTY-SEVEN

He had disturbed her, disturbed and confused. She'd grown used to passes being made but this was quite different, and what did he mean by her being ideal. It didn't have a right feel about it but she couldn't deny that his timid yet evident adoration fulfilled a need in her as much as the usual clumsy approaches failed to. She turned the card over, read the scant words for the umpteenth time: *C. G. Maxwell, Photographer.* The address was simply, *The Hut, River Road, Brighton,* and beneath a telephone number in fancy italics. C.G.? Charles George? Well Charles would be about right, proper charlie, yet she reproached herself even as she thought it. She flung the card down, exasperated, changed for work and went off in an uncharacteristic huff.

'Mucky pictures I'll bet,' Frankie uttered darkly, 'you want to be careful. Saw you in that bit of a bikini I expect.'

'But that's just it, I don't think they would be,' she protested, still only half-believing it herself. The twins' reaction was equally sceptical.

'Don't you go. He might be one of them pervert things. There was this woman in Bayview Road……'

It took a week for her to make up her mind and in the end vanity won. She had enjoyed the flattery, the new power it gave her, a power she only dimly understood. When she saw the ramshackle wooden building though, she nearly walked away again. It was indeed little more than a hut, a single storey clapboard house in an unkempt patch of land. The white paint was faded and peeling. She told herself to be brave and knocked firmly on the door. It opened, revealing his white face and an expression of complete astonishment.

'All right then,' she said tartly, 'but you better had be what you say you are.'

'You came!' he gasped, dumbfounded, 'I didn't think……' He seemed frozen by her appearance and stood with the door still half-open, then remembering himself, threw it back. It crashed against something behind as a gloomy, cluttered interior was revealed. 'Sorry,' he said eagerly, 'please come in, bit untidy I'm afraid.' But she was already backing off.

'No, not now. I just came round to say that I would and to fix it up.'

'Oh I see,' he fiddled with his glasses.

'Well, when then?'

'Anytime at all that would suit you, anytime,' he answered enthusiastically, then pondered. 'I will need to get things set up though. Would Thursday be convenient. About seven o' clock.' She knew that it would but made out she was searching a mental diary.

'Should be. Yes I think so. How long will it take only my boyfriend says he'll bring me and wait in the car.' It was impromptu and ill-conceived, an instinctive insurance thrown in just in case the dire warnings were justified. She had no idea how she would carry it off.

'Yes indeed,' he said in his peculiarly dated way, and without any sign of having understood the implied suspicion, 'about an hour or so?'

'Thursday then, at seven.'

'Good. I shall look forward to it, if you're quite sure it's convenient.' She nodded and turned to leave. As she reached the gate he called after her.

'Miss!'

'What is it?'

He smiled bashfully, 'I don't know your name.'

'Jennifer Robin. Jenny,' she laughed, 'what's the C.G. stand for?'

'C.G.?' he looked perplexed, then with a spark of realisation, 'You mean me! It's for Christopher. Chris for short.'

'What about the G?'

He looked acutely embarrassed, 'No.......Please.......'

'Go on, what is it?'

'You won't laugh will you?' he entreated, then admitted wretchedly, 'Gladstone. Awful isn't it?'

'I won't tell a soul.'

He was the most self-effacing person she had known and appeared to have no sense of himself at all, other than as someone who would inevitably blunder or say the wrong thing. His whole manner was permanently apologetic; a bank of sorrys built up in advance against the certainty of their future need. It gave her a mastery over him, too tempting not to exploit.

They were both nervous that first evening, she of his motives and he simply of her presence. She fibbed about the boyfriend and said he'd dropped her off at the end of the road and would pick her up at eight on the dot. Yet as the evening progressed she was reassured by Chris's continuing vulnerability, more certain that he wasn't, after all, a wolf in sheep's clothing.

The inside of his house had been hastily tidied. There was even, to her surprise, a vase of flowers, so fresh they must have been cut that day.

She was self-conscious, embarrassed in front of the camera, and clumsy and wooden in response to his suggested poses. She knew it would be a complete disaster and her smile would look a ghastly, forced grimace. Yet Chris seemed more than pleased with her efforts and took great pains to encourage and make her feel confident.

Later he made tea and brought it in on a tray. The house was really one large room with tiny ones jammed up against it; a kitchenette, a poky bathroom where she did her make-up and what she supposed was his bedroom, though that door was shut. It had a dowdy, well-used feel and was crammed with photographic equipment.

They sat and drank the tea, the session over. Small talk was not easy. He greeted her questions with a short, nervous laugh and had a way of not answering which began to irritate her. After a while she realised that far from being evasive he was just hopelessly, irredeemably, shy and believed himself of no interest at all. When a car horn fortuitously gave two sharp bursts a little way off, she gratefully jumped to her feet and said it must be her boyfriend. He leapt up at the same moment and began to ham-fistedly help her on with her coat.

'I'll have them ready by Sunday,' he said enthusiastically, opening the door, 'if you'd like to see them that is. I mean if that would be all right. Or, or, I could bring them to you if you'd prefer.'

She said she would have to check and telephone him and experienced an unpleasant satisfaction when his face fell. As she left he said, almost plaintively, 'You will call this time though won't you?' and, as if in contrition, she promised.

'Cross my heart and hope to die.'

★ ★ ★

'Told you they would!' He was beside himself with excitement as he spread the photographs out on the bench between them. 'Look! And what about this one, it's a beauty!' Despite herself she could not disagree. The stranger who looked back at her so confidently from beneath a deep gloss, this familiar yet unknown creature, was a beauty. He had performed a kind of alchemy.

'Do I really look like that?' she asked circumspectly.

'Course you do,' he said, surprised, 'it's you.'

'It's just I don't feel that's how I look.'

He laughed diffidently, opened another folder of prints.

'It is absolutely you,' and he stared at them, rapt by her and by his own craft.

She had arranged to meet him in the ornamental gardens by the seafront and waited out of sight, making sure he arrived there first, before sauntering over.

'Don't you like them?' he asked suddenly, his excitement checked by her questions.

'Oh yes. It's not that. They're very, very good. Really professional.'

'Really?'

'Really,' she insisted, 'it's a bit of a shock that's all.' She examined one of the prints, 'I didn't know she was me.'

'But other people, not just me, must have said.'

She gave a small smile, 'Yes, they have a bit. I wasn't sure if I believed them though.'

He looked down at his hands, the slender, splayed fingers. 'You really must, I think. You are you know.' She didn't know what to say and he fumbled awkwardly putting the prints back into their folders. 'There is one thing though......' he ventured diffidently.

'What?'

'I think you'd do better as a blonde.'

Her unrestrained laughter across the elaborate flowerbeds and newly-shorn lawns made people stop, look at them and smile fondly, imagining that they were courting, a couple. Bewildered he stood up, then sat down again quickly.

'Sorry. I shouldn't have......none of my......that was wrong of me.' And still laughing she twinkled at him.

'Oh no, not wrong, not wrong at all!'

★   ★   ★

It had been long enough. The trail, had there ever been one, must long since have had gone stone cold. It would be all right now. The hair she had regularly dyed was now so much a part of her that it was hard to recollect her true shade, especially at the chemists where she was bemused by the choice; strawberry, ash, platinum, straw, ice.

'Everyone's going blonde this year,' the woman assistant remarked cheerfully, 'must be that actress.'

'Actress?'

'You know, the one that can't sing.'

Eventually she chose a tint called Morning Sun. She didn't recognise it as her own natural colour. It was someone else entirely she remembered it from, Annie. The next day, newly flaxen, she went to a hairdresser and, after mulling over endless style books, finally and triumphantly found a full, tumbling bob cut just to the jaw. It took an age to find, not because she didn't know what she wanted but because she was so absolutely certain.

'Are you sure?' the hairdresser asked, 'all this lovely long hair you got, seems such a shame.' Jenny insisted and when it was finished sat quietly serene, looking into the mirror and remembering an old, old friend, one inviolate day, and wondering where the *Typhoon* was now and whether its crew remembered a skinny Devonshire girl and wondered of her too.

'Well if I say so myself,' the hairdresser said, pleased with her handiwork, 'you do look a treat. You got the face for it though. Take anything that face.'

Back at the restaurant even Mac emerged to see what the fuss was about and, unconsciously quaint, pronounced her the 'Belle of the Ball'. Mrs. Norman nodded, mute and approving, from the door of the kitchens while the twins bombarded her with questions about where she had got it done and who by and how much. It was Frankie, for once standing back and unusually quiet, her smile infused with the merest sliver of a mysterious self-reproach, whose words meant most.

'You look,' she said softly, 'like I always wanted to.'

When she returned to Chris's house a few days later he could only gape at her, open-mouthed.

'My goodness! What a shock! Isn't it......don't you......?'

'But do you like it?'

'Yes!' he enthused. 'It's absolutely wonderful, even better that I imagined!

This time she forgot the boyfriend charade and he made no mention of it. When she remembered it was too late to resurrect him. She thought it would look clumsy and obvious.

During the second session, or 'shoot' as he self-consciously called it, she began to feel more comfortable about the whole thing. Perhaps along with the new blonde hairstyle she had also acquired a little of Annie's ease and self-possession. It was, after all, just acting really, pretending, but no longer at pirates.

'Why do you do this?' she asked during a break while he changed films. He looked fleetingly alarmed.

'What?'

'Take photos like these.'

He wound on the new film thoughtfully, 'Oh I see. To try and capture it I suppose. Beauty I mean, before it's gone.' As before, he made tea when the photography was over. This time, out of devilment, she questioned him directly about himself. He squirmed at first but after a while began to unbend. He was born and brought up in Harrow, where his 'folks' lived, yet oddly the cosy word was spoken without fondness. Haltingly, he revealed that he had gone against his parents' wishes to become a photographer. He even relaxed enough to laugh, in a stifled way, when he told her that their ambition for him had been to become a barrister.

'Can you imagine me doing that?' She couldn't but it was evident from his silence, as he looked dejectedly down at the thinning rug, that his stand had cost him dear.

When she met up with him a few days later in the same ornamental garden he was even more serious than usual. He handed her the new prints apprehensively.

'I think you've got it,' he said gravely.

'What?'

'A look. I think you've got it.'

'Flash sod,' Julia snorted as a small green sports car gunned its engine noisily in the road outside.

'Who is?' Jenny asked, emerging from the kitchens with a tray of cutlery.

'Him,' Julia pointed towards the car, 'just been in to see Mac. Smarmy bugger.' Jenny caught a glimpse of a sandy-haired man in a sheepskin coat and tweed cap before the car sped away.

'Never seen him before,' she said without interest and began to lay out the tables. At the other end of the restaurant Frankie was doing the same.

'Parliamentary candidate isn't he. Too bloody young by half. Only been on the council five minutes.'

Julia inaccurately mimicked a public school accent, 'Trust I can count on your support ladies,' then the voice dropped, 'all smiles and jam tomorrow, just like the rest of them.'

'What did he want Mac for?' Jenny asked idly.

'Vote catching isn't he. Came out of the office all smiles he did. Mac's in that chamber of whatsit, you know.'

'After a dibble in the till more like,' Frankie said, wearily scornful as she clattered cutlery onto a table, the perpetual cigarette dancing between her lips, 'campaign funds and all that. Scratchin' each other's backs I expect. We'll be doin' the mayor's tea parties next,' she smirked, then added darkly, 'or up at the Masonic.' She sliced her hand across her throat like a knife and dropped ash onto the fresh white tablecloth, 'Oh bugger it!'

But it was an agitated Mac who came out of his office an hour later, one who, unusually, failed to acknowledge two of his regular customers as he hurried out, saying he would be gone for most of the day.

'Urgent business,' he frowned, 'regrettably.'

In the fortnight that followed, Jenny occasionally bumped into Chris as she walked the seafront on her evenings off and they would spend half an hour dawdling and looking at the sea. She didn't tell him where she lived or worked. She thought the pedestal he had perched her on would crumble if he discovered she was just a waitress. Not that he ever asked. It wasn't in him to be that forward. She teased him sometimes now, and once or twice took it too far. She didn't know why she did it and afterwards always felt mean. There was however, a pleasing thrill in seeing how far she could push him, just how much he would take.

There was something else about him she hadn't reckoned with, something wholly unexpected. He had, without knowing it, pricked the bubble of her solitude and in doing so made her recognise it, made her see clearly the habitual distance she kept between herself and others, even Frankie. It was part of the penalty for keeping her guard up. That he had done this, in innocence and guilelessly, made her both resent him, in a tiny unacknowledged part of her, and want more of him, or at least his apparently inexhaustible attentiveness.

This evening though was different. He was sitting on the sea wall, and looked desperately gloomy.

'You look like you've lost a shilling and found a tanner,' she remarked brightly but he scarcely looked up. When at length he did his face was so disconsolate she immediately sat beside him, concerned, 'What on earth is the matter?' He swallowed and would not look at her.

'There's something I should have told you. I'm very sorry. I had no right.'

'What is it for goodness sake? It can't be that bad surely.'

'But I should've asked,' he said, 'it wasn't right to just go ahead without asking and I knew it wasn't. It's unforgivable of me.' She waited while he calmed himself, drew breath and continued. 'The last batch of photos. I couldn't resist it. They were so good. You were so good. I sent them off.' He gazed up at her distraught, as though he had just confessed to murder. She shrugged, looked puzzled.

'Well, so what. Sent them off where anyway?'

'To a magazine. And now, now they want to print some of them. And that's not all, they want to take some more of you. Here's the letter.' He handed her a brown envelope, 'I'm sorry,' he said in a muffled voice, 'really sorry.'

It began as a far distant wave, slowly gathering speed and swelling, becoming louder and more powerful until it crashed in a tumult of sparkling exhilaration inside her.

'Me?' she said at last, almost lost for words, 'in a magazine. Me?'

And below them, along the beach, a fretful black dog barked ceaselessly and without reason at the approaching waves.

★   ★   ★

It was to be a celebration. He had insisted, in a gush of words brimming with relief. A treat, the very best, supper in the Kings Crescent, silver service and everything.

She had dallied past it more than once and soaked up its sumptuousness. It was a large, imposing Victorian hotel. Beyond the glass doors she had seen the field of thick maroon carpet stretching away, the polished wood and gold fittings and everywhere vases of fresh flowers. There was even a top-hatted doorman in green livery piped with silver.

She had bought a new outfit, a tailored cream suit, and was putting the final touches to her make-up. The photograph of Daddy at her bedside smiled up at her. What would he have thought about it all she wondered, what would he have said. She had long since put aside the night visitor. It had drifted from her. She remembered, and clearly, but through the years it seemed after all more likely that it had been an invention, conjured up out of her unhappiness. When she looked back, it was fondly, wistfully indulgent of her child-self. Every so often, at night, in the moments before sleep claimed her, she could feel herself stretching back into the past, and would come to again with a start, stare wide-eyed at the shadowed ceiling before sliding into the blue and green of her chosen, happier memories.

When she met Chris on the promenade, he looked ill at ease in a grey suit and blue, diamond patterned tie. The recalcitrant tufts of hair had been greased and brushed flat but still threatened to spring up. She eyed him critically.

'Not bad. You'll pass. There's a mark on your tie though so keep your jacket buttoned.' Obediently, he fastened it.

'You look absolutely stunning,' he said reverentially, 'absolutely first class.' She nodded a small, pleased acceptance of the compliment and they set off in the summery evening to walk the half-mile to the hotel.

'I really thought you'd be angry with me,' he said, still edgy.

'Perhaps I should,' she teased, 'taking liberties like that.'

It was to be a curious, stilted treat. From the moment the doorman called her Madam and opened the door, she was secretly entranced. Chris, on the other hand, was clearly unnerved, daunted by the atmosphere of grandeur. They were seated by a window overlooking a gently melancholic sea. Chris looked round furtively, dropped his head between his shoulders and whispered across the table.

'I did a wedding here once. Two hundred guests. Must've cost a fortune.'

'Don't whisper,' she said, 'you're not in church.'

The discreetly affable waiter asked if they would like a cocktail. Chris's glasses flashed as he shot her a strangled look. He opened his mouth but could say nothing and it was Jenny who answered.

'Yes please. Martinis?' she hazarded. The waiter nodded approvingly and went away.

Martini. It was wildly sophisticated. She had never had one before. Chris tasted his suspiciously while she sipped with assumed familiarity. She knew he was hopelessly uncomfortable, yet when it was time to order he visibly screwed up his courage and said he would order for them both. He plainly thought it was what he was meant to do. Her heart sank as he gingerly settled for the dullest thing on the menu, roast beef.

'And to drink Sir?'

Chris blinked, ran a finger round the inside of his collar and strained as if to loosen it.

'Champagne,' Jenny said decisively.

He hardly spoke during the meal and looked increasingly diminished. She knew too, that he was secretly taking a lead from her because he was unsure which cutlery to use.

The champagne brought back sweet memories of her first taste. She wished Annie and Jerry were there. They would know about things and not be intimidated. They would cheerfully insist that she try exotic and unpronounceable delicacies from the menu. She could almost hear Annie's voice; 'But you must darling, simply must. You haven't lived till you've tried these!' And there would be laughter, and gaiety, not Chris's cowed silence.

Over coffee he said, 'I've made a set of those prints for you. I thought you'd like to have them. We could collect them if you like. It's only just round the corner.' She nodded agreement and thought again of the magazine, and the letter that lay on her dressing table together with her half-written reply. She would finish it later and post it in the morning. First thing. Before they changed their minds.

To his credit Chris left a handsome tip and on the way out she thanked him for the treat.

'My pleasure,' he said, more relaxed now they were leaving. 'It was the least I could do, the very least. Jolly good wasn't it?'

As they walked to his house through the fading light, the sea air added its own potency to the cocktail and the champagne. She felt she was floating just above the sun-bleached pavement. Not drunk but just a bit merry, and it made Chris's pale, earnest expression, as he dogged her steps, absurd and out of place. She wanted to be swept along by excitement and fun and by people who knew how to live and enjoy, who weren't downcast by life.

It was dusk when they arrived. He unlocked the door and ushered her in with a self-conscious, 'Ladies first.' She sat on the sofa and sighed contentedly. There was a pleasant humming in her ears and a deliciously languid feeling in her limbs.

'Would you like some of this?' he ventured, proffering a squat bottle, 'A sort of nightcap to round the evening off.'

'What is it?'

'Peach brandy. It's very nice.'

Sweet peaches of remembered fruitful summers, the smell of green orchards.

'Yes, thanks.'

He poured it into two unmatched tumblers and passed one to her. Standing before her he raised his glass.

'Well then, here's to you, your future.' The drink was sugary sweet and left a stickiness on her lips. She wasn't sure she liked it. It was disappointingly unlike peaches. He went and got the folder of prints and put it down on the sofa beside her.

'I can make some enlargements if you'd like. Just let me know which ones. Free of charge,' he joked feebly. He was hovering about her, darting like a dragonfly, dancing attention.

'Why don't you sit down?'

'No really, I'm all right standing.' But he looked far from all right. His face was full of a pent-up misery. She put down the half-empty tumbler.

'I ought to be going now, thanks again for everything.'

'No! Please don't go yet!' The words were wrenched unwillingly out of him. He pushed his hair back with a worried sweep of the hand, releasing the oiled tufts. 'This is it, isn't it? It'll all end now, I know it will. It'll all end and I'll be on my own again.'

'What are you talking about?'

He did not answer but suddenly slumped to the floor and hugged her knees, his face buried in her lap, sobbing like a child.

Dumbfounded, she looked down at the top of his head, at the ridiculously unleashed shock of hair. He stared up, cheeks flushed and wet, made an ungainly lurch and kissed her; a hard, dry kiss, one she neither returned nor, in her shock, stopped. Then frantically, like a bird pecking, he kissed her eyes, her nose, her chin. His hands were fluttering over her, running quickly up and down the sides of her body, flickering at her breasts. She shut her eyes as the kisses rained onto her, numbed by his frenzied pawing. The weight of him, of his slender frame, pushed her down into the sofa as he scrambled on top of her. His shaking hand, clammy against her thigh, darting uncertainly between her legs and, frighteningly, she felt her own unbidden, unwanted, responding wetness. His hand was scrabbling between their bodies and she felt the pull of fabric beneath her skirt. She opened her eyes, saw his contorted face above her, gasping as though in pain, eyes screwed shut as his hips jerked and bounced against her. Then suddenly he shuddered and collapsed, panting.

It had been just seconds. Repugnance swept over her and she shrank inwardly, recoiled. She didn't quite know what had happened, all she knew was that it had been so fast and so unexpected. Something slid from the sofa and landed on the floor with a sound that was oddly delicate in the electric silence. She looked down. It was the photographs. Then, galvanised, there was a swift snapping to inside her. She pushed him off and he rolled to the floor and stayed there.

'What did you do that for?' she shouted furiously, and the words seemed to club him. He ducked, hid his face and huddled in silence. Her crumpled skirt was pushed up around her hips. She pulled it down indignantly and glared at him. 'You shouldn't have done that! I didn't want you to, I didn't say you could!'

His voice, thin, muffled, 'Sorry!'

She grabbed the photographs and hurled them at his crouched, slight body. The folder came open and they fell limply about him, onto the rug. He didn't move and she backed away, fists clenched with rage. She got her coat and went out into the now cold night. She was still simmering as she stalked past the brightly-lit hotel, and didn't see the constable until it was too late. He was young and there was a pale wisp of moustache on his upper lip, an unwise attempt to insist some gravitas on his otherwise puppyish features. Clearly delighted by this chance encounter he took it upon himself to escort her home. When they reached her front door he stepped back and saluted.

'There you are Miss. All safe and sound. Can't be too careful you know.'

Very early the following morning, well before work, she bundled every single item she had worn the night before into a bag and, on the way to the beach, dumped it in a waste bin.

She swam far out and looked back at the coastline. It had been her fault. She had known all along that she could twist him round her little finger and had used it, mercilessly, teased and tormented him as if it were all a game. But it wasn't. It had all gone horribly awry. She was angry with herself but angry with him too. After all, he must have planned it. Perhaps it wasn't really all her fault, not all of it.

She kicked for shore and swam back. The letter was with her towel and she would post it on the way to work. Unable to sleep she had finished it late at night in a lukewarm way, no longer with expectation.

CHAPTER TWENTY-EIGHT

'Telephone for you!' Mollie called up the stairs. As Jenny came down she added in an animated whisper, hand clapped firmly over the mouthpiece, 'It's that magazine!'

It was a woman's voice, brisk and nasal. Could she be available in a week's time? They were keen to do some beach shots and possibly some around the Pavilion if the weather turned. Oh, and what dress size was she? And was she agency?

When Jenny put the telephone down her head was reeling. She could barely keep up with the torrent of questions from Mollie. Later she arranged with Mac to have the day off and during the week bought new make-up and practised in front of the mirror, the radio on for company. She didn't walk the seafront as usual, didn't want to run the risk of bumping into Chris. When the day finally arrived she was surprised and touched to find a small poesy of freesias left for her. The card with them read simply, *From Frankie.*

She hadn't known what to expect but imagined a glamorous crew of sophisticated professionals. The reality was very different. A woman in her late forties, a touch overweight and with greying hair pulled back in an inappropriate girlish ponytail. She introduced herself as Evelyn but the photographer called her Evie. He was old, even older than Mac, Jenny thought. A few strands of ginger-grey hair were stretched preciously across an otherwise bald head, already shining with perspiration. There was a mottled, beaten look to him, one she recognised; he was a drinker. His name was Ted and he called Jenny 'love'. They arrived in a small van with no windows in the rear and nothing on it to indicate that they were from a magazine or important. Ted wheezed as he unloaded the equipment and fell behind when they walked a short distance along the beach, looking for what the woman called 'a good location, right backdrop.' As Ted eventually lumbered up to them, burdened with cameras, cases and tripod, he was out of breath and deathly pale.

They had brought with them several changes of costume and a few small props. Evie asked, with a shame-faced grimace, if she wouldn't mind changing in the back of the van.

'Won't peep,' Ted said with a hoarse guffaw, 'promise!'

She went back and climbed in while they set up the equipment. The van's interior had a whiff of chemicals that made her wrinkle her nose. Incongruously, a small mirror had been fixed inside though she had to crouch down to see herself in it.

They wanted to do the beach shots first, while it was sunny, and had brought a bikini for her to wear. She struggled into it in the cramped interior, carefully putting it on beneath her skirt and top before removing them, just in case anyone could see in. The bikini was spangled with gold thread and felt scratchy. It was smaller than the one she had bought and the top was under-wired, pushing her breasts up uncomfortably. It definitely wasn't for swimming in and she was sure Frankie wouldn't think it decent.

The sheer volume of shots Ted took surprised her. It was quite different to Chris's careful staging. Every time she moved, it seemed, there was a click and a whirr. She was photographed leaping up against the blue sky with a multi-coloured beach ball, relaxing in a deck chair and peeping out from behind the spun pink froth of an enormous candy floss. Finally, she was posed kneeling and leaning seductively forward over a bucket and spade.

'But it's pebbles, not sand!' she protested, laughing.

'No one's going to notice that,' Ted said, winding on quickly, 'you'd be surprised what people don't see if they don't want to. Now squeeze those elbows in towards each other a bit, that's it, lovely, and give us that little girl look again.' The camera worked ceaselessly. Even when she thought they were taking a break, and she was sat on the beach pushing back her hair, it clicked and then clicked again as she turned round to look.

'That'll be a good one,' the man grunted, pleased with himself.

She changed into a long turquoise dress for the final sequence beneath the pier, and was made to lean up against one of its massive gnarled legs and look out to sea, the wind blowing through her hair.

'That's it, now give us a dreamy face, all wistful like,' Ted barked. 'You've just met Mr. Wonderful and he's pushed off to sea. Yep, like that, good……good. Chin out a bit. Lovely.'

When it was over, and Ted laboriously loading up the van once more, Evie took out a notebook.

'Just a few details about you.'

For no good reason Jenny found herself blushing at the innocuous questions, yet the photography had been easy, almost enjoyable.

'And what's your ambition?' the woman asked finally, still smiling, pen poised. Jenny floundered, stuck for an answer.

'I don't know,' she hesitated and laughed shyly, 'isn't that silly?'

'Don't worry,' Evie reassured, 'I'll dream something up.'

After they had gone she felt unexpectedly flat, at a loose end. It had all been a bit too businesslike. She half hoped they might let her keep some of the clothes but instead Evie gathered them up carefully and packed them away. It wasn't so much that she wanted them, especially the uncomfortable bikini, though the dress had been nice. It was just that now it was all over there was nothing. She cheered herself up with the thought that it was only a week or so before the magazine came out. She'd have something then. At least, she cautioned herself, she would if they used the pictures. Evie had said she would let her know.

When the brief letter arrived it was surprisingly formal and signed by someone else, not Evie. A selection of the photographs would, it said, be used in the forthcoming issue and a cheque for ten pounds was enclosed in payment for the work she had undertaken. There was a receipt too. She looked at the cheque with delight. She hadn't thought about getting paid for it. After all it wasn't like work.

'Money for old rope, eh?' Frankie said later. 'Well why not. Good for you. Give yourself a treat.'

A week later, early in the morning, she went to the local newsagents.

'Have you got the latest *New Britain* please?' she asked with affected coolness.

The elderly shopkeeper sighed, bent and cut the string from a newly arrived bale of magazines on the floor, extracted one and handed it to her disinterestedly, without any hint of recognition. She wouldn't have noticed anyway. She paid and left the shop in a daze. It was her face on the front cover.

★　★　★

'Christ!' Frankie closed the magazine, looked again at the cover then at her. Jenny felt the sinking weight of her disapproval. It was true the gold bikini looked more skimpy, more revealing, than she remembered. But censure hadn't been uppermost in Frankie's mind. 'There's a whole page of you inside as well,' she continued, flipping the pages. When the rebuke did come it was with a teasing gleam, 'But look here young lady, that bikini thing don't leave much to the imagination. Surprised a scrap like that didn't fly orf with you runnin' and jumping about.' She looked at Jenny, the banter and the voice softening, 'Famous then aren't you?'

'Course not,' Jenny was shyly dismissive, 'it's only a magazine.'

'They'll be coming here in droves I'll bet,' the baiting was back as Frankie drifted towards the kitchens with a loaded tray 'coach loads of 'em. That'll cheer old Mac up anyway.' And she disappeared, pushing open the swing doors expertly with her rear end.

Frankie was the first person she showed it to. The magazine had stayed hidden in her room for days, challenging her to own up to it. In the end, she told herself they were bound to see it anyway, far better to meet it head on.

After her own initial shock, panic set in, the renewed fear that she would be recognised. For some time she had given it scant thought, so long had passed and she looked and was quite different. Seeing herself paraded on the magazine cover though had shaken her. Then she told herself she was just being stupid, no one could possibly identify her from it. Yet it unsettled her. She thought it would just be a little picture, hidden away inside, not that she would be beaming from every news-stand she passed.

She was, nevertheless, diffidently pleased with the images. They had enhanced her somehow, by some magic in the laboratory, made her more blonde, more tanned. The day itself had been transformed into high summer, much brighter than it had really been.

The article, under the banner headline, *Holiday Great Britain*, was titled: *Lookaround Brighton*. It listed the standard attractions as well as some selected hotels and restaurants. There was a piece on the continuing controversy over the fate of the pier and a eulogy on the marvels of the Pavilion. The photographs of her were used to give it, as Evie had explained, 'human interest'. In the captions she was *local beauty Jenny Robin,* her age given wrongly as nineteen, although she herself had anyway lied about it.

When she's not dazzling customers with that winning smile at one of the town's seafront restaurants, it went on, *lovely Jenny enjoys nothing more than the delights of Brighton's famous beach where she hopes one day to land a special catch of her own – and what a lucky fella he'll be!*

So that was it. That was what her life amounted to. She cringed at the chirpy, provincial enthusiasm, and was embarrassed. The photographs made her look good but the writing made her silly dumb blonde. She was cross she had let it be like that, hadn't had answers ready, and it set off a dull, incipient realisation; she had been drifting, lying low, and been diverted. As she lay in bed that night, a part of her, long submerged, surfaced again. She had too successfully put the dream of going home to one side. Unrealizable before, it had been waiting and came back now with a vengeance, firing her determination to have again what had been taken from her: Hadley, home. She had been dazzled by a little freedom and blind to the real one, in a way still just as much imprisoned as she had been in London. To be free she had to return and lay claim. Only then would she win. She was no longer Jennifer Hawker, a frightened child. She was Jenny Robin, a woman. It was not enough to chide herself for her inconsistency, her lack of action. She must choose who Jenny Robin was to be, what she would become, and no longer be hostage to a dead man, a ghost.

She turned on the bedside lamp and Daddy smiled at her. Picking up the photograph she searched his face, then slowly put it down again, smiling sadly at the lost childhood imagination that could summon him up and had such blind faith in his indestructibility.

'I will win,' she promised them both. 'I shall have it back. I'll make a way. It belongs to me.'

★   ★   ★

'That nipper's been back,' Julia whispered suspiciously, her voice thick with rumour in the making.

'What nipper?'

'You know, flash one with the sports car. Dunno what he said but old Mac looked proper out of sorts.'

Jenny had only a dim memory of the green racer that had scorched off down the road and was too preoccupied to take much notice of gossip. Her own schemes, so clear in the night, remained still just schemes and she was troubled by not knowing what to do next, where to begin. Unexpectedly the first inkling of an answer came that evening. She walked along the front, her old walk, half-looking out for Chris. She didn't exactly want to see him but equally no longer wanted to avoid him. Part of her too, wanted to flaunt the magazine, as if that would re-establish something, something about her, although she could not put a name to what that was. Perhaps if she just bumped into him, by accident......

Yet there was no sign of him and as darkness fell she found herself wandering, with guilty compulsion, towards his house. She stopped in the road outside and peered furtively round the hedge. The place was in complete darkness. She crept towards it, peeped through a window and found it deserted, no longer crammed and cluttered with his paraphernalia. It had all gone. There was not a trace of him anywhere. He had disappeared. She walked back telling herself she didn't care anyway, but it left her feeling hollow, a touch resentful, and by the time she was at her lodgings, she was unreasonably piqued and deflated.

The telephone rang just as she passed it, making her jump. She picked it up and gave the number. A woman's voice said, 'Jenny?'

'Yes?'

'Well you are a popular girl. We've had a small avalanche of enquiries since the last issue,' and then added, as an afterthought, 'It's Evie. *New Britain*.'

'Oh hello!'

'Look sweetie, it's your choice but as well as the usual creeps and cranks we've had several trade enquiries. Do you want us to pass on your number?'

'Trade?'

'You know, agencies, that sort of thing. What do you say?'

'Well, I don't know.'

'It's up to you.'

'All right then, if you like. All right.'

'Fine darling, we'll do that. Now just remind me of your address and I'll get some copy prints sent for your portfolio. Did you like them by the way?'

She came off the phone unsure what to make of it all; portfolios, agency, trade? It was a baffling new language. She doubted whether anything would come of it anyway. There were more important things for her to think about now.

Two days later she returned home to find a message from Mollie. It was written in large capitals. A company called Chelsea Film had telephoned, and they wanted to speak to her. Would she call next morning and ask for Mr. Blake. Mollie had written IMPORTANT across the top and underlined it heavily.

She made the call from work. Mac was out again and Frankie shooed her conspiratorially into his office.

'Go on, go on. He'll never know. Won't be back for ages.' She was still waiting at the door, arms folded, wreathed in blue smoke, when Jenny came out.

'Well, what did they say?'

'They said they've got some work for me.'

'And?'

'Modelling. For a catalogue, about three days.'

'What sort of catalogue?'

'Clothes, fashions.'

'How much?'

'I didn't ask. They said the usual rate.'

'And what did you say?'

She hesitated, 'I said yes.'

That evening she flouted her own unspoken rule, the one that kept others at arms length and, at Frankie's insistence, went out with her for a celebratory drink. Frankie drank whisky, steadily and with a well-practised hand. Jenny asked for a martini and was served a tart, bitter liquid from a green bottle, quite unlike the one poured for her from a silver shaker in the Kings Crescent.

'You never know, this could be the start of something,' Frankie said, well into her third Scotch. 'You grab it if it is. You don't want to drift along like the rest of us and end up in the back of beyond.' She nudged Jenny in the ribs, 'If you've got half a chance take it and make something of yourself. You've got nothing to lose.' And she clinked her tumbler a touch too fiercely against Jenny's glass.

★   ★   ★

She was encased in one of the most elegant dresses she had ever seen, a slender, electric blue sheath. At least, elegance was what she saw in the dressing room mirror, that and her own slightly startled expression. What the reflection concealed though, was a knobbly spine of wooden clothes pegs running down the back of the dress, tugging and pulling it until it was like a second skin. A sour wardrobe mistress had spent half an hour putting them into place. By the time the woman was satisfied Jenny's back and calves ached from standing and she hobbled to the set like a geisha. She was also self-consciously naked beneath the dress. The same woman had rebuked her for showing lines.

She stood dumbly in front of the cameras while a make-up man put the final touches to her face. Then briskly, and without a word, he covered up the scar beneath her forearm.

The three days, cadged from a benign but distracted Mac, were disappointingly low-key. She hadn't shown it at the time but Frankie's pep-talk had fired her up and, with her own reawakened dream spurring her on, she wanted some momentous hand of fate to swoop down and show her the way, the answer. Instead it was quite mundane. She caught a train, and then a bus, each morning to a jaded but still palatial country house just outside Reigate, which was being used as the location. The day was spent scrambling in and out of clothes, being fussed over by the make-up man, and then photographed. There was no glamour in it and only the meagre satisfaction of knowing that someone, the absent Mr. Blake she supposed, wanted her face, her body, in his catalogue. They were constantly pressured by the expense of hiring the location and had to scurry about and miss breaks to meet the deadline. It was all rush, all haste. Apart from her there was one other model, a woman called Rose, who treated her disdainfully despite Jenny's deference. Rose was, after all, older and a proper model. The woman made it absolutely clear that Jenny was merely an unimportant adjunct to her own central and starring role in the enterprise. Yet it was Jenny who was photographed the most. Rose wore a perpetual scowl that magically evaporated as soon as she was before the camera, replaced by a smile of such sweetness it was hard to believe she was the same person.

It wasn't until the last afternoon that the mysterious Mr. Blake turned up. He was much older than Jenny expected, more like a businessman or bank manager. He introduced himself in a slow, polished voice and was clearly embarrassed when Rose flounced past and snarled at him sulkily.

'Law against using children isn't there?'

When the three days were over she felt tired and dispirited. At the end she was given an envelope and caught a late train back to Brighton, gazing out at the darkness, brooding and absorbed. When she was back in her room she opened the envelope. As well as a receipt it contained, in cash, as much as she earned in a fortnight at the restaurant, including tips. She put the money back in and wrote on it: *Hadley.*

They phoned again, a week later, and asked if she would do another shoot, this time a weekend. She hesitated. The anonymous but enthusiastic voice on the other end promised, 'it won't be boring like that old catalogue thing. That's just bread and butter stuff. This is different, you know, classy.' Still she demurred, sounded unconvinced, and said she would think about it. When they called back the next day she bluntly asked for twice the money. There was a pause, a muffled murmuring as a hand went over the mouthpiece. Then the voice returned, bright but a shade taken aback.

'Yes, well......Mr. Blake says we can agree on that, so......yes......'

'OK then,' she said dryly and hung up the phone. It had worked.

★　★　★

'Who is she?'

It was an imperious voice that honed in on Jenny like a pointing finger. The precise enunciation silenced the crowded set for a few moments until a hum of activity, more subdued than before, started up again.

The question came from a short, fleshy man wearing a burgundy turtle-neck and black corduroy trousers. He had a neatly trimmed beard and receding hair clipped very short, like a crew cut. He was looking straight at her, oblivious or indifferent both to her unease and the intimidated hush that followed his loud interjection. Jenny tried not to look but his fixed stare drew her back to him. A woman with a clipboard standing next to him whispered something.

'Who?' he said again, his eyes still intent on her. 'Jenny who?' She turned her back, cross and flustered at his arrogant ill-manners and his air of dismissive flamboyance. It was a relief when he strode from the set with the clipboard woman in tow.

'Who is that rude sod?' she asked one of the other models. A kind of classroom glee, laced with relief, had broken out and there were whispers and sniggers in the room. The girl looked at her in surprise.

'Tilden,' she answered.

'Tilden who?'

The girl gave a short, derisive laugh, 'Oh no, not Tilden who, or Mr. Tilden and especially not dear Tilden. Don't you know?' The name had a vague familiarity but Jenny could not pin it down.

'Well, what is he then?' she asked peevishly. The girl sighed impatiently, took a dress from the rack and brandished the label at her. There was one word stitched across it in black thread: *Tilden*.

'You must have heard of him for God's sake. He's famous. He owns all of this.'

The penny finally dropped. Of course, she had seen it all over the place, in fashion magazines and clothes shops,

'But I thought it was just a trademark, not a real name, not a person.'

'It's all of them,' the girl said shortly, putting the dress back.

Deflated, Jenny said, 'Isn't Mr. Blake in charge then?'

'Blake?' the girl snorted, turning away, 'he's just Tilden's runner.'

Jenny filled a paper cup from an urn and retreated thoughtfully to a quieter corner with the tepid, indeterminate brew.

It had been six weeks since she upped her price and the company had called on her several times. She had been quietly warned off letting the other girls know about her hike in pay; although she anyway kept herself to herself. The brown envelope had swollen and with it her restlessness. Although uncomfortable about taking more and more time off from what she still thought of as her proper job, her modest portion of fame had, as Frankie predicted, boosted custom and with it the pool of tips they all shared. The local paper ran a small piece about her and she was photographed standing outside the restaurant with Mac.

'Best advert he's ever had,' Frankie drawled. 'Gawd knows why his face is so ruddy long.' A niece of Julia's was recruited to help out during Jenny's absences. All the same, Mac did seem increasingly preoccupied with some deep and secret concern.

She still swam almost every day but was aware of a needling disenchantment with the town and its docile sea. It was tamed here, hemmed in by the pier, and she longed for the landscapes of home and for the remembered seas that effortlessly imparted the gift of belonging.

The Spindrifter

'Tilden wants to see you!' It was an urgent, whispered summons. The woman with the clipboard was standing over her. She looked nervous, her mouth forcing an uncertain smile. 'Please come now if you will.' Jenny stood and followed her. A hush had again descended over the set and she had the irrational but disconcerting feeling of having broken some school rule and being led away for punishment. The woman marched quickly along the corridor with Jenny in tow. They stopped in front of a plain white door. The woman cleared her throat, knocked sharply, then opened it and ushered her in.

'Stand just there,' the voice ordered. He was sitting cross-legged on a large desk, genie-like, elbows on knees, fingers pressed together under his chin. She did as she was told, hoping her obedience was offset by the impassivity with which she returned his gaze. He stared at her silently; piercingly intense, small green eyes, a look simultaneously appraising and challenging. The tips of his fingers slowly brushed the tailored beard as he coolly assessed her. 'Now turn around.' Again she acquiesced and found herself staring at a blank wall. Blind to what was going on behind her she felt vulnerable, awkward. 'You may turn back,' he said as though granting a favour. As she did he slid from the desk and began to circle her contemplatively. He came just up to her shoulder but held himself very straight, stiff-backed. The woman with the clipboard stood pensively by the window, pen poised, waiting for instructions. He stepped backwards, folded his arms and began to stroke the beard again.

'Take off your dress,' he said evenly.

'Drop dead!'

It came out hotly, instinctively, and the moment it did she regretted it. It belied horribly the cool and sophisticated appearance she had tried to project. She wanted to have said something clever, some quick, smart retort. He looked at her impenetrably then began to laugh, a low, satisfied chuckle.

'Perfect,' he purred, 'absolutely perfect.' He strutted up to Jenny and planted himself squarely in front of her, arms still crossed, the green eyes now faintly ironical.

'Beauty is a strange and unpredictable currency,' he said. 'Do not for one moment allow yourself the illusion of thinking my request voyeuristic or prurient. That would indeed be folly.' A curiously prim smile briefly illuminated his face. A secret joke, she thought, and probably at her expense. She looked down at him, into the unyielding eyes. There was something so detached and impersonal in the way he scrutinised her that, against her better judgement, she was inclined to believe him. He backed away and perched on the desk again, still studying her, waiting.

It was a test. A dare, to see if she had the nerve. She looked away from him, past the woman and out of the window. With icy defiance she unzipped the dress and let it fall with a soft swish where she stood, now completely naked. Slowly half turning her head, she cast her own long, remote look of appraisal over him.

If he was taken aback it did not show. When at length he spoke it was as though to himself, in a voice less domineering.

'Quite the young Amazon,' he mused, 'fabulous tone. Outstanding, outstanding.'

Then, without warning, and to her utter amazement he did something quite extraordinary. Jumping to his feet he bestrode the desk like a podium and in ringing tones addressed a vast, invisible, imaginary throng.

'I have seen the future!' he proclaimed, 'and it is not in Paris, Milan or New York. It does not wear Chanel or Dior. No!' He paused for breath, or effect. Jenny wanted to giggle but the sight of the woman, scribbling as though possessed, quashed it. He opened his arms expansively. 'The future is here. It is nineteen years old and the clothes it wears will no longer grotesquely ape those of the so-called great houses. Instead they will come from ordinary shops in ordinary towns. I will create those clothes and give my name to them.' He looked down at her and his voice dropped a tone. 'I have seen the future,' he said again, 'and this is its face.'

With surprising agility he leapt from the desk, took hold of her by the shoulders, eyes burning into her own. 'This is the look of tomorrow. I have found it.' He laughed, soft and sardonic, and his expression changed to amusement, eyes crinkling, glittering as if at some inner joke. 'I'm right aren't I?' he whispered. 'Tilden is right. It's you Jenny Robin.' Despite the laughter there was such certainty in his voice that she found herself nodding dumbly, still completely bewildered by what she had witnessed, and wholly unsure just what she was giving her assent to.

He stalked back around the desk, picked up a handful of photographs and shuffled through them disinterestedly. He was again brisk and decisive, the high melodrama gone in a moment. 'These to go back in the file,' he said to the woman, dropping the prints onto the desk. 'Put your dress back on now,' he added, turning to Jenny. But she ignored him, had glimpsed the photographs, and came forward, uncertain, disbelieving, and picked one up. It was her, and it was one of Chris's pictures.

'Where did you get these?' she gasped.

He shrugged, 'Left at reception some time ago, together with an appalling ragbag of a magazine. You were on the cover. Left anonymously I might add. People are strange and do strange things, sometimes those things are also fortuitous.'

She struggled with a feeling of revulsion that somehow the whole tawdry episode with Chris was revealed in the scattered prints and had been seen by these strangers. Sombrely, she pulled up the dress and fastened it.

'Now,' Tilden snapped, 'to work quickly. The hair is good but not good enough. More bounce and uplift. Get Wilding on to it.' The woman was again writing furiously. 'And I want a dozen designs from make-up by the end of the week.' He was pacing up and down, face set in concentration. 'You haven't done this work for long have you?'

'Not very long, but I've watched and learnt and......'

'No!' he thundered. 'Unlearn, unlearn everything! I have no use for a stiff mannequin. All that is finished now. It is dead. I want the life in you. That is what is required. Every woman in the country will want to look like you, move the way you move, even speak like you. We will make them spellbound precisely because you will be different.' He leant over the desk and glowered ominously at her. 'Unlearn everything,' he hissed incisively, 'and be different.'

Her head was spinning. She couldn't take in what he was saying or what it meant. The handful of inexplicably tell-tale photographs were whisked from the desk. Everything around her was moving too fast and she felt pummelled by it.

'Look,' she said, disturbed and perplexed, 'what is all this about, what do you want me for. Is it another shoot or what?'

'Another shoot?' he echoed dismissively and drew himself up to his full height. 'This will be an adventure. The biggest of them all, the best of them all.' He paused and gave her a caustic, sidelong look. 'Dare you?' he drawled provocatively.

'I don't know......'

'Dare you?' he insisted.

'All right,' she said weakly, both baffled and intrigued, and still without a clue what it was all about. A smirk of satisfaction came over his face.

'I thought you would.'

'But what is it then?'

'An assault upon this fair island, an attack on sensibilities. We will outrage and enchant, we will beguile and affront and, most of all, we'll keep them guessing. Do you begin to see?'

She began to say no but, as if suddenly bored, he fluttered a hand at the woman and said without interest, 'Jane will answer all your questions. She is remarkably good with the, uh, detail.' He strode to the door and as he opened it turned and with a slight, playful smile muttered, 'You will, of course, make a great deal of money.'

★   ★   ★

A hum of giddy excitement and daring anticipation stole slowly over her as she sat on the train going home. She couldn't quite believe her luck and was brimful of herself. But even as the day's events unfolded again in her mind, uppermost was a tantalising vision of Hadley, now perhaps becoming dazzlingly attainable.

As Tilden had said the woman, Jane, proved to have a remarkable facility for detail. Jenny listened, abstracted, as she went over point by meticulous point of Tilden's 'adventure.'

She would be required to leave Brighton and move up to London as soon as possible. A company flat would be placed at her disposal. In return for what Jane called a generous commission, she would be the exclusive model for Tilden's new look, an extensive and radical collection which she would also undertake to endorse and promote as and when directed, at all times.

'Body and soul stuff rather,' Jane grimaced apologetically, 'I'm afraid your feet will hardly touch the ground.'

'I see,' Jenny said thoughtfully. 'So it's a whole new fashion, to catch the mood of the times.' It was a phrase she had read somewhere and repeated now uncertainly.

'No,' the woman smiled indulgently, 'not to catch it, to manufacture it.'

Jenny was to understand that she would be at the behest of the company and would also be expected to attend launches, promotions and special events to present Tilden's creations.

'However,' Jane said matter-of-factly, 'the rewards, as indicated, will be quite considerable.' A two year contract would be drawn up in due course but, in the interim, a retainer would be paid to her now as an indication of good faith. Jane wrote out a cheque there and then. Jenny accepted it but thought it impolite to look at the amount. The woman relaxed as the business was concluded and leant back in her chair.

'He's been looking for you for rather a long time you know.'

'Has he?'

'Oh yes. We've all been under orders to scour the country. Pure chance he was here today really and spotted you himself. It's better that way. It has to be his idea. I'm sure you will have gathered he can be a teensy bit difficult, shall we say, but I can at least promise you an interesting time with us.' She seemed amused by the prospect and lit a cigarette. 'If I might just offer one piece of advice?'

'Yes, please do,' Jenny was quietly euphoric.

'He must have things his own way. It's the price one pays. And he likes to shake things up a bit. Anyway, hold on to your hat.'

And now the slow train was rattling her back to the prosaic, the humdrum. She wondered what Frankie and the others would think and had a guilty pang. Mac, having put up with her increasingly frequent absences, would now lose her altogether as well as the cachet of her local celebrity. But soon dreams of home once again filled her. Two years, Jane had said, two years and she would be rich. In her mind's eye Hadley was always empty, waiting for her to return, although common sense told her that other people must be living there now. It didn't matter though. If you were rich you could do anything, get anything, and it seemed such a small thing to want, just an ordinary house that was anyway hers by right. Not at all a grand dream.

It was dark when the train shambled listlessly into the station. Dreamily, hugged by the night, she made her way back to her lodgings. She had not been there long when the telephone rang in the hall and Mollie called her down. She picked up the receiver in the same pleasantly muzzy haze of well-being that had cocooned her on the journey home.

'Hello?'

It was Frankie.

'It's Mac,' she said in a hoarse, detached voice, 'he's dead.'

CHAPTER TWENTY-NINE

Mac had killed himself that afternoon. While she had been eagerly absorbing her future, Mac had relinquished his own. He had left the restaurant at midday and driven out into the country, parked his car by the side of the road and, in a small, still clearing, hanged himself with a towrope.

The two women stood disconsolately outside the locked restaurant in the damp early morning. A hasty sign on the door read *Closed. Re-opening soon.*

'Why did he do it?' Jenny asked sadly, 'why?'

Frankie shrugged, 'Don't know. No note or nothing. Always kept himself to himself did Mac. Money probably. Usually is.'

'But business has never been better, he said so himself.'

Again Frankie shrugged. She looked particularly gaunt and sallow. Mac's death had affected her far more than she was owning to. She looked at the sign and said gloomily, 'Don't suppose there'll be jobs for us when it does,' and she reached out to Jenny, a simple clasping of hands, eyes averted, nothing said.

She could not tell Frankie about Tilden and the gilded adventure she was set to embark on. Frankie looked sombre and crushed as she lit a cigarette. Jenny decided to tell her later, over the weekend. They parted awkwardly, the place that had brought them together now out of bounds and Mac's lonely suicide somehow a silent admonishment. They each knew, and for different reasons, that their own friendship was changed by it.

On the way home Jenny struggled to come to terms with her own enormous good fortune while the others had been pitched so suddenly, and in such terrible circumstances, out of work. She felt stricken too at the manner of Mac's death. They had all, at one time or another, taken advantage of his good nature, and made jokes behind his back, albeit without malice. More than that though, her feelings of guilt and sadness came from the realisation that, now he was gone, none of them really knew anything at all about him. As Frankie had once said, he was a loner and that was how he had died. Nobody, she thought, should die like that, without friends. What should have been her triumphant first step on a golden ladder had been unexpectedly cast in deep shadow. Now especially, she could not wait to get away.

She had told Mollie the previous evening, or at least told her a more modest, muted version of Tilden's grandiose scheme. On the way home she stopped to buy a gift for her, a silver powder compact in a blue velvet pouch, as well as a suitcase for herself. She spent the afternoon packing, carefully wrapping the photograph of Daddy in a patterned silk scarf and solemnly stowing her childhood mementoes with painstaking care, drowning out other, darker thoughts with a babble of chatter from the radio.

When everything was more or less done, she sat dejectedly on the bed and looked round at the empty walls. She had found a kind of happiness here, an equilibrium, even though she recognised it too as a self-imposed limbo. And now another departure. Where she should have been elated she was instead downcast and melancholy.

'For God's sake, buck yourself up!' she scolded, clenching her fists. Then decisively, swiftly changed into her bikini, threw a dress over it and, grabbing a towel, walked quickly to the beach.

The day was cool and overcast and she was the sole swimmer. Neat piles of deckchairs remained undisturbed and the ice-cream kiosk was closed and shuttered. It always gave her a small swell of pride to be the only one who dared go in on days like this. Sometimes people would stop and watch, point her out to each other and shiver. She knew it was a kind of showing off but didn't care. She swam out then turned and floated on her back, looking up at a rolling mass of pale grey cloud.

Not tomorrow, she thought, but the day after that, she would be back in London and she would be someone else. She was curiously neutral about returning to the city she had so hated. It seemed she had left one London, a place of unhappiness and disillusion, but would go back to another, a different one that held out the promise of so much. There was an irony, a justice, that the city which had so diminished her should now play a part in returning what she had lost. She looked up and into the future, at a swirl of opportunities, possibilities, she had never dreamt of. She was free to become......to become whatever she wanted. It was all just around the corner.

'I am what I will be,' she laughed, and an answering breaker at the shore crashed its approval.

She rolled over and began to swim back, cheered by the cool sea and its silent encouragement. As she neared the beach she noticed a man standing motionless far up by the deckchairs. He was quite plainly watching her. Too distant for her to see him clearly, he was dark and stocky, solitary and anonymous, the collar of his coat pulled up around him. She felt put out by his spying, not so much by him looking but by the brazen, shameless way he was doing it. She waved with enthusiastic mock gaiety, to embarrass him, so he'd see she knew what he was up to, but the man remained quite still, unmoved.

'Bloody cheek!' she said to herself and, changing stroke to a fast crawl, swam quickly to shore. When next she looked he had disappeared.

★   ★   ★

That evening found her with quickening impatience and time to kill. A sea fog had descended and she wandered aimlessly along the deserted promenade. Despite herself she couldn't stop thinking about the puzzle of Mac's suicide. It was such a forlorn act. She sat down on a bench and looked out at the intense night. The shroud of fog gave it a pensive, muffled stillness and she shuddered at the image of Mac that refused to leave her. She forced herself to think instead of the future, of Hadley, remembering it room by room, inch by inch, and walking once more along the secret ways of childhood. In her mind she clambered through the woods, recalling the rich greens and the mingled scent of salt, trees and earth. Then along the dusty lane to home, glitteringly white in the sunshine, through the special gate and past the beech tree Daddy had climbed to make a swing for her. Up and up he had gone, vanishing among the branches so completely that she was frightened for him and wanted to call out.

Dad. What on earth would he have made of all this, of what she was doing. Would he have been proud? Again she was a child, looking out of her bedroom window at the clear night sky and listening with rapt attention as he gave names to the stars and, in remembering, tears splashed down onto her folded hands. She wiped them away. She hadn't wanted to cry, hadn't meant to. She was glad of the fog now, it hid her from anyone seeing. She took out a handkerchief, wiped her eyes and thought wryly that the stars were in hiding tonight. No way of knowing then, which was the right way home.

And then, out of the dark, out of the mist and out of the blue, strode a tall, square figure, hauntingly evocative, the glow of a cigarette reflected in the glinting, braided peak of a familiar cap as he stopped in front of her. Startled, jolted back to the present, she froze, not daring to look up but staring transfixed at the double row of shiny buttons on his jacket. An electrifying, timeless silence, a wreath of blue smoke curling slowly around the mist.

'Are you sure you're quite all right?'

It was a warm, gently concerned voice and to her astonishment not one she recognised.

★   ★   ★

Peter. Woozily half-awake she studied him as he lay, still sound asleep, beside her in the bed. He was so neat, so precise, even in sleep. Neat was just the right word, she thought, for the handsome symmetry of his face; the pleasantly shaped brown eyes, each with a scattering of small wrinkles at the corners when he smiled. She loved the way his short black hair was clipped tidily around his ears and the evenness of the blue beard shadow which had appeared overnight, a curve running down from each cheekbone that might have been drawn with a compass. His face was lightly, evenly, tanned, a line encircling his neck where the colour stopped and below the flesh was paler and smooth. Everything about him was just so and he glistened with an effortless, youthful polish.

He had been so kind too, so gentle in a shyly attractive way. Yet what she liked most, what had given her the greatest pleasure, was that he so clearly and charmingly had been utterly smitten by her. She found it completely compelling, gave a wriggle of pleasure and snuggled down into the unfamiliar and particular warmth of a shared bed, breathing in the smell of him, the man smell of soap and tobacco, metal buttons and polished shoes. Beyond the hotel window a chirruping glee-club of starlings announced the morning and she felt a puff of hope that more than just a new day might be heralded. It was just idle day-dreaming of course, but nonetheless she found herself wondering what being with him would be like, about a shared future, a lieutenant commander's wife. She laughed at her flight of fancy but in the cosy morning it did seem rather appealing, the prospect of a lifetime soaking in that delightful attentiveness.

The night before, when he had appeared from nowhere and her imagination briefly got the better of her, he was chivalry itself. He insisted on buying her a brandy and that she take his arm as they walked.

'You still look a little shaky,' he said solicitously and she felt garlanded by his gallant consideration. It was a little unnerving to find herself once again in the Kings Crescent, but Peter was so kind that she soon relaxed and found herself rather enjoying answering his questions. He wanted to know all about her and leaned forward in his seat, head tilted eagerly. He was fascinated when he found out she was a model but professed himself unsurprised and asked all sorts of technical questions about the photography that she could not answer. She did not tell him that until a few days before she had more properly considered herself a waitress. Instead, and knowingly, she gave a vague impression of having always been 'in the fashion lark', only now she was about to embark on a London career. He looked especially pleased and said he often went to London and perhaps they could meet for tea.

'Perhaps,' she flirted assuredly, briefly puzzled that an invitation to tea sounded more genteel than romantic. When he suggested dinner at the hotel she secretly jumped at it, though the cool, elegant young woman he asked paused, mulled it over, before accepting.

He was a training officer at a land base. Over dinner, he made her laugh with tales about new recruits but always he came back to her and always with that same bright attentive light in his eyes, an unconcealed fascination that made her feel powerful, important, desired. At the end of the meal he lit a cigarette and said quietly, straightforwardly, that she was the most beautiful woman he had ever met. She purred inside, accepted the compliment with simple grace, charmed by him and cupped in swirling cigarette smoke. There was no question but that they would be lovers. A soft intensity between them had developed and deepened during the evening and the looks they now exchanged sparkled with a sensual intimacy. When he asked if she would stay, covering her hand with his own, it was not with an expectation that she would but with the unspoken acknowledgement of a great favour to be granted or withheld. He had looked boyish then, and vulnerable, as he waited for her answer.

She admired the unabashed aplomb with which he booked them a room, the ease with which he wove a tale about his 'wife' being slightly 'under par' and how it would anyway be much better to stay over than travel on in 'this damned fog.' The reception clerk nodded in sage and unsuspicious agreement.

'Quite the best thing Sir, by far.'

It had been hard for her not to giggle as they went up the stairs, especially when the clerk said he hoped she would be fully recovered by morning.

Peter. The luxury of him, of letting go at last. The sweet pressure of his delicate hands running over her and the shattering crush of coupling as she grabbed at his back, clawed at his shirt and pulled him into her. How she had revelled in him, and afterwards in his astonished male delight at being the first.

She slipped quietly from the bed and went into the small adjoining bathroom, anxious to look her best when he woke. She was dressed and sitting in front of the mirror as he began to stir, rolling over in the bed and flinging an arm across where she had lain. She smiled as the brown eyes flickered open, closed again, and a hand came up to rub his face. He yawned, a glorious, straining yawn, one arm outstretched, groping the air, and suddenly there is a flashing glint in the mirror. She stares, sees the circle of gold on one of his fingers, dropping into her consciousness like a white-hot, molten fragment and at the same time a cold enmity erupts inside her, and a loathing with herself for not seeing, not choosing to see. The wedding ring gleams in the reflection, mesmerising, and in looking she sees only herself now, blinded by empty, useless pipe dreams, by betrayal bitterly revisited.

He is shaking himself slowly awake, a smile spreading over his face as he looks at her, then swings his legs out of the bed and sits, contented and trim. She remembers his gleefulness at being her first lover, a grubby plus to his faithless conquest. He is still smiling as she rises and with slow deliberation moves across to the bed and stands over him. He does not see the small manicure scissors as she stabs savagely down into one of his still strange, pale thighs, feels the flesh bend and puncture, leaving the stumpy blades embedded. A startled yelp and for a moment she is hypnotised by the thick, fat bubble of blood oozing slowly from the wound. Then his howl of pain and incredulous, 'Jesus Christ!', still ringing in her ears as she slams the door unrepentantly behind her, takes the maroon-carpeted stairs two at a time until at last she is out again, confronting the cool morning and the white breaking waves racing each other to shore.

Early that evening, alone once more, she plunged into the purling, steadfast sea, salt-scourging herself of both deceptions.

★　　★　　★

It was a Mercedes, dark green and discreetly opulent. Inside, the upholstery was rich cream leather and the steering wheel and dashboard were crafted from the same highly polished walnut. The driver, equally discreet, called her 'Miss' and loaded her single case into the cavernous boot. She had butterflies in her stomach but was determined not to show it, even to him. At least, she thought thankfully, Tilden didn't make the man wear a chauffeur's cap. That would have been altogether too much.

After her not altogether successful, purging swim, she had gone back to her lodgings and seethed in silence, feeling foolish and humiliated, let down by her own absurd, brittle pretending. He hadn't even been free. It had been a game to him, a one-night stand. She could hardly bring herself to use his name, the name she had cooed and whispered in the night. She had to put it behind her, not think about it and keep on.

Later she called at Frankie's and told her about Tilden and the move to London. Frankie started to brew a pot of tea than abandoned it and instead took out a bottle of sherry. The news floored her, especially when Jenny said she was leaving the next day.

'Tomorrow? Oh my Gawd. What with you and poor Mac gone place'll be like the Marie Celeste. Oh Lor'!' But as the sherry worked its sweet sorcery she became more philosophical. 'Good thing though. At least you got something to go to. 'Course it don't matter much for me at my age but it does for you. Told you didn't I that this modelling game might turn up trumps.'

Jenny smiled, 'I know. I'm so lucky aren't I?'

Frankie gave her a withering, reproachful look, 'Never mind that,' she said severely. 'You make your own luck.'

The sherry, honeyed and cloying, disappeared rapidly, most of it into Frankie though Jenny too felt pleasantly tipsy. She gave Frankie a gold cigarette case; a farewell, she emphasised, but not goodbye present. The woman was almost in tears as she turned the gift over in her hands.

'It's proper lovely,' she said admiringly, 'something to remember you by. Proper lovely.' She excused herself and went into the next room. When she returned her face was set in its familiar firm, practical expression. 'Now I got nothing to give you 'cause I didn't know you was off and anyway, I reckon there'll be plenty of men up there falling over themselves to offer you the earth. You won't be needing nothing from me to clutter everything up. There is one thing that always comes in handy though. You take it and that's enough said.' Brusquely she thrust a roll of banknotes, held by a rubber band, towards Jenny.

'But I can't take that Frankie,' she gasped, 'it's yours. You'll need it. I'm perfectly all right for money. It's just too kind. I can't......' she jabbered helplessly.

'It's a hundred pounds,' Frankie said flatly, 'and you take it. You don't need it now but you might one day. It's not for spending, it's for safe keeping, in case you need to get out quick or something like that. Now that's enough about it.'

It was an emotional leave-taking. They hugged in the doorway.

'I'm not going to come and see you off tomorrow because do's like that make me cry and old women look daft when they cry,' Frankie said. 'You look after yourself. I'll be thinking of you. And watch yourself up there, it's a funny old place.'

As Jenny turned to look back and wave at the spare, resilient figure, she could see Frankie was mopping her eyes. Her own too were unashamedly damp.

'And never mind about no luck!' Frankie called after her. 'You make it happen!'

Frankie's roll of cash, together with her own, was now in the handbag Jenny clutched as the big car pulled away, its quiet, powerful engine effortlessly gliding her to the start of the adventure. Mollie is smiling, waving a handkerchief from her doorstep. She is saying something Jenny cannot hear through the insulated luxury of the vehicle and then it is anyway too late, the car has moved on.

The Mercedes made a stately sweep along the promenade. Ensconced grandly in the plush interior and remembering another, and far less welcome, departure, Jenny turns to watch through the rear window as the sea recedes. Picking up speed the car turns inland and away.

Three hours later she was alone in the strange new flat Tilden had provided. Fresh flowers greeted her with a card which read, *Welcome to London, city of fools* and signed with just the initial: *T.*, although she recognised the writing as Jane's. Outside was the usual rush of traffic, but an unexpected cool silence within perturbed and bothered her. Ignoring the large and expensive radiogram in the flat she rummaged through her case – until she found her own small, familiar radio and switched it on.

CHAPTER THIRTY

A deafening roar was rapidly closing in.

'What the hell is that?' Jenny exclaimed, but even as she turned to look out of the rear window eight or nine motorcycles flashed past them in a blistering blur, thundering off down the road. Tilden watched intently.

'Ton-up boys. Sleek aren't they?' he purred glutinously, green eyes narrowing as the leather-clad warriors disappeared into the distance.

His homosexuality had come as a complete, and shocking, surprise to her although now, looking back, the only surprise was that she hadn't realised it straight away. But then, when she first came to London she was an innocent abroad. He had changed all that. Life had bolted away with her, sprinted ahead and outstripped the wildest of her hopes and dreams.

The Mercedes cruised swiftly towards the city. Beside her, in the back, Tilden was dozing, his head lolling against the cream seat. It had been a tumultuous nine months with barely a pause for breath. Whatever her private misgivings he had been proven emphatically, triumphantly right. She recalled with amusement their first encounter, after she had arrived.

'There is one matter,' he said loftily, 'I must clear up immediately. You will doubtless be privy to rumour and speculation surrounding my so-called Christian name. For reasons I fail to comprehend it is a subject my employees appear never to tire of. I would advise you to remain uninvolved in these pointless intrigues. I am simply Tilden.' He gave a stiff bow, like an old-fashioned stage musician, but remained straight-faced throughout.

It was a speech she now knew he delivered to everyone who came to work for him and it was a skilful piece of self-publicity. The unknown name was indeed an inexhaustible and irresistible source of conjecture and amusement in the corridors and offices of Chelsea Film and it bound the staff in a curious, loose loyalty. It cast a wider fascination too, together with his dynamic and temperamental persona, his uncompromising utterances and, it had to be said, his genius for equally uncompromising design.

She took an instant, and undisguised dislike to the look he created for her, holding up the first of the boxy, bright orange dresses and glowering at it.

'It's horrible! And far too short. I can't wear this thing!' But instead of being angry he'd been amused.

'Precisely. It is vulgar and brash. You, on the other hand, are not. The fascination will be in the paradox.' And he laughed, a sardonic snort. 'You shall go to the ball Cinderella. I do not simply make clothes.'

Everything he did was an outright departure from whatever else prevailed, as far removed from the exclusive formalism of the established fashion houses as it could be. If there were gasps of outrage and disbelief from one half of the country, the other half, the young, loved it instantly.

They were, as he had so confidently predicted, both right and ripe for it and the indignant disapproval it aroused served only to increase its desirability and unite the gathering rebellion. It was a badge, Tilden said, that left no one in any doubt about the wearer.

He arranged massive publicity: advertisements, billboards and posters, each with a single, arresting image of Jenny, sultry face half in shadow, wearing the dress she so disliked and leaning against a crumbling, red brick wall. A white poster next to her, deliberately tattered and askew, announced simply in bold type: *STEP INTO TOMORROW*. And that was it. No explanation, not a single clue as to what on earth it was about. Word of mouth, Tilden assured her, was the best advertisement.

The high street copies of the collection, sold only in rationed bundles, were an instant sell-out wherever they appeared and Tilden ensured that their appearances were random and unannounced. She was genuinely baffled by her rapid rise to celebrity status and the attendant autograph hunters and fan mail, some of which made her squirm with embarrassment.

'After all,' she said, 'it's not as if I actually do anything is it?' But he just shrugged airily. 'It's for looking right, at the right time. For being a focus, an aspiration. What they are buying is a piece of you and what they think you are, not a yard of cloth. And,' he chided her in a told-you-so way, 'it's not for doing, it's for daring to be different.' Still, she remained part-detached from it all, as if it were happening to someone else and not her.

The publicity for the first show called it *TILDEN'S NEW LOOK: INTO TOMORROW* but the newspapers swiftly and more succinctly dubbed it 'the Jenny look.' She half-suspected Tilden himself planted the idea with them, although for what reason she did not know.

Again, for that first show, he departed completely from convention. No catwalk, no commentary, no endless parade of models. Instead it was held in a basement gallery. Androgynous, faceless, matt-black dummies, robed in his creations, were placed like statues and surrounded with paintings by Mondrian, Klee and Miró. 'All fakes,' he muttered cheerfully. Perversely low lighting and an ethereal Debussy, relayed through hidden speakers, all contributed to an eerie, crypt-like atmosphere that Jenny, startlingly long-legged in the short smock, floated through. It all proclaimed, and loudly, that risks were being taken, a challenge thrown down. It was less a show than an event and it translated into inch upon column inch of valuable publicity, fuelled by the growing controversy.

Fleet Street, quick to pick up on the new phenomenon, canvassed the high and mighty for their mostly scandalised opinions and printed them, together with pictures of Jenny and the rapidly growing band of ordinary young women in shops and offices who were now revealing previously undreamt of amounts of thigh. For weeks the press itself had no clear opinion and neither condemned nor condoned, but as a languid summer gently unfolded and the craze, as they called it, showed no sign whatever of abating, it came down firmly on the side of what best sold newspapers.

Her first brush with reporters at a press call had been a disaster. Nervous and brittle-bright, assailed by quick-fire questions, she gushed, looked awkward and gauche. Afterwards she meekly endured a blistering rebuke from Tilden. It rankled with her all the more because she knew he was right. Bloodied, close to tears, but stubbornly unbowed, she rose to it, fed off her umbrage with him and the curious tension that existed between them. Under his impatient, often irascible, tutelage her public self became sharper, more defined. She discovered in herself a gift for dry, sometimes pointed wit, born of her frustration at, initially, still being cast as dumb blonde, little more than a clothes horse, albeit a particularly attractive one. That and her growing realisation that Tilden was right; to break the mould she had to dare to be different. Determined not to let herself down again she found out, somewhat to her astonishment, that she could get away with it. If anything the humour sealed their complete triumph and won her the affection as well as the admiration of the public. When a leading interviewer asked her, with unconcealed sarcasm, 'How do you justify earning reputedly huge sums of money just for your looks?' she sweetly squashed him, answered deadpan.

'How do you, for asking such clearly unimportant people as me questions like that?' And in the brief, caught-off-balance silence that followed she heard, with quiet satisfaction, Tilden's mischievously delighted off-stage chuckle, and felt a proud tingle at a balance beginning to be redressed.

An already receptive public gleefully seized on her pawky retorts. She rationed them though, sprinkled the quips thinly and never allowed them to take over. When the second press call came round and she was asked what she really thought about 'these short skirts', she countered with arch good-humour.

'There's not really a great deal of room for thought, is there?'

It provided a counterpoint to Tilden, notoriously difficult and cavalier but especially with the press. After one radio interview, in which he had been more than usually overbearing and contemptuous, she rounded on him in frustration.

'Why do you do it, why?'

He winked, flashed a rare grin, and in a broad Liverpool accent which dumbfounded her, said, 'Boredom girl, and because I can,' adding in his usual clipped and haughty voice, 'besides it's what they want.'

She would never discover if the accent was real or assumed. Like her, he was skilfully evasive about his background and the few glimpses she had into his private life revealed little.

From the beginning there was a tacit acknowledgement between them, recognition of a shared thirst. With him she supposed it was success, the power it gave him. He was addicted to the dazzling lustre of recognition and would go to any lengths to secure it. As she came to know more of him she saw it as a craving, ultimately a weakness. Even so she admired his single, often bloody, mindedness and learnt to trust his shrewd judgement. She couldn't say she liked him. She knew he had no idea at all what it was that drove her, what she was thirsty for, and was equally certain he didn't care. It was enough that she was, and he could harness it to his plan, his adventure. Although they invariably appeared together in public, and the schedule he concocted hectic, in her rare free time she hardly ever saw him and suspected he had another, secret life. Often she was alone at the flat. Impeccably furnished, it boasted a library she frequently dipped into. And there was the radio, which still and always would hold an attractive mystique for her, even though she had herself been on it many times now. And sleep. Away from all the cameras and questions, away from the crowds of look-alikes, the bliss of aloneness.

All her public appearances, even those which seemed casual and spontaneous, were planned, rehearsed. Tilden was particularly adept at spreading rumour that she might just be at this opening or that concert. He spared no expense either in providing her with every comfort, yet she recognised in the disinterested largesse that he was equally adroit at protecting his own interests. After a while she apprehended the obvious, something which, in her shyness and early naivety, she failed to understand; however domineering and autocratic he might be, however arrogant, he needed her. Without her, as he himself insisted, there would be no Jenny Robin look. No one else would have done. And it had all been such a crowning success. She had become an industry; the clothes, the hair, the make-up and personal preferences, and she drifted through it in a haze, at the centre but distanced. They might well be Tilden's means but she had shackled them to her own secret ends.

Confined inland, she took a solitary dip three or four times a week at a private health club. She sent postcards to Frankie and received friendly, stilted letters in reply. The restaurant and much of the surrounding area had been sold off to a property developer and turned into offices. Frankie and the twins had set themselves up selling lunchtime sandwiches and drinks to all the clerks and typists. Jenny liked the letters and read them over and over. They were a necessary lifeline into another, more normal world.

Occasionally she spent weekends at a country house in Hampshire that Tilden rented but hardly used, preferring instead to stay in London. It had its own pool, stables and a staff of three. She enjoyed its hidden-away tranquillity. She was closer there to home and her heart would leap with a sparkle of anticipation whenever she saw a road sign magically proclaiming THE WEST.

For if sometimes she chafed at the strange brew of being privately secluded but publicly owned, if sometimes she became impatient at the waiting, it was offset by the acclaim and admiration, the attention she so liked. But more importantly, it was held in check by the regular, gratifying statements from her bankers and her certainty that she would soon be home free.

The car slides to a smooth, hushed halt outside her flat. Tilden rouses, yawns and stretches as she gets out into the darkness.

'Goodnight fair demotic princess,' he says sleepily, 'sweet dreams until tomorrow.'

★　★　★

It was as she quietly celebrated the first year of her contract, with the country still firmly bewitched, its mood that of an unending, carefree party, that the crash came. It came out of nowhere. The whole edifice gave way at the foundations, collapsed and cracked up.

'Tilden's sold us out!' a distraught Jane wailed angrily as she stood at the door of Jenny's flat. 'And he's gone, flew to Spain last night. The company was about to go bust and he's sold the only asset it had left, his bloody name and us along with it. And now he's run away, the bastard, and left us in the lurch!'

Jenny stared in disbelief at the red-eyed woman who, trembling with rage and frustration, lit a cigarette and blew smoke nervously. 'I can't believe it,' she continued, shaking her head, 'I can't believe he'd do it. He hid it from me, from the accountants, everyone. And after all we've put up with. I could kill him!'

Jenny sank into a chair as Jane paced the room, smoking furiously. Eyes fixed dumbly at the floor she said slowly, 'Oh my God, what's going to happen?'

Jane blew her nose.

'I don't know, I just don't know. But it's all over,' she said despairingly.

Again Jenny contemplated the floor. For a year she had allowed the dream-like unreality of Tilden's adventure to use her. Now, tumbled unceremoniously out of it, she felt a cold wave of blunt, indignant obstinacy. It wasn't going to end. Not now. Not when her fingernails were scraping at the edge of her dream. It would end when she wanted. That was the plan, her plan.

'Whatever happens,' she said flatly, 'I shan't sink with him.'

They shared a drink in silent alliance, Jane still stunned, Jenny blindly, intractably, determined. When Jane left, promising to phone as soon as there was news, she immediately telephoned her bank and asked for a verbal statement. She knew it was panic, a madness. Tilden could not have spirited away her money as well, but even so. A calm voice assured her that it was intact, safe, as she knew it had to be. She'd just wanted to be sure of it.

For days there was nothing from Jane. The gossip columns were full of Tilden's dramatic flight and speculation about the future of what they called his 'fallen empire.' From somewhere in Spain he issued lofty statements, hinting at a conspiracy of traitors and citing the irreconcilability of 'my art with the deadening weight of commerce.' It was all good copy. Jenny recognised immediately that he was already scheming, about to start up all over again, this time in exile. Not only was it clear that he had manipulated them all, it was clear to her that he was simply bored with the tedium of his own success. In another context he once said to her artfully, 'Lay a false trail, throw up some ghosts, allow others to create the myth.' He was evidently following his own advice. Unlike Jane, she did not hate him. She had, after all, been complicit in his scheme and used him just as ruthlessly.

She lay low, long days stretched into a timeless limbo. A clutch of reporters took shifts at the door of her apartment building. Somehow her private phone number was discovered and it rang incessantly. Eventually she covered it with cushions and left the answering machine on.

On the fifth day she played back the messages. Hidden amongst the demands for press quotes and offers of money to tell her story was Jane's voice. In stark contrast to her visit she sounded positively ebullient.

'Jenny! It's all OK. Everything's fabulous. They're going to carry on, the people who bought us I mean, England Holdings. They've got some great ideas. They want to re-vamp you!'

Moments later, and as fresh as a breeze, she emerged from her flat and smiled brightly at the startled band of reporters.

'Good morning,' she announced. 'Tilden is finished. But Jenny Robin is just beginning.'

★   ★   ★

'You really do have the most extraordinary eyes,' the stranger murmured admiringly, 'azure oceans.'

'Oh yeah,' she said bluntly, in a voice deliberately bored and disinterested, not pausing as she put the finishing touches to her make-up. She had heard them all before, all the clumsy chat-up lines, the veiled and not-so-veiled propositions. 'Who are you anyway?' she asked, as the man continued to stare in fascination at her reflection. 'I should clear off before security spot you. You aren't allowed back-stage.' It was a charity function she was due to open. Already she could hear the hum of the audience as the theatre filled up.

The man looked contrite, 'Forgive me,' he said in a voice ringing of public school, 'dreadful of me, forgotten my manners. I'm Edward England. England Holdings.'

Abruptly she stopped applying eye-liner, swivelled round to face him and smiled wryly.

'My new boss!'

He waved a hand in horror, 'Oh, please don't think of me as that. I know nothing whatever about this business. Not really my line. I leave that to my people. Sound investment though, if carefully managed. That's what I do really, just move money about. I've heard of you of course.'

'Have you?' She returned to the mirror. He settled himself on a packing case, took out a silver cigarette case and lit one.

'Well, who hasn't? The most photographed face in the country.'

'The most over-exposed,' she retorted dryly. He laughed, a brittle ripple.

'Maybe, but it's certainly been your passport to glory.' He was in his forties, tall and rangy, his sandy hair was thinning and he had pale lashes around chestnut coloured eyes. He wore an expensive, slightly showy Italian suit and silk jacquard tie. Not at all her type. 'Well,' he clapped his hands lightly together, 'what chance of dinner later on, to cement our new partnership?'

'Absolutely none,' she replied affably, sweeping through the stage curtain and out into the dazzling light beyond.

In fact, thanks to Jane, she knew more about him than he might have supposed. Following Tilden's departure, Jane made it her business to investigate the fitness of England Holdings.

'It's a conglomerate,' she said knowledgeably, 'fingers in all sorts of pies. They've got a name for buying out and selling off the juicy bits, or acquiring the badly run but potentially lucrative. That's us I suppose. We had the success all right but that little bastard pissed away the profit.' She pored over newspaper clippings and what were to Jenny incomprehensible company account sheets. 'Quite ruthless really,' she said with admiration.

'What about him?'

Jane looked up, 'The Honourable Edward?'

'Is he?'

'Oh yes. Been an M.P. for a year or two. Strictly backbench. Doesn't poke his head above the parapet much. Now where's that......' she rummaged through the clutter of papers on her desk. 'Ah yes, here we are. Wykehamist, then Sandhurst and a stint in the Horse Guards. Father was the tea planter, Randolph England. Pots of loot that boy wonder inherited as the only child. Spoilt rotten I expect. Moved into property development along the south coast, mostly leisure industries. Was a town councillor in Brighton......'

'Brighton. Really?' Jenny interrupted.

'Yup. Now member for Brighton and Hove. Not much on the personal front. Single, I think, in case you're interested.'

'I'm not.'

'Oh well,' Jane returned to the papers 'Pretty mercurial rise up the ladder. Seems to put his money where his mouth is. Hasn't backed a loser. Not yet anyway,' she grinned.

Tilden's melodramatic disappearance forced a moratorium on Jenny's frantic timetable, yet it was used to full advantage. England, or his 'people', employed an advertising agency to promote their own new look and a team of designers to manufacture it under the strictest secrecy.

She received a letter affirming that her contract would continue as before, under the same terms and conditions, and even, to her surprise, sealing England Holdings good intentions with a substantial one-off bonus. They planned for her to stay out of the public eye for a month prior to her re-launch. The lease on the country house had been acquired, along with everything else that once made up Tilden's sprawling dominion, and she took herself off to it. It was the first long break she had had and she sank gratefully into the calm of the countryside. She saw little of England himself. Despite her rebuff he remained amiable and charming, though clearly out of his depth with the fashion scene. As she found out more about the company, mostly from Jane, she saw that he was however, almost uncannily astute in his financial dealings and was reassured that her own plan was out of jeopardy.

He asked her out again, in a casual way, but, gently turned down, seemed now to accept it. There was a faint, unappealing craftiness to his flirting which, coupled with the pale eyes that slithered over her, she disliked. Something below the surface of him left her wary, in spite of the urbane exterior and polished manners. She had learnt the hard way to recognise and trust her own instincts. Neither did she approve his taste for flashy cars and the ostentatiously wealthy trappings he surrounded himself with. Besides, she wanted no complications, and there was to be no false modesty this time; she was their main asset, and to be that suited her just perfectly.

★ ★ ★

Two events occurred in rapid succession that were to make her pause for thought and reassess him. The first was that he made Jane a company secretary and turned over to her a handful of shares which, although worth only a few hundred pounds, ensured her place in the new order. It was a move Jenny thoroughly applauded. After years of unrewarding worry, toil and frustration under Tilden's regime, it was at last a recognition of her loyalty.

The second happened a little later. The new look was ready and England wanted her to look at the sketches. When she did it was with dismay.

'Well what do you think?' He was seated behind a leather-topped mahogany desk. Another man, dark suited and thick-set, was in the room with them, though she was not introduced and he remained silent throughout.

She flipped through the thin portfolio impatiently, 'I think they are unoriginal and unexciting,' she said firmly, scrutinising the parade of short, patterned pinafores. 'This is Tilden by any other name but without flair, imagination or the lack of compromise. It's all been done before. And better.' She closed the folder and dropped it onto the desk. England took a cigarette from a box, lit it and leant back, unsmiling.

'Is that really what you think?'

She nodded solemnly. He put his hands palms down on the desk and spread his fingers. Then, without a trace of emotion, said simply, 'I see. Thank you. Leave it with me,' and motioned for the silent man to show her out.

Later she found out from Jane that within half an hour of that meeting he had, without hesitation, dismissed the entire design team and postponed the launch. A search was instituted for a new designer and after several anxious weeks a tiny, intense Japanese woman was given the commission. In a single long weekend she took literally hundreds of snapshots of Jenny and then silently disappeared into her studio.

Meanwhile, the advertising agency swung into action to minimise the effect of the postponement. Using Tilden's own technique they produced a barrage of publicity that just showed Jenny's face, lit from below, head down but eyes looking boldly up. In soft monochrome and again without reference to her or any product, it said enigmatically, *SOME THINGS ARE WORTH THE WAITING…..* It was a stark image, full of dramatic impact. Stripped of colour it trumpeted a new direction, hidden but about to be revealed. When, a fortnight later and again in his plush office, she first saw the Japanese woman's drawings, she knew it would work. They were as different from Tilden as he had been from everyone else. The skirts were longer, to mid-calf, close fitting and then flaring out, and teamed with a matching bolero-style jacket. It was a return to the fluid elegance she so liked. It wasn't playful or fun, it was sensual, sophisticated. There was a touch of the Edwardian about it. It was stylish. It had class.

'This is it,' she said with conviction. 'Not everyone will be able to wear it but they'll all want to.'

A slow smile spread over his face, 'I did so hope it would be.'

And then he did something else which surprised and pleased her. When the first outfit was produced it bore, instead of Tilden's name, a black label embroidered with the delicate outline of a small golden bird and the words, *Jenny Robin*. She was quietly, diffidently, delighted but asked him why he had gambled on dropping Tilden's still influential association with the new look, especially as he had spent so much to acquire it in the first place.

'By buying the rights,' he explained gravely, 'I have the freedom to choose. Tilden, on the other hand, has no such freedom. I have chosen not to use the name. In my view you're the main attraction. You eclipsed him and it's you the public want. You've won that for very good reason and this is just a small recognition of it. Of course, there will be a percentage increase for you personally, a perhaps more substantial reward than one's name on a label?' he queried mildly. She nodded and thanked him. If it was largesse it was soundly wrapped in good economics. As she stood to leave she gave an impish grin.

'I wonder what he'll think about it. Tilden I mean, not even using his name anymore. He's gone rather quiet lately hasn't he? I suppose the papers have done it to death.' England was holding the door open for her and smiled fleetingly.

'Possibly,' he drawled, 'I did send a representative to explain our position.'

'Did you?' she said surprised.

'Oh yes. Just a quiet chat. But I expect you're right. Life moves on in Fleet Street.'

CHAPTER THIRTY-ONE

The up-market move did not create quite the same instant sensation as its renegade precursor. Yet it lit a slow fuse and the women left out in the cold by Tilden's brash unconventionality breathed a huge sigh of relief and snapped it up. And if it failed to sell in quite the same spectacular numbers, its equally sophisticated price tag ensured a fatter profit. For Jenny the public fascination ground on unabated. At a press call after the launch a chorus of reporters, barely able to conceal their disappointment that the famous legs were not on view, pressed her with, 'What do you think of it Jenny, really?' She looked down at her well-covered knees and through the window at an overcast, unseasonably cool day.

'It's wonderful,' she enthused, 'absolutely wonderful. And it's warmer!'

England, unlike Tilden, kept himself out of the public gaze. The Jenny Robin collection was for him one of many enterprises. Surprisingly though, as the weeks went on he began to relax and enjoy himself in the unlikely role of fashion house proprietor, establishing a closer contact. 'Keeping tabs,' he called it amiably to Jenny.

Although she saw him more often he was careful, after that early rejection, not to impose. She appreciated his funny, old-fashioned manners, even if they did sit uneasily with the business ruthlessness Jane delighted in describing. With Jenny he was always courteous in a faintly stiff, quaint way that she found herself quite enjoying. He took great pains to make sure she had everything she wanted and there were other small, diplomatically handled considerations that, little by little, began to make her wonder why she had found him so off-putting; a champagne party in her honour after the launch, good luck telegrams before guest appearances, plump asparagus brought especially from a farm he owned when he discovered she had a passion for it. And ten weeks after the launch, just when the giddying round of promotions was beginning to take its toll, he insisted she took a long break at the country house and ordered her schedule to be re-arranged. Gratefully she agreed and, armed with a box of books she'd promised herself to read, was driven down in the powerful Jaguar that had taken the place of Tilden's Mercedes. Sitting comfortably in the back and feeling pleasantly pampered, she mused idly that perhaps she had misjudged this Edward England, tarred him with an unfair brush. When she arrived in Hampshire a crate of champagne had beaten her there.

★   ★   ★

'How often have I said to you that when you have eliminated the impossible, whatever remains, however improbable, must be the truth?'

She smiled to herself, pushed up her sunglasses and put the book down on the wicker table at her side. She liked this rogue scholar of Baker Street, with his precise addictions, disdain and disguises. Much better than the films.

She closed her eyes against the sun and felt deliciously lazy. It had been a week of soft Hampshire sunshine. The garden, a wide expanse of luxuriantly bursting green, breathed an air of attention and care. Behind her the pool tinkled invitingly and birds sang in the sheltering trees, their feathery tops swaying in a languid breeze. Blissful peace. A whole week of early nights, of swimming, sunlight on her skin and country sounds in the morning when she woke. Best of all its closeness to home, almost as if Hadley was just beyond the hills, witchingly westward, a few miles away. Long ago though she had foresworn any half-measures, any notion of travelling down like a tourist to gape at it. There was to be no compromise. It had to be whole, the going back, not just a visit. She had promised herself. And anyway it was less than a year now, just months that was all, just months.

'Lotus eater!' The voice startled her, drifting across the sweeping lawns, and was unmistakable. She sat up, perched the dark glasses back on her nose and looked for him. He was strolling towards her, hands in pockets and casually dressed. It was the first time she had seen him not wearing one of his sharp-cut suits.

'Had a spot of business in this neck of the woods,' he said, 'and thought I'd drop by, hope you don't mind?'

She thought fleetingly that she scarcely could as he paid for the rent but she was by now so serenely relaxed that in fact she didn't mind at all.

'What business?'

'Trout farm,' he said, 'not far from here.'

'Good God, what's that?' she laughed.

'Exactly what it sounds like,' he answered genially, 'it'll be big business though, in a year or two.'

'I'll take your word for it. Sounds absolutely dreadful to me.'

He plonked himself down in a chair opposite her, one long leg crossed loosely over the other. 'And talking of business,' he said, 'a small celebration is in order.'

'Really. What?'

He shrugged as if it were not really that important, 'Oh, small matter of clocking up our first half-million in sales.'

'Half a million? Pounds? I had no idea that many had been sold. I mean it's hardly......'

'Been a runaway success? That's where you're mistaken. Not so much noise about it all I grant you but it's selling, and to the right people.'

She smiled at him, 'And who are these right people?'

'The ones who live on easy street. Tilden sold his for a fiver and sold thousands but they cost damn near that to make. That's why he went broke. Ours might be considerably more expensive but the kind of women who are buying come back for more and tell their friends. We did a little bit of research. You've moved up a notch or two Jenny Robin. You rule the smart set now and that's where the money is.' He stood up, 'Any of that bubbly left?'

'Oh yes, sorry, I forgot to thank you for it.'

He waved a hand, brushing away the oversight. She often forgot to thank him for things, there seemed to be so many things to thank him for. She stood and pulled a towelling robe over her bikini, aware that he was studiously not looking at her, and they sauntered idly back to the house.

The champagne was in the refrigerator and he fetched it while she found glasses.

'Turn the bottle and not the cork,' he said with a funny downward smile, screwing the green bottle round. A soft pop as the cork came away, a wisp of smokiness from its neck but no rushing plume of effervescent wine. 'There!' he said triumphantly, 'only good advice my old pater ever gave me.'

'I've heard that before,' she proffered up the glasses, 'but I quite like it when it goes whoosh. It's more exciting, more like a proper celebration.'

'Well,' he pondered, cocking an eyebrow, 'I did say something about a celebration didn't I? Let's see, how can we put some fizz back?' He pretended to ruminate for a moment, 'Oh yes, nearly forgot, follow me,' and marched off through the house, Jenny in tow.

'What is it?'

'You'll see,' he strode on ahead and threw open the front doors with a flourish. Outside on the gravel drive, immaculately new and shining red, was a compact, low-slung sports car. He flung an arm out to it, grinned at her.

'What……do you mean?'

'It's for you. Little bonus. Keys are in it, go on, take her for a spin. Drives like hell. You'll love it.' He stood gazing at her and, she thought, despite his easy manner, looked shyly expectant.

'But I can't……' she began.

'Absolutely no argument,' he said good-naturedly, 'it's all signed, sealed and delivered.'

'No but……'

'That's right. No buts.'

'It's not that,' she said at last, then added hopelessly, 'you see, I can't drive.' And from him a roar of unexpectedly infectious laughter which, despite her embarrassment, she could not help but echo.

'Right then, that's settled,' he said briskly, as they ate a light lunch by the pool, 'I shall teach you. Have you roaring around in no time.'

'Is roaring obligatory?' she laughed.

'It is rather, in one of those things. Good lark though. Shakes the old peasants up a bit, especially out here in the sticks.'

'I like the sticks,' she said with mock indignation. 'I'm not sure I want to shake things up.'

'Absolutely,' he agreed a shade hurriedly, missing the tease in her voice, 'nothing like the old countryside.'

'With its rolling acres of picturesque trout farms?'

He leant across to her, quizzical, not quite sure, 'You're not taking the……'

'Piss?' she interrupted pertly, 'I most certainly am.' They both laughed, the champagne fuelling a new light-heartedness between them. Later they dozed in the mellow afternoon sunlight. He was still napping when she roused and, peeling off the robe, knelt by the pool, examining her reflection in it, her mirroring eyes an arresting, enigmatic blue. She smiled at her good fortune, plunged in and swam underwater to the far end. When she surfaced he was watching her in admiration.

'Bravo!' he exclaimed, and gave a little round of applause.

'Come on then!' she shouted cheerfully, splashing him. 'In at the deep end!'

He shrugged nonchalantly, 'No costume.'

'There's bound to be a spare in the house,' she chivvied. 'Go on, Mrs. Oliver will find one for you.'

'No, I don't think so.' He had stepped back from the edge and his hands were jammed firmly in his pockets once more.

'Oh go on,' she urged. 'It's lovely in.'

'No, no really, I'm fine.'

She had been kicking up a great ball of froth, but now stopped, conscious of a distinct uneasiness he was trying to conceal. The water around her seethed as the surge subsided.

'You can't can you?' she asked flatly. 'You can't swim.'

He pulled an awkward face, squirmed. 'Well, no actually......'

'It's all right. It isn't a crime.'

'No, no, of course not,' he agreed quickly, looking away from her, 'just one of the things I never got around to that's all. All the same one does feel a bit, well, foolish.' His voice trailed off and he looked down at the chequerboard of coloured concrete slabs surrounding the pool. She glided smoothly towards him.

'You aren't frightened of it are you?' she asked, quietly forthright.

He gave a quick, strangled laugh, 'That would be silly.'

She rested her elbows on the edge and peered up at him, 'Prove it then.'

'But......'

'No buts. Get a costume and prove it. You teach me to drive and I'll show you how to swim. That's fair isn't it? Don't worry, I won't let you drown. There isn't a deep end. I was fibbing.'

He swallowed, cast round anxiously as if for escape but there was none. Ensnared by his own maleness, he attempted to put on an unconcerned face yet there was a marked reluctance in his step as he trudged back to the house.

After what seemed like an age he returned, wearing a pair of striped shorts and carrying a towel. His skin was painfully white and he was altogether thinner, more angular, than she would have thought. At her instigation he sat on the side and dangled his feet in. Perched awkwardly above her, with the dread prospect of four feet of warm water below him, he looked utterly daunted. But his vulnerability touched her, and she spoke to him gently and held his hands as he let himself gingerly into the pool with a gasp. She showed him how to float, then made him try. It was painfully slow. He flailed nervously in the shallow water while she coaxed and cajoled as if he were a child. She was aware, too, of enjoying being in control as, stripped of clothes, pride and dignity, he succumbed to her coaching. Time and again his long body folded in panic and he went under, splashed up coughing and gulping mouthfuls of the chemically sweet water. Time and again he meekly allowed her to persuade him to try once more, his red-rimmed eyes searching for reassurance. When at last he managed it she clapped and cheered enthusiastically. He struggled to find his feet and a broad smile spread across his face.

'I damn well did it!' he puffed incredulously, 'I damn well floated!'

'And that's the hard part,' she lied, 'once you can float swimming is dead easy.' It was a lie his new found confidence swallowed whole. Half an hour later she had him spluttering along in a kind of flat-out, desperate side-stroke, mightily pleased with himself, his humiliation assuaged by the few yards he could now splash across the pool. Even so, he looked relieved when she said that was enough for one day and heaved himself thankfully out of the water.

Where his progress had been agonisingly torturous, hers in the red sports car was spectacular. She listened carefully, absorbed by the strangeness of it. When she turned the key and the engine answered with a low, purring growl, she felt the new thrill of a harnessed power that was hers to compel. Soon she was driving in eager, occasionally lurching, spurts round the drive, with only the odd scrunch of gears that made him wince visibly. As the afternoon slipped into early evening he also, but to her disappointment, announced that that was enough for her first lesson. He was genuinely admiring of the comparative ease with which she'd mastered the car and she allowed herself to bask in it.

'I expect,' he said later, over dinner, 'you think me a prize chump, getting into a funk like that in the pool.' She could tell from his expression that he was hoping to be proved wrong.

'Not at all. Lots of people are frightened of water. I don't like heights very much.'

'Really?' he sipped at his ruby wine. 'You see, it's not that I'm cowardly about it……'

'I didn't think you were.'

'No, but I do want you to understand.'

'I understand that you are protesting a little too much,' she said tartly. He was silent and looked down at his plate. It irritated her, this trying to re-cast the afternoon, turn what she had seen so plainly in his face into something else.

'Why do all men think they've got to be Tarzan,' she said, exasperated, 'it's just not important. Besides, you've beaten it and that is important. You need never be frightened of it again.'

He gave her a quizzical look, 'What is then, for you, what is important in a chap?'

The word darted unequivocally from her, 'Honesty.'

He nodded and smiled self-consciously, 'You are quite a formidable lady,' he said quietly.

'Is that a compliment?'

'Very much so.'

Dinner over, they sat out in the shadowed but still warm garden, chatting over brandy, wrapped in the delicious honey cool of an English summer evening. After a while he went back into the house for his jacket and something warm for her. The moon had appeared, cradled in a treetop, and the glowing light from it filled her glass. She drank as though it was a potion and, childlike, intoned, 'The moon was in my glass and now it's in me.' She looked up into the night and smiled. The moon was still there but perhaps she had stolen a slice of it.

He returned, smiling, and slipped a cardigan around her shoulders. She reflected that like this, relaxed and at ease, he looked younger, not unattractive. She wondered too, if she had been a little hard on him over dinner. He had after all been very kind.

Eventually he looked at his watch and sighed, 'Much as I hate to, it is time for me to go. Thank you for such a splendid day.'

'Sure about that?' she teased.

'A mostly splendid day,' he corrected himself, 'and instructive.'

She thanked him again for the car and told him it was altogether too much, too extravagant and not deserved, protests he brushed away lightly. He would drive it back to London and send the Jaguar for her when she wanted to return.

'And remember,' he said, 'there's no rush. You're on holiday, enjoy it.'

She walked with him to the front door where he stopped and gave her a quirky, self-deprecating look.

'I was frightened,' he admitted. 'I always have been.'

'But you won't be again.'

He looked doubtful, 'I'm not so sure.' Tentatively, he leant forward and brushed her forehead with a kiss. 'Thank you for the lesson.'

CHAPTER THIRTY-TWO

The fine limpid weather broke the following week, with two days of constant rain and a low blanket of grubby cloud. She returned to a drab London and resumed her schedule.

For ten days she didn't see or hear anything of him and, when eventually she did, it was in the least likely setting. The regular swim at the health club had become a necessary, if solitary, counterpoint to her dislocated life. Lost in thought she ploughed up and down, trailing a churning furrow behind her. As she completed her thirtieth length a voice, close by, took her by surprise.

'Thought I'd catch you here.' He was squatting at the edge, grinning down at her and wearing dark-blue, monogrammed swimming shorts.

'Edward!' She trod water and looked up. 'What are you doing here?'

'Come to show off,' he said mysteriously and lowered himself in. He pushed off from the side and swam a passable, if laboured, breast stroke to the shallow end where he stood and bowed.

'Fantastic!' she called, pleased for him.

'That's about all I can do at the moment,' he puffed, 'been taking a few lessons. Wanted to give you a surprise. Don't think I'll be challenging you to a race just yet.'

'I'm impressed, and you will if you keep that up.'

He had another surprise for her too, tickets for a first night and this time she didn't refuse. A week later it was a film premiere, then a garden party, and his company, always fastidiously attentive, brought home the extent of her loneliness. When she didn't see him, she missed him. When she did it was always fun, always something new. The mistrust she had felt, the circumspection, melted away. At his invitation she toured Westminster, leaving a minor commotion in her wake. She asked politely what it was like and was mildly shocked by his blasé answer.

'Parliament? Best club in the land. Awfully good fun. Not to be taken seriously of course.'

'I thought it was.'

'That's the mistake most people make.'

A month later, after an evening at the theatre, she finally invited him in for coffee. They sat on the sofa and talked about the play while the coffee percolated. Then very softly he lifted her arm by the wrist, laid it across his lap and ran a finger lightly over the scar.

'Shame about that,' he crooned, 'how the devil did you come by it?'

But she did not answer. Instead, unplanned and on inexplicable impulse, a kind of abandoned devilment, she found herself leaning to him, pushing him back against the sofa, kissing him deeply, irrevocably.

Later, as he lay on the bed and she straddled him, sure as a cat in the dark, she did not hear the low murmur as he pressed his face against her breasts.

'Caught you, Jenny Robin.'

★　★　★

'You are a pig,' she said cheerfully, smiling down the phone, 'leaving me on my lonesome so long.'

'I'm sorry darling. This week's been hell. I'll make it up to you I promise. Look, there's something I want you to see.'

'Oh yes,' she feigned suspicion, 'not another racehorse is it?'

There was a pause, 'Rather more legs,' he said cryptically, 'and right up your street I should think.'

'More than four?' she snorted, 'go on, what is it, tell.'

'Lots more than four,' he laughed, 'and no, it's meant to be a surprise.'

'Beast, all these secrets.'

'All will be revealed.'

He arranged to pick her up later in the day after she had opened a supermarket. Opening shops was one of the duties she truly disliked but tried to carry off with good grace. There was something so remorselessly downbeat about them, no matter how many balloons and flags bedecked the place. The managers too all seemed to be smooth, plump men in florid ties who were full of a fragile bonhomie. It was as though they all belonged to the same club and were rather pleased to have been accepted as members.

The Jaguar arrived and she got in, lit a cigarette, and thought about the phone call. Edward really could be the limit. A week with no word whatsoever and then it was all flowers and champagne. He was always up to the most unlikely things as well, like the racehorse, now stabled in Hampshire. He had wanted to re-christen it after her but she forbade him.

She had no idea at all where their relationship was going. For her it was a pleasant diversion and she suspected it was the same for him. Neither of them had talked of love and she knew she did not love him. But it was good to see out the last few months less alone, less isolated inside her fame. He made it all so easy too, everything was sparkling froth, cascading on a wave of laughter, parties and night clubs, all of it shimmering and irresistible. She liked him, and he had been good to her, but the fling was to be enjoyed for what it was and then ended. She would miss him when she went home, but this life would be finished then and she could, would, take no part of it with her. That wasn't in the plan. She had more than enough money, far more in fact than she would ever need. The percentage increase he had given her had paid off handsomely, in addition to her already generous salary, all of it carefully nurtured and prudently invested. She could, she knew, go now, but she would keep her side of it, the contract. It was only right, only fair, and at the end of it, somehow, home.

She felt in good spirits when the car pulled up at the supermarket and was unaffected by its depressingly familiar resemblance to a modern hospital; a less inviting place to shop at she could not imagine.

Predictably, the manager belonged to the same wearisome affiliation, though he was plumper and prematurely balding. Plainly star-struck, he hid it behind a clumsy, well-mannered flirtatiousness. It grated, as it always did, but she smiled, laughed at his feeble jokes and admired the flat, squat, spiritless building of which he was so proud.

A small podium had been set up outside and a crowd had gathered. A banner stretched across the back of the podium, replicating the label from the Jenny Robin collection. Below the shop's name it said *We Value You With*

The Best Value. She grimaced at the slick sentiment and at seeing her name yoked to it. It was a detail Edward insisted on always getting right, the facsimile label, and in one shape or another it had followed her around half the country.

She was to stay out of sight while the now edgy manager had his brief moment of glory. He climbed heavily onto the podium and, tapping the microphone, eulogised the shop, the town, the people and the products. He looked suspiciously evangelical with his arms uplifted, exhorting belief. There was polite applause as he finished then, winding himself up like a showman, he announced her with an amateurish flourish. She took her place beside him to more enthusiastic and sustained clapping. Right at the front she heard a woman turn to her companion.

'In't she lovely eh? In't she though? Just like her pictures too.'

The faces spread out before her looked up expectantly, urban faces, overfed and under nourished.

'It's lovely to be with you,' she began, 'especially on such a smashing day.' She looked up at the robust blue sky and felt the heat of the sun. 'And you'll be pleased to know, I'm reliably informed that this shop is positively bulging with ice-cream, particularly important to those of you under three feet tall.' A murmur of approval went up. She was all right, one of them, set apart by her looks but down to earth enough to know that hell was standing in a sweltering crowd with a fractious five-year old. 'So I won't hold you up any longer,' she continued, 'it's lovely and cool in there and I know it will bring an interesting new dimension to your weekly shopping, so it gives me great pleasure to announce your first supermarket in town well and truly open for business.' The manager stepped up smartly and handed her a pair of gold-coloured dressmaker's scissors. She snipped the pink ribbon to obviously genuine applause. As much as anything, she thought, probably because she'd kept the whole thing mercifully brief. Released, the hot, agitated crowd surged forward through the glass doors, thrown theatrically open by the manager who, inspired by her, was now bellowing, 'Free ice-cream for the kiddies!'

At the tail end of the crowd a few stragglers, a sprinkling of the merely curious, and a handful of passers-by who had stopped to watch, began to disperse.

She shades her eyes. The manager is beside her again but she does not hear what he is saying. At the very back a fleeting glimpse of a man, arrestingly still in the middle of the crush, looking directly, particularly, at her; face hidden in the shade of a cap, a collar pulled up around him, for incredibly, in the blazing sunshine, he is dressed solidly in a dark reefer jacket. Something in the stance, in the calm reckoning......something......then he is gone, vanished into the glaring heat and the blur of moving people. Minutes later, bustled as she is into the unremitting babble of the shop, the mystifying, freakish image is lost too from her mind.

★   ★   ★

It was late afternoon by the time they arrived. She was delayed by the supermarket manager who, flushed with triumphant conviviality, seemed unfortunately to now regard her as a personal friend. When finally she extricated herself he was becoming sentimental, holding her hand and gallantly kissing it several times before at long last closing the door of the idling Jaguar for her. He waved, a forlorn, pear-shaped figure, until they were out of sight. She reflected wryly that supermarkets were one thing she would not miss in the slightest.

When Edward collected her at the flat he looked bumptious and tapped the side of his nose with a finger when she asked where they were going.

'Wait and see, my girl, wait and see,' he said, irritatingly. It was though, pleasant to drive away from the city in his own rather more powerful sports car. An hour later they crested a hill and looked down on a town, and a seashore that was unmistakable.

'Got it!' she clicked her fingers. 'Brighton, your constituency, lots more legs than four, and right up my street because it's where I came from.'

'Did you?' he replied offhandedly, 'I never knew that. Brighton belle eh?' She gave him an emphatically withering look and at the same time felt oddly let down that he didn't know.

'You're right, and you're wrong,' he continued, again infuriatingly self-satisfied. 'It is Brighton, my patch, but that's not what we're here to see.'

She hid her annoyance with him behind dark glasses as they went on into town. He stopped the car at the seafront and sat next to her in silence, surveying the scene. To Jenny it looked the same, just dressed up for summer as usual in the familiar, garish colours she remembered. Yet now she saw it with different, changed eyes; it had a reek of usedness, or used-upness. She wondered what Frankie would think if she turned up on her doorstep with an M.P. but straightaway thought better of it. Frankie wouldn't appreciate it nor, maybe, him either. She smiled as she recalled Frankie's dire warnings about London. She must write to her soon.

'Well,' he asked at length, 'what do you think?'

'Think of what?' she retorted, a touch huffily. 'Tired old Brighton, nothing new as far as I can see.'

'Look again.' His voice was terse, eyes narrowed.

'Oh Edward!' she exclaimed petulantly, 'I'm too hot and bothered for these games. Just tell me!' But instead of answering he pointed slowly across the water.

'There,' he drawled lasciviously, 'just look at that long, gorgeous creature.'

'Oh no, not the pier,' she groaned. 'You aren't serious surely. It's a wreck, a joke.' It was true. The pier, once stately and magnificent, had for years been derelict. With its mid-section blown away during the war as a precaution against invasion, it now stood crippled and rusting, fenced off with warning notices.

He stared entranced at the massive, desolate platform jutting out across the sea. Eventually he turned to look at her with an ill-concealed air of vexation.

'Can't you see it either? She's a lovely lady in need of a facelift that's all.' He punched the starter and sped them towards it.

They parked close by and scrunched along the beach. When they reached it he placed a palm gently against one of the encrusted iron legs and looked up in wonder. 'Beauty isn't it?' he murmured.

'Faded beauty,' she said, unimpressed, 'and beyond redemption. What on earth will you do with it anyway?'

'Do with it?' he echoed sharply, 'Open it of course.'

'Edward, look, it's a mistake. Don't. Please.'

'Too late. Work starts Monday.' He reached out for her hand. Reluctantly she trudged with him to the padlocked entrance. A new sign had been put up on the high fence that enclosed its landward end: *Danger. Unsafe Structure. Trespassers Will Be Prosecuted. Property of England Holdings.*

'It says it's dangerous,' she protested.

'That's just to keep the buggers out. Follow me. You'll be all right.' He unlocked the padlock and swung the gate open. It screeched on its hinges as he ushered her through. She followed him carefully as they picked their way through the debris of collapse and neglect, along sun and salt bleached planking.

'Can't go inside yet,' he warned, 'surveyor says the roof is hanging on by a thread. Should be all right if we go along the side.'

Everywhere was rust and decay, the huge mock palace perched on top of the pier was crumbling, the once white paint flaking, exposing rotten wood. Windows were smashed and boarded up with odd bits of timber. The farther out to sea they went the more precarious it felt. She noticed a torn poster still stubbornly clinging to a hoarding: ......*the master of magic and illusion. Matinees every day except Monday. Book now for a spectacle guaranteed to amaze and astound you*....... She snorted glumly and pointed to it.

'End of the pier show circa 1939.'

But he was too engrossed to hear. 'There'll be kids' amusements by the entrance, then a sort of shopping market. Not tat but classy. A coffee bar, two restaurants, a ballroom cum nightclub and, at the end, a casino and swimming pool,' he enthused.

'Swimming pool?' she queried. 'This is the seaside for Gods sake. Who's going to use that?'

'Well it won't be the ruddy municipal baths,' he exclaimed impatiently, 'it'll be up-market, a club with its own bar, very exclusive.'

'Edward, this is all going to cost an absolute bomb,' she said sceptically. 'A fortune, on top of what the damn thing must have cost to buy.'

He stopped dead, became uncomfortably bullish. 'Correct. More like two fortunes. Listen, I don't spend in order to lose and this isn't some kind of whim. I don't rely on guesswork. I've sunk everything into it and it's going to be a sensation.'

She bit her lip. A gust of wind whistled through the empty building and something inside swung to with an echoing crash.

'No need to get shirty about it,' she said, peeved.

★   ★   ★

He kept a flat on the outskirts of town and they drove there in an uncomfortable silence. It was their first quarrel and she thought he had been unnecessarily brusque. His grand plan seemed to her dangerously ill-conceived, uncharacteristic of the astute businessman she had come to know.

The flat was surprisingly small and also served as an office.

'I don't use it much. Just the odd night here and there, when I have to. Useful though.' He poured them both a drink and sat moodily nursing his. Five long minutes passed. She spoke, gently.

'It's just such a gamble that's all. I'm frightened for you.'

'Don't worry about that!' he snapped. 'You'd be all right anyway. Beautiful people always get by!'

She sighed, got up and went to him, knelt and put her hands on his knees, 'That isn't what I meant. I'm sorry if I upset you.'

The last of the sun faded from the room. Slowly he reached down, placed his hand gently against her upraised face. 'I just got rattled that's all. Bad case of ruffled plumage,' he said with a frown, but echoing her conciliatory tone. 'Stupid of me I know. It's just that I can't bear being taken for a fool. Not by anyone. My father was especially good at it. I've had enough to last a lifetime.'

'I didn't take you for a fool. I just thought……'

'That it was a rich man's folly?'

'Perhaps,' she admitted.

He leant forward purposefully, 'Jenny, I haven't climbed to the top in order to slide down again. That just wouldn't do.'

She got up and re-filled her glass, 'How can you be so sure it will be a success?'

'I can guarantee it.'

'But how?'

He smiled, 'Because there'll be nothing like it, no competition, not within striking distance anyway. You see I've spent the last few years acquiring everything around it that might be a rival, or might become one. My people went over anything that came up on the market. I knew the pier would eventually be put up for grabs. I told you it wasn't a nine-day wonder. I don't operate like that. It's been a waiting game.' He held out his glass and she filled it for him, then moved to the other side of the room and sat behind his desk. She picked up a gilt paperknife embossed with a regimental shield and drummed it absently against the telephone and a small tape recorder next to it.

'When I was here the council couldn't make up their minds what to do with it,' she said thoughtfully, 'there was just endless bickering. You must have been very sure of yourself.'

'I didn't need to be,' he smiled wryly, 'tweaked the nose of the council boss instead. The chap happened to have a bit of an Achilles' heel that I helped him out with, you might say. Got him on my side. Easy really.'

'When I left there was an outcry because they wanted to pull it down,' she said, perplexed.

'Ah yes well,' he was his old self again. 'That was part of the plan. We knew there would be opposition to the development plans from the nostalgia merchants so we got the council to announce that it would be demolished unless someone stepped in to save it.'

'And that's where you come in.'

'Not really, not yet. I submitted outline plans and an offer. That whipped up the opposition lobby who formed themselves into a preservation society. Raised enough cash to have a survey done and promptly went green at the gills when they found out how much it would cost just to have it made safe. Backed off pretty quick I can tell you.'

'And then?'

'Well, I got it put about in the local rag that I wasn't all that interested anymore. Went coy on the idea or that's what it seemed. Got the demolition estimate put about as well, which was pretty staggering, I can tell you. It was plain sailing from there.'

She cocked her head to one side, 'I don't follow.'

'Simple. I let them simmer for a bit then put in another bid. Lower than the first but considerably more than pulling it down would have cost the dear taxpayer.'

'So they had no option but to accept?'

'Exactly. None. Went through on the nod,' he sipped his drink triumphantly.

'You devious sod,' she said admiringly, in spite of herself and the uneasy feeling his underhand playing left her with.

'I'll grant you that,' he chuckled, 'although I prefer to think of it as being creative. Heaven helps those who help themselves. Anyway, that's how I know it will be a success.

You see, there'll be nothing quite like it.' He tipped back his drink and got up, 'Come on, let's eat, I'm starved.'

They dined at an Italian restaurant within walking distance. He was, after the essay in skulduggery, positively animated and expounded on his vision for the pier. She was relieved they had patched things up and asked facetiously, 'So I should be jealous of this other woman? She seems to be making great demands on your attention.'

'Course not,' he smiled.

'I must admit that, years ago, I used to think it was pretty wonderful. That's before I saw it up close.'

'It?' he said, 'She, you mean.' A dreamy yet intense look came over him. 'That's one of the problems. Can't for the life of me think what to call it. Any ideas?'

She thought for a moment, then hazarded jokily, 'England's End?'

'Sounds like Somerset Maugham.'

'E.M. Forster you mean.'

'Do I? Yes you're probably right.' He fell silent then said, 'But seriously I am rather stuck.'

She racked her brains but finally admitted she hadn't a clue.

'Ocean Palace,' he declared firmly, 'that's it. Ocean Palace.'

She wrinkled her nose. It did not suggest to her the classy exclusivity he wanted.

'Bit ordinary. Besides it's not an ocean.'

'Doesn't matter,' he sounded a shade exasperated, 'don't split hairs.'

He ordered another bottle of wine while she toyed with her salad. She hadn't seen him quite like this before, snappish and changeable. It disturbed her.

'Are you all right?' she asked quietly.

He looked up surprised, 'Yes. Yes of course. Why do you ask?'

'You seem a bit, well, touchy. It isn't like you.'

The corners of his mouth dropped in a look of contrition. He reached across the table and covered her hand with his own. 'I am sorry. You're right, I know. I always seem to get like this when I've just closed a deal. I don't know why. Makes me a bit prickly I'm afraid. Forgive me?'

'Forgiven,' she said gladly, happy he could tell her, 'you don't have to be the perfect gentleman all the time.'

He seemed more at ease afterwards and they laughed together on their way back to the flat. The wine and the cool, sea-scented night air liberated a careless nostalgia in her.

'Can you hear that?' she asked.

'What?'

'Stop. Listen,' and faintly, from a distance, came the soft suspiration of the sea. 'It's one of the best things in the world, walking with the sound of the sea.'

'Yes,' he said, 'it is pleasant.' Then gathering her up he kissed her almost ferociously.

'Steady on!' she laughed and breaking away from him began to run. 'Come on, race you back!' She sprinted lightly through the darkness, aware of the heavy pounding of his feet as he tried to catch her but it was she who reached the doorway first. When he caught up he was flushed and gasping.

'Jenny Robin!' he panted, 'you'll be the death of me!'

Back in the flat he threw himself down in a chair, still puffed out, while she rifled through some records and put one on. When she looked round he was proffering a decanter.

'Like a loosener?'

'Aren't I a loose woman already?' she asked coquettishly, vamping it up.

He smiled to himself and poured the drinks, 'No, and I don't think you ever could be, quite.'

'Why not?'

'You never completely let go, even in bed.'

She was astonished, felt put out, rebuked, 'I don't understand.'

'It's what you are. You're all of a piece somehow. I can't really describe it. Very beautiful and......self-contained.'

'So I'm not passionate enough, is that it?'

He put up his hands in protest, 'No, no, don't get me wrong. I'm sorry. I'm hopeless at explaining things like this.'

She shrugged, piqued, and said in a bruised voice, 'I am as I am.'

He sighed deeply. 'Look, take no notice. It's not important. I've made a complete hash of it and a complete hash of today.'

There was a stiff, embarrassed silence in the room, accentuated by the cheerful music. After a while he got up, moved across to the desk and sat behind it. Opening a drawer he took out a small silver box.

'Time to cheer ourselves up,' he said, 'one for me and one for you. Try it?' Inside were two hand-made cigarettes, their ends twisted like the touch-paper of a firework.

She picked one out and examined it. 'It's a reefer isn't it?'

'Devil's own brand,' he laughed, 'do you dare?'

'What will it do?'

'Much less than you think.' He lit his own from a brass table lighter, inhaled deeply, then languidly slid the lighter towards her. 'Well?' he inquired, softly challenging.

Calmly, she lit the slender white tube and heard it fizzle. It tasted dry and gave off a rubbery smell. He sat casually smoking and watching her with cool, amused eyes.

She licked her lips, 'It tastes funny doesn't it?'

'You get used to it.'

'Where do you get it from?'

'Uncle of mine,' he said, grinning as she raised her eyebrows. 'I know, sounds unlikely doesn't it. Strange old boy. Picked up the habit in Egypt between the wars. Grows the bloody stuff on his estate. Got a greenhouse full. Swears by it.'

She slumped back in her chair and thirstily downed a glass of wine. 'Nothing's happening,' she said, squinting at the glowing tip of the makeshift cigarette. 'I had an uncle once. He went to Africa. Frightened the natives I bet. Wonder what happened to him. He wasn't really an uncle, not a proper one.'

'Best sort to have, one who isn't related.'

She got up, fetched the decanter and sat on the floor with it. Filling her glass, she slopped some of the wine on the carpet.

'Whoops, just my luck.'

He leant back in his chair, 'I'd say you've had a pretty extraordinary run of luck, all in all.'

'Very lucky,' she agreed readily, 'must have a guardian angel.'

He smiled indulgently, 'Mumbo jumbo all that, don't you think?'

'Yes, I suppose it is.'

'Pure hokum. Take my word for it.'

Her mouth was becoming dry and once more she drained her glass and re-filled it. The small flat was beginning to feel hot and claustrophobic. She got up with a lurch and flung open the window. Far off, in the deep darkness, she could hear the dolorous milling of the sea. When she sat down again a gentle buzzing in her ears made her think of bees in the summer. She squashed the stub of the reefer into an ashtray.

'Well,' he said, 'at least you can say you've tried it. Got to try everything once.' She looked at him, sitting upright at the desk, and wanted to laugh. He looked for all the world like he was about to interview her for a job.

'Must one?' she smirked. She felt tipsy but it was nice tipsy, as if she could talk and talk all night. 'Like what?'

'Dunno,' he said blankly, then 'oh, you know, all the cliché things, all that rot. Have to live a bit, experience things, don't you?'

'And have you then, experienced things?' She held up her glass and peered at him through the straw-coloured liquid. It made him look small, terrifically far away.

'Not everything. Shot a chap once though. Strangest bloody feeling that was. Didn't kill him. Thought I had at the time. Out in Cyprus it was, during the troubles.'

A taut coil inside her was unwinding, leaving a limpid space, a space where there was no longer anything at all to worry about. She could out-dare him, this man, she could trump him, make him sit up and take notice.

'I have.' Her voice was husky and seductive, luxuriating in the sure prospect of besting him.

'Have what?'

'Killed someone.'

He was still smiling but his eyes crinkled, alert and quizzical, and he put his glass down quickly. 'What?'

'Killed someone. Little me.' She smiled playfully, rolling the cool tumbler across her brow. 'All by myself.'

'Enlighten me,' he drawled lazily, intrigued.

CHAPTER THIRTY-THREE

It was a pale blue envelope addressed in an unknown hand. She opened it curiously.

Dear Miss, it began, *we are writing to tell you the sad news that our mother and also your friend, Mrs. Frances Hellman, passed on at her home last Wednesday. It was very peaceful although we had no idea she was ill. Right up to the end she spoke about you and said she hoped all your dreams came true and that you remembered her. She liked all the postcards you sent and had them on her mantelpiece......*

The thin notepaper shook, rustled in her hand. Pierced by inconsolable grief, she wailed loudly and unashamedly. Frankie gone. Dear, true Frankie of whom she knew so precious little, and even now another twist in the script. There were children after all. Grown-up children whose existence she had chosen to deny. She cried for Frankie and for all she would now never know, and in her loss was recognition of the slenderness of certainties.

A week later she attended the funeral but stayed in the background, veiled and unrecognised. Her heart yearned for Frankie's droll dubiety, the gruff good heart, but she did not want to mingle or ask questions that might explain the enigma Frankie had left behind. If she hadn't wanted her secrets known, Jenny had no wish to uncover them. After the last of the mourners had gone she left her own deliberately incongruous tribute; wild flowers, gathered from hedgerows, less artificially vibrant than the florist's wreaths, but more true.

The following day Jane arrived at the flat. She breezed in and whacked down a brown folder on the table.

'There you are,' she said, 'just needs signing. Nice little surprise in it for you too!' and she winked, grinned hugely.

'What is it?' Jenny asked unenthusiastically, still oppressed by Frankie's loss.

'New contract of course. Had you forgotten? The old one expires in a week. It's very generous, Edward drafted it himself. You'll be very pleased I think.'

'No, I don't think so.'

'Oh you will. It really is most generous.'

'I didn't mean that Jane. I meant I don't want it.'

'Don't want it,' Jane looked stunned, 'but you have to.'

'I don't have to and I won't,' Jenny said wearily, 'I'm going to retire.'

Jane laughed anxiously. 'Retire? Oh come on, you're pulling my leg!'

'I'm perfectly serious.'

'But why for God's sake? You must be crazy! You're at the very top, why?'

'Nowhere else to go then is there, except home.'

'Home?'

'Along the coast,' Jenny said simply, 'I was happy there. I want to be free now, free of what I am.'

Jane patted her hands and looked worried. 'Look, I won't say anything just yet. I'll leave it with you for a day or two. Read it through. You'll change your mind, I know you will. You're just feeling a little low or something I expect. Promise me you won't decide just yet?'

Jenny nodded, unsmiling, and the woman left the folder where it had been dropped and where it would remain untouched.

★ ★ ★

'The car will pick you up in half an hour. He's very anxious to see you. Please Jenny, think again.'

'Jane it's final.'

The woman at the other end of the telephone gave a crushed sigh, 'Well at least hear him out, please, will you do that for me?' Jenny agreed, not from any doubt, but for Jane's sake, to appease her. Inside she was calm, absolutely sure.

The sky, earlier overhung with thin cloud, began to clear as the car cruised out of London. When they arrived in Brighton they stopped not at his flat, as she had expected, but at the pier, now enclosed in a towering skeleton of scaffolding. Its two sections had been bridged and a pile-driver shook the air as massive new iron legs were rammed into the seabed. It swarmed with workmen and a relentless cacophony of hammering and sawing enveloped it.

'Jenny!' It was a warm greeting as he emerged from the still fenced entrance, now crowded with lorries and trucks, timber, bricks and sacks. He kissed her lightly on the cheek. 'Come see the phoenix rise!' It was as though nothing had changed and he made no mention of her reason for being there.

With the now familiar keen enthusiasm, he took her on an exhaustive tour of the work in progress; the hollowed-out theatre that would become a ballroom, the as yet unfitted restaurants, even the kitchens and toilets. Finally, at the seaward end, he proudly showed her the partly-built exclusive club and its newly-installed but empty swimming pool. She thought it was rather small but didn't say so.

'Sooner it's up and running the better,' he chortled, 'great isn't it? Course there's an awful lot still to be done. Haven't even got the roof on the pool yet.'

She smiled. 'Best toy you've ever had I should say.'

He led her back through the noise, the piles of rubbish, and the overwhelming smell of new paint to where his car was parked by the entrance. Usually gleaming, she saw with amusement that it was streaked with mud, and building dust lay thickly on the bonnet and roof.

'Phew!' he said, 'good to be out of that racket. Come on, let's go where we can talk.'

They climbed into the car and drove to his flat. Along the way he kept up a commentary about the pier and what was left to be done, but still did not touch on her decision. When they arrived he fixed them both a drink and settled himself behind his desk, uncharacteristically cluttered and piled high with plans and papers.

'Now then,' he said amiably, 'what's all this nonsense Jane's been telling me?'

She was suddenly drained, 'It's time that's all, time to bow out gracefully.'

'Absolutely not,' his voice was even, controlled. 'I can't allow that.'

'Look Edward, don't take it badly. It's not that things aren't going well or I'm unhappy or anything like that. It's been great fun but I have to stop. I promised myself. I'm not going to defect or anything, just retire, settle down. I want out.'

'Retire? Your whole life is ahead of you.'

'And I want it for something else.'

'No. Not possible. Not remotely possible.'

'Please don't make it difficult for me, don't let's have a scene.'

'Talking of which,' he said, 'this is not the time to play the prima donna. I've made a substantial investment in you.'

'I know, I know,' the beginnings of a dull headache throbbed at her temples, 'and you've made a lot of money out of me, your investment has been repaid.'

'Not in full,' his voice was still cool and even. 'I rather think you owe me a little,' he opened a folder and pushed it towards her. 'Sign and we'll forget all this silliness.'

She looked up at him sadly and shook her head, 'Oh Edward, I didn't want it to end like this. I don't want things to go sour, please.'

'Now listen to me very carefully,' he insisted. 'In front of you is an eighteen month contract. It will provide you with a very great deal of money. If at the end of its term you still wish to retire,' he spoke the word without irony, 'I will be prepared to discuss it. But right now you will pick up that pen and sign.'

'You can go to hell!' she exploded, a sharp pain twisting across her eyes. 'I didn't think you'd be like this. I trusted you. I thought you'd understand!'

'And I thought we understood each other!' he snapped back. 'I shouldn't have to remind you that in your business a face, even one such as yours, has a limited life. Time marches on. Tick tick tock. I'm telling you, you are not quitting now, not while the going is still so very good.'

'Edward, I won't sign anything and I won't be hounded like this. I'm leaving. It's over.'

'You fail to comprehend. Let me make it even plainer. You will do precisely what I tell you, now and for the next eighteen months. You have no choice. None.'

'Of course I've got a choice!' she flashed back. 'I can just disappear if I want to!'

'Disappear?' he gave a brief, withering laugh. There was a sure swagger now in his tone. 'One of the most famous faces in the country? Wouldn't stay hidden for long now would you? You will sign. I won't ask again.'

She jumped up angrily, her hand screwed itself into a tight fist at her side, nails digging into her palm. 'I've had enough of this! What can you do anyway, sue me on some……some technicality. You wouldn't have a chance.' She strode quickly across the room. 'And anyway, think of the publicity!'

She pauses, fingers around the handle, ominously aware of his silence. From behind her the click and purr of a machine as it is switched on and then a voice spluttering out into the room, turned up insistently loud, inappropriate to its intimate tone. Her own maddening, intoxicated giggle, her own teasing voice, trying to out-do, to be enigmatic.

'Killed someone……Little me……All by myself.'

And in the background, almost inaudible, the sea.

★　　★　　★

'Fool, fool, fool!'

Alone in her flat she beat her fists in fury against the wall, pressed them to her temples and shook her head. One stupid unguarded moment, tricked by so foolishly wanting to eclipse him. She had handed him her freedom, her future. It was unbearable, unendurable. One deft, unseen flick of a switch and she was inescapably shackled to him, powerless.

For days her anger boiled then, abased by her own blameworthiness, it cooled and became instead a spike that pierced her and remained poisonously in the wound.

One act of stubborn defiance. A week later, confined in a stuffy city studio, she refused the ritual smear of panstick over the scimitar scar. And kneeling, not in submission but as though to pounce, raised the arm across her forehead above an unsmiling, expressionless face, revealing the old wound, unmasking herself. The photographer, taken aback, rapidly snapped a dozen shots of the disturbing, unconventional pose.

When the picture was published she was summoned. She had not seen England since hearing her own slyly recorded confession played back. Determined not to appear weak or wretched before him she stopped outside his office door and composed herself. Then, without knocking, marched in, prepared to face him out. He was on the telephone and glared at her as she stood before him, disdainful and statuesque. He gestured her to sit but she remained obstinately standing as he continued his conversation, his voice not betraying the displeasure in his face.

'Quite. I do agree. About three months if it runs to schedule. Well I've had my eye on the spot for some time and snapped them up. No, not really. Just one sticky bugger early on took a bit of persuading. Isn't there always? Very good offer too but the blighter still wouldn't shift. Beggars belief doesn't it? Look, can you just hold on a moment?'

He put his hand over the mouthpiece. In front of him was an open magazine with the photograph prominently displayed. He jabbed it with his forefinger.

'This,' he said slowly, 'will not happen again. Ugly scars are not good for business.' He waved her away and returned to the telephone, 'Now, what was I saying, oh yes......'

Back out in the corridor she took a deep breath, leant against the wall and pressed her brow despondently against its coolness. She could still hear his brisk voice.

'Well in the end we dug around a bit. Turns out that our immovable friend had a run in with the law a good few years back in bonny Scotland. Caught in flagrante delicto with a schoolboy.' He laughed, male and unsavoury, 'Yes, that's right. Wasn't at all pleased when it was gently pointed out that the great and the good of our fair resort might take a dim view of such behaviour if it was ever made public. Not at all good for trade eh? Anyway, silly bugger only went and topped himself didn't he. Yes, absolutely. Tinpot place it was too as restaurants go, hardly the Ritz. Unbelievable!'

Mac. It had to be Mac. She shuddered, felt sick, repulsed by the obscene intriguing, and realised bitterly how wrong she had been. She hadn't misjudged England. She had been right about him all along and misjudged herself. Fool for letting him catch her, fool for succumbing and fool for being thrice fooled, and bested. And now Mac, horribly compounding it all.

'Had a tiff have you?' Jane remarked, friendly and unknowing, as Jenny passed through the office, her face set in a scowl.

'Something like that.' She found it hard to be civil, even to Jane.

'Looks like it too. Want to talk?'

'No. No but thanks. It's over that's all. Has been for some time.'

Jane pulled a face, 'Oh dear. Sorry. I thought something was up. You did say he wasn't your type.'

'I know. I should have listened.'

She left the building and took a taxi to her flat. When they arrived she told the driver to wait, went inside and packed a towel and swimsuit into a duffel bag. Back in the cab the driver turned to her triumphantly.

'You're that girl from the magazines ain't you? Knew I knew. Where to then love?'

She lit a cigarette and rued the face that could not, as England said, simply disappear. Rummaging in her bag she found dark glasses and put them on.

'The seaside,' she said in a small voice.

The cabbie chuckled, gazed at her in the rear view mirror, 'Riviera then or what?'

'I don't care. You choose.'

He scratched his head, nonplussed, 'You 'avin' me on?'

'No, I'm serious. You choose.'

' 'Ow about Southend then, that do yer?' he asked, perplexed.

'Perfectly.'

The taxi gave a catarrhic growl and headed off eastwards, weaving pugilistically through the heavy traffic. On arrival he parked facing the water and smacked his palms against the wheel as he surveyed the depressingly urban foreshore and the unedifying grey water beyond.

'Lovely innit? Just right for a paddle.'

She lied and agreed, unpacking her bag.

'Flat as piss on a plate,' the cabbie murmured to himself with obscure satisfaction. 'You goin' in then?' he asked, glancing at her doubtfully in the mirror.

'Of course.'

He honourably made himself scarce while she changed and picked her way down to the water. It did not look in the least bit inviting. Even so she waded in and, with diminishing enthusiasm, swam out and round a small buoy that clanked tunelessly. A clamouring wail of gulls filled the air and a lump of blackened wood drifted past her, running with the tide. It wasn't working. There were no answers here. No easing of her mind. When she emerged the cabbie was sitting on the shingle, an ice-cream in one hand and a cigarette in the other.

'Fantastic you is,' he announced cheerfully, 'could've been in the Olympics or summat. You wait till I tell the lads who was in my cab today.'

She dried herself and sat in the sun, bitterly disappointed that the sea, too, now seemed to have deserted her. After a while she put her dress on over the sun-dried costume and got the cabbie to drive her back.

A few days later she was scheduled to do a promotional shoot for the half-completed pier and was driven down to Brighton. It was still scaffolded but gleaming and risen, yet now she saw it as a graceless monster. There was something oddly stillborn about it too. It exuded a rigid air of a particular kind of pleasure. And she hated it because it was his.

Predictably, she was to be photographed in a bikini, surrounded by workmen in grubby vests and hard-hats. But if the intention was to trade on beauty and the beast, the reality was altogether different. The workmen did not leer, or, as she might have expected, whisper coarse comments to one another. Instead they were shy of her, unexpectedly bashful and gentlemanly, and had to be gently coerced into grouping around her. It was as the shoot came to an end that England appeared, exuding good humour.

'Jenny! Lovely to see you.'

She eyed him coldly. That was it then, in public at least nothing must seem to be different. He bent to kiss her cheek but deliberately, in front of the workmen, she pushed past and coolly walked away; a small but infinitely satisfying retaliation.

Back in London that night she took a long, deep bath. A book remained unread on the linen basket as she searched her mind for some solution, some way to extricate herself and fly away. Lost in thought, she did not hear the key turn in the front door nor the soft approaching footsteps as she gloomily swished the foaming water. The bathroom door, already ajar, was suddenly and violently kicked open and she shrieked in terror. But already England was on her, lunging forward and grabbing her arms, dragging her from the bath.

'Bitch! You bloody little bitch!'

She slithered soapily from his grasp and fell heavily to the floor. On her knees in an instant, she scuttled past him into the bedroom. The stone is there, on the bookshelf, smooth, round and ageless, deadly ally. She stretches for it, feels its coolness as her fingers brush desperately against it and then horror as it rolls away from her, drops to the floor and rumbles beneath the bed. His cursing behind her, itself like a blow. She turned to face him, eyes burning as he looks down at her nakedness and vulnerability.

'You won't!' she spat, 'You won't touch me, not ever again. I shan't let you!'

'Oh no, not for that, you mistake me,' he muttered grimly and dived at her again. Quickly she rolled away, struggled to her feet and was sent sprawling by a punch between the shoulder blades, knocking the breath from her. Then he was astride her, forcing her round. He is trembling and white-faced, breath hissing through his teeth, the pale eyes a milky fixed stare skimming at the edge of madness. 'Enough of this,' he whispered fiercely, 'do you understand. Enough of this.' And raising his hand he slapped her face with the back of it, a single, vehemently unrestrained, blow.

He got off slowly, as if spent. Absurdly he straightened his tie, then walked shakily to the door and, without looking back, pulled it shut behind him.

For a moment she lay where he had left her, then leapt to her feet and rammed home the door bolt and stands there trembling. A bitter yellow taste rises up through her, into her mouth. She rushes to the bathroom and vomits over and again until her stomach knots, achingly empty. She leans over the bath and splashes the tepid water against her face. Painfully she pulls on her bathrobe and shuffles to the bedroom. There she gathers round her the handful of objects which define her exile; a small, china windmill, the cigarette tin from her handbag where she always kept it and the framed, smiling image of the lost seaman to whom it once belonged, the stone, a shell, the yellow blouse and twisted gold ring, a letter, photographs, and finally her spade. She sits on the floor amongst them, in darkness and in silence.

CHAPTER THIRTY-FOUR

She woke to find her back sore and stiff, an angry bruise on her shin and absolute bleakness within. Crushed by England's sudden flash of violence she felt herself cast even further adrift, floundering. Everything, all hope, had been snatched from her and was held unassailably by him.

With quiet despair she began to automatically clear up. She emptied the bath and returned the unstarted book to its place, then carefully put away her treasures. After that, she examined her face in the mirror. The slap had left no mark but the troubled night had stamped dark shadows under her eyes and her skin was an unhealthy, bilious colour. She turned away from it, went to the kitchen and made coffee. Staring blankly at the delicate primrose yellow wall, she smoked and remembered summers of long ago filled with certainties and truth. The gentle metallic chink of the letterbox barely registered and she did not hear at all the soft intrusive flutter of the real, the ordinary, as the day's post tumbled onto the doormat. It was much later when she noticed and picked it up. There was the usual envelope from work with trade magazines, circulars and press cuttings but also, unexpectedly, a picture postcard. She stared at the glossy image. For a moment she thought it must be a ghastly coincidence but, if it was, it was too horrible, as if someone knew and was playing a mean, spiteful trick. The picture was of a technicolour Devon coast; red cliffs, the sea an impossible blue, a ketch leaning gracefully into the wind. She flung it down angrily, as though it were cursed, then snatched it up again and flipped it over.

A steady, attractive hand, fluid and devoid of flourish. Black ink. Five words. She read them and shrank.

I love you Jenny. Dad.

★   ★   ★

It was a sick, evil joke. It could only be that. One of England's dirty tricks. God alone knew how he had found out about Daddy. She might have been unbelievably stupid but she had at least stuck to her war orphan story, just adding in Kit as her guardian, so how the hell did he know? But then she had seen and heard just what he and his 'people' were capable of, what lengths they would go to.

Fuming, though with no clear idea of what she would say or do, she telephoned the office only to be told he had left the country that morning and wasn't due back until the weekend, something to do with buying some specialised equipment for the pier. She hung up in frustration and looked again at the card. There was no stamp or postmark. He probably got one of his hacks to deliver it. Even Jane perhaps. No, not Jane. That was unworthy.

That night she slept fitfully and, in the morning, struggled to shake off a muzziness that the troubled small hours had left her with.

Again the usual, regular envelope lay on the mat bearing her office mark. Inside was another postcard, innocent-looking, a simple greeting from someone's holiday. She grabbed it up, her anger returning, clearing her mind instantly. That same unknown, despised hand:

Jenny, please will you meet me at the Greenwich Observatory, today at 1.00pm. I'm sorry for the shock and that clumsy card. I could think of no other way. Love always, Dad.

She scowled at it, turned it over. Another improbable West Country scene, the red cliffs at Jacob's Ladder beach, hopelessly re-touched and over-tinted.

It was a cruel and hateful act. Why was he doing it? What more could he possibly hope to gain? There was nothing else he could take except her sanity and she wouldn't allow him that triumph to crow over as well. She would go, go and face it. He wasn't going to best her again, not ever. She was too strong for that, no matter what he did, what vicious game he played. And if anyone did show up, which she doubted, she would be cool, contemptuous and show she couldn't be broken.

The morning was still and brilliantly clear. It shimmered with the promise of scorching temperatures to come. She arrived early and sauntered in the park, watching people to see if they were watching her. Despite her grim determination to debunk England's ugly game her nerves were wildly on edge. She tried to calm herself with tea and a cigarette in the café, then resolutely made her way up to the Observatory.

It was just before one when she reached it. There was no one there, no one at all. She laughed out loud and felt both foolish and disappointed, foolish for going at all, disappointed at not being able to vent her anger.

Shading her eyes she looked at the mast atop one of the towers and at the red globe suspended there. It quivered and slid heavily down the spar: one o'clock precisely. There was a curious, rasping sound from somewhere behind her, a dry cough and then a cracked male voice.

'Jenny.'

She spun round. A man was standing some way off, square and shadowed. Despite the day and the season he was wearing a dark coat, the collar turned up. The dazzling sun was full in her eyes and she could not see his face. She yanked the postcard from her pocket and brandished it at him.

'Did you write this?' she demanded, flaring up, all thoughts of staying unruffled now completely forgotten.

Again he made a strange noise in his throat, a scraping gulp, 'Yes, that was me.'

'Well you've no right, whoever the hell you are! No right at all! I know what you're up to, I know who put you up to this and it's outrageous and disgusting and you should be ashamed!'

'I am Jenny, ashamed that I didn't come home to you.'

'Oh for God's sake drop it, can't you, it's pathetic!'

The man drew himself upright and for a moment she felt unguarded. Once more that harsh cough.

'I'm very sorry. You must be terribly distressed. That postcard. I could think of no other way to do it, no gentler way to try and bring us together again. I don't know who it is you're so angry with, but you have a right to be angry with me.' He stopped and she could hear his quick, laboured breathing.

'Oh, very good,' she said scornfully, and began a slow hand clap, 'very, very good. What are you, an out of work actor or something? Paid you a few dirty quid did he? Well I can see why you're out of work. Not very good are you, not very good at all!'

The man stepped hesitantly forward and when he spoke his voice was soft, almost a whisper, 'You must prepare yourself.'

Her hands fell to her sides. She stood open-mouthed as he approached, unveiled from the burnishing glare of the sun. 'Oh my God!' she said in horror. He stopped three paces from her. The face, unflinchingly disclosed, was savagely disfigured. A web of thick, red welts spread up from the neck and across what had once been recognisable as a face; a complex, fearsome network, twined and interweaving. It was bloated, puffy, looked unnaturally large. The mouth was a shrunken slit, the nose a piece of distorted flesh, the eyes impenetrably dark, narrowed and misshapen. Between the welts the skin had a spectral opacity. It was a colossal, unbearable mutilation.

'Fire,' he said, answering the unaskable.

'Oh God get away from me!' she gasped, recoiling. 'Get away, get away, stop it!' Her voice began to break and she turned from the hideous mask.

He spoke, 'I didn't want you to know. I didn't want you to see. I didn't want you......I couldn't. Perhaps you understand now, why it was so difficult.'

She began to sob, 'This is obscene!' but the man continued, gently, falteringly. She forced herself to turn back and look.

'Because of this and because I was lost, I knew I would have to prove who I am and I have no proof, other than what I am.' He broke off and coughed several times, struggling to catch his breath. She had an unlikely flicker of something like sympathy at his wretchedness but he straightened determinedly.

'Sorry, sorry,' he wheezed, 'worse inland.'

She looked at him intently, no longer afraid or overcome by the terrible, stricken face. Very quietly she asked, 'Who are you, what is all this about?'

'I was,' he said with difficulty, 'James Hawker, Commander James Hawker, someone I haven't been for a very long time. We lived in a house called Hadley, the three of us. You called your mother Liddy.' He paused, 'I could go on.'

'She's dead,' Jenny murmured weakly, bewildered. Everything seemed to be happening in a swimmy slow-motion.

'I know,' the man said sadly, 'I know.'

'But anyone could find out those things!'

'No. They couldn't.'

She was weeping and didn't care. Armed by past betrayal she shouted, 'You aren't Daddy, you're a fraud, a sham. It's a trick, I don't believe in ghosts!'

'No ghost,' his voice was patient, even. 'Not a trick.'

She squared up to him, tormented and beside herself, 'I don't believe you. It's a lie!'

The man raised a hand to his face and she saw that it too was swollen and caustically scarred with burns. The fingers brushed his brow in a gesture of weary defeat. 'I can't blame you,' he said sorrowfully. The mutilated hand reached out slowly, cupped itself around the nape of her neck and with exquisite tenderness gently ruffled her hair, 'I never did bring you the treasure house of the world.' He looked away and in the downcast shape of him is an immense, lost tiredness and in herself the sudden release from another, older tyranny.

'Daddy!'

She stands before him, reaches into her handbag. Then with both hands outstretched in a small, earnest gesture, offers not fruit to a false castaway but instead an old, battered cigarette tin, and with it, herself.

'I missed you Daddy. I missed you!'

★   ★   ★

A child's fragile dream-wish, once denied, now made flesh. The salt taste of tears as she moves to him, by this resurrection forever to be set apart from the ordinary mechanics of the everyday. A shy, unpractised embrace, at last connecting. Silence in place of the inexpressible. Inside she is dead calm yet spellbound. She gazes up, looks upon the grotesque, reticulated human landscape until at last she reaches out, touches the loved, ravaged skin. He takes the worn tin sadly and in a breathless rush she speaks.

'I kept the secret of you in there, when they wouldn't believe me and I was all alone.'

He looks down at it, runs a finger across its battered surface and in a voice of wondering gratitude says, 'Thank you, thank you. Not alone, not any more.'

Unable yet to confront the enormity of his returning and the extreme, violent transformation that rendered him unrecognisable, all of her questions were held in suspension, held against each gilded moment of silence when they simply looked at each other and breathed the same air.

It was much later, after they had drifted in an entranced daze back to her flat, unaware of the startled looks on the faces of passers-by, that the questions began. Hastily, she loaded them with gin.

'Oh Daddy, where were you, where have you been, what happened to you?' It came out in a flood as she sat hunched on a chair. He looked down at his maimed hands, took a deep rasping breath and began.

'There was a voice from nowhere. It said, "There is another death."' He gulped at the gin, spoke to himself, 'No, not that, not yet. It's the detail you want, the facts before we come to the heart.' He glanced at her, began again, 'We were patrolling the Baltic, rounding up the straggling ends of them, the Nazis, when it happened. None of us saw or heard a thing, no kind of warning at all. So long ago now, so much time since. It was the middle of the night. A torpedo hit us, absolutely square amidships. I was on deck at the time. All I can recall is complete disbelief. It wasn't supposed to happen. They were meant to be on the run and the war all but over. Anyway, there was a shuddering impact and then a curious sort of lull that went on forever. Then the whole ship reared up beneath me. Wrenched apart as easily as a child pulls the wings from an insect. I grabbed a life-jacket and put it on, exactly as if it were just another drill. I still hadn't grasped the reality of what was happening. I was removed from it, at a distance, watching. The blast came right up under me, unbelievably fast and powerful. A deafening roar and then a screaming column of fire that picked me up and put its face to mine before it threw me aside. It ripped up through the ship like the devil's breath. It filled my whole body. I breathed it in.'

He shuddered and poured more gin into his glass, 'Blasted through us as if we were just a toy boat made of folded paper. Incredible, unbearable heat, an inferno. I clapped my hands over my face and was overwhelmed by a sweet smell of burning, an awful charred smell. It was me. That and the smell of blazing diesel oil and hot metal. There was thick smoke belching all around and I was bellowing but it was a puny sound inside that roar. It was the last loud noise I ever made. I must have jumped over the side although I was hardly aware of it, and blacked out before I hit the water. One thin sliver of a memory is all that remains before they found me, a brief moment of consciousness or something like it. I was lying on a beach, utterly alone, and the sand was scraping at my face. I was convinced I was still on fire but couldn't move. Then nothingness, absolute nothingness.'

'When I came to everything had been stripped away from me. Everything I knew or believed, all expectation. I had no memory, not of the ship, the explosion or being burned. I was newly arrived on a different planet, without any clear idea of where it was I had come from. I looked up at a vaulted sky of bent, interlaced branches covered with sack-cloth. Through it I could see a light like a bright coin. But the strangest thing was that I was cocooned in complete tranquillity, absolutely serene. All I had to do was lie there and enjoy that circle of light. Nothing else mattered.'

'It was the sun of course, although it was a long time before I was myself enough to know it. Then there was a woman at my side. Most curious face, Slavic, stony. No beauty I can tell you. She cut off what remained of my uniform and discarded it. She spoke a harsh language I did not recognise. I thought she was talking to me but there was another woman behind her. She never took her eyes from mine.'

'When I was naked they began to anoint me with a thick, yellowish paste. They covered every part of me and it felt cool. Then they put a leather skin over me, very carefully, and went away. I was alone again with the light.'

'When I next came to the first woman was there. She had my head cradled in her lap and was spooning some liquid into my mouth. It tasted dreadful, old bark, leaves and pencil shavings all mixed up. At first I gagged on it but she persisted, a few drops at a time. It must have been some sort of infusion, though of what I had no idea. I remember once regaining consciousness and panicking because I was alone and in darkness. The light had gone, my friend had vanished. I tried in vain to sit up then fell back to dreams.'

'My notion of a self, myself, returned only gradually, sometimes in a leap, at other times a sound or smell would hint at something familiar. The same thing happened each day; I was re-anointed, given water and force-fed the ghastly cold tea. Once a man came in and gabbled something to the woman. He wore a black trilby that was too big. The sight of him made me want to smile but I found my face wouldn't work. Nothing moved in the way it should. Then one day they carried me out into the light. It was dazzling, beautiful. They laid me down and I saw for the first time where I was. It was an encampment at the edge of a forest, tents and wagons. They were gypsies of some kind, thirty or forty of them. I could hear children, dogs and voices. Lying on my back I looked up at the tops of trees moving like delicate feathers against the blue sky, casting flickering shadows about me. After that they took me out every day except once when rain spattered on the roof of the tent. But such clear moments were rare. I was barely conscious most of the time and when I did surface it was slowly, not like waking but more like moving through a procession of shrinking dreams. Time passed in a blur of voices, voices I could not answer or call to. Instead I listened to the buzz of life; the wind at night, birds in the morning, the rustling of the forest and creatures calling in the dark. It was like being a child again and hearing a language I'd once known but forgotten.'

'Over the days they gradually propped me up so that I could see more and encouraged me to move for myself a little. I remember the first time I became aware of my hands. They were like blackened lumps of wood. I held them up and looked in wonder, as if they were not mine but belonged to somebody else. Then I remembered the ship, the explosion, and covering my face with them. It slowly dawned on me that my face must be injured too, because of the way it felt wrong when I tried to move it and because they'd continued anointing it long after they stopped with the rest of me. But I wasn't prepared for what I finally saw. It loomed out at me from a bowl of water; monstrous, grotesque, a gargoyle.' He raised his head almost defiantly. 'A part of me detached itself then. I was no longer anything I recognised. Not me, not English, not human. And I felt ashamed, smothered by shame. My burning face had been fixed, set in that instant when I hit the water, sculpted by the sea into this. I was wiped clean of all I was in a second, by a nonchalant touch of fate, and made different, freed. From that moment I forgot……no, not forgot, put into cold store all that remained of my old life. It was a specialised sort of amnesia. The past was in suspension, in paralysis. I sank into the strange anonymity this new disguise forced onto me and in that descent there was a relief of sorts. I believed then I could never come home.'

'I had extraordinary dreams, drifted in and out of them. Dreams of being in flight, of being always in that moment of jumping from the ship, and I would wake in terror, dripping with sweat. Then, after a few days, it changed inside me from a feeling of horror to one of exhilaration. It became a brilliant, pure moment of absolute transition, dropping down through the air, a moment I could repeat indefinitely, over and over again. It was a madness, a fever, and it nearly swallowed me. The gypsies realised something was wrong and the woman took to sitting up with me at night. Her presence was calming. The dreams stopped.' He looked up and directly at Jenny, 'Do you know, not one of those people betrayed the slightest flicker of revulsion at my face, not even the children.'

'A few days later everything suddenly changed. All the usual noises stopped and something else took their place, a rush of activity as they hurriedly struck camp. They found clothes and with considerable difficulty dressed me. The woman and three of the men carried me deep into the forest and put me under a huge tree, nestled amongst the thick roots that broke up through the ground. They gave me food and water, a blanket, then stood jabbering and looking down at me helplessly. Finally, the woman grabbed a stick and scratched something in the earth, then pointed back through the forest. It was a swastika. She gestured me to stay put and with one of the men's watches let me know that they would return later. Then they were gone, vanishing silently into the green.'

'But they didn't come back. Much later I tried to find where the camp had been. There was a word they used and I thought it might be the name. I found something that sounded like it in Poland, along the coast, but if it ever was the place I could no longer tell. Something had certainly happened there. The ground was burnt, scalped, and the whole area was unnaturally still. I asked in the nearest village but the people weren't keen to talk and I don't think it was just my appearance that was frightening them. I only had a phrase book and the things they did say seemed vague and contradictory. One man looked up the word for plague and jabbed at it repeatedly with his finger. All I could get from the local policeman was that it was a bad place, rumours of witchcraft and magic, that sort of nonsense. I never found out what happened to the gypsies. There was something uncomfortable about that village and I was glad to leave it. I'd like to believe that the gypsies got away but I have seen enough to doubt it. The whole country was riddled with Nazis on the run and they left a trail of barbaric reprisals, acts of staggering cruelty. I hope those gypsy people escaped. Were it not for them I too would certainly be dead.'

'Left alone I was nursed by the giant tree, held in its improbable cradle. It was immensely peaceful there and I had no inclination to move. It felt secure, safe. As time wore on, I became more attuned to sound, the hidden life of the forest around me; the snap of a twig or brushing of leaves as an animal passed by in the entangled distance, burrowing and scurrying noises, insect hum. The forest was full of life and not secret after all.'

'As the days passed though I became frightened. Out of the blue a terror struck me. The forest would kill me. It was a dense green tomb gradually engulfing me, absorbing me into itself. Worse, a part of me wanted that slow obliteration, even welcomed it. That was the part of me that had no wish to ever come out and have to reveal myself. The great tree towered over me, its branches moving slowly. I was petrified by the thought of there being no trace of me, ever, that this was the last place I would see. I tried not to but I must have slept. I had the idea that if I closed my eyes, dropped my guard for one moment, that would be it.'

'When I woke the next morning a hare was sitting up, not three feet away and it looked right through me as if I was already invisible, already part of the forest. A leaf fluttered down and without thinking I reached out and caught it. The hare was gone in a second.'

'And then the damndest thing happened. A voice, an English voice, clear as day from behind the tree, "There is another death." '

'I couldn't believe my ears. I thought someone, somehow, was hiding. I wanted to shout out but couldn't, I hadn't yet got my voice back. Then it came again, lucid and friendly,"Imagine. From the deep past I stretch into the future and hand you an empty plate, a perfectly ordinary white plate, and I say here is your freedom, now show me what you will put on it, what you will choose." And that was it. I was complete astounded. It put the fear of God in me. I waited for someone to appear but no one did, there was just the rushing of leaves where the voice had been. Then I got angry and thought that some practical joke was being played on me, though God alone knew how. I realised I was still holding the leaf but it was crushed now and my hand wet. What the hell did it mean? It kept going round and round in my head but I couldn't make any sense of it. In that stillness, denied past and future, I made myself sit up. Then I tried to stand. Time and again I fell but I couldn't give up. I had to find out. It took me all day to crawl over the roots to the other side of the tree and, of course, there was no one there, no marks on the ground, nothing. I couldn't believe it was just my imagination. Even now, after all these years and against all reason and logic, I still believe it wasn't just a voice inside me. But at least I had moved and could move. I fell into an exhausted sleep and when I awoke it was night. I put my hands against the tree and scrabbled until I was upright. I thought I had conquered the world. Then a few steps and each day a few more. I was stronger than I thought, physically at least. Five days later I struck out and headed south. I never heard the voice again, but if I ever did I would know it at once.' He paused and lit a cigarette. 'Shouldn't smoke really, sometimes though……'

'What do you think it meant, the voice, about another death?'

There was a long silence then he shrugged, 'I don't know. A warning about not giving up or giving in? I just don't know. It sounds crazy but all I can think is that it was the future, a future, reaching back to me in some odd, inexact way, holding out an offer. Either that or I just plain cracked up for a bit. It's a mystery.' He half-smoked the cigarette then ground it out in an ashtray.

'After two days I found a road running through the forest. I followed it from the cover of the trees. After a while I came across a crashed motorcycle. A dead man lay close by. It looked like he had driven straight at a tree. The forest had already begun to claim him, there were flies and maggots all over the body. The motorcycle was wrecked but in the panniers I found identification papers wrapped in an oilskin pouch, an expensive Leica camera, some tins of iron rations, a few rolls of film and a half-empty bottle of vodka. There was money and cigarettes in his coat pocket. I worked out from the papers that he had been some sort of correspondent. His name was Christian Jianou. I took his things. In a way I suppose I stole him back from the forest. I decided there and then that I would try and pass myself off as him. After all language isn't a problem if you can't speak and I thought I could always play act at being deaf. It seemed worth a shot. Anyway, I had little alternative. I sat with him for a while and smoked one of his cigarettes. It seemed the proper thing to do, a sort of communion. The cigarette made me throw up and put paid to that. Empty stomach. The food the gypsies left me had run out and for a couple of days all I had eaten were a few berries. So I left him and carried on. Later I had the film in his camera developed. The photographs were taken in the camps, the death camps. Shadows of people, skin and bone, grey, sunken eyes devoid of emotion staring at the camera, the awful striped uniforms so grotesquely like pyjamas, piles of bodies, barbed wire. And in the emaciation an unintended, horrifying dignity. He must have been there when they were liberated. I sometimes wonder if he hadn't deliberately pointed his motorcycle at that tree. It might have been the only way of freeing himself once and for all from that nightmare.'

'After a day's walk I came to a small town. I watched it for hours from the edge of the forest and ate some of the iron rations. There didn't seem to be any Nazis there. I entered it and went back into the world with my new mask. It was turmoil. People were walking about dazed. The war had ended. I had no need of my masquerade. It was all over.' He grimaced, something she was beginning to recognise as his smile, 'Finished but not done with.'

'I went to a café for food and for the first time came up against what I knew I would meet for the rest of my life, revulsion. I ordered by pointing at things on the menu and hoping for the best. I hung around the town for a few days, sleeping rough in the forest, before moving on. This time I knew it was safe to follow the roads. On that first day I discovered I could whistle. I didn't try to, it just happened. Old habit. From then on my voice began to come back, just a whisper really for a long time. I put one of the rolls of film in the camera and began to take photographs because what I was witnessing was quite extraordinary. I was no longer alone on the road. There were refugees, thousands of them, all displaced, disconnected. Alone, in pairs or small groups, sometimes a whole tribe, were criss-crossing all over Europe. I discovered, too, a sort of release in my disfigurement. No one stopped me or questioned me. One day a long convoy of Allied troops passed by. I heard their voices speak my language, recognised the subtle inflections in their banter, and felt completely estranged from it and from them. I would continue my masquerade. There was no way back.'

'I felt too that I was continuing his work, the dead motorcyclist, almost repaying him for the things I had looted. Over ten days I used up all his film. Eventually I reached Vienna. His money was beginning to run out but I wanted to see the photographs I had taken, see if I'd done him proud or not. I found a small camera shop and left the film with a tall, elderly man, the first I had met who did not recoil, although he didn't smile either. When I began to mime what I wanted he spoke to me first in French and then English, very fluent, a touch of Oxford. Off the top of my head I gave my name as James Christian. It's been my name ever since. When I returned he looked me over solemnly and spread out the photographs. "Unusual subject" he mused, "these are mere snapshots, of course, but in one or two you have perhaps caught something, a look of true actualité." He took me to his apartment above the shop and offered me tea. As we drank it he asked if I was looking for work. Of course I said yes, thinking it would probably be something menial in the shop. But that wasn't what he wanted at all. He wanted me to continue taking photographs. I explained that I had only a rudimentary knowledge and reminded him that even he had called them snapshots but he dismissed it, saying that was merely the technical which any fool could master. I asked him why. He seemed surprised and said for the future, so that everyone would always have to know what had happened. I asked him why me. He looked at me and said baldly, "You have the perfect passport."

'He was as good as his word, arranged new identity papers for me and everything, and for a year I travelled Europe, recording a continent ripped apart, the most appalling destruction imaginable. Not just to towns and cities but to the spirit, the misplaced optimism of ordinary humanity. I sent the films back to him and, whenever I returned, he always seemed pleased with them. He never asked me about myself, nor I about him. He was kind in the way of straightforward human decency. He arranged for a doctor he knew to perform a small operation on my throat that made speaking easier for me. I wouldn't want to misrepresent him however. He had a severity, a dry asceticism about him, always. I could not say we were friends. One day I came back and he was dead, sitting upright at his desk. There was a half-empty glass of something beside him and at first I thought he had killed himself but they found nothing at the post-mortem. Natural causes, they said, by which time I knew better. I had gone through his desk to try and find someone to contact. What I found was his will and a letter to me. In it he said he was leaving me everything because, as he put it, I had 'stumbled on a mission.' He had no one else. He had lost his wife, five children, two brothers and a sister in the death camps. There was one proviso, that I continue the work and send the photographs to an organisation in London. I did exactly as he asked. Whatever the doctors said, it was a broken heart that killed him. Of that I'm certain.'

'I sold the shop and carried on as he had wished, sending off batches of the photographs every now and then. I based myself in Paris, as much as anything because I could speak a little French. After a year I was contacted by the London organisation who said my pictures were to be shown as an exhibition. I became quite well known after that, or at least my name did. Obviously I avoided any risk at all of appearing in public. As time went on though, there was less and less to photograph. Europe soaked up those people like drops of water into a sponge. I began instead to specialise in portraiture; politicians, academics, artists, people of influence. Freed from my own vanity I became fascinated by faces and was always trying to crack it, to get at some truth about them through the camera. I warned my subjects first and, of course, they were all too polite, too civilised, to refuse. Yet because of me, my face, something new was disclosed in theirs. I became a fashion, never seen in public, just a name it was the done thing to have been photographed by. Over the years I had more exhibitions and books of my work were published. Time passed. I led a comfortable existence, if very private. My work was acclaimed and I was in demand. I amassed a respectable, no a large, fortune. No distractions you see, just work.'

'One day I decided to move to a bigger studio and spent weeks going through my back catalogue, putting it in some kind of order. Late one night I came across the prints from that very first roll of stolen film. They shook me to the core. For the first time I saw mirrored in them my own loss. All those bewildered faces, touched by sheer hopelessness, by fear, by all that the licensed barbarism entails. Faces unmarked but just as disfigured and, in all probability, with nothing whatever to return to. It struck me then, like a thunderbolt, that I did, I could. I had chosen life all right, freedom, but the plate was still empty. I broke down and wept, and the shame left me in those tears just as I had left the forest. I realised then that I had been trapped by it, by my own humiliation. I was ashamed of what happened to me because I thought it was some kind of retribution for my part in the carnage. But the shame is not mine alone even if I am its manifestation, its badge. It is for us all to share.' He stopped and drained his glass, reached for another of her cigarettes and lit it.

'That was three years ago. I've been searching for you ever since. I came back for you.'

She looked at him gravely, immersed in his naked story.

'Are you angry with me?' he asked.

'Yes……no.' She looked uncomfortably down, overcome by an urgent need to have her experience, her existence, made whole and explicable. 'When I was little I thought you'd come back, returned somehow from the other side, to watch over me. I even saw you and heard you, but then I grew up, grew out of it. You were though, weren't you? You've been there all the time. Looking after me.' She gazed hopefully up at him, 'Say you have,' she entreated.

He reached across, touched her face, 'I'm sorry. I wish I could, but it wouldn't be true.'

Crestfallen, she said quietly, 'I want it to be though.'

'And I'd want it to be so, but I can't lie to you.'

She swallowed, 'How did you find me?' Her own voice sounded infinitely small. Again he stubbed out the cigarette half-finished.

'I'm not sure I did. It seems more that you found me. I came back to England, to London, and then headed straight home. Nobody recognised me of course. I said I was trying to locate a family who lived at Hadley during the war. It's interesting, people are very helpful towards this face now, or at least want to be. Anyway, nobody seemed to know very much. Then I came across Frank Martin. Do you remember him? He's had some sort of stroke or something and it was pretty hard going. He told me about Liddy and that you'd gone off with a cousin. I thought at first he was a bit confused and meant Richard, but he was adamant that it was a much younger man.'

'He wasn't a cousin,' Jenny whispered.

'No, I didn't think so,' he patted her arm gently. 'He wasn't the first,' he reflected sadly. There was an awkward silence which he broke, 'Liddy wasn't always what she seemed I'm afraid. She was lonely and liked it when a fuss was made of her, needed it perhaps.'

'I know,' Jenny said hollowly.

'Well,' he continued, 'then it was a dead end. Frank Martin didn't know where you'd gone, nor did anyone else. I returned to London, hopelessly flat and dejected. But then came a shock, one hell of a jolt. The answer was staring me, literally, in the face.'

'But how?'

'Well, photographs and portraits were my business after all. Everywhere I went or looked I kept seeing this one remarkable face. I saw it in newspapers and magazines, on billboards and buses, everywhere. A face that was impossible to ignore, inescapable. Those arresting eyes seemed always with me and they belonged to a woman called Jenny. Perhaps it was some, I don't know, sixth sense, or a spark of instinct that this extraordinary creature might just be my lost daughter, but I think it was much more down to earth than that.'

'What do you mean?'

'I recognised you. It was that simple,' he seemed almost puzzled, 'I hesitate to say it, but you look like me.' There was a short, broken laugh and he added ironically, 'Not as handsome of course.' He became serious again, earnest, 'I wanted to believe it. I wanted it to be true. I found out all I could about this Jenny Robin, then I saw a newspaper announcement that you were to open some shop. I went along and saw you. I still couldn't be sure, of course, couldn't be certain. But later I came across this.'

He reached into his pocket, took out a page from a magazine and unfolded it. It was the photograph of her England had so resented; unsmiling, full of mute dissent, flaunting the scar.

'Liddy wrote to me about the air-raid and your cut. She said it would leave a mark. So, against the odds or in spite of them, I'd found a Jenny who was more than just familiar, and who was war wounded, like me. You know, I would've sent a message every day for the rest of my life, and waited at that same place every day for the rest of my life,' he paused and gazed at the picture, 'because when I saw this I knew beyond all doubt. I'd come home.'

He looked up and out of the window to where an ill-tempered dawn was just breaking.

CHAPTER THIRTY-FIVE

He stood wearily and rubbed his arms, 'Enough, that's it. Cold, always cold. Never can get warm enough.' He went across to the sofa and sat heavily, closing his eyes.

She fetched a blanket and covered him, then watched as he fell asleep. She was numb, shattered by his story, reduced to wordlessness and overcome by what he had endured. She wanted to soak all of him in and cheat the lost years. Yet within minutes she too was fast asleep in her chair.

When she woke he had gone. For a moment her heart plummeted at his absence, as if something had been scooped from her soul. But on the table was a note, written in the hand she had so recently hated. It said he would be back later, that he needed to get some medicine. Then, less prosaically, 'This returning, it's better by degrees.'

He came back during the afternoon and looked altogether brighter, restored. He had a taxi waiting and cheerfully hauled her off.

'A mystery trip,' he said, 'something I want to show you.'

The taxi took them to a small, down river marina. He paid the driver then stood for a moment, inhaled deeply.

'Easier here. Easier to breathe.'

Taking her hand he led her across a maze of pontoons to a neat, clinker-built motor launch. Across the bow was the name, *Kingfisher.*

'Elegant isn't she?' he asked proudly. She nodded enthusiastically, and fleetingly recalled another happily trim craft.

'Is this where you live?'

'Sometimes.'

The launch was beautifully fitted out and she explored it with a child's wide eyes, 'She's just perfect!'

'I can't handle sails anymore but this is the next best thing.' He excused himself and went below as she sat in the spacious cockpit, eyes closed, enjoying the gently purling river as the afternoon sun bounced softly off the water. He emerged with a bottle of champagne in one hand, two tumblers in the other.

'Never more appropriate,' he said, twisting the cork. The champagne gushed out, spattering onto the deck. He poured it, handed her a glass and raised his own, 'here's to…'

'Choosing!' she pre-empted.

'Choosing,' he repeated warmly. He sat beside her and together they looked across the breeze-stippled creek. 'And I'm glad all my fears for you were groundless.'

She pursed her lips as the shadow of her entrapment reared up, intruded into the intensely private world of the previous twenty-four hours.

'It isn't quite that simple,' she faltered.

He looked at her enquiringly, 'But you're famous, very famous.'

'Famous for being, not doing,' she said bitterly.

'From what I've seen and heard that sounds as if you're being a bit hard on yourself.'

'It's not just that.'

He looked thoughtful and when he spoke his voice was softly encouraging.

'Your turn then, to start at the beginning.'

She looked down, drew breath and began. It came out in a torrent, long pent-up and, before now, impossible to share. A torrent that rushed from her so quickly that more than once he had to interrupt, ask her to repeat or clarify something. She left nothing out. It was all laid before him. As she talked evening fell and they were in darkness. The inky river glittered around the boat when she finally told him about England.

'That's who I was so angry with when I met you. Oh God, I'm trapped! I could kill him!' She was trembling and her eyes filled with tears of frustration. She banged her fists helplessly against the gunwale. 'I've been such a fool...... I am such a fool!'

'A dangerous business that, laying down absolutes about oneself......'

'But I am!' she insisted abjectly.

For a long time he was silent, then he turned to her, 'What is it you want?'

'I just want to go back!'

Another loaded pause, 'You can only return, ever,' he admonished gently, reaching for her cigarettes and lighting one, 'and that is a different thing altogether.' The flare of the match illuminated his face and his eyes were shining, impenetrable. 'This man, this Edward England,' he enunciated the name with undisguised distaste, 'has taken hold of your life. Listen carefully, I'll ask again, what is it you want to do?'

'Take it back!' she smouldered, without hesitation.

★   ★   ★

Two days on, as a gauzy, late afternoon mist began to fall, the launch slipped its moorings and headed down the estuary towards open sea. Jenny watched as her father steered a course past Tilbury and Sheerness then on towards Dover. He looked at ease on the water, the edge of self-consciousness gone. He was whole man again and not freak or victim. They had spoken little since she'd unburdened herself to him, and he had passed no judgement. She wanted desperately to ask about Hadley but dare not, held back by some unnameable superstition. He had anyway been busy making ready for the voyage.

'Do you blame me?' she asked uneasily, when they were well under way.

'Blame you? For what?'

'Kit, that I killed him, do you blame me?'

He gave her a searching, quizzical look, 'No. I don't. I might have done the same, who can say. And who is to say what might have been if you hadn't. Besides, how could I condemn you for what I too have done in one way or another?'

'But that was wartime.'

'Does that make a difference? I don't think so.'

'War is different though.'

'No,' he said flatly, 'it isn't. Just sanctioned.'

'You don't think we should have fought?'

'On the contrary, I don't think there was any option but to fight. All oppression must be resisted, especially that of a dangerously insane clown. What I'm saying is that we should stop fooling ourselves about the cost of it, the price to be paid. That's what I really saw all those years ago, the terrible cost. The cost to men, women, children, the winners and losers and to the future, all that such action lays down for generations to come. It doesn't end when we've won and the flags go up. It carries on long afterwards and marks us as people and as countries. But back then I could see it in unforgiving close-up, impossible to ignore. That's what I was trying to show.'

'What's the answer then?'

'I haven't got any easy answers for you Jenny. In the end it must come from each of us, as individuals. If there is an answer it will be in ideas, not nations, and it'll need insight as well as intelligence. That and being genuine, authentic, not fooling ourselves anymore. A failure to see disfigures us more than any fire can. Once we do see clearly, wholly, we must keep faith with it or we remain free of tyranny but enslaved by its shadow.' The lumpy sea swashed against the bows and above a trio of gulls kept pace with them.

'Is that what you believe?' she asked.

The answer was concise, unequivocal, 'Yes.'

They fell silent, then as if to lighten the mood he said, 'And singing in the rain. I believe in that too.'

'What?'

'You know, laughing in the face of adversity and all that. Not quitting. I mean look at us.'

She smiled briefly but still looked downcast.

'Jenny,' he said quietly, 'you were just a child.'

'I know. At the time I didn't feel anything except glad. But I still have to live with it don't I?'

'Yes, you do. But most of all you have to live. Fallon denied you that. I think what you did was neither right nor wrong, a crime of passion if you like, but it's dead wood now. Look at it for the last time, understand it, and cut it away.'

'Se déraciner,' she sighed, remembering again one golden afternoon, 'change one's life, uproot oneself. I should have listened a long time ago.'

'And isn't that exactly what you did? Imperfectly perhaps, but nonetheless……' He spoke mildly, 'You're in danger of feeling sorry for yourself.'

'Yes,' she answered unrepentantly, 'I am.' He laughed and turned a few degrees to starboard, taking them ever closer to their destination. It was nightfall when it came into view, just as he said it would. A long, low line of distant flickering lights over the leeward bow, faint in the deepening fog. He pointed to them and tapped the compass.

'Dead reckoning,' he said cheerfully, 'better than creeping round the coast.' Too cheerfully, she thought with apprehension. She had become increasingly uneasy and tense during the voyage and, she brooded, with good reason. A chalky moon wavered delicately over the bay and drifts of sea-fire brushed past the boat.

It was a further full hour before the launch nuzzled silently against one of the columns supporting the pier. She knew England would be there. Jane had told her the week before that he'd had his things moved from the flat while it was decorated and had settled himself temporarily in what was to become the private club at the end of the pier. It had come up casually, when the two women met to discuss Jenny's schedule.

'He can't keep away from it,' Jane gossiped. 'I think it's the new love in his life. Silly aren't they, men?' Then, realising her blunder, she'd said, 'Whoops. Sorry! Me and my big mouth……'

Jenny had noticed a light as they approached and now she could hear music, jazz, from above. They had cut the engine while still some way off and allowed the launch to drift in on the tide. The underside of the pier resembled a huge cavern, echoing with the wet clap of the sea and mournful creaks from the structure. An iron stairway, like a fire-escape, led upwards from a small landing stage. They hauled the *Kingfisher* gently towards it with boathooks, through a maze of pillars and a network of taut guy wires. There was a soft bump as the boat came up against the steps and her father quickly secured it. He put a finger to his lips and motioned her to go first. His eyes were coal-black and hooded. As she slipped past him he cautioned in a whisper, 'Tread softly.' The metal hand-rail was clammy and the steps clanged faintly beneath her feet. As she climbed the jazz beat grew louder, an inappropriately spirited accompaniment to their purpose. Below she could hear Daddy's laboured breathing as he followed. At the top was an iron gate. She reached through the steel bars and slid back the bolt. It opened out onto the main deck where a viewing area had been created. Behind it, surrounded by white painted trellis and flooded with light, was the swimming pool. It had a roof now, supported by unclad metal girders but the glass panels that would be its walls and finally enclose it had yet to be installed. Beyond, the great complex of the pier loomed up, its gold domes aping the town's Royal Pavilion. They waited while her father caught his breath then stepped cautiously towards the floodlit pool from where the music and a tinkling of idle water came. She peered through one of the diamond-shaped gaps in the trellis fence.

He was there, alone, floating on a blue airbed in the middle of the pool. A record player had been set up on a crate and, next to it, was a rattan chair and a small, round table strewn with papers, anchored down by a champagne bottle. Across the pool was the clubhouse and through an open doorway she could make out an unmade folding bed, open suitcases and half a dozen cardboard boxes stacked untidily against a wall. His lair looked uncharacteristically makeshift against the opulence of the pier. Further down was an arched opening in the fence. She touched her father's arm and pointed. He nodded and together they padded quietly towards it, Jenny in the lead. She could see now that England had his eyes closed and was half-smiling to himself, a glass in one hand resting on his chest, the other upraised, conducting the music. That smile, self-satisfied, impenitent. She gave an involuntary shudder, collected herself resolutely. Daddy was behind her as she stepped through the archway and, charged with a shimmering fury, strode to the record player and yanked the needle brusquely across the disc.

'Edward!'

Her voice was like a blade cutting the sudden silence in half. Startled, caught off guard, he jerked upright, grabbed wildly at the airbed and tumbled awkwardly into the water. Scrambling to his feet he stood waist-deep and dripping.

'Jenny! Jesus Christ you spooked me!' He pushed the hair back from his eyes as the airbed bobbed away and rode the ripples to the side of the pool. 'What the hell are you doing here, how did you get in? It's all locked up.' For a moment he looked taken aback, unsure. It quickly turned to annoyance. 'Well?' he demanded.

'We want it back,' she said coolly, staring him down.

'We? What we?'

It was then she realised she was alone. Daddy had vanished completely. She faltered, caught herself faltering and, inexplicably alone now, drew herself up. 'You stole something from me. I want it back!'

'Do you, and what might that be?' He chuckled unpleasantly and swished at the water as if it were of more interest to him than her presence.

'The tape. I want it.'

He stopped moving, returned her stare with his own, 'I don't think so. Not in my interests at all. Let's face it, careless girl, as far as I'm concerned you were collateral on a bad debt and that debt is not yet made good. I'm hardly likely to turn in the insurance now am I?' He laughed, overtly scornful. 'Now I should just run along and behave yourself. Unless, that is, that's not all you've come for......' the drawl slid away, primed with salacious opportunism, and he gave her a questing, sideways look.

'Don't flatter yourself. Not for one minute.'

His face became stony, 'Strictly business then. Well Jenny Robin, I should fly away before I lose my rag. You don't want that to happen, do you?'

Out of the dark a harsh, rasping cough. England twisted abruptly, the water swirling around him. 'Who's there! Come out and show yourself, come on!' he barked.

A figure rose up out of the gloom: monstrous, forbidding and, as Jenny now apprehended, unpredictable. He emerged slowly from the shadows, revealed by the floodlights until only his face was still hidden.

'Who the hell are you?' England roared, then his mouth dropped open as the figure sauntered forward into the glare, the magnificent, unashamed face vibrant with intent. England recoiled, backed away, 'What the......'

'I'm the bogeyman,' Jenny's father whispered evenly. He was idly folding a piece of white paper and there was something held in the crook of his arm. His eyes twinkled.

He had made a little triangular boat, a child's plaything. 'Reconsider,' he said icily.

'What?'

'Reconsider.'

'And if I don't?' England snorted.

'A little mayhem.'

England began to move towards them, striding through the water, 'I've had just about enough of this……' A droning blare came from a lightship far out at sea and then another.

'Not wise,' her father said, and when she looked, saw he was holding some sort of gun in one hand. England saw it too and stopped dead, the cockiness checked. The gun was lowered slowly until it hung loosely at her father's side. He toyed with the paper boat then sniffed the air ostentatiously. 'The wolf at your door,' he said quietly, 'has slipped in through the back.'

'What do you mean?' England fumed, then he too sniffed, baffled by a strange, pervading odour that had suddenly rolled in and over them, like the mist itself. 'And what's that bloody smell?'

'Fuel oil. You're swimming in it.'

England looked suspiciously down at the water surrounding him. He dipped his hand in, breathed at it. 'What have you done?' he asked guardedly.

The disfigured man gestured casually into the shadows, 'I opened the drain tap on a large storage tank over there. Just to see what was in it. For central heating I think? Such luxury. I watched it trickle away. Imagine my surprise when I saw where it trickled away to. Bad planning that, or perhaps the fault was in the design all along.'

'Daddy,' Jenny whispered anxiously.

'Daddy?' England parroted, bewildered, 'What d'you mean Daddy, what the devil is going on here?'

Her father bent down, launched the little boat and watched, absorbed, as it glided out from the edge then bobbed its way back and clung to the side like a nervous beginner, 'It's simple. The tape.'

'When hell freezes over!' England spat sourly.

'Your choice,' the scarred man shrugged. There was the scrape of a match against the poolside. He lit the paper boat.

'No!' England thrashed in the water, struggled to get away from the fragile burning craft. A harrowing hiss as the yellow flame touched the oily water. And fizzled out. Jenny's father stood, stepped back a pace, then overtly, almost luxuriantly, extinguished the sputtering match between his fingers. He stared grimly down at England's ashen face. 'It would take more than that to spark it,' he said, as the small floating pyre pirouetted in the pool, 'I know about these things.' Then ominously he held up the weapon. It was a flare gun.

England shook his head, looked at them with incredulous disbelief, 'You must be stark, staring mad the pair of you, completely insane! You'll never get away with it,' he blustered. 'Now look, I've got people coming you know. Anyway man, for God's sake, you'll be blown to pieces too.' A frozen look came into his milky eyes and he began to back away.

Her father screwed his face up into the agonised grimace Jenny knew was a smile, 'What can fire do to me now?' He lifted the gun high and brought it slowly down until it pointed straight at England. 'Boom,' he croaked.

The man in the pool shrank down, raised his palms towards them urgently. 'Stop pointing it at me for Christ's sake!'

'Jenny's tape.' The voice was still raw, but now there was something different about it, and about him, a piercingly chill edge, implacable, mesmeric. 'You are just one moment from extinction.'

England looked down, powerless, his voice sullen, almost incoherent. 'In a box, through there. Take it, take it and go!'

Jenny ducked into his temporary quarters and began to rip open the boxes. One of them was half-filled with spools of tape. She heaved it up and took it back out. England stared at her resentfully, his mouth a thin scowl. She lifted the box high over the pool and upturned it. The tapes clattered out in a rush and splashed noisily into the water, spattering at her legs. They sank slowly to the bottom, began to unwind and ribbon off, like sea-snakes.

'Come on Jenny, we're finished here.'

'Finished but not done with,' she uttered softly, then held out her hand. 'Give it to me Daddy, the gun. It's my time to choose.' Far off, the lightship rolled out its echoing siren. He looked into her unreadable eyes and without a word handed her the pistol. It was smooth, imbued with a deadly weight. 'You go and start the boat,' she said, 'be ready for me.' He gave her an almost imperceptible nod and was gone, melting back into the shadows.

She clutched the gun in both hands, brought it up and took aim. The curve of the gleaming barrel all but obliterated him from her sight. 'You fool, for thinking you could beat me. Tick, tick, tock.'

'Jenny, I……' he began, suddenly earnest, 'Look, can't we……' he blinked rapidly, arms dangling at his sides. Then an odd, blank look came over him and he shivered in the shiny, lacquered water. 'You're going to kill me aren't you? What kind of creature are you?'

The gun quivered eagerly in her hands, 'I am what I will be. But I won't be trapped.' Her face twisted in triumph, distorted by a graceless snarl. She had him now. She had won. He was held suspended between existence and oblivion, trapped by a tiny squeeze of her forefinger, a squeeze as thin as the skin of a bubble. Her finger closed on the trigger and she sensed the gun's mechanism stiffen. Yet then, from out of the blue, a voice, and with it her own unexpected, perfectly still moment of pure transition. It wasn't enough. This could never be enough. The smooth, hard stone in her soul must be put away for good, returned to the deep, or she would forever be sullied, diminished by a snatched moment of blind vengeance. If she killed him something in her would be laid waste too and would always remain so. She saw it clearly now as she looked down the fat barrel.

'Get out!' she hissed. 'Jump!'

For a scant second he stared at her in glazed astonishment, a string of saliva quivering from his chin. Then, as though scalded, he surged awkwardly away through the tainted water. He reached the side of the pool, looked anxiously back over his shoulder and hauled himself out, dripping and vulnerable. Like a startled animal he crashed through the white fence and ran, bare feet pounding against the deck as he raced to the end of the pier and flung himself at the railings, scrabbling to get over. She saw his white back and a face filled with terror as he glanced at her. She swung the pistol round at him and screamed.

'Jump, jump, jump!'

Then, a pale blur, he leapt and was gone, dropping down through the darkness.

She swung back, aimed the gun at the translucent, impregnated water, her own captured voice now immersed by it, at the still churning place where he had been, and squeezed, broke the bubble. The flare crumped from the barrel, screeched hungrily across the surface of the water leaving a white hot trail of burning phosphorus. It slammed into the pool and sent up a glittering, loaded spray. There was a moment of intense seething, then an unbearably loud thump, like the sound of a vast turning sail, as a bellowing wall of glacial white flame erupted. The clamouring blast struck her like a blow from a giant's hand, immensely powerful. She was hurled back by the sheer unleashed force of it roaring up into the night. Flames ate up the surface of the pool and leapt out over the sides. She struggled to her feet and dashed across the deck. Behind, the gathering inferno exhaled greedily and she felt the scorching heat of its breath at her back. She threw herself at the railings and swarmed up them. For an instant she balanced hazardously, crouched on the top rail, then sprang to her feet, pushing up and leaping off. The air rushed past her as the raging fire above pounced on the fuel tank and it exploded, rocking the mist-dampened night and robbing the bay of all tranquillity.

She hit the water and went down like a stone. Touching bottom she kicked off hard and rocketed up through the muffled gloom. Surfacing beneath the pier she could hear the furious tempest, see its consuming brilliance through cracks in the burning deck. The *Kingfisher* was already sliding towards her and she heard his urgent voice.

'Quick, over here!'

She kicked out and glided swiftly across the water, clambered up the rope ladder and tumbled breathlessly into the cockpit, trembling and numb. The engine throbbed with quick acceleration as the boat shot out into open water and the pier was riven by an abrupt chain of sudden, thundering explosions.

'Are you all right?' he struggled to make himself heard above the din of the blistering fire storm. She nodded dumbly and stared over the stern. The pier was engulfed in flames, plumed with acrid, billowing smoke. Then came a hollow, wrenching groan of buckling iron, like a great wounded beast baying in the night. Fire bells pealed lamely from the shore as a final, deafening blast ripped up through the heart of the structure, blue-flamed, unbelievably volatile. There was a long, stricken wail as it began to break up, showering burning debris into the sea.

She ducked instinctively, turned away, but could not anyway have seen the fragment of cheap-gilded finial, ripped from one of the domed roofs, as it shot up into the air and curved in a deep parabola. It plummeted down with a whistling scream like a hot, spent firework and struck her in the back, punching the breath from her. She gave a startled cry and somersaulted backwards over the gunwale, into the sea and under, churning over, wreathed in seething foam. She breaks the surface, gasping for air, and is once more assailed by the uncontrollable holocaust of the pier and by the screaming pain between her shoulder blades.

Already he has turned the boat and is coming alongside. He hurries from the wheel but she is dangerously at the edge of consciousness. She raises a desperate hand and feels the playful tug of her own looming extinction plucking from below. She closes her eyes, mouth filling with the taste of sea salt.

'Jenny!'

Her eyelids flicker and struggle open. Daddy's face above. One strong hand reaching down, connecting, straining to haul her to safety and struggling with his own fragility. She rises from the water, falls back again. She can see his eyes burning with determination. And then a roar came from him, an awesome sound, unbelievably loud and dominating the night, an extraordinary roar torn from the depths of him. In that moment he became an incandescent flash of existence, triumphantly alive again. A spark, an invisible, jagged shaft, flashed between them, filled with his indomitable spirit. With one last bone cracking heave she was free, water streaming as he pulled her up and out, streaming and cascading back into the racing sea.

They fell back into the cockpit and lay struggling for breath. After what seemed like an age she began to feel herself slowly revive and it was she, awestruck, who spoke first.

'That was my dream. I dreamt that years ago. I never knew who the woman was, and all along it was me. It was me.'

And far off now, already in her past, the gutted remains of the pier yielded in torment and collapsed, as the once cheated sea claimed it for its own.

CHAPTER THIRTY-SIX

S oft seas. The haunting air of a summer night far from shore. Jenny sits in the cockpit enveloped by a blanket, the wound cleaned and dressed. He had wanted her to go below and rest but she insisted on staying above, close to the calming rhythm and scent of the sea. She drifts unknowingly in and out of consciousness, the silence broken only by the steady chug of the engine and by her father's ragged, intermittent cough, made worse by the smoke and exertion.

He stopped the engine, put over a sea-anchor and settled beside her in the darkness for several hours, both lulled by the soothing swell and a breeze that snaked over them, pungent with distant lands. When he roused at first light, his body shook with the effort and he struggled to shake off exhaustion as he pulled in the anchor and resolutely resumed the wheel.

All through the day the *Kingfisher* plied on and hardly a word passed between them. For a long while the fire still filled her mind, but as the day wore on its now intangible smoke drifted away, leaving her clear-sighted and restored, eyes once more sea-stark, face upraised to the sun.

'Land!' his voice rang out clearly as he pointed into the distance. She shaded her eyes and peered at the horizon. It looked like a shadow at first, then like a low tumble of clouds where sky met sea. As the boat closed on it she saw first a broad sweep of white merging farther to the west with a distinctive iron red and above, spilling down, an intense, unmistakable green. She gazed, overcome, at a scene released from the confines of memory and returned.

'Daddy?' she whispered in a voice so small, so brought to timidity, that she knew it would go unanswered. From that first sighting her eyes did not leave the land as it grew nearer, took on familiar shape and form. She neither dared ask nor believe. Even as the *Kingfisher* gently entered her own bay, sliding surely between the rocks, she could not bring herself to believe.

The engine slowed to idling and then stopped. He stood before her, an immense wistful quietude emanating from him as he held out his hand.

'Step ashore?'

Tentatively, eyes wide, she reached out and took it.

'Have to wade from here I'm afraid,' He sounded quietly calm, almost amused.

She looked down into the clear sea and hesitated, turned to him for courage. His face curled into what was once a grin.

'No monsters Jenny. Not here.'

She climbed over the side and slipped shyly into the warm embrace of this, her ageless, much-missed friend; a silken greeting, assured, unchanged. In a daze she waded to shore, hands trailing, held by the sea, staring up at the remembered, beloved landscape. Emerging, she looks down in wonder at the sand, spellbound at the sight of her own castaway's footprint, and is once again bound unerringly to this place. And the word she cannot speak, that her mouth will not form, comes to her across the still evening air.

'Home Jenny. We're home.'

Home. Home again. Home at last. The word flew through her mind like a greenwood arrow.

Together, in silence, they leave the beach and the hypnotic cadence of the waves and climb up through the eloquently shade-dappled woods and into the lane. It was no more a dusty track but long since metalled, although the green arch of foliage above and the verdant overspill at its verges had softened it.

She felt unsteady on her feet, whether from the sea or her own unravelling emotions she could not tell. It would be just ahead, around the curve. So close. Achingly close. A few last steps.

Hadley.

Exactly as remembered, each detail carved by loss in her memory, now rendered absolute and abiding. Hadley.

She stands awkwardly by the old gate, the special gate, afraid to open it, still mute and overwhelmed. She struggles, finds an anxious, childlike voice.

'Can we……can we go in?'

He reaches past her, gently swings it open, and in the faraway voice of someone once cast up on another, less manifest shore, a voice filled with an unsoundable ocean of penitent sorrow, he speaks.

'It is yours. At long last I have brought for you the treasure house of the world.'

★   ★   ★

News of the fire, and of the pier's destruction, came over the radio and, though no cause was ever found, it was widely held to have been started by an accidental fire in the paint store or where the welding equipment was kept. A nearby resident babbled excitedly, 'Ain't seen nothing like it since the Blitz!' and England, who had survived, was interviewed at the scene. He pronounced himself devastated, said lamely, 'I was extremely...... lucky,' and perhaps in his voice there was the trace of a new inflexion, some understanding. Her father looked at her levelly then and said quietly, 'I think perhaps you hit the mark somehow.' She never saw or heard from England again.

She returned to London only once, to collect her belongings from the flat, hurrying there and back in a day. It was already another world to her, as unreal as fiction.

Her true identity remained undiscovered and the people of the village threw a shyly proud and protective cordon around this exotic and celebrated woman who had given everything up and come to live amongst them. Only once was she recognised. Mr. Martin, frail now and wheelchair bound, pushed half-heartedly through the village by a young man in a T-shirt. The old man's face lit up at the sight of her and the toothless mouth grinned.

'Come 'ome then? And all growed up!' But the young man put a finger to his temple, screwed it round and mouthed, 'Gaga,' and carried on. And one day in Exeter a woman sidled up to her and asked flatly, 'Ent you that actress off the telly?' and she'd felt a momentary rush, the old need for acclaim. But it was an outworn need, past its time, and truthfully she answered, 'No. Sorry.'

From time to time offers came for her story. She refused them and they gradually petered out as the next big thing moved in to take her place. Together the two of them lived a life of seclusion, steeped in each other. Sometimes they went to Liddy's grave and laid wild cowslips and primroses there. Once Jenny asked, 'Do you forgive her?'

and he had looked questioningly down at where Liddy lay; fragile flesh no longer enticed, and perhaps a little surprised at himself, answered, 'Yes,' and then presciently, 'but not here Jenny, for me. Not here.'

Almost a year and then he was gone. Radiant days billowing with a love resurrected. And if that last, colossal effort of pulling her from the sea was what finally broke him, he was accepting of that brokenness, completed somehow by it, a half-circle made whole. Towards the end he squeezed her hand weakly.

'I'm not ready for it you know. I think I'm scared of dying,' and she could find no words to comfort him. Then he had given her an already distanced smile and said, 'Once, when I was a boy, I saw a kingfisher. Just a turquoise flash along the river, three or four seconds and it was gone. I never knew they were so small.' He paused to clear his throat, 'I didn't ever forget that sight, not ever. So damned small and brilliant.' Later he asked, 'Will I dream?' and she smiled, nodded in quick, infinitely sad assurance and said yes, the best of dreams. Just before he slipped away he became suddenly alert and clutched her arm. 'Listen! Can you hear it, that voice?' and then slowly he laughed; warm, confident and liberating, snatching away sadness.

Afterwards, she sat with him for a long time then went out into the garden. It was a glorious day. All of a sudden she rushed back in and raced up the stairs to her room. Nervously she went to the window, hands clasped before her, and flung it wide open. The old tree outside was still, unmoving. She leant out and whispered.

'Daddy?'

Then louder, 'Daddy!' a single word flung in aching hope. A silent pause then, slowly at first, up from the distant blue sea, across the green land, came a single, delicious, answering breeze, ruffling her hair and finding its way home, always and forever.

★   ★   ★

Autumn winds assemble. A click, a soft mechanical purr in the night. She dips towards the small microphone and confronts a ghost.

'It's been two years now since he went and there has been nothing since. Nothing and everything, but no night visitor. I believe now it was perhaps the manifestation of our separation, our severance, a manifestation inside me but no less real for that. This is how I remember Daddy. I remember the height and breadth of him standing over me and laughing. I remember the shine and leather smell of his shoes, his cap on the hall table, a ribbon of blue cigarette smoke making a shape around his smile. And then later that great challenging roar, his monstrous head thrown back. It was the sure voice of his humanity and every now and then I find a smaller, still struggling, voice inside me and I ask him, have I chosen well?'

'I have his photographs. They are chilling. I take my own now in this, my tiny speck of the world. He recorded the brutally dispossessed and, now my wandering is over too, I peer through the lens of my camera to try and find what it is, ancient, compelling and indefinable, that ties me to this landscape, bound by a sailor's knot. The photographs I take are good enough in their own way but I never quite capture the mystery. Sometimes I think I come close and so I continue.'

'This is no longer a secret place, or if it is, then it's a secret shared by many. In winter there are echoes of what it once was but I don't need them. I remember. It is always mine, this land and sea, but mine to share, not own. I swim with others now, holidaymakers, and I tell their children not to be afraid of monsters.'

'I have found a redemption in my retreat, my connection to place, and he is still with me in every stem, root, stone and tide. I am here because it fits my soul and I shall be here until last breath. He came back for me you see, and I'm not alone, not anymore. He came back. Imagine it.'

'Some men a forward motion love,
But I by backward steps would move,
And when this dust falls to the urn
In that state I came return.'

Lightning Source UK Ltd.
Milton Keynes UK
18 September 2009

143895UK00001B/41/P